INSIDER

K.B. GAZEENA

Cover by MiblArt

Edited by Isabella Betita

Paperback ISBN: 979-8-9924516-1-0

Ebook ISBN: 979-8-9924516-0-3

To my parents, who made it all possible

Chapter One

THE SOLDIERS COME TO Beijing at nightfall. They pour from their vehicles like a swarm of red ants, unfurling into narrow alleys and rousing families from sleep to scan their Identifications.

The Hyperrail, trailing a stark white ribbon of light through a corridor of skyscrapers, is bustling with passengers even at this hour. But the soldiers aren't here for the busy citizens traveling in luxury or the ones sleeping soundly in the upscale towers. They're looking for the people who hide in plain sight, who live their lives in the cracks between jurisdictions and owe their allegiance to no corporation.

The residents of Beijing's darkest corners reach out across Mindlink to warn each other of the arriving force. Yang Lin is among the last to get the message through the web of neural implants. Although she grew up in this neighborhood, she has few close ties, and the soldiers are almost to the door of her apartment building when Sammy Chen's name flashes in her peripheral vision. She acknowledges the call and Sammy's translucent avatar appears in front of her. The real Sammy is a skinny kid with awkwardly long limbs and poor posture who buses dishes at the restaurant where Lin works. Sammy's avatar looks a bit like Sammy but with rippling muscles bursting at the sleeves of his designer shirt. The other half of him goes straight through her bed, causing his legs to appear fuzzy and distorted.

"The Directorate soldiers are here in Fengtai district," says Sammy, and Lin sucks in a breath. "They're checking everyone's Identification." With a subvocalized command, she ends the call as abruptly as it started and turns to the other side of the bedroom. Sammy's name blinks again but she ignores it.

"The Directorate is coming!" Lin yells through the neural implant. Lin's mother, hunched over a desk in the corner, doesn't respond. Sabohat Iskakova's hands are spread flat on her desk, her eyes vacant, her lips and fingers twitching almost imperceptibly. She's working.

Lin grabs her mother's shoulder. Sabohat blinks twice and shakes her head as she files away whatever project had consumed her attention and refocuses on her daughter.

"It's the Directorate soldiers." Lin speaks aloud this time, but barely above a whisper. "They're here in Beijing again. Nearby."

"I knew they'd be here soon," Sabohat says, nodding with a slow calmness that makes Lin's breath short. "They've left us in peace for too long."

Lin runs to a chest between Sabohat's bed and her own and throws open the lid. Inside is a handful of lethal devices that Sabohat herself designed. She's one of the most skilled weapons engineers on her planet and this one, but her own collection amounts only to a handful, since bringing her inventions into physical existence takes resources beyond Sabohat and Lin's means. Lin fingers a small drone, feeling it request a connection with her implant, but sets it aside in favor of a long glove—she likes to keep her weapons close to her body. She starts to pull it over her hand, but Sabohat snatches it from her.

"Don't be stupid," Sabohat says. "You could lose everything. And what are you planning to do, take on the entire army?" Still, she slides the glove onto her own arm. The fabric changes color to match her skin tone. From a distance, it would be hard to tell that she was carrying a weapon at all, but the darts fired from her fingertips would be deadly at a short range. With her other hand, Sabohat grips Lin's arm.

"I'll go alone. There's no reason for you to risk your citizenship."

Lin ignores her. "Are we in the clear?" They've had the stairway bugged since they moved in. Sabohat's eyes glaze over for a moment while she checks the feeds from her implant, then she refocuses on her daughter.

"It's clear," she says. "They're not here yet. I'm going." She heads for the door, swinging her left leg in an awkward gait. Lin grabs her mother's cane and pushes it into her hand, then they hurry out of the apartment.

Hanting Community, where Lin and Sabohat live, is a block of ancient, boxy buildings. At only eighteen floors each, they're dwarfed by the modern towers hemming them in, their concrete gray exteriors all but invisible next to the advertisements that leap in three dimensions from the sides of the newer corporate buildings. The community is forgotten property, not owned or coveted by any of the Big Three corporations, and for some of Hanting's residents, invisibility is ideal. While most are simply too poor to afford better, Lin knows more than one resident without Big Three citizenship, though she's never bothered to dig for the reasons why. Minding your own business is an unspoken rule in the community. Maybe they're felons on the run, or maybe someone in their family was punished with exile generations back. Or maybe, like Sabohat, they were born on another world.

The narrow halls of Hanting are illuminated only by moving lines of light slipping through the windows. Lin guides her mother with a soft hand on her back, watching over her shoulder and wishing she had a weapon. She looks at the closed doors of her neighbors' apartments and feels a twist of guilt at not warning them, not sharing her escape plan. But the more people attempting to hide, the greater the chance that they will all be discovered. As Lin follows her mother into the dark stairwell, she hears footsteps echoing several flights below.

"Go," she says, and they begin climbing the eleven flights to the top floor. Sabohat moves slowly. An accident decades ago left her with a permanently twisted leg, compounded by the usual joint aches from growing to adulthood on a high-gravity planet; Lin often hears her stifled moans at night when spasms grip her back. Now, with ten flights to go, her right hand, still in the glove, clutches the railing and her left is white-knuckled on her cane as she limps up the steps. The footsteps grow closer.

"They're going to catch us," says Lin silently. Sabohat doesn't look at her as she continues her labored ascent.

"Probably," comes the curt reply in Lin's mind.

"I'll take care of it," says Lin, and turns back down the stairs. She just makes it around the corner and out of sight of Sabohat before she almost collides with two soldiers on their way up. One is tall, with a deep tan and black hair shaved close to his skull, the other soft-faced with blond curls tied at the nape of his neck. Below their matching headlamps, shadows cut harsh lines across their faces. They both wear the deep red of the Directorate.

"Oh! Hello, officers!" says Lin. Her voice rings too loudly in the stairwell. Are Directorate soldiers called officers? She thinks that's what they say in the dramas. The tall soldier stares in her direction silently. As a member of the Directorate military, his implant is equipped to scan her Identification.

"Yang Lin, 23 years old," he says. "Server at a Tier Three Xinqi Tech noodle house." He's quiet again, presumably reading further. Then his eyes focus on hers. "Congratulations on your new job," he says. "That's quite a promotion." Lin nods mutely. The soldiers brush past her.

"Wait," she says. Her mother hasn't had enough time. The soldiers pause and look back at her, just a hint of impatience in the tight line of the tall one's mouth. Lin climbs the stairs to block their path again, desperately grasping for a way to stall them for even a few seconds.

"No one here has done anything wrong," she says. "They all work for the corporations. I'm sure of it. They're my neighbors, I know them." Truthfully, Lin has barely exchanged a word with anyone else in Hanting. The blond soldier raises his eyebrows at her.

"People always think they know their neighbors," he says. "And their friends, and their family. But in your new position, you'll learn pretty quickly that everyone has their secrets."

"Not these people." Lin grabs the railing with her left hand and plants the right firmly on the opposite wall, as if she could actually hold these two men back with her own arms. She tries to look casual, but they notice her stance and their eyes narrow.

"We already know there was at least one offworlder living here," says the tall soldier. "Third floor, New Palu accent and messed up skin and everything." Lin's throat constricts. Mr. Tomasy and his niece often play mahjong with Sabohat and her friends in the evening.

She doesn't trust herself to say much, so she simply responds, "Oh." She keeps her arms extended for one more tense second and then lets the soldiers pass. They continue their upward march without a backward glance. Lin messages her mother.

"They're coming now."

"It's OK. Only six more flights." Six. Sabohat is still barely halfway to safety. The soldiers aren't moving fast at least, unaware that they're hot on the trail of a non-citizen, and they'll have apartments to check along the way. Lin lowers herself to a sitting position, leaning sideways and pressing her cheek against the cool concrete wall. Above all else, she hates this helpless feeling, the loss of control.

"Go fast," she says to Sabohat, if only because giving the instruction, useless as it is, makes her feel that she is doing something. Then she waits.

Several painful minutes later, a shape materializes before Lin. A gray star with eight points radiating from four arms, centered around a glowing sphere with a hint of gold. It's Sabohat's avatar. The custom among Rogovan refugees on Earth is to represent themselves with symbols rather than human forms, as most Earth-born do. Like so many Rogovan customs Lin has grown up with, she doesn't understand this one. Why appear to someone at all, if not to give the illusion that you, yourself, are standing in the room with them? But tonight, Lin feels only relief at seeing her mother's avatar.

"Did you make it?" asks Lin.

"I did. If you're coming up here, wait until you know the soldiers are gone." The star blinks away. Lin closes her eyes and exhales. She returns to their apartment, the small rooms empty without Sabohat's presence, and sits on her bed to wait. Through the walls she can hear neighbors chattering excitedly, probably reliving the moment the soldiers stopped at their doors. When the silence of night is thick again and the feeds show two figures in Directorate red departing the building, she quietly climbs to the eighteenth floor.

Between two apartments is the battered metal door of a supply closet, so old and caked in grit that it looks as if it hasn't been used for decades. In the gleam of Lin's flashlight, however, it's clear that the dust around the edge was recently disturbed. Lin grabs the handle with both hands and drags the rusted door open with a piercing screech of metal on tile, revealing a closet draped in a faint mist of fallen dust. An antique-looking mop sits in a bucket so dirty it has sprouted a miniature forest of creeping white mold. An early model Cleanerbot rests in the corner, decapitated. Blending into the gray mess, invisible at a cursory glance, is another door, light and wooden, which Lin slips through.

"Where are you?" she asks Sabohat through her implant. Lin walks carefully beside the wall, her hand trailing through dirt and mold as she finds her way. A light comes on a few meters in front of Lin, and she can finally see her mother sitting against the wall, the glove folded in her lap.

Sabohat pats the ground beside her. Lin sits and puts a hand to her chest. She can't seem to calm her speeding heart.

"How long are you going to stay in here?" she asks aloud. Her voice bounces around the bare walls of the room. She and Sabohat don't know why the building has this chamber. It's possible some of their neighbors know about it, but not the ones who need it. Like Mr. Tomasy.

"Another thirty minutes to be safe," says Sabohat. She turns off her small flashlight and slides it into her sleeve. They sit in silence, staring blindly into the dark. After several minutes Sabohat says,

"You can't ever get complacent, Lin. The Directorate hadn't been here for years and people were saying they wouldn't come again. That the military wasn't concerned with us anymore. But I knew they'd be back."

"I know," says Lin.

"You can't think they'll never hurt you because you're a citizen," Sabohat says urgently. "They haven't done it yet, but they could. Don't forget that." Lin is quiet. Sabohat grabs her leg suddenly. "Lin, how did you know they were coming?"

"Sammy Chen told me."

"How did he know to warn you? You haven't told him about us?"

"Of course not. He was probably just telling everyone he knew." Lin can feel her mother's frown.

"You can't be so trusting, Lin. Sammy may just be a busboy, but his cousin heads an R&D division of Xinqi Tech. Tier One, even." Lin pulls out of her mother's grip.

"It's just Sammy, Mom. Everyone has a cousin high up in Xinqi or an uncle working on a big project for Wonju. He warned me, and I warned you, and now you're safe. That's what matters." Sabohat reaches a thick arm around Lin's narrow shoulders and squeezes her close.

"Yes, you're right, of course. My daughter has saved me again. What would I do without you?"

When Lin doesn't say anything, Sabohat turns on her light again and peers into her face. "What is it?" Lin doesn't look at her so Sabohat speaks directly into her mind. "Something's bothering you, I can tell."

"What would you do if I weren't here?" says Lin. "In Beijing, I mean. Would you be alright?" Sabohat laughs, startling her.

"I would miss you very much. And I would be fine, because I always have been, through darker years than you can imagine, Earth girl." She gives Lin a warm smile. "What is this about?" Lin leans into her mother's soft hug.

"I took a test," she says. "Actually, several tests. With Hauser Incorporated's Internal Security division." Sabohat's eyes widen, shadows arching across her forehead in the muted light.

"Internal Security?" she asks. "Those are the soldiers for Hauser." Sometimes Sabohat's understanding of Earth terminology is surprisingly weak. The knowledge gap is intentional—she knows what she needs to know to stay undetected by the corporations but laughs at the idea that she should memorize names and titles in a system she despises. "No, not soldiers—enforcers. Only the Directorate can officially have an army, since they oversee all of the corporations. The corporations just have enforcers. They're like... like the police you told me about on Rogov, I think. A Hauser enforcer protects Hauser citizens and stops crimes against them."

"So these tests you took, they were to become an enforcer?"

"Yes."

"And?"

"And I passed. They offered me a position. Tier One citizenship at Hauser. If I accept, I'll leave next month for four months at one of the Hauser training bases in North America. Then I'll be assigned somewhere else—could be anywhere." Sabohat lets out a happy shout and then claps a hand over her mouth.

"Lin, that's incredible! I'm so proud of you! Hauser is great. Weren't they the first to develop the Lundberg engine? Lundberg is a bit behind what Rogov has, of course, but still good. And you'll be Tier One! It's really an amazing opportunity."

"Are you sure it's OK?" Lin searches her mother's face, puzzled. "I would be there, working with them, the corporate leadership that you hate so much. Serving in a Xinqi restaurant is one thing, but my entire job will be to protect Hauser's interests. I would work with the top tier of the corporation, even bunk with them. People who want to hurt you." Sabohat leans back against the wall.

"I do hate them," she says softly. "For what they do to us Rogovans. For what they did to your father. But he and I... we came to this planet for a reason, even knowing we weren't welcome. We wanted you to have everything we never had. And now here I am, still fighting these old battles, still working to resist their power. But you shouldn't worry about that. You just rise as far as you can." She turns off the light and they sit silently, pressed together in the dark.

Chapter Two

JUST WHEN IT SEEMS all hope is lost, Cenric Smith is saved. His rescuer is not his father or anyone in his family, not even someone in debt to his family. For Cenric, who rides on the shoulders of generations of influence, the support comes from an unexpected source. A friend.

He's headed to the suite of the Vice President of Internal Affairs when it happens. He doesn't know what he'll do when he arrives, since the VP has already refused to accept his messages several times. Cenric tells himself he is driven by righteous fury. He will demand vindication, he will order the VP to reinstate him. But beneath his anger, a hot shame boils in his stomach. He pictures his family line like an ancient pyramid, standing on the solid base of his ancestors, narrowing, weakening as it approaches the peak, until Cenric, wavering at the apex, crumbles to dust.

In the low gravity of Mars, Cenric's stride across the Hauser Incorporated campus is light and airy, a feeling incongruous with his rage. A name appears in his vision field: James Lyon, Director of Global Oversight. Cenric pushes the message away. He can still feel it nudging his mind. What can Lyon want except to remind him of his disgrace?

James Lyon witnessed Cenric's fall, his humiliation. He'd been the one to find Cenric outside the Hauser suites, lying prone in the lush Martian grass, his mind locked in the thin blue haze of shav and sinking quickly into some deeper and irreparable state. Lyon quickly procured an injection that left Cenric unpleasantly lucid as the drug flushed out of his system and groaning in a pile of his own vomit. On his knees, looking up at the older man, his friend and mentor, Cenric did something that still causes him remorse. He pled. He begged Lyon not to report the incident.

"I can't lose my membership here," he said. Lyon looked at him long and sad and claimed he would say nothing about it. But Lyon lied, because this morning Cenric received notice that he was no longer welcome at the Mars Congress. He was given twenty-four hours to leave the planet. Cenric clenches his fists as he bounds lightly across the lawn.

The trees on Mars are like the people: stronger and better cultivated than elsewhere. Across the planet, the evergreens cluster in thick forests, but here on the Hauser campus, they stand in straight, disciplined lines, as if even they respect what happens on these grounds.

The quarterly Mars Congress—invented as a strategic business summit—is now a time for each corporation's most influential members to rub shoulders. Where else can Hauser's VP of Household Electronics share a drink with Wonju Bank's Head of Asset Management? For one Earth month out of every three, a few hundred of the most important members of each corporation—and some lucky bodyguards and personal assistants—come together to lounge by the pool or golf on the planet of luxury. It's where Cenric belongs.

In the center of the Hauser campus is a fountain, a basalt canal circling a statue of Hauser's three founders. The founders gaze into the distance, chins lifted, broad-shouldered and brave in the face of a collapsing civilization on Earth. The figure on the left, Tiana Williams, is Cenric's ancestor.

Cenric tries the VP one more time without success. Lyon's name pulses in his mind again and Cenric huffs. He acknowledges the message.

"Calling to apologize, I hope," he says when Lyon appears before him. Like everyone employed in the top tier of Hauser, Lyon's primary avatar is an official portrait. Anything else would be crass. He's wearing a Hauser dress uniform and his hair is impeccably styled. As Cenric continues his march to the VP's office, Lyon levitates at his side.

"Apologize?" says Lyon. "I want to offer you an opportunity." Cenric scowls.

"After you ruined my career?" His advancement has already peaked if he's no longer welcome at the Congress.

"What are you talking about?" asks Lyon. Cenric resents being forced to say it aloud.

"My Mars Congress membership was revoked. Or did you already know about that?"

"I did see that Congress membership had been removed from your profile, but I had nothing to do with that. I promised I wouldn't say anything."

"And now I know how much your promises mean. I thought I could trust you, but here I am, exiled from Mars." Something else that Lyon said registers with Cenric. "Why were you looking at my profile, anyway?"

"That's what I wanted to talk to you about. I want to offer you a position working with me on a project. A somewhat secret project. As a benefit of the position, your Mars Congress membership will be reinstated. I, of course, never miss a Congress, and I'll need you with me as much as possible. The VP understands and has agreed to the condition."

Cenric stops walking. Lyon's avatar stops, too.

"What kind of project?" Cenric asks.

"It's classified, above your old security clearance. I'd really rather talk to you about it in person. What I can say is that there's a group of people trying to destroy everything we've built here, and I mean to stop them." The facial expressions of Lyon's avatar shifts to reflect his seriousness. "Cenric, this job won't be easy, but it's a chance to take down a real threat to Hauser. To all of the Big Three. And I think you're perfect for the role."

Cenric's chest swells as he envisions himself as the bringer of justice, the savior of the Big Three. He would surely get the Gold Award, Hauser's highest honor, at the annual banquet. From there he could have any position he wanted in the company—maybe even be elected to the Directorate. But tugging at his mind is a sharp suspicion of Lyon's true motives for choosing him, especially now, after the night by the dormitories. Is Lyon feeling guilty for reporting Cenric's breakdown? No, his angle is likely the usual one.

"Is this because of my father?" Cenric asks. Lyon's avatar looks amused.

"Absolutely not. Anything I give you, any friendship we share, is in spite of your family name."

"I've been told my Hauser citizenship could be in jeopardy if I'm not gone on the next shuttle."

"Check your official records. Your Congress invitation is reinstated, and the transfer to my division is already done." Cenric accesses his personnel file on Mindlink. His title has been changed. Special Program Expert, Global Oversight Division. And yes, there's the Mars Congress icon. Cenric lets himself feel the first small flutter of hope.

"Global Oversight Division," he says, trying out the title.

"Do you know what that means?" Lyon asks. Cenric flushes, realizing he isn't really sure what kind of work Lyon does, only that his role is a very important one at Hauser. Lyon laughs lightly. "Of course you don't—no one does. I think I was given this title as a first step toward retirement. It mostly means I poke around at various reports and make sure Hauser is still running smoothly. Which it always is, naturally. But recently I found something. Something that even the Directorate has missed." Cenric is startled.

"The Directorate? If the Directorate has missed a threat, shouldn't we report it to them? If it involves all of the Big Three, it would be their jurisdiction."

"What we've created here at Hauser, what the Big Three have created...our order, our stability, our prosperity. We have to protect it ourselves.

We can't leave our well-being in the hands of the Directorate. Who are they but a bunch of politicians in a world that's moved past politics?" He waits a moment, maybe to see if Cenric will flinch at the insult to his father, his avatar still hanging emotionless beside Cenric.

"This is big, Cenric. A real threat to the world as we know it. I haven't shared it with anyone else yet."

Maybe, Cenric thinks, he will claim his place atop the family pyramid after all. Maybe he'll rise above it. His father is the crumbling stone, not Cenric.

"Tell me more."

"Do you watch the news feeds, Cenric?" Lyon asks.

"Sure. I watch the Hauser reports, at least."

"Good. What have you heard lately about offworlders?"

"Offworlders? That's the threat you're talking about?"

"It relates to that. Just come to my suite. It's best if we talk about this—" Suddenly, Lyon disappears. Cenric looks around the Hauser campus as if he might catch the avatar hiding around a corner. He messages Lyon again. Then a guttural wail rises inside Cenric's mind, rattling his skull. He covers his ears instinctively, but the unearthly scream is unmuted. Could it be coming from James Lyon? He calls Lyon again when the wail subsides, but there's no response.

Come to my suite, Lyon had said. Cenric first met James Lyon in a social room on Mindlink, created for Hauser Mars Congress members to converse while spread across the Earth. Later, Cenric and Lyon frequently chatted at mixers and banquets on Mars, and of course, there was the incident with the shav. But Cenric hasn't been to Lyon's suite, the quarters where he lives and works while on Mars. He pulls up Lyon's file. He's listed as staying in Smith Tower. Cenric turns and heads for the Smith, breaking into a run and taking the steps to the building three at a time. Once inside, his neural implant displays arrows that guide his way to the corner suite on the top floor.

A pair of medics rush into the opposite end of the hall. They're rolling a Surgerybot between them, its four metal arms curled above its cylindrical body, poised like a scorpion's tail. Cenric stands aside to let them pass, but they stop in front of Lyon's door, which slides open automatically in deference to their medical clearance. He follows them to the suite's doorway, then stops. Behind Lyon's desk, the Surgerybot's limbs do a delicate dance, flitting across something on the floor that Cenric can't see. The medics stand beside the machine, watching its movements. A hand, tinged blue, flops out from behind the desk. With each jab of the Surgerybot, the hand twitches.

The Bot's arms slow to a halt. The medics both nod in unified acknowledgment of a communication that Cenric can't hear.

"What happened?" he asks. The medics jerk around. They are similarly sized with matching chin-length dark hair and they stare at Cenric with the same wide eyes.

"James Lyon is dead," says one.

"Who are you?" says the other.

"Cenric Smith," says Cenric, and both medics' faces flicker in recognition. "Lyon was just talking to me a minute ago." He looks at the hand, outstretched from the desk, fingertips curled upward. One of the medics goes vacant-eyed, nods, then refocuses on Cenric.

"Hauser's Chair of Internal Security will want to talk to you about your conversation with the deceased. Wait for her here." Numbness creeps through Cenric. The Surgerybot clanks from behind the desk, the sound of its titanium body unfolding into a stretcher, and the medics bend and hoist the body onto the bot. The stiffening blue hand now hovers a half meter above the floor.

James Lyon's lolling head gapes at Cenric as the medics slide it past the desk, clouded eyes rimmed red, pink foam crusted around his open mouth. The door swishes shut behind the corpse, leaving Cenric alone in the room with a sharply sweet smell slinking into his nostrils.

He looks around. Lyon's suite is much bigger than his own, with many more rooms. The front room, where Cenric stands and where Lyon died, is arranged like an office. The walls are sterile white, the decor sparse except for a few small backlit display cases hanging on the wall at eye level. Cenric examines the contents of the nearest one. In the glow of a yellow light, a peculiar ceramic creature meets his eyes from behind its elongated nose. An elephant, Cenric remembers from the recordings he was shown as a school-child, a minuscule representation of a massive beast long gone. Across the statue's wide forehead is an inscription, *IES Talwar*. The aesthetic and the abbreviation are familiar to Cenric. The piece is from a space vessel belonging to the lost Ganges Fleet.

The next case holds a thin, silk glove, laced in an intricate pattern of geometric shapes in primary colors. This one has a placard. *Woman's Evening Wear, Rogov Planet*. Cenric wonders why Lyon, who had recently spoken so passionately about protecting the people of Earth, apparently took an interest in extraterrestrial civilizations. Hadn't he said that offworlders were a looming threat?

He walks behind the desk, where his eyes lock on a small splash of dark pink on the floor, a lone pool of the foam that cascaded from Lyon's mouth. Cenric feels weak and has to steady himself on the desk, which hums to life at his touch. The surface of the desk is a glowing monitor displaying a list of several files. One of them is called "For Cenric Smith." Cenric touches the file to upload it to his neural implant. The request is rejected with a buzz at his fingertips. He jabs it twice more in frustration, but the outcome is the same. The privacy settings won't allow him to take it. Footsteps approach down the hall. Cenric impulsively swipes the original file into the trash.

Lyon called the project a secret, which means it's only for Cenric to know about.

The office door slides open to reveal a tall woman with a strikingly angular and contemptuous face. Cenric hasn't met her before, but he doesn't need to consult his implant to put a name to the fiery hair and mismatched eyes. Moll Mackenzie, Chief of Internal Security, Hauser legend. Naturally, she, too, is a member of the Mars Congress. Cenric wishes he wasn't meeting such an important Hauser executive in his current flustered state. Moll Mackenzie lets her gaze float down his body and back up to his eyes before she speaks.

"The medic said you were with James Lyon when he died."

"I wasn't with him," says Cenric. "I was talking to him."

"About what?"

"I'm going to work for his division. He was telling me about my assignment."

Moll Mackenzie's mouth twitches slightly into something not quite a smile. "Funny, I heard you were leaving the Congress early," she says. Cenric clenches his jaw. He is gripped by a sudden fear that Moll Mackenzie can take this from him, that with Lyon gone, his place on Mars will be ripped away after all.

"I'm staying here," he says. "Continuing my work for Lyon."

"How well did you know him?" Moll Mackenzie asks. Cenric thinks of drinking with James at the Hauser pub, discussing his plans for the future. The first time the older man struck up a conversation, Cenric was wary of his motives, but there was something about Lyon's warm tone that melted Cenric's reserve. When Cenric talked about his stalling finance career and confessed that he hoped to make more of a mark on Hauser and the world, he knew that Lyon genuinely believed it would happen.

"Not well," he says. "I was only transferred to his division today."

"Did anything seem strange about your last conversation?"

"No. I mean, not until... at the end, there was a sound. Like screaming." Moll Mackenzie nods.

"It happens when minds are connected and one is dying or in extreme pain." Cenric shudders to think he witnessed Lyon's life being ripped from his body.

"Why are you asking me about this?" Cenric asks.

"We don't know if this is a suspicious death yet," says Moll. "If it is, we'll have to talk to you again. For now, go home and thank the stars over Mars that your daddy saved you again." Cenric looks down and doesn't correct her.

***

Back in his own small, single-room suite, Cenric slumps at his desk. A brush of his hand brings the desk display to life. Ten figures rise from the back of the workspace and straighten their translucent bodies to meet Cenric's eyes. At the far left, Tiana Williams grins, content with her exalted position in history. Her son, Romey Williams, Hauser's second chief executive, stands beside her. Cenric slides his gaze past his father on the far right to the empty air where he himself should stand.

He slams his fist into his desk. Pain shoots up to his elbow, but the ten smug figures on the desk barely waver. *For Cenric Smith*, the file in Lyon's suite had said, taunting him with proximity to his secret mission.

There's suddenly not enough air in the room. He tosses his chair back and storms to the dresser, tearing through clothes with shaking hands until he finds a small white patch of shav. He presses it to his bicep, closing his eyes and sinking to his knees. The edges of the room blur, and the floor beneath him curls into peaceful, rolling waves as the stress of the last few hours floats away.

Tomorrow, his work will begin. He'll hunt down the truth about James Lyon's special project. He'll be the one to bring justice to Hauser and another generation of glory to his family name. But tonight, he'll allow himself to fall into this old habit just one more time.

Chapter Three

When Lin opens her eyes, the world has shrunk. She can feel, before she even tries to reach out to the neural web, that she's been cut loose from billions of other connected minds, severed from Sabohat and the streams of information that make the world navigable. The clean white walls of the hospital operating room are the edge of her existence, the sound of the doctor laying a hand beside her on the operating table her only input. Lin closes her eyes again.

"Strange, isn't it?" says the doctor. Lin can hear the warm shape of a smile in his voice. "They make us turn off our implants sometimes in medical school to make sure we can operate without looking up information or using a Surgerybot. It's disconcerting, I know. But don't worry, I have your Hauser upgrade implanted and ready to go."

"Turn it on," says Lin hoarsely. She feels exposed, lying belly-up on the steel table.

"I will in a minute," says the doctor. When Lin opens her eyes again, the steepled fingers of a Surgerybot hover gleaming above her face. She turns her head to see the doctor. His sharp jawline and deep brown curls remind her of the actor Mads Gupta in his famous role as a rugged captain in the Ganges Fleet. In the film—based on true events—the fleet of would-be colonizers leave Earth for a string of planets they call the New India Belt but disappear instead into the cosmos, never to be heard from again. This young doctor has both the broad shoulders and the confident eyes of Gupta's captain. Lin sends out an inquiry about his identity, then remembers she's offline. The silence is deeper than an absence of sound.

"My name is Doctor Rajan Singh," says the doctor, smiling gently at her. "Junior Neurotechnologist for Hauser Medical Center in Beijing."

"Can you turn the implant on now?"

"Pretty soon. But I have to warn you first. You're Tier One now, so you're getting a top-of-the-line implant and access to a lot of information most people don't have. I had a look at your old implant, and..." He frowns. Lin can tell he's trying to be tactful. "I don't usually see implants quite so old or... inexpensive in new Tier One recruits. With this new model, the line between projection and reality will be less clear. Most citizens have had the implant since their childhood so the adjustment period is longer, but for you, it might be overwhelming."

Lin glares at him. "Just turn it on."

The operating room melts into a swirl of colors and floating objects, like streams of paint circling a drain. A cacophony of sounds swells until Lin is afraid she'll choke on the noise—the rattle of the Hyperrail, a summer storm, voices shouting in languages she doesn't know. She grasps for something solid to steady herself, but the arm that extends before her isn't flesh but a cartoon animal's claw. Lin shouts and tries to run. The air is soft and gelatinous, filling her ears and rippling through her chest. Her ankle knocks against metal, sending a painful vibration up her leg, which is somehow not below her body, as she expected, but hovering parallel to her face. Lin flails her arms, her real arms this time, and clutches the side of the operating table just in time to realize she is falling from it. Strong arms catch her and steady her by the shoulders.

"Breathe," says Dr. Singh. "And think about where you are. Hauser Medical Center in Beijing, in an operating room. Table and Surgerybot behind you, me in front of you. Your feet are on the ground. Your hands are," he takes them in his, "here. Now open your eyes."

Lin hadn't realized they were closed. Stupid. She forces her eyelids open and finds the concerned eyes of Dr. Singh mere centimeters from hers. She yanks her hands away and leans heavily against the operating table.

"Do you have the implant under control now?" asks Dr. Singh. Lin flushes at the thought of him watching her stumble blindly.

"Did it malfunction?" she asks.

"Unlikely," he says. "If you take it slowly and get used to it, you'll find that there's a reason that Xinqi and Wonju are jealous of Hauser's implant tech. Are you ready to try again? Here. Lie back down on the table." Lin looks at him warily but reluctantly follows instructions. "There's an orientation video preloaded on the implant. Anyone who changes citizenship to Hauser receives it. Do you see the file?"

Lin closes her eyes and scans the directory of files on the implant. She finds and launches the video, bracing for another flood of sensory overload. Instead, she finds herself suddenly facing the stage of an auditorium designed in the grandiose style of old America, where Hauser was founded. She opens her eyes. She can still see the operating room behind the projection.

The man on stage is immediately recognizable from the history books. Matthew Renard, one of Hauser's three founders, stands at a podium and looks out over the sea of empty chairs with a bold smile. Lin closes her eyes again to focus on the details of the illusion. The visuals provided by her old implant would have looked hastily rendered and artificial, but now she can see the texture of the red velvet curtain behind Renard and the small flowers etched in the gold balcony rail.

"Less than three hundred years ago," Renard begins, his voice booming through the cavernous auditorium, "the nation-states of our planet had fallen into chaos. Resources and space were scarce. War and disaster were frequent. Almost two hundred governments existed at the time, each concerned mostly with the problems inside their own borders. They failed to cooperate, letting scientific progress crumble in the face of petty squabbles over small patches of land and local resources. The people of that time had stopped working for a better future."

Though the projection puts Lin in a back row of the auditorium, Renard seems to lock eyes with her. "In the midst of these dark times," he continues, "three small technology companies formed an alliance. From the nation called China, Xinqi Tech. From Korea, Wonju Systems. And from the United States, Hauser Incorporated." The moment Renard names Hauser, the sound of applause swells out of the empty seats surrounding Lin.

"Of the Big Three," says Renard, "Hauser was the leader from the start. It was Hauser that suggested it was up to the innovators, not the governments, to save the world. It was Hauser that led the other corporations into the future." Lin raises her eyebrows. That's not exactly what she learned attending Xinqi school as a child. She distinctly remembers stuffy old Mr. Magri lecturing his virtual classroom of ten-year-olds that only Xinqi had the foresight to step in and provide social services for its people while the old government systems collapsed around them. While Hauser and Wonju were solely focused on selling their fanciest tech, droned Mr. Magri, it was Xinqi that used that tech to build a new life for its growing force of employees.

"These companies looked beyond the designation of nation-state borders and came together to develop the technology that allowed us to terraform our subsidiary planet, Mars, and later expand into the galaxy." Renard leaves the podium and walks thoughtfully to the front of the stage, gazing into the distance, his expression twisting into something almost comically dark.

"Some chose to leave us during those difficult times. They fled to faraway worlds rather than working together for the progress of Earth." Lin is glad her mother isn't listening. Sabohat sees the original colonists as the brightest and bravest that Earth had to offer at the time, not fleeing from their homes but daring to seek a new path for humanity. "But we at Hauser never lost hope for our beautiful home planet. Today, life here is prosperous, and despite our humble beginnings, Hauser, Xinqi, and Wonju employ almost 100 percent of the world's population." Almost.

"Yang Lin," continues the recording of Renard, startling Lin with the use of her name. "You have been chosen as an heir to the dreams of Hauser's founders. You will protect our cooperative way of life and contribute to the advancement of life on Earth. Together, we will create a better future for all of our citizens."

The hall and Renard dissipate. Lin opens her eyes and sits up, shaking her head. Dr. Singh is still standing beside her.

"It's a little much, isn't it?" His eyes have a conspiratorial shine that makes it impossible not to smile back.

"Yes," she says, surprised. Dr. Singh seems like the type of successful citizen that would buy into the hype.

"The implant also contains some new nanotech. Over the next few months, it will gradually have an effect on your physique and senses. Better vision, especially at night, more muscle mass, a quicker response time. Basically, you're becoming the ideal enforcer."

"I understand," says Lin. "Am I finished then?"

"Just a few questions," he says. "To complete the medical history. I can see from your file that you're adopted, right?"

"Yes," says Lin. True enough.

"Do any records exist in the Big Three systems for your biological parents? I couldn't find any link to them."

"No," says Lin. Also true.

"OK, it's not a problem, but we need to know as much as possible for the health records. To analyze risk. Have you always lived here in Beijing?"

"Yes." That one is a lie. She was born light years away, on a small ship traversing deep space.

***

Lin hires a slow taxi home, the kind that meanders through Beijing's alleyways and points out the best local vendors. The taxi's computer would typically convey its recommendations directly to the passenger's implant, but Lin still doesn't quite trust her new hardware.

"I'd like a baozi," she says. "A handmade one, not from one of the automatic stalls." The taxi sends her request ahead, and by the time it pulls up to the food cart window, a plump woman with scarce teeth has a steaming bun ready to hand Lin. Lin takes a chewy mouthful and leans back to watch her home city out the window. The trees in Beijing are tumultuous, huddled low and wrapping gaunt arms around every building, springing through sidewalks no matter how often they're stamped down. The flora in Beijing originated from the same genetically engineered seeds that were used throughout the galaxy, designed to germinate in anything resembling soil and quickly evolve into something new. Earth's original plant species succumbed to Terratech centuries ago, taking most of the animal kingdom with them. Each of the Big Three corporations would love to claim the dominant Terratech strain as their own patented invention, but speciation is so rapid that no one knows where each new variety came from. In Beijing, Terratech plants grow deep, tenacious roots that hold fast when sandstorms rage over the surrounding mountains.

Soon, Lin will leave Beijing. She doesn't know many people who have left home, especially among the poor residents of her neighborhood. Even

Lin's Earth-born and well-to-do classmates from Xinqi public school, despite being raised on the rhetoric of a borderless world where geography is meaningless, mostly live near where they were raised while working online for the Big Three.

This state-of-the-art implant is where her new life begins. It will make her better, stronger, more successful in her new role at Hauser. Lin breathes deeply and uses the implant to search the first thing that comes to mind. Rogov. Her parents' home planet materializes in the taxi, spinning lazily to display its arid, cratered geography. No lights or other signs of human habitation appear in the image—but then, Lin suspects that whoever created this informational listing didn't want viewers to dwell on the people who make their home on Rogov's parched surface. She quickly closes the search. The corporations claim not to monitor Mindlink and even that their implants are impervious to spying, and Lin has never heard of any refugee or criminal being caught due to their activities on the neural web, but she's always been skeptical. Now that she's in Tier One law enforcement, her implant might be under more scrutiny. She opens a more innocuous file: her own personnel record. Citizenship: Hauser, it declares, and lists her title as Internal Security Enforcer Trainee followed by her citizen ID number and employment and educational history. Adjacent to this block of information is her own official portrait. It isn't an exact representation. Lin doesn't actually own a Hauser dress uniform yet, and she's never smiled in such a dizzy way. Lin examines the woman in her new avatar and imagines meeting her in public. Who is she? She looks like a person whose eyes would glide past Lin on the Hyperrail on her way to some important meeting. Someone who lives in luxury and has no worries of Directorate soldiers and suspicious neighbors. Someone who would turn on Sabohat in a heartbeat.

***

The dim light of Hanting Community is warm and comfortable compared to the stark Hauser Medical Center.

"I'm home," Lin subvocalizes before she turns the door handle to her apartment. She always gives a warning before she enters, so her mother knows it's only her, although Sabohat never seems worried.

"And here she is," says Sabohat aloud as she enters. Lin pauses just inside the door. Seven people are gathered around the kitchen table. Lin only recognizes a few individuals, but she knows their type—not quite Earthly in body, in style, in mannerisms, in accent. Lin and Sabohat's kitchen has always hosted people like this. She grew up studying or playing games in the bedroom to the background music of raucous laughter from Sabohat's circle of friends. Lin never joined them. She wasn't forbidden, but she felt as unwelcome in that world as she was in the virtual clubs her classmates frequented in their free time. Sabohat's associates were always kind to Lin, but their kindness came with weighty expectations. If she slipped and used the trending local slang or spoke a little too warmly about the other kids at Xinqi school, her mother's friends shot each other disapproving looks.

Sabohat herself never questioned whether Lin was offworlder enough. "We Rogovans" was a favorite phrase. "We Rogovans know how to work hard," she beamed at Lin when Lin got her first raise at the noodle house. And when Lin helped her fix an issue with their Hanting security feeds, she said, "We Rogovans are good problem solvers."

But Sabohat also pushed Lin to assimilate. She talked often about what Lin could achieve and how successful she would be—if she fit in on Earth. The result of this was that Lin had learned to fit in a little too well for Sabohat's friends' tastes, so she avoided any more than cursory contact with the offworlder social group.

Today, the meeting lacks the usual smiles. Lin realizes she hasn't given any thought to what kind of shadow the visit from the Directorate soldiers has cast over the community. She steps closer to the table, and the murmur of voices fades. The offworlders are all watching her.

"Any news about Mr. Tomasy?" Lin asks. A few people just turn away sadly, but Sabohat's friend Jul shoots her a stony look. Lin has known, and feared, Jul for years. Like most Rogovans, Jul is thick-bodied and short, compacted by Rogov's high gravity. But where Sabohat's wide stature gives her a soft plumpness, Jul looks tough as a boulder. A long, graying braid runs down her back and a geometric pattern of tattoos creeps over her high collar.

"He's gone," she says, in a tone that tells Lin she shouldn't have asked. She seems angry at Lin for some reason. "To a camp maybe. Or he's dead. We don't know. We never know." Sabohat speaks more softly.

"This is just the way it is, Lin. The Directorate comes, and people like us disappear. We don't know where. We don't know if there's any logic to who they take. We've tried in the past to find out, but all we've ever learned is that they're not here anymore."

"We shouldn't accept that," says a young man in the corner. He's tall and lean—not Rogovan, then. From New Palu, Lin is certain, like Mr. Tomasy. Sabohat heaves herself from her chair and stumps across the kitchen with her cane to stand beside the man.

"Lin, this is Emas," she says. Emas steps forward and extends a hand, which Lin takes awkwardly and shakes. Such an old-fashioned gesture.

"I've heard a lot about you," he says. "Sabohat just told us about your new position. It's exciting to have one of our own in the first tier." One of our own. There's an assumption in his voice that Lin doesn't trust. Sabohat pats Lin on the back.

"It's an impressive achievement for anyone," she says.

"But we can use this," says Emas. The intensity of his eyes makes Lin blush. There is a trace of light blue liner around them. "Lin is going to have a level of access that we've never had. It's a great opportunity, and right when we need it."

Lin looks at Sabohat for an explanation. "Lin isn't a part of this," Sabohat says to Emas.

"A part of what?" asks Lin, but she knows there are many things she has never been a part of. Not her mother's social circle of offworlders who gather to share rumors about anti-refugee actions and memories of people back home, and not the professional network for whom Sabohat does engineering work in exchange for small sums that go into Lin's account with strange tags like "housekeeping." She isn't a colonist, a rugged survivor with old stories to share, a proud alien.

Emas, obviously proud, locks eyes with Sabohat. "If the conversation is over, I'll be on my way," he says. "Thank you for dinner, Sabohat." He turns to Lin. The dark hair covering one side of his face shifts, giving a peek of mutilated purple flesh on his cheek. The toxic clouds of New Palu maim many residents. "Yang Lin, I have an offer that might interest you."

"What kind of offer?"

"It's an invitation, actually, for a virtual social room. A group of us refugees meet on Mindlink. We talk about life on Earth and what we can do to make it better. Or sometimes we just talk, have fun." Emas doesn't seem like the fun-having type. He reaches into his pocket and pulls out a small piece of paper, which he hands to Lin. It has two strings of handwritten numbers on it. "That's the address and the password," says Emas. "Commit them to memory, then destroy the paper. You'll be able to access the group because I invited you and my identity is verified. The group is hosted on an unlisted server and every now and then we change the location, so you'll get a new login. One of the group members, probably me, will let you know the new number in person."

"Why so much secrecy?" Lin asks. It doesn't sound like he's really talking about a casual social club. "Do you think that the Big Three are monitoring Mindlink groups?"

"Maybe," says Emas. "Probably not. We're more worried about strangers infiltrating the group. This way we don't have any lurkers that we've all forgotten about."

"OK. I'll check it out sometime." Emas switches to speaking through his implant.

"And this is my ID number," he says, "Contact me whenever you like." Lin looks back at him silently. He nods, and then turns and leaves the apartment.

The small kitchen is silent for a moment in the wake of his departure. Then one woman, rice spoon frozen midair, speaks in a voice too loud.

"Young people and their virtual rooms." The crowd in the kitchen bursts into laughter, relieved to pretend that they had only been sharing friendly banter all along.

"So, Lin, what do you think of Emas?" says Sabohat, eyes sparkling. Lin's face flushes as several women giggle.

"Ha, look at her," crows Jul.

"Those New Palus aren't the same as us Rogovans, but they're like us," says Sabohat, and then nudges Lin. "And easy on the eyes, right?"

"Yes," says Jul. "Of all our plentiful resources in the colonies, our beautiful faces are the best of all." The whole group laughs for reasons Lin can't entirely explain. The woman with the rice grins.

"If you want to see easy on the eyes, wait until you see my nephew. I'll be happy to introduce you as soon as he gets here." She giggles again but the others are suddenly hushed, darting glances around the table. Sabohat pulls out a chair and ushers Lin into it with a soft hand on her back.

"Lin, something is happening. Something very big."

"What?" An inexplicable dread boils in Lin. Her mother's face is too solemn and she seems reluctant to speak, so Jul jumps in.

"A Rogovan ship is on its way to Earth. *The* Rogovan ship, the flagship of the original fleet that settled the planet. It's finally space-worthy again and almost three thousand Rogovans are making the trip here. They've already been traveling for many years, and according to the latest message, they'll be here in just a few months." Lin grips the table as she stares at Jul, then cups her mouth as the bile rises from her stomach. She doesn't trust herself to speak. She stands, accidentally spilling someone's cup of water. She starts to wipe it up, then hurries from the kitchen and shuts herself in the bedroom. She curls on her bed, facing the wall.

Lin can hear the thump of her mother's cane approaching the door. Sabohat knocks.

"Lin? Can we talk?" Lin doesn't answer, and after a moment Sabohat sighs and goes back to the kitchen.

***

Three thousand Rogovans is an unprecedented onslaught of refugees. The vessel that brought Lin to Earth carried only seventeen crew members, each of them recruited for the trip because they had something special to offer. Lin's mother designed the ship, and her father Hayato secured his passage by mining for various rare materials needed for construction.

For the first eight years of their long deep space journey, they were the only seventeen people in their world. Then secretly, lovingly, in a stolen moment in crowded quarters, Sabohat and Hayato brought another refugee into existence.

A makeshift drawer was her cradle. The other refugees held her, kissed her, played her recordings in English and Mandarin and Korean so she could learn those languages with the accents of Earth. They placed drops of their own sweet water ration on her lips. *You are the future of the Rogovan people*, they whispered. She was called Nadya then, like so many Rogovan girls are, to honor the brave and desperate scientist who led the first settlers to Rogov. Later, they took that name away and gave her one more common on Earth.

Earth was the only home Nadya ever knew, even before she knew it. She was told from birth that she would have a good and happy life there. The refugees on the ship knew their chances of surviving the landing were slim, and several regretted leaving their loved ones behind for such an uncertain future. But when little Nadya was present, the word "Earth" was always spoken with a smile.

TEDI, the unfeeling artificial intelligence that guards the skies for the Directorate, spotted the Rogovan ship as soon as it entered orbit. Eight Rogovans were killed in the first blast. The others, including Sabohat, Hayato, and seven-year-old Nadya, made it into the landing shuttle and blazed into the atmosphere trailing fire, crashing in the desert of North America. Two of the refugees were killed on impact. Hayato died more slowly, the charred skin on his face oozing blood as he rasped for his family to run for their lives. Sabohat took Nadya's small hand in hers and fled into the desert, spending the night huddled together in a cave for warmth.

***

Now, lying on her bed, staring at the wall, Lin can't seem to catch her breath. She presses her eyes closed, trying to squeeze the vision of her father's death from her mind. Instead, she sees it multiplied by three thousand.

Chapter Four

VEDRA RUNS LIKE HELL. The blaze from the compound blisters her back and sends her shadow stretching ahead of her down the dark stone tunnel. Vedra grips her son's hand and tries to tug him along faster. Temar is weak, born in low gravity and spoiled by his father. She'll see that change now that Fenton is dead.

"Come on, sweetie, we just have to make it to Daddy's fliers."

"Do you even know how to fly them?" Temar snivels.

"I'll figure it out," says Vedra. She always figures it out.

A scream from the compound echoes through the tunnel. Vedra looks behind her. No one else is coming.

The tunnel widens into a cavernous room that houses Fenton's six fliers. Vedra has never been allowed to see the sleek planes come and go, but she knows that Fenton and his men use them to bring goods to ships waiting nearby. They make those trips often—that means there must be plenty of passing ships. One of them will take her to a better place. Or a worse place, as such things usually go, but at least she won't be burned to death.

A crash and a sound like splintering glass come from the compound. Time to fly herself and Temar off of this flaming world before she roasts with it. The stone walls of the flier dock are taller than the halls of the compound, with none of its ornate furnishings. The fliers sit in a row in the center, gleaming black. Vedra goes to one and runs her hand over its smooth exterior. How do you open the thing?

"Going somewhere?" says a voice. Vedra spins. Leaning against the last flier in the fleet is Myat Shin, a recent acquaintance of Vedra's recently scorched husband. Until now, Vedra has only seen Myat from a distance, lounging in the banquet hall with the rest of Fenton's men when Vedra served them dinner. The man caught her attention, though, and while they had never exchanged a word, there was something intriguing about the set of his broad shoulders, alert and poised while the others slouched and belched and splashed wine onto her dress. She asked one of the other women in the compound about him later and learned his name and that he was a freelance pilot Fenton had hired.

Myat takes a few steps toward her, his eyes wary but his hands not reaching for his weapon. Vedra pushes Temar behind her.

"I'm just looking to get out of here," she says.

"You know how to fly one of these?" says Myat. His voice has a surprisingly warm tone, though his accent in Anglian is fishy. Perfect, but forced, in complete contrast of her own sloppy brand of speech.

"Sure," says Vedra. Myat's look is skeptical.

"Fenton teach you?" he asks. They both know that would never have happened. "Look, I have a ship out there, waiting not far from this asteroid. I can take you. It's your only option for surviving."

"I get that the odds aren't good," says Vedra. "But Temar and I are going off on our own. We don't need anything from any of you men." Myat approaches them swiftly until he's right in Vedra's face. Vedra does a double-take. It appears she was hasty in the "man" part of her evaluation. Myat looks at her with soft cheeks and full lips.

"Damn, you're a girl."

Myat smiles slightly and winks at Vedra. "I'm Myat," she says, pressing an unseen button on the side of the flier and a hatch springs open. "Get in."

"Why should I trust you?" says Vedra.

"Your husband did."

Vedra laughs. "Well that's one strike against you," she says.

"I'm the only chance you and your son have to live. And we've got about five minutes," says Myat. Another tortured scream from the compound drains Vedra's bravado.

"Come on, Temar," she says. He doesn't move, except to tremble. His eyes are wide and unblinking. Vedra scoops him up in a mess of gangly limbs and climbs into the flier with him. There are only two seats, so she holds him in her lap on the passenger side. She runs her hands over his long limbs, quaking now with shock. Fenton promised him time in the gravity simulator but rarely gave it, leaving him too thin and frail. His lips are looking a little blue. Vedra strokes his hair.

Myat swings into the pilot's seat and runs quick fingers across the console. The flier hums to life and taxis towards the rock wall with increasing speed. For a moment, Vedra thinks Myat means to smash the flier right into the stone, but as she braces for impact, a thin, glowing line appears in the wall. It's the edge of a large door—perfectly camouflaged in the stone—which slides away to reveal a long runway. Myat taps a few buttons and the flier accelerates rapidly, crushing Vedra painfully between the seat and Temar. The last thing she hears before she blacks out is her son screaming.

***

Vedra wakes with a mouth full of cloth. She groggily tries to pull it away from her face and finds her hands bound to her sides. Vedra jerks, wide awake now, and when she moves, a sharp pain attacks her chest. All she can see from her captive position are padded grey walls.

"Hey, Myat!" she yells, spitting out the cloth. "Show yourself!" Myat's high cheekbones and short dark hair float into view, her face close to Vedra's, her back against the opposite wall.

Or is it the ceiling?

Vedra realizes only then that she has gone from the low gravity of the compound to true zero gravity. The cloth binding her is a sack holding her in place while she sleeps.

"I'm sorry," says Myat. In the cramped space, Vedra can feel Myat's breath on her skin. "I should have realized the high pressure in the flier would be hard on your son." Vedra squirms in the sack, ignoring the burn in her ribs. Her head swims and she balls her hands into fists.

"Where's Temar?" she demands. "Is he alright?"

"He's right there," says Myat. Vedra turns her head to the side and sees her son sleeping in another sack beside her.

"I gave him some medicine to build up bone and muscle density," says Myat. "I gave you a bit too, although I don't believe you came from low gravity originally." It's a half-question that Vedra doesn't answer. Myat continues, "It will take a while to heal his fractures, but he'll be fine." Vedra finally manages to work one hand free and reaches out to stroke her son's cheek, then turns back to Myat as she unzips her sleeping sack.

"Where did you get that kind of medicine?" she asks.

"I'm a trader," Myat answers. Vedra narrows her eyes. Fenton was a trader too, not to mention the owner of a valuable mine. He was rich enough to employ dozens of men like Myat, but even he could have rarely procured such potent pharmaceuticals. Not that he would have given them to his son anyway.

"Where are you from, Myat?" Vedra asks. The woman has the look of an Empire man. Myat looks at Vedra for a long minute before answering.

"Pluto," she says. "Before the colony there was abandoned."

"And then you joined the Empire." Vedra thinks she sees a smile tug at Myat's mouth.

"The Empire?" Myat asks. "You mean the Big Three corporations? I've never even been to Earth." Vedra searches Myat's face for a hint of whether she's telling the truth, but she's perfectly expressionless. Vedra will have to remember not to trust Myat no matter how many gifts the pilot makes to her and her son.

"Where are we going?" asks Vedra. As if it matters.

"There's a station not far from here called Emberaz."

Vedra shudders. She would rather avoid any station. "How far is it?"

"We can get there in less than twenty days." Myat uses the Anglian term for an Earth day.

"Day?" says Vedra. "And you say you're not Empire."

"Days are the standard measurement on space vessels throughout the galaxy," Myat says with a smile. "A trader might schedule meetings with people from many different places with different systems of measuring time, so we've all taken to using a standard—'Empire' or not. Fenton used it too, I promise." Vedra eyes her skeptically. Myat grips Vedra's arm.

"I'm sorry that you lost your husband," she says. Vedra wants to say *I'm not*, but she just nods. Myat's eyes are soft and soulful, and Vedra is now one hundred percent sure that despite the style of her clothes and hair, Myat is a woman. Vedra has spent her life around men, and none of them have ever looked at her with Myat's compassion. She obviously pities Vedra the widow. If only she knew.

***

The fire was an accident, mostly.

Or if anyone was to blame, it was Fenton, who surely must have known that their home was lined with veins of combustible minerals. But that didn't stop him from presenting Vedra with four giant torches to light the banquet hall. He had seen similar decor when he visited the palace of Dieter Juergen—his biggest mining rival—and he couldn't stand to lose to the competition, even in matters of ambiance.

So Vedra hung the torches on the hooks installed by Fenton's men and twisted the bases, laughing in delight when the flame bloomed from each one. She was setting dinner on the table when one of the hooks fell, sending the torch tumbling. A line of fire, like a writhing orange snake, crept out from the fallen torch, following some invisible path across the floor. Vedra grabbed a pitcher of water off the banquet table and held it above the flame, poised to extinguish it.

Then she stopped.

She lowered the pitcher and stared at the burning line, now creeping up the wall and branching into five sizzling fingers. The middle finger touched a large tapestry, which caught fire instantly. Vedra set the pitcher back on the table.

The banquet hall was the center of the compound and the only hub between its three wings. The fire was spreading slowly in the low gravity, but of the three passageways leading out of the hall, the entrance to the one nearest the fallen torch was already mostly obscured by inky smoke. It led to what Vedra thought of as Fenton's wing, where the men lived and where Fenton entertained guests and conducted business.

The second exit, which would also be impassable within minutes, led to the only way off of the compound—the fliers. Black smoke swelled up to the hall's arched ceiling. Vedra coughed and wiped greasy sweat from her forehead.

"My god!" Fenton's voice made Vedra jump. She could barely make out his wavering outline behind the door to the first wing. "What are you doing? Get some water and get us out of here, now!" Vedra grabbed the pitcher again and tossed its contents at the burning wall, but the small splash of water did nothing against the raging fire. She looked over her shoulder. How long did she have before the third passageway was also cut off?

"Vedra!" yelled Fenton. "Don't you dare leave me here!" Vedra took two steps backward, then turned and started walking toward the passageway. Just as she was about to leave the hall, she was knocked to the ground, sending the pitcher clattering. She tried to scramble back to her feet, but a rough hand grabbed the back of her head and shoved her face into the gritty dirt floor.

"Where do you think you're going?" growled Vedra's husband, his rank breath close against the side of her head. How had he gotten through the wall of flame? As she kicked and flailed against his heavy body, a stench like overcooked meat reached her nostrils. Vedra imagined herself burned to death, trapped below Fenton, their bones piled together for all time. Temar would die here, too. Even if he escaped the fire, no one would come to this godforsaken place to save him.

She reached her arm around his head and yanked on his ear, causing him to loosen his grip just long enough for her to pull herself forward and grab the pitcher. He dragged her back to him and she swung blindly upwards, feeling a satisfying thunk. Fenton's hand lifted from her neck. Vedra pushed him off of her and stood up, gasping for breath before looking back at her husband. Fenton was writhing on the ground, flames reaching around from his back and clawing at his chest and neck. Vedra turned and ran out of the banquet hall.

This passageway led to the women's chambers, mostly empty now as the few other women in the compound performed their various household tasks. The wife of one of Fenton's top men came running toward Vedra in the direction of the fire.

"Turn around, Linnea!" yelled Vedra. "We don't have much time to get out of here!"

"Barnet is in there," Linnea said as she passed Vedra. "I have to help him."

"There's nothing we can do for them," said Vedra. "But I know another way out." Linnea slowed to a walk and gave Vedra a long look over her shoulder. For a moment, Vedra thought she would have a partner in her escape, then Linnea started running toward the banquet hall again. Vedra didn't wait to find out what happened when she got there.

Temar was curled up asleep on Vedra's bed in the women's chamber. She could smell the smoke even from here. Vedra shook her son gently, and Temar moaned and sucked his thumb. He was such an infant. At his age—six Anglian years, maybe eight Earth years—Vedra had already seen her mother killed and spent two months in station jail for theft. Temar spent most of his days with her in the women's chambers, sipping tea and listening to music, except for when Fenton wanted to show off his son to some business partner.

"We have to go," said Vedra, yanking the boy out of bed. He blinked lazily at the strands of dark smoke beginning to billow into the chamber.

Vedra's escape plan was a passageway only she knew about. She grabbed a small table and dragged it across the room to the opposite wall, barely noticing as a lamp and tablecloth clattered to the floor. Above the table was a tapestry. Vedra climbed onto the table and flung the tapestry aside, revealing a chiseled hole, barely large enough for someone Vedra's size to squeeze into. Vedra had found it just seven months earlier. She didn't know who had made it or why it was hidden, but she knew immediately it could be useful.

"I don't want to go anywhere," said Temar.

"You don't have a choice. Come here," Vedra said. Temar still sulked, but he shuffled to her obediently and let her pull him up onto the table with her. There was barely space for both of them, and Temar clutched her waist as the table rocked.

"Now climb on through this hole," said Vedra. "I'll give you a push. It's bigger on the other side, I promise."

"No." Temar dug his fingers deeper into Vedra's flesh. "No way. I'm staying here." Vedra looked at his terrified face and sighed.

"Okay, I'll go first," she said. "But you have to promise you'll come right after me." Temar nodded.

Vedra crawled into the small opening. It was narrow enough from top to bottom that she immediately felt her breathing constrict, and for one terrible moment, her hips lodged between the stone walls and she couldn't move in any direction. Then with a final heave, she tumbled forward into a larger tunnel, just tall enough for her to stand. Vedra turned and reached her hands back through the narrow space.

"Come on, baby," she said. Temar shied backward, looking over his shoulder as if he were considering choosing the flames over escaping.

"We have to go," said Vedra, trying to sound calm so her son didn't panic. Temar just stared back at her. "Now!" she yelled, and Temar immediately reached up to grasp her hands. Vedra pulled his skinny body through the hole easily. Then she helped her son to his feet, grabbed his arm, and ran like hell.

***

Myat's ship is a piece of junk.

An incessant background chorus of grinding and clanking rings against Vedra's skull. Every surface is dull gray and layered in grime. Other than the tiny compartment where Vedra awoke, she's only seen one other room. It's bigger and would be more comfortable for travel than the sleeping space, if only it weren't littered with empty crates and piles of rope, some of which are secured while others spin about hazardously.

"Is this ship safe?" asks Vedra, eyeing what appears to be a melted hole in the wall of the larger room.

"We'll make it to the station," says Myat.

"Wonderful."

Myat points at a door above Vedra's head. Just when she thinks she knows her up from her down.

"Let me show you something," says Myat. She pushes off of the wall floor and lands next to the door. Vedra follows. On the other side of the door are two chairs protruding from the left wall. Vedra reorients herself once again—chairs mean down. Each of the chairs has a small touchscreen console attached to the arm, and a large monitor, currently turned off, hangs above them. Myat slips into one chair and buckles a strap across her chest, then gestures to the other chair. Vedra straps herself in too. What would Fenton think to see her now, sitting at the controls of a spaceship? Myat taps her chair's console and the monitor above them flashes. Vedra leans back to look at it. A lumpy brown rock floats in the middle of the screen.

"That's the asteroid," says Myat. "That's where we came from."

"That little chunk?" says Vedra. "I don't see anything."

"If we were a little closer, you could see the remains of the original scientific outpost," Myat says. "They're the ones that spun up the asteroid to have livable gravity and built the first few rooms of the compound, like the flier bay. They were there to study its unique composition. The, uh... flammable parts."

"What happened to those people?" asks Vedra.

"Fenton did," says Myat.

Vedra stares at the asteroid on the monitor. She never thought of the compound as a pockmark on an unremarkable little pebble. It was her entire world.

Chapter Five

PEOPLE ARE EVERYTHING, OR so Cenric has been told by his father since he was a child. Cormand Smith has always cultivated relationships like a master gardener of people, tending them diligently for years until they bear him valuable fruit.

Cenric has tried his hand at horticulture as well, but inevitably one mistake, one blight of angry words, leaves the whole relationship withered and barren. That's why Arthur Adeyemi is so puzzling—he's like a weed that Cenric can't seem to kill with neglect.

Even for an official portrait, Arthur's avatar smiles a little too widely.

"Hey, Cenric, some friends and I have a weekly poker game going. We start it up every Mars Congress—it's so fun to play in person! Harder to bluff with your real face than an avatar. We meet in Douglas Hall. You should join us! Today's your day off, isn't it?" Cenric runs a hand over his face. He doesn't know why Arthur always expects these things of him.

"It is my day off, but I have extra work to do," he says. Cenric doesn't actually have work. Since Lyon's death, he's been stuck in a strange limbo. He hasn't been reassigned, but he doesn't know what his job for Lyon's department actually is, only that he alone has been tasked with taking down a major threat. "What about the investigation?" Cenric asks Arthur. "Has Mo looked into it?"

"Yeah, he said he would. He's not working on the Lyon case but he's going to try to find out what they know so far." Arthur's partner is a detective with the Hauser enforcers who, thanks to Arthur, somehow always gets assigned to the Mars Congress.

"It's important," Cenric reminds him.

"So you keep saying."

Cenric and Arthur met fifteen years ago when they were both just out of school and assigned to the same small Hauser division developing kitchen software. Arthur coded from Lagos and Cenric ran financial analysis from his hometown of Denver. Arthur was a genius programmer and the darling of the department director. In fact, everyone on the team loved Arthur, though it seemed to Cenric that the hours Arthur spent on banal socializing in virtual clubs and even during work meetings were a fatal flaw in an otherwise talented individual. So Cenric was surprised that when he finally made it to the Congress—after years of coveting that most prestigious of Hauser perks—he found Arthur already there, now working as a highly-respected lead engineer in the Terratech division. He was even more surprised when Arthur remembered him and instantly considered him a friend.

Cenric doesn't reciprocate the feeling, but somehow he keeps finding himself pacing the hallways late at night, sometimes high and sometimes mortifyingly sober, raving to Arthur's avatar about how his father is like Nero fiddling in the fire. In the morning, he always vows to avoid Arthur. It never works.

"Last chance to join the poker game," Arthur's smiley avatar says.

"I have work to do," says Cenric again.

"No problem," Arthur says. "I just thought maybe you'd like to get away from your father. I saw him headed for your tower."

"Cormand?" says Cenric. "He's here at the Congress?"

Arthur's smile wavers. "I assumed you knew. Doesn't he come every session?"

"For just a day or two. He wants us all to fight for his time."

Cenric ends the conversation and Arthur and his shining white teeth blink out of sight. He calls his father's implant. No answer. Most people allow their family members a direct line—the ability to speak into each other's minds at any time. Not Cenric's father. His time is too valuable.

The door chime trills and the surface of Cenric's front wall displays a portrait of Cormand Smith. Beneath the image is Cormand's name and designation: Senior Hauser Representative to the Directorate.

"Come in," Cenric subvocalizes, and the door opens at his command.

Cormand is a physical version of an Official Portrait; everything about him is stylized for maximum professional effect. His light brown skin is flawless and his hair thick and black. He and Cenric could both pass for thirty-five, although in fact, Cormand is almost eighty years older than his son. Looking young is important in politics, as is looking affable. Cormand is a bit on the portly side, and a bit unkempt. Those who meet him usually believe him earnest and genuine and are tempted to forget that he's one of the most powerful men in the galaxy.

"What are you doing here?" Cenric asks, standing. Cormand steps into Cenric's quarters and runs his eyes across every surface. "Taking a break from campaigning?"

The Big Three corporations are set to choose their representatives to the Directorate in a few months. Cormand doesn't have to worry. He's been one of Hauser's four representatives since before Cenric was born.

"I don't campaign, Cenric," says Cormand. He sits on the sofa, crossing his arms over the ample swell of his belly. "I try to make visits to all the major Hauser facilities—including the Mars campus—to lend my support and find out what concerns our people. This week I thought I should come here because I heard about a murder, of all things."

"Lyon," says Cenric. He paces in front of the sofa.

"Yes, and when I looked at his file, I saw you were working for him. What kind of project could a man like Jim Lyon want you for?"

"It's —" Cormand cuts Cenric off.

"Sit down, son, you're making me nervous." Cenric sits back at his desk.

"My work for Lyon is *classified*," he says, lingering on each syllable. He waits for some reaction from Cormand, but Cenric's father simply holds his gaze until Cenric confesses. "I don't know what he wanted me to do. He didn't tell me before he died." Cormand chuckles with what seems to Cenric like satisfaction.

"Well, knowing Lyon, I suppose it was something far-fetched and unnecessary," he muses. Cenric bristles.

"It's about a threat to Hauser. To all of the Big Three." He recognizes that he's only echoing Lyon's last words. He scans his memory of that final conversation, trying to dredge up some morsel that will prove its importance to Cormand.

"What have you heard about offworlders lately?" he asks. Cormand looks at him for an uncomfortably long moment.

"Offworlders, eh? Is that what this is about?"

"Lyon talked about offworlders when he offered me this job," he says.

"It's true that the threat from the colonies is growing," Cormand sighs. "Unfortunately, now is not the time to crack down on offworlders. Frankly, Hauser should be more worried about its own future rather than throwing resources into investigating problems happening outside of its limits. "

"But they're breaking the law. Our laws! And no one is stopping them, including the Directorate!" To Cenric, who until his conversation with Lyon had given no thought at all to offworlders, this suddenly seems like the pinnacle of injustice.

"Of course, of course," says Cormand with a wave of his hand. "I didn't mean to upset you." But Cenric won't be soothed. He feels a fire rising in his core.

"They're breaking our laws," he says again, slamming his fist on the desk. Cormand doesn't flinch at his outburst. In fact, he looks mildly amused. Cenric doesn't care. He knows he's on the side of righteousness. "Someone has to stop them. I have to stop them. That's what Lyon wanted me to do." He feels sure of it now. Why else would Lyon bring up offworlders immediately after mentioning a threat to Hauser?

Cormand smiles his infuriatingly amiable smile, the one that makes his constituents imagine he's just a regular bloke like them and not a magnate who has been in power for decades.

"Law isn't everything, Cenric," he says. "People are everything. Why are the laws made? Because the people want us to make them. Why are the laws followed? Because the people believe in them. Just try to get anything done without people on your side. You've never known much about people, have you? Maybe that's my fault." Cenric prepares to launch his defense when he remembers something else his father said.

"What do you mean, Hauser should be worried about its future?" he asks.

Cormand frowns at him, looking him up and down. "Nothing you need to worry about," he says.

Cenric simmers.

"I'm Hauser Tier One," he insists. "I'm a member of the Mars Congress." His father must know how many people would kill for Cenric's position.

"Yes, you are, somehow," says Cormand. "Alright. This is for your ears only though." Cenric sits straighter.

"I understand."

"Hauser is hemorrhaging citizens. Everyone on Earth wants to join Xinqi or Wonju these days. They offer better compensation and more perks, especially in the top tier, and let's be honest, Hauser has focused on turning a profit in food and household conveniences while the other corporations make real innovations. Consequently, the Wonju and Xinqi representatives to the Directorate don't take us Hausers seriously. The other representatives hold the power and my hands are tied. For example, it's been four years since any of the Directorate military's contracts were with Hauser divisions."

"How is that possible?" demands Cenric. "Hauser has led the world since after the dark years. Since we ended the dark years."

Cormand shakes his head. "Attitudes like that have made us less vigilant. We think that all we have to do to maintain our position is keep doing what we are doing. But these days, our products are mediocre and we're hopelessly bloated with excess departments and committees." He gestures at Cenric as he mentions bloat. "We're doing very little that really matters to the world. What we need is a new innovation, a new way that Hauser adds value to the world. Otherwise, we'll become obsolete."

"What about stopping the alien threat?" Cenric asks, his voice an eager growl. "Wouldn't that be a kind of innovation? Isn't stopping that threat more important work than Xinqi is doing with its new propulsion systems?" Cormand looks at him sharply for another minute, then sighs and claps a hand on Cenric's shoulder, making him flinch.

"Well, this is exactly what I've been talking about. You just don't understand people."

"Huh?"

"Take your head out of the sand, Cenric. Public opinion is shifting and you haven't even noticed. The people don't have stomachs for public executions or military action against colonists anymore. A lot of them are downright sympathetic to the colonies. There was even that drama recently that everyone was talking about—what was it, pretty Wonju biologist falls in love with a reformed hit man from Britton, her family doesn't approve, and so on and so forth. The point is, in this particular climate, putting all our eggs in the 'alien threat' basket would be a terrible choice for Hauser."

"It's not right," says Cenric. "They are a threat."

"I know, I know. But you'll never get anywhere if you ruffle too many feathers. Listen, if it makes you feel any better, I'm actually on a committee in the Directorate that's investigating what to do about the colonists. At this stage we're just commissioning research, developing training plans for Big Three enforcers, talking to experts, things like that."

"And if the colonists attack Hauser property, like in 2312? Will you be 'commissioning research' on what to do about that?"

"What are you going to do, Cenric, go to war with them yourself?"

"Why do we care what the people want?" Cenric glowers. "We built this world. Hauser built it and our family built it. We've always known how to take care of it."

Cormand chuckles.

"You sure know the propaganda by heart, son. Tell me, why do you think Hauser, Xinqi, and Wonju became the Big Three?" Cenric glances at the space on his desk where Tiana Williams would stand if he turned on the display.

"We invented Terratech. When the world had turned against scientific progress during the dark years, our founders came up with the innovations that made it possible to inhabit Mars and later the colonies. The money the three corporations earned from selling terraforming and spaceflight technology—along with our advances in climate control and food production—allowed us to provide for the rest of the world. We are what we are today because, after the rush to the colonies, everyone still here on Earth wanted to join us and be a part of our new prosperity."

"You sound like a school child," says Cormand. "Yes, we had new technology. So did others. A startup in Geneva had something very similar to Terratech and a state firm in Tehran had spaceflight better than ours. But we managed to outsell them. How? Because we understood people." Cenric closes his eyes as he feels the beginning of trembles in his hands.

"Father," he begins, searching for an excuse to get rid of Cormand, trying to think about something other than where he could get a hit of shav. Before he can come up with a reason to make Cormand leave, Cenric's father interjects in a completely different tone, low and conspiratorial.

"Okay, Cenric, listen closely." Cenric opens his eyes and sees Cormand is leaning forward, looking at him intently. "The truth is, the offworlder threat is very real." Cenric leans in, too, matching Cormand's posture.

"I knew it." This isn't the first time he's seen this look on his father's face. When Cenric was younger, before his career trajectory flattened and before the first time Cormand caught him with a shav patch on his arm, Cenric lived for the moments when Cormand deigned to throw him a scrap of insider information. He imagined that it was just the beginning—that Cormand would entrust him with more and more Big Three secrets until he was part of the inner circle himself.

But it has been years of waiting for that opportunity. Years of fearing that his place on Mars was in jeopardy and that he'd never rise to his rightful rank.

"In fact, we've heard rumors of a vast alien plot. Something very big, organized by all the offworlders hiding here on Earth."

"That's what Lyon was talking about! A big threat to everything."

"But the Directorate simply can't look into it now. We can't go against public opinion."

"But—"

Cormand holds up a hand and says, "That doesn't mean that you can't." Cenric's hands suddenly slow their quaking.

"It doesn't?"

"I'm going to get you an assignment as an intelligence agent. I know you don't have the training, but they'll give you a chance because of me. You'll be looking at satellite images of Hauser properties. Ostensibly, you'll be looking for drugs and other low-level crimes against Hauser so that we can send enforcers in. But you keep your eyes open for any sign of offworlder activity. And if you find anything, you let the Directorate know. No, let me know personally. I'll make sure we actually do something about it."

Cenric swells with pride.

"Thank you, Father," he says.

"Don't worry about it," Cormand says. "We both know that finance wasn't your strong suit anyway."

Cenric's hands are shaking again.

***

Cenric paces the well-worn angry path in his quarters. He tries to read the file he's been sent about his new position, but his mind is a jumble of fragmented thoughts and ideas racing by too fast for him to tie them down. Sweat beads on his forehead.

Arthur Adeyemi's name appears in front of him again.

"Arthur!" he says. "Law or people?"

"What?"

"The old man says people, but what does he know? Hauser won't fail, it can't. Wrongdoers need to be stopped." Cenric feels the words tumble out of his mouth before he has time to arrange them sensibly.

"Cenric… I don't know what you're talking about. Listen, I want to tell you, there's been a development in the Lyon case. He ingested some kind of poison in his tea. The thing is, the chemical used isn't something the team has seen before."

Cormand has no sense of the greater good, Cenric thinks. He only cares about his position on the Directorate, not protecting the people that he's there to serve. And it's not just Cormand—the Hauser elite have all lost their way. Only Cenric sees what's happening. Only Cenric understands that it's time to fight for Big Three civilization itself.

Arthur is still speaking in his head. "Cenric, do you hear me?"

"He doesn't see how weak he is," says Cenric. "He thinks I'm the useless one."

"OK, Cenric, I'm going to go. I'll talk to you later."

Cenric yells and kicks the wall.

***

In the morning, Cenric reports to his new supervisor, Bao Ding. Bao is ineffectual, with none of Lyon's vision. How he ended up at the Mars Congress at all is astounding. He has Cenric scanning satellite data for abnormal activity at unclaimed properties. *Cenric*, who holds Hauser's fate in his hands.

"Skip the residentials," he tells Cenric. "You want a good bonus this year? Find me some illegal weapons or drugs. Abandoned warehouses or tunnels are the usual culprits."

As far as Bao Ding knows, Cenric is like any other intelligence agent. He doesn't know about Cenric's special project for Lyon and for the Directorate and Cenric doesn't tell him. The project is his and he won't relinquish any bit of it to his inept boss. Every day he checks in with Bao Ding and listlessly seeks out petty criminals, all the while thinking about his real mission.

Three long weeks into the deep monotony of his new job, he finds what he's looking for. He starts a Mindlink call to his father, then cuts it short before Cormand can answer.

He can't give the Directorate a half-formed thought. He needs to learn more. He needs to find out everything he can about this offworlder plot, and then he'll let his father and the Directorate know that he's saved the day.

Justice for Hauser.

Chapter Six

MOLL MACKENZIE'S RIGHT EYE shines steely green. The left is a gray digital prosthetic. She stands waiting for the elevator in the lobby of Fern Valley Luxury Apartments, a smirk on her face and a small handgun clutched beneath her jacket. The elevator doors slide open and Moll steps in. The elevator's only other passenger, a stooped old woman, tips a cheery smile up at her.

"I don't think I've seen you around here before," she says. "Which floor do you live on?" In one lightning-fast movement, Moll Mackenzie whips the pistol from her jacket and shoots the old woman through the ear.

"She's made her first kill," says Lin, watching a feed of Moll's actions on her implant.

"Damn it," says the woman standing next to Lin. Kirs Jonas is tall and sturdy with the palest skin and hair Lin has ever seen. "Why did she shoot that lady? She's supposed to be going after the VP of Hauser R&D. The old woman wasn't going to stop her."

"She's putting on a show for us," says Lin. The two of them stare up at the apartment building, its forty floors of luxury living space a smooth cylinder gleaming in the sunlight. The skyscraper is surrounded by a circular, 8-meter-tall wall flashing Hauser-branded advertisements for Cleanerbots and smart lighting systems at a rate that makes Lin's head swim. On the feed, Lin catches the occasional glimpse of artful Terratech gardens in the center of the tower. She's been told that the wealthy residents of the building might go months or even years without leaving the idyllic atmosphere of Fern Valley. Almost everything they need is contained inside, and the rest can be delivered by one of the carrier drones Lin sees coming and going from the apartment windows.

"We still can't get any of our own drones to approach the building?" Lin asks.

"No," answers Kirs. "She's somehow screwed with the building security system so it won't let enforcer equipment approach."

"Or enforcers," comes a voice in Lin's implant. "We haven't had any luck getting in." In the distance, Lin can see the owner of the voice, a tall man with a beard and a long nose. Bogdan and his shorter but equally long-nosed brother, Boyu, are working on getting through the single gate in the wall.

Another of the enforcer team is crumpled dead on the ground, electrocuted by the security system when she tried to climb over the wall. Residential security systems aren't made to be so lethal, but Moll has hijacked this one and made it a formidable obstacle for the enforcers.

Moll Mackenzie exits the elevator on the twenty-ninth floor.

"Isn't the VP on the thirtieth and thirty-first?" Lin asks.

"I think he has a human security team that he uses in addition to the building security system," says Boyu. "The elevator wouldn't let her off on his floors. The building doesn't think she's a threat, but his people might have identified her. Yeah, look, the door to his apartment from the stairwell is locked down too. That buys us some time."

"Unless she kills some more random elderly people," says Kirs.

"We can't use our own drones," says Lin, "but can we use those?" She gestures to a sleek white carrier approaching a window on the seventeenth floor, its dangling arms wrapped around a stack of packages. In the time they've been watching, she's seen several of the same machines come from a large warehouse across the street.

"They seem to be mostly delivering groceries," says Kirs.

"Perfect." Lin takes off at a sprint toward the warehouse. The building is unlocked so Lin goes straight inside. At first, she thinks there's no human supervisor at all. Small, wheeled robots cut orderly lines across the warehouse floor, carrying packages of food from somewhere deeper in the building. When they reach the loading bay, where Lin now stands, the bots open their top hatches to offer their cargo to the waiting drones, which wrap their four metal arms around the payload and lift off through a chute in the ceiling.

Lin strides to the nearest drone and kicks its load of food onto the floor.

"Excuse me! What are you doing?" Lin whirls, raising her rifle. A short, wiry man with disorderly dark curls hurries across the warehouse in Lin's direction. He stops in his tracks for a minute as he takes in her weapon, then shakes his head and continues toward her. "I'm the manager here," he says. "Please put the groceries back on the Delivery Bird immediately!"

"I'm a Hauser enforcer," says Lin. "I will need to borrow this machine. It's a matter of life and death."

The manager eyes her skeptically. "How do I know you're really an enforcer?" he asks.

"Do you have an Identification scanner?" asks Lin.

"Of course not," the manager says, seemingly indignant that she would even ask. "I have no need for that kind of security." Lin sighs.

"Moll Mackenzie just made it to the thirtieth floor," Bogdan says in Lin's head. "Is she going to take on the whole security team with just that little pistol? Oh god, she's got a grenade! Shit. It's carnage over here."

Lin glares at the manager. "People are dying," she tells him, "right now. I don't have time for this."

"The thing is, this is a Xinqi facility," the manager says, punctuating his words very clearly, as if he doesn't think Lin will understand. "But if you really want me to, I guess I can help you out and get in touch with my boss. He'll be able to contact a Hauser rep to check your credentials. But I can't contact Hauser directly—there's a chain of command."

"Fine," says Lin. "Do it."

"We finally got through the gate," Boyu announces. "But the elevator isn't working and the stairs are blocked off." The manager is now silent, staring blankly ahead for what feels to Lin like hours.

"Excuse me?" she says. "Can we speed this up?" The manager doesn't respond. Lin goes back to the drone whose packages she previously toppled. It now hovers motionlessly, the hooks at the end of each dangling arm swinging just above the floor. Lin grips one of the drone's arms in each hand and slides her feet into the hooks. There's just enough space for her to crouch below the whirring wings.

The drone doesn't move.

Lin hops off with a grunt of frustration. The manager is still staring into thin air, presumably chatting with his boss.

"OK, I've confirmed your Identification," he finally announces, beaming and waiting like he expects a reward for the accomplishment.

"I need this drone to go to the thirty-first floor of Fern Valley Luxury Apartments across the street," Lin says.

"Carrying what items?" the manager asks.

"Just me." She climbs back onto the drone. "OK, I'm ready." She watches as the manager types the address into a keypad on the drone.

"Manual override," he explains. For a few seconds, nothing happens, and Lin is about to chastise the manager when the drone blasts upward through the ceiling chute and into the brisk air outside. Lin barely maintains her grip on the drone's arms as the air rushes by her face.

"No way!" comes Bogdan's voice in Lin's implant. "I didn't think you were actually going to ride the thing!" The swaying of the drone's arms in the wind turns her stomach and her knuckles ache from her tight grip. From below, the drones seemed to move slowly, but now the speed takes her breath away. Lin briefly looks down at her team, thinking that they look like nothing but tiny figurines on a gameboard, then she blinks and refocuses on her destination. The drone stops about twenty meters outside the VP's window, waiting for someone to open the window and accept the groceries.

"I can see her," Lin tells the team. "I think I have a shot." Inside the VP's apartment, Moll is crouched behind a desk, her back exposed to the window. Lin very slowly removes her right hand from the drone's arm and raises her rifle, propping it against her chest. The rifle is old-fashioned and unwieldy—it doesn't even interface with her implant. It's not what she would normally choose, but she's confident she has Moll Mackenzie's head in the scope. She tightens her grip on the left arm of the drone so that the recoil doesn't knock her out of the sky, and fires. The window shatters.

Moll stands upright just as Lin pulls the trigger. The bullet pierces her shoulder. Lin waits for the blood and the scream of pain, but Moll turns and returns fire through the broken window, hitting Lin between the eyes.

Lin lowers her weapon and waits. Moll Mackenzie blinks and the training simulation melts away, leaving only a small room with a few rows of chairs. Lin knows the skyscraper was never really there and her feet never left the ground, but the crisp images and sensations of her new implant, indistinguishable from reality, are still startling. She rubs her forehead where the fatal shot entered.

Kirs, Bogdan, Boyu, and a handful of other trainees are sitting in the chairs, all looking slightly dazed. Moll Mackenzie stands at the front of the classroom, arms crossed.

"The simulation was rigged," Lin says to Moll. "I hit you in the arm. In the real world, it might not have killed you, but it should have made it impossible to shoot so quickly and accurately." Moll Mackenzie's expression shows only the slightest trace of amusement, then she lifts her shirt over her head, crumples it, and tosses it aside with a flourish. Boyu blushes and looks away. Moll slowly rolls up each pant leg. The trainees stare.

Moll Mackenzie is a patchwork of shining titanium and heavy muscle. Her right arm and shoulder, right leg and hip, and left leg up to the knee are as synthetic as her eye.

"No wonder you beat us," says Bogdan. He sounds both awestruck and miffed. "You have an advantage. You're almost a machine."

"It's a disadvantage," says Lin. Sabohat has taught her all about the pros and cons of weapons and other devices that interface with the brain. If the connection is disrupted, or certain hardware damaged, the limbs would be dead weight. Moll Mackenzie scans the line of trainees.

"It doesn't matter if it's an advantage or a disadvantage to me. What matters is that you gauged the situation incorrectly, and you failed. Seventeen people died. Go again. Now."

Before she can process Moll's words, Lin is standing outside Fern Valley once again. In this round, she heads immediately for the warehouse, not wasting any time on discussion. But Moll changes her tactics as well by avoiding exposure at the window. By the time Lin lands with the drone and bursts into the apartment, the VP and all his staff are dead. The simulation disappears again.

"There's no way to get there in time," Lin says to Moll. "At least, not if you know in advance what we're going to do."

"There's one way it works," says Moll. "I'm going to show it to you. You don't need to do anything this time."

The program starts again, but this time the trainees themselves are part of the simulated images. Lin sees herself sprint toward the warehouse.

Real-Lin floats through the air beside simulation-Lin like an avatar. Simulation-Lin enters the warehouse, but instead of going for the drone, she finds the manager and shoots him dead. Then she manually overrides the drone, flies it to the twenty-ninth floor, intercepts Moll Mackenzie, and kills her with a single bullet to her natural flesh before she has a chance to take on the VP's team. And then simulation-Lin is gone and real-Lin is back in the gym.

Moll Mackenzie raises her eyebrows at Lin's consternated look.

"You killed the manager," says Lin. "Or, I did, I guess. He was innocent."

"It's cruel," agrees Moll Mackenzie. "And you would face legal consequences for doing it. But I've run this simulation for years, and it's the only way to lose only two lives—the manager and the old woman."

"But there's no way to know that!" objects Kirs. "You can't just go around killing people because it may or may not be efficient."

"That's true," says Moll. "But if you don't, you'll be responsible for many more deaths."

"So what's the lesson?" asks Lin. "Kill first, ask questions later?" Moll shakes her head.

"The lesson is that as an enforcer, sometimes there are no good options."

$$* * *$$

"Training is going really well, Mom. How have you been?" Lin asks Sabohat over their direct line, but Sabohat isn't there. It's early morning in Beijing, and Lin's mother is either still asleep with Mindlink messages silenced or working and ignoring all distractions. Lin sighs and sits heavily on a bench. She's near the center of the Hauser training base, a silent stone in a current of chattering trainees and instructors. Fort Omar is Hauser's largest training facility, a city in its own right, home mostly to citizens who specialize in law enforcement, medicine, or other professions requiring in-person interaction.

The hum of conversations around Lin has an unfamiliar shape. Like any educated citizen, Lin can converse in all of the Big Three languages without relying on neural implant translation, and she also knows a bit of a minority Slavic dialect common on Rogov. But at home, she speaks Mandarin with Sabohat, and her beloved Beijing has a Mandarin undercurrent. Here among Hauser citizens, the background noise is more English than anything. A few words drift to her out of the jumble.

"Hey, it's Lin." Kirs Jonas leads the bearded brothers to Lin's bench. Kirs is Lin's bunkmate, but in the three days they've roomed together, Lin has avoided all but the simplest pleasantries. Kirs told Lin when they first met that she was previously Tier Two local security for an entertainment club in her hometown of Calgary. She also said, in her overly chatty way, that she would love to join the Directorate military.

"That's got to be the ultimate enforcer gig," she told Lin, who held back a shudder.

"How do people get that job?" asked Lin, and Kirs laughed.

"I don't actually know. I don't think anyone does, really. And what do our Soldiers in Red even do all day? You could go for a year without hearing anything about them. But I still think it would be a great job. Directorate is basically the tier above Tier One."

"I suppose," said Lin. She hasn't talked to Kirs much since.

"We're headed to the mess hall," says Kirs now. "Join us for dinner."

"I'll just eat back at our quarters," she says with a shake of her head. Kirs rolls her eyes.

"Come on. We want to get to know you better. You're my bunkmate and you're the only person in training I never talk to."

"The food in the mess hall isn't so bad," says Bogdan. Lin looks at each of them. She's already sick to death of her small, spartan quarters. One dinner with her fellow trainees won't hurt.

"OK," she says, and is startled when Kirs and the brothers cheer.

On the way to the mess hall, they talk about their instructor, Moll Mackenzie. "She's been that way for fifty years. She helped stop the Vancouver uprising and took a bomb for it. She's fierce," says Bogdan.

"Fiercer than me, anyway," says Lin. "I'm going to run some extra simulations tonight and try to improve before the next session."

"You're so serious," Kirs snorts. But Lin frowns. Given the opportunity for a Tier One career, who wouldn't try to do their best?

At the doorway to the mess hall, there's an Identification scanner, there to make sure only Hauser personnel can enter the premises. As always, Lin holds her breath as the red light from the scanner finds her.

***

Lin's identification is legitimate; it's a thing that can't be faked. The nanotech in her body communicates her identification code to the scanner while simultaneously monitoring her DNA to ensure the tech hasn't been transplanted into someone else.

The only way to become a citizen of the Big Three corporations is to be born to citizens, who then submit their children's DNA to their corporation's HR department at birth. The only exception: children under ten years old who are abandoned, for whom no parentage can be established, can be adopted by citizens and have their DNA permanently entered into the system.

Lin's legal parents are Yang Zirong and Wang Qing. She was nine when the adoption was finalized, already too tall to tuck her head under Sabohat's chin but filled with childish terror of everything and everyone. Her name was Nadya Iskakova.

"Hello, child," said Zirong when Nadya and Sabohat arrived at her stately home. Zirong and her wife Qing had the matching faces of longtime spouses, although Qing dressed delicately in a qipao and kept her thick hair coiffed, while Zirong had a more modern look and a sharply professional demeanor. "What's your name?" Nadya stared back at Zirong and clutched Sabohat's sleeve.

"She doesn't talk much," said Sabohat. "The poor thing has been through too much." Qing came forward and knelt in front of Nadya, taking one of the girl's hands in her soft palms.

"Sweetheart," she said. "It's OK. We're going to keep you safe here. Just tell us your name." Nadya's mouth wrapped around the N before she recalled what her mother had told her.

"My name is Lin," she whispered. Qing nodded, and before Lin could even flinch, she slid a needle from her sleeve and drew a bit of Lin's blood.

"We'll register her tomorrow," said Zirong to Sabohat.

From that day on, Lin bore the name of an Earth citizen. From that day on, she took responsibility for Sabohat's safety. She enrolled in Xinqi school online and learned the things that Earth children learned. She was still always afraid.

***

The scanner detects Lin's citizenship and lets her through. Inside the mess hall, she and her training-mates line up for a bowl of mushy soup, squirted from a vibrating pink tube. Bogdan catches Lin poking a tentative finger at it.

"OK, the food really is that bad," he says. Lin smiles a little.

"It's nutritionally optimized," says Boyu seriously.

"I don't get what training was all about today," says Kirs as they take their seats at a long, crowded table. "Does she really expect we're just going to shoot people just because we think it might be the most strategic choice? That can't be what she's supposed to teach us. I'm missing something."

"More importantly, have you heard the rumor about Moll Mackenzie?" asks Bogdan.

"Do you mean that her cybernetic eye is actually a laser weapon? Someone told me that on my first day here. Don't mess with Moll Mackenzie—one look and it's all over." Kirs slaps a hand on her chest like she's been shot and drops her head to the side, tongue hanging out.

"No, no one actually believes that."

"Her eye is too small to be an energy weapon," says Boyu.

"Thank you, Boyu. No, I mean her big secret."

"Which is…" prompts Kirs.

"She's an offworlder," says Bogdan. Lin stops with a spoonful of soup halfway to her mouth.

"Don't be stupid," says Boyu. Bogdan laughs and his eyes show he isn't serious. Still, he continues.

"Lin, do me a favor and look something up. Moll Mackenzie's background file." Lin pulls up their training instructor's profile on her implant and scans it. She doesn't see the big deal. Official profiles don't contain any confidential information, just employment and educational history and any citizenship changes. Then she realizes what Bogdan means.

"There's nothing before about sixty years ago. Ten years before Vancouver. Nothing at all about her schooling."

"Right," says Bogdan. "Alien."

"It's a pretty big leap from missing educational information to 'Moll Mackenzie is an offworlder,'" says Kirs.

"Sure," says Bogdan. "But that's not all. My friend Ryan knows Cass Brandt who works at the armory here at Omar, and apparently, Cass says that Moll is super secretive about her background. She won't tell anyone where she's from or when she became an enforcer or anything."

"The colonies are pretty violent. It would explain why she's so tough," Kirs speculates.

"Not all the colonies are violent," Lin says, then bites her tongue. She pokes at her soup.

"Sure, Rogov is a bunch of elite scientists or something. But Moll Mackenzie could definitely be from Britton. Those people are fierce with a capital F," says Boyu.

"Yeah, maybe," says Lin. Moll seems completely Earthly to her. The colonists Lin knows, even when they think they're blending in, just can't help but let a little bit of alien shine through. New Palu refugees can't bring themselves to wear the dull colors fashionable on Earth and Rogovans talk with their hands in ways Lin is sure Moll Mackenzie never would. You can always hear traces of an accent on certain words, even decades after they arrive on Earth. But if Moll's English pronunciation had ever deviated from Big Three standard, Lin would have noticed it in a heartbeat.

"Where are you from, Lin?" says Boyu.

"Beijing," says Lin.

"I love Beijing," says Kirs. "My aunt used to take us there all the time when I was growing up. My absolute favorite place we would go to was Jing Lan Teahouse. Have you been there?"

"I don't believe I have tried that one," says Lin. A teahouse like that is out of the price range of Tier Three servers, and out of the realm of possibility for non-citizens like Sabohat.

"More importantly," says Bogdan. "How did you start training already so good at this stuff? Flying in that drone today was amazing."

"Seriously, Lin," says Kirs. "You've been the best at pretty much everything." Lin's cheeks burn.

"I just like games," she says. "Like the simulations. So I get a lot of practice on those. It's not like I was really flying on the drone."

"Nice try, but we've already seen that your combat and weapons skills are top-notch in real life too," says Kirs. "I thought maybe you were already an enforcer before you came to Hauser. Weren't you Xinqi before this?"

"Yes," says Lin. "But I wasn't an enforcer or anything like that. I just worked in a restaurant." She expects some condescension, but none comes.

"Is it weird to switch citizenship?" says Bogdan.

She suddenly smiles, thinking of something she's noticed. "You're all Hauser by birth?" They nod.

"What is it?" asks Kirs. "Tell us."

"Well, the jargon is different," says Lin. "Like... say you get demoted to a lower tier. In Xinqi the boss will ask you to 'step back to seek new opportunities,' but in Hauser, I recently heard someone say—"

"Rebalancing the corporate workflow!" Bogdan and Kirs chime in unison. As they all laugh, Lin lets the tension of the last few days melt out of her. At least she's found a couple of people here who aren't so bad.

"This is how we can tell if Moll Mackenzie is an offworlder," says Bogdan.

"Are you still on about that?" laughs Boyu.

"Figure out what lingo she's using. If she's really from the colonies, she won't speak perfect Hauser."

"She can't be from Britton," says Boyu.

"Oh yeah?"

"Britton is one of the farthest colonies away—it takes over twenty years to travel in-between. And like you said, Brittons are violent. Everyone knows that their long-distance ships are practically war zones in and of themselves. So it's reasonable to assume that they don't take babies along, or at least that an infant wouldn't survive. So let's say she was twenty or so when she left, forty-five when she arrived sixty years ago. That makes her one hundred and five, which I don't believe for a minute. She barely looks eighty. Therefore, not an offworlder."

"This guy doesn't even know what a joke is," complains Bogdan.

Kirs looks at them pensively. "I don't really get it about the colonies," she says.

"What about them?" asks Lin.

"Well, they don't all seem that bad. Britton is obviously a hellhole. But like Boyu was saying, Rogov was founded by top scientists. And I've seen pictures of the mountains on New Palu. Absolutely breathtaking scenery. But it sounds like practically everyone is trying to leave, even though over thirty percent of the refugees who come here are killed trying to enter orbit. So what's the point? Why travel for so long just to die?"

"Because the survival rate on New Palu is worse than thirty percent." Lin suddenly feels very tired. She excuses herself and dumps the soup in the recycler.

***

Alone in the room she shares with Kirs, Lin examines her body in the mirror. The nanotech is beginning to work. Where before she was long and lank, now her body is thickening with muscle. She hasn't turned on the light yet, but the contours of her reflection are clear due to her enhanced vision.

Lin sits on her bed. On her neural implant, she enters the address and password of the virtual club Emas invited her to. The shape of a new room appears, bending and blurring where its imaginary edges conflict with real objects in Lin and Kirs's room. Lin closes her eyes so she can only see the virtual room—tall log walls in the style of New Palu architecture, a round table, and five avatars seated around it. Lin is sitting in a sixth chair.

"Education is key," one of the avatars is saying. "Whatever risk we take to show our citizen connections the truth about the Big Three is well worth it." The avatar speaking is nondescript—not recognizably male or female, dressed all in black. Probably factory default. The voice is also featureless except for a lilting accent that Lin can't place.

"We have a new guest," says a different avatar, presumably the room's moderator. This avatar appears as a massive woman with a pile of glittering silver hair on her head. The other members stop their conversations. "Please introduce yourself. No surnames—we value privacy here."

"I'm Lin."

"You're Emas's friend," says a male voice, this one coming from a purple spiral. Rogovan, with the typical inexplicable need to avoid taking human form in an avatar.

"I know Emas," says Lin.

"Lin has a Tier One Hauser enforcement position," says the spiral. "And she's Rogovan." Lin finds it disconcerting that the group, which supposedly "values privacy," already has these details.

"Rogovan?" says the silver-haired woman. "I wouldn't have guessed it." Lin's personal avatar is a simple representation of herself, not unlike her official avatar, but less airbrushed.

"I'm David," says the spiral.

"Lin, I'd be fascinated to know what you think about our obligations as members of the offworlder community," says the default avatar. "What initiatives do you undertake to influence citizen opinions?" Lin hesitates. It's better not to reveal too much about herself, even online.

"I'm sorry," she says. "I don't think I should be here." She exits the room and opens her eyes back in her Hauser quarters. As she gets ready for bed and crawls under the covers, a call flashes to her left. Emas Day. She answers it.

Emas's personal avatar surprises her. It's simply himself, but with a short Earth-style haircut and smooth, unscarred skin.

"Sorry I left the group," says Lin. "I just don't think it's for me."

"It can be a little intense," he says. "I hope you'll give it another try, though." Lin props herself up on her side so that Emas appears to stand beside the bed.

"Look, Emas," she says. "I don't want to be part of any special group. I'm glad that you all have a way to connect with other colonists if that's what you want, but all I want is to stay safe and do well at my job." She expects him to argue, but his avatar nods.

"I used to feel that way," he says. "I came here five years ago. I wasn't looking for a fight. I just wanted to get away from... this." He gestures at his face, although in the avatar Lin can't see the boiled skin.

"It's pretty bad on New Palu then?" asks Lin. Emas is silent for a moment.

"I'm not sure anymore that it's better here," he says. "At least there, everyone's in it together. You never lived on Rogov, did you?"

"I was born on the trip here," says Lin. Emas smiles slightly.

"That explains it then."

"What?"

"The way you are. Able to pretend you're like them." Lin doesn't know how to take that.

"What changed your mind?" she asks. "About being part of the cause?"

"I got tired of losing people." Emas's avatar looks her in the eyes. "We have to fight back," he says. "We don't have a choice. You'll see it eventually."

Chapter Seven

EMBERAZ STATION IS A place that sells pleasure. Vedra knows it immediately, having come of age in the same sort of place, although the station of her childhood dealt in pleasure of a different type. She hesitates before the door to the main station hub, struck weak by the knowledge that her son has none of the fortitude needed to survive here.

"Myat," Vedra hisses. Myat stops and their two armed escorts stop, too. Temar keeps walking until Vedra grabs him by the bicep. "How long are we going to stay here?"

Myat regards her slowly.

"I'll be off in a few days. You can stay here or arrange transport somewhere else if you'd like."

"What?" The witch. Vedra fights panic.

"I thought that's what you wanted when you tried to take that flier."

"Well, yes." Vedra can't admit that, faced with life on a station, she would rather go anywhere else with anyone, even a friend of her husband's who is probably Empire.

"I'm sure this place is nice," says Myat, and starts walking again. Her boots clank loudly on the metal walkway. This station's gravity is the heaviest Vedra has experienced.

They're escorted to a room decorated with cheap lanterns, strings of mismatched colored lights, and a badly engraved sign reading "Reception."

The reception desk, the only piece of furniture in the room, has a jagged hole in its front with singed edges. From behind the desk scampers a fat man with a jovial smile and graying scruff that stretches down his neck and beneath the collar of his shiny, patterned garb. He extends a hand to Myat, who stares at it for a minute before accepting it, and Vedra, who ignores it. He pats Temar on the head. Vedra scowls.

"Doolig!" says the man, and for a moment Vedra thinks he speaks a language she's never heard. Then she realizes it's his name, and he's speaking her variety of Anglian after all. "I'm Doolig Sater! Welcome to Emberaz."

"Thank you," says Myat. "I'll need to refuel before I continue on my way."

"No problem," says Doolig. "And what can I interest you in while you're here? Let me show you a few of our offerings." A line of seven men and women emerge. No, girls and boys—they're all much younger than Vedra. She stares at them. Have they spent their entire lives here, or were they purchased or lured from some other hellish place?

"Don't worry, these are the discounts, won't hardly cost you a thing." Then Doolig runs his eyes up and down Myat. And does it again. "Eh, on second thought, he might be an Empire man, eh?" He shoos the wretched things away. "We have better stock. Just let us know what kind you want then."

"Not now. We'll just take two rooms if you have them." Myat flashes something silver that makes Doolig's eyes light up.

"Two rooms?" asks Vedra, looking at the shabby surroundings. "We're not staying with you?" Myat raises her eyebrows.

"Is that a problem?"

"Of course not," Vedra says. "You're going to give me your weapon, right? I have a child to protect."

Myat turns back to Doolig. "One room," she says.

A girl, tall but young, with long dark hair like Vedra's, leads them across the station to their room. The station is even uglier than Vedra's birthplace, which at least, due to the nature of their business, had plenty of greenery. The room itself is small, without much furniture except the bed. Vedra sits gingerly on the stained and tattered blanket.

"Can I go play?" says Temar. "Are there other kids here?"

"You stay away from everyone on this station," she says sharply. "This is a dirty place." Myat lets out a single bark of laughter.

"I never took Fenton's wife for a prude. They're selling sex. Everyone likes sex, what's the problem?" But Vedra can't find the words to explain that nothing on a station like this is given freely. Everything is an unfair transaction, with winners and losers.

"It's not the sex that makes it dirty," she says.

***

Myat disappears into the filthy bowels of the station. Whether to refuel the ship or partake in the pleasures, Vedra doesn't know. But she and Temar are tired and soon they're curled in the bed together in the dark. When Myat comes back, she can sleep on the floor. After all, she'll have plenty of space to herself on her ship after she abandons them here.

The door slides open. Vedra opens her eyes, expecting Myat's muscular silhouette, but sees a shorter, rounder figure instead. She bolts upright. Doolig enters the room and the door closes behind him.

"You can't have me," Vedra says. "I'm done with men like you."

"Eh, I don't want you," says Doolig. "You're not what our clientele is looking for." Vedra wraps her arms around Temar, who's just waking up. Doolig leaps onto the bed with surprising agility and tries to pry Temar away from Vedra, but she kicks at his stomach and groin. He doesn't loosen his grip.

"Mom, get him away from me," cries Temar softly. Vedra sighs. The boy is so naïve.

She knows that's not his fault—he was barely a minute old, his warm little body nestled in her tired embrace, when she heard Fenton and his men yell and clash their glasses together in a drunken toast outside the birthing ward door, celebrating the arrival of Fenton's first son.

Vedra swore then that she would do everything in her power—limited as it was—to keep Temar from knowing the hard truths of the world. He wouldn't spend his childhood trying to bring in enough money to avoid punishment and he'd never think about survival and escape plans.

But in protecting Temar, Vedra worries that she's left him unable to protect himself. She lets go of her son and tackles Doolig. All three of them fall from the bed to the floor and Temar slips away and huddles in a corner.

Vedra straddles Doolig and presses down with all her weight on his neck. He sputters and gurgles, but manages to flip her onto her back. Vedra locks her legs around him before he can go after Temar again, grabbing the sides of his face as she pushes her thumbs into his eyes. Doolig screams, then falls heavily onto Vedra. When Vedra wriggles out from under Doolig's body, running to hold her crying son, she sees a wide hole spurting blood from his back. In the doorway, Myat holsters her weapon.

"You could have shot me!" she yells at Myat, still shaking from nerves.

"I wouldn't have."

"I had it under control! I didn't need your help."

Myat shrugs. "This was faster." Footsteps echo loudly in the hallway, getting quicker as they approach.

"They can't already know he's dead, can they?" asks Vedra.

"Depending on what kind of implant he had and whether there was an alert set up, then yes, they could know," says Myat. "In any case, it looks like we're not staying here tonight. Let's go."

Vedra follows Myat into the hallway, holding Temar's hand tightly. They turn right, away from the footsteps, in the opposite direction from which they came.

"Are we going the right way?" asks Vedra.

"The whole station is a circle," says Myat. "Either direction will get us there. Let's just hope they aren't smart enough to come at us from both sides." They run past dozens of doors, each so identical that Vedra is sure that they've gone all the way around at least once. They don't see any of Doolig's employees, just a handful of other guests, all of whom avert their eyes as if two women and a child sprinting down the hallway is private business that doesn't concern them. Finally, Myat stops in front of one of the doors. Vedra almost smashes into her from behind.

"Let me go first," says Myat. She opens the door and steps through, gun raised. Vedra and Temar follow. They're in another hallway, but this one ends in a solid wall, and the only other door is a round hatch in the floor. Myat pulls it open.

"This is the way to the ship?" Vedra remembers arriving at Emberaz, Myat expertly matching the curve of the spinning station until a docking seal locked them into its rotation and its centrifugal gravity pushed her into her seat, and she remembers Myat opening a hatch above the cockpit and pulling down a ladder, which they climbed into the station. But she was so preoccupied with anxiety at the time that she forgot to pay attention to where the ship and the ladder were in relation to the rest of Emberaz.

"Yes. Hurry."

The three of them climb through the hole in the floor into and down the ladder. The hatch above closes and another below them opens with a hiss, allowing them to descend into Myat's ship. Myat rushes to the controls and within minutes, Vedra finds the weight on her frame lifted. She drifts into the cockpit and straps Temar into a small seat that folds down from the wall before taking her own seat next to Myat.

"We're detached from the station," Myat says. They sit in silence for a while.

"Thank you," says Vedra.

Myat looks a bit surprised, then says, "You had it under control."

"I mean, thank you for not leaving us there," says Vedra.

"I wouldn't have," says Myat. "I just had no idea it was such a horrible place."

"Aren't all stations?" says Vedra.

Myat leans forward to look at Vedra's face. "Of course not. If you'd been to other stations, you would know they're usually very nice." Vedra huffs and looks away but Myat, still watching her, raises her eyebrows.

"You have been to another station."

"Born and raised," says Vedra. "Well, not raised. Born and tolerated for a while."

"You grew up in a brothel?"

"No, the station where I lived was different. But it was also the same. We were a drug center. You know, traders who had managed to grow Terratech into something smokable would trade it for synthetic drugs they couldn't manufacture on their own world, stuff like that. Sometimes we did easy things, like packaging the products. Other times, it was more dangerous. We weren't real children." Vedra pauses and realizes that somehow Myat's hand has wrapped itself around hers.

"I feel for those kids, the ones Doolig showed us. Eventually, I started to have too much of a mind of my own, and my father started to think it wasn't economical to keep me. I knew if I stayed, I wouldn't be long for this world." Myat squeezes her hand. "Finally, a visitor was my way out."

"Fenton saved you," guesses Myat. Vedra pulls her hand away.

"I saved myself. I knew how to make a man like that want me. And I went someplace better. I was barely older than Temar, but I had some skills. Not like him." Myat glances at Temar.

"He doesn't have to be skilled. He has you," she says. They sit in silence a while.

Vedra wants to take Myat's hand again, but just says, "Where are we going to go now?"

"I think," Myat says, leaning back in her seat, "our only choice is to go to Earth."

Vedra stiffens. "Are you crazy?" she says. "We'll be killed before we can even say 'Earth.'"

"Don't worry, I have a plan. It won't be a problem."

Not a problem? Damn. For a minute there, Vedra had almost trusted her.

Chapter Eight

THE FOOD IN THE mess hall never gets better, but Lin warms to the afternoons spent chatting casually with Kirs, the brothers, and occasionally other training-mates. She forgets, more often than not, that she's only playing a role. That she's not actually one of them, that they could—and probably would—take everything from her given the chance.

"That simulation this morning really made me think—" starts Bogdan today.

"Be careful," says Lin. "Moll Mackenzie says that using undeveloped skills is dangerous."

Everyone is silent for a moment, and then Kirs and Bogdan burst out laughing.

"She has a sense of humor after all," says Kirs. Lin looks at the slush in her bowl.

"Kirs," says Boyu, "is that a Guardian necklace?" Kirs fingers the pendant around her neck. Lin has seen it before and thought it was simply a blue jewel in a gold frame, but now she sees that it's meant to be an eye, the jewel acting as its pupil.

"What's a Guardian?" asks Lin.

"It's a cult," says Boyu.

"It's a faith," says Kirs, "that happens to not be very popular anymore. A lot of early Hauser citizens believed."

"What's it about?" asks Lin. Religion is almost unheard of among Rogovans, and Lin doesn't know anyone with a faith.

"We all have Guardians watching over our life," begins Kirs.

"What are they, exactly?" interrupts Boyu. "I never got this part. Ghosts? Gods? Extraterrestrial beings?"

"Well, I don't know exactly." Kirs touches the pendant again. "I just know that we have several of them, and they try to tell us to do different things. So it's important to follow the right Guardian."

Bogdan's avatar materializes in the center of the table. The friends open up a direct line to each other when they meet for lunch, and Bogdan is projecting himself into all of their minds at once.

"Wooooo, Kirs," the avatar warbles, "Follow me as your Guardian and we will..."

He apparently says the next part only to Kirs, who snorts with laughter and slaps the real Bogdan on the shoulder.

"But how do you know which one to follow if they're all telling you different things?" asks Lin.

"It's not a real thing, Lin," says Boyu.

"Just follow your intuition," says Kirs. "You'll know."

A name appears in Lin's vision.

"Moll Mackenzie is calling me," says Lin, turning away from the table to answer the call. Moll Mackenzie's official portrait looks just like her, down to the fake gray eye, but somehow the fire is gone from her features.

"Yang Lin, congratulations. You've got your first enforcer assignment."

"Now? But training isn't over," says Lin, subvocalizing to Moll to keep the conversation private from her friends.

"It is for you," says Moll. "We're short of personnel right now and you're at the top of the training class. I'll tell you about the assignment in person. Pack your things and be in my office in an hour."

"I won't be coming back?" Though she doesn't speak aloud, her startled expression seems to register with her training-mates, who stop talking.

"I should hope not. As of this moment, you're a rookie enforcer, not a trainee," answers Moll Mackenzie and severs the connection. Lin turns back to the table.

"I'm leaving," she says. "I have my assignment." She looks at each of their faces and reminds herself that it's better to cut her ties with them before they get too close, but the lump in her throat doesn't dissolve.

***

"You're going to be the personal bodyguard for one of our Hauser VIPs," says Moll Mackenzie when Lin arrives at her office, leaning back in her chair, feet propped on her desk, arms crossed. Lin tries to keep her eyes off of her instructor's right hand. It looked as real as the left at first, but now Lin can't unsee the slight mismatch. "It's a short-term gig while she's at a hospital in San Antonio for a few weeks. We don't usually use rookies for VIPs, so after her hospital stay, you'll be reassigned."

"Did she have a bodyguard before?" asks Lin.

"She's gone through a few," says Moll. "She doesn't exactly have a reputation for being easy to work with. But the hospital is in a low-crime area and she hasn't had any threats against her, so I wouldn't expect it to be a challenging assignment."

"I understand," says Lin. She waits to be dismissed. Moll lowers her feet to the ground and sits straighter, eyeing Lin curiously.

"You didn't even ask who the VIP is," she says.

"Oh. Right. Who is it?" asks Lin.

Moll Mackenzie sends Lin the personnel file for a woman named Abena Owusu, Hauser Senior Vice President of Public Relations. It's a title with "future Directorate representative" written all over it. There's an icon on the file that Lin doesn't see too often, indicating that Abena Owusu is part of the Mars Congress, which as far as Lin understands, is some kind of resort the leaders of each corporation frequent while their subordinates pick up the slack at home.

"Now go," says Moll Mackenzie. "She's waiting for you." Lin nods and starts to go, then turns back to Moll.

"Was there a reason you called me here in person? You could have told me this over the network."

Moll Mackenzie shrugs. "No reason. I'm old, and when I was young, we used to wish each other good luck in person." Lin takes a chance.

"Where was that?" she asks. "I mean, where are you from?"

"You've heard the rumors, then?" Moll Mackenzie laughs, an unpleasant sound that makes Lin blush. "What do you think, Lin," Moll asks. "Am I an offworlder?"

"How could I tell?" asks Lin.

"You tell me," says Moll. "Consider it your last training exercise." Lin just stares at her, afraid to say anything. "Just go."

As Lin heads to the train station, she wonders if Moll was intentionally avoiding the question about her hometown.

***

The flowers and fruit trees in San Antonio are Terratech, but unlike in Beijing, the flora in San Antonio strikes her as uninspiring. The trees lack distinct character and the flowers are all the same pale shade of yellow. Once, alone on a side street, Lin pulled over to pick one of the blossoms, but even the aroma was lackluster.

Her assigned VIP is a more interesting specimen. Abena Owusu is at the San Antonio Hauser Medical Center to receive life and fertility-lengthening procedures, and likely cosmetic career-lengthening procedures as well. She travels with her own security detail, a secretary who appraises her each morning of new developments in all the corporations, and a woman she calls her cousin who massages her back and strings her hair into long braids while she undergoes treatment. When Lin is introduced to her on her first day in San Antonio, Abena somehow keeps her sharp eyes glued on Lin even while she reads Lin's file on her implant.

"You came here from Xinqi," she says.

"Yes."

"I myself have recently moved to Hauser from Wonju. Before that I was Xinqi, and before that, Hauser again. Born Xinqi. If I never have to watch another orientation video again, it will be too soon."

"Why have you changed citizenship so many times?" asks Lin. Abena smirks in a way that makes Lin feel smaller than before.

"Do you buy into this idea of company loyalty? It's bullshit, of course. Not all of us were born into the right part of the world to be a Cormand Smith with seven generations of claws sunk into Hauser affairs. But if we have the right skills we can take advantage of the opportunities that arise." By the time Lin has thought about this and started nodding, Abena has lost interest in her and ordered her away.

"I know you were assigned here to guard me," she says. "But I have my own team. Relying only on people I trust has kept me alive for a hundred years. So you run along. You might as well go out and enjoy yourself. I won't tell anyone that you're not standing outside my door all day."

Lin's days are dull and lonely. Occasionally, she'll accompany Abena on a shopping excursion, vigilantly watching for threats that never emerge. But most mornings, she reports to Abena's room knowing that her charge will send her away with another exasperated hand wave. She goes home to her tiny apartment, where she watches security feeds of the hospital on her implant until she's too restless and claustrophobic to sit still. Then she rides her standard-issue enforcer motorcycle through the district, looking for signs of trouble and reporting to Internal Security on the neural network when she finds none.

Once, she sees a woman with long braids walking down a side street. Even approaching her from behind, there's something about her barrel-chested figure, the way her plump body moves beneath her oversized dress, that makes Lin's breath catch. She thinks of the question Moll asked her: How would she recognize an offworlder? Through a lifetime of experience, of course.

Lin wants to greet the woman, to make a connection, but she's sure that any attention from a Hauser enforcer would be nothing but terrifying, so she simply rides on.

***

Emas contacts her on Mindlink.

"I have a new number for you," he says. "So you can access the group. Otherwise you'll be shut out in a few weeks."

"I told you I don't want to be a part of it," Lin says.

"I know. You don't have to spend time in the room just because you have the number. But you might want it at some point."

"Fine," says Lin. "But you can't send it over Mindlink, right? And I'm guessing you can't ride the Hyperrail to San Antonio." Buying a Hyperrail pass requires Identification. "So I guess we're out of luck." Emas's avatar looks a little sad and Lin softens.

"It would have been good to see you," he says. "But no, we only have a few group members who are able to travel between continents using connections to illegal transport groups or forged train passes. They make sure the chain of in-person connections is unbroken. A guy named Roil is ready to hand the number off to you. He got it from his cousin, who's a smuggler, who got it from her friend in South Asia who—"

"I get it," says Lin.

"Right. Anyway, that's all. Roil will get in touch." But Emas doesn't hang up. Lin waits.

"I think you might like the group if you gave it a chance," he says. She starts to object, but he cuts her off. "But if you don't want to talk to them, you can talk to me. No matter how well you fit in there, it must get lonely to spend all your time with citizens."

"It does," she says, surprised at his empathetic words. "Training was OK. Those people weren't so bad. But now that I'm in San Antonio, it's hard." She tells him about Abena and the way she makes Lin feel useless.

"She doesn't know how lucky she is to have someone so hard-working and skilled protecting her," says Emas. Lin wonders if her avatar is blushing.

"Thanks." She suddenly wants to keep him on the line. "How are things in Beijing?" she asks. He sighs deeply.

"It's tense here," he says. "Everyone is so worried about the ship. Those of us from the other colonies don't know anyone on it, of course, but so many of the local Rogovans do. They're all sick over it. I'm sure your mom has told you." Lin doesn't admit that she hasn't talked to Sabohat about the Rogovan ship at all. "Well, I suppose I shouldn't keep you too long. But get in touch any time."

"Hey, Emas," Lin says just before he ends the call. "It would have been good to see you, too." His avatar melts away, leaving her staring at the blank wall of her apartment. The little room feels more like a cage than ever. She may be "hard-working and skilled" and a Tier Once citizen, but she can't do her job as an enforcer, can't protect her mother, and can't help the Rogovans. She thinks about the refugees in Beijing and everywhere, anxiously awaiting the day their friends and relatives enter dangerous skies, and wants to scream.

When she first met Emas, he was excited about her Tier One position and how the colonists might be able to use it. Like most offworlders, he overestimates what a rookie enforcer can do. But now Lin wonders if she can help in some small way after all—maybe get some intel for Emas and the group, at least. She does have access to the official Hauser citizen directory, and her Tier One position even allows her to see the profiles of certain key Directorate members, so she could start by finding out who in the Big Three is involved with monitoring for alien vessels or managing TEDI. Lin shudders thinking about someone with the job of ensuring that colonists die trying to reach Earth.

She opens the directory on her implant and searches job descriptions and departments for every relevant term she can think of: offworlder, alien, TEDI, astrosecurity, Earth defense, and so on, but nothing comes up. She'll have to try a different strategy. Lin dials Internal Security.

"Hauser Internal Security Dispatch. Hi again, Lin." Lin diligently calls in everything she observes in San Antonio, as pointless as it is.

"Hi, Martin," she says. "I just have a couple of questions this time."

"Go for it."

"If I were to find an offworlder living in San Antonio, I should report it to you, right? And you would let the Directorate know?"

"Of course. Do you know of any aliens in your district?"

"No, no, I was just curious. Who deals with issues related to offworlders? Is there a specific department for it, or a person?"

"I don't know. How is this relevant?"

"So you don't have a specific number that you would call? For example, if I knew about—"

"Lin, if you've found anything, you need to let us know. Otherwise, your assignment is to protect Abena Owusu. We don't need anything else from you."

"I get it, Martin. I haven't found any offworlders." There really isn't anything she can do.

Lin meets Roil on a public street the next day. She's never seen him before, but she could have recognized him a mile away with his eyeliner and his high-collared, colorful tunic that probably hides scarred skin. It amazes Lin that everyone else on the street isn't pointing and saying "he's from New Palu!" But they don't know the signs like she does.

Lin considers destroying the paper without looking at it, but she reluctantly memorizes the number before tearing it to shreds.

***

Lin has been in San Antonio for two weeks when she gets a message telling her to rush to the medical center. Her heart pounds, thinking that something has happened to Abena while her bodyguard was aimlessly riding around town. But instead, she finds herself responding to a disgruntled elderly patient who has climbed onto the roof of the center, possibly to throw himself off. He's convinced that his cancer is incurable, although nanotech is already at work dissolving his tumor. Lin learns all this from a report sent to her implant as she races up the stairs to the roof. When she arrives, a young woman is already standing near the door. She sags in relief when Lin arrives.

"Oh good, you're here. I'm so afraid he's going to jump."

"Did you try to stop him?" Lin asks. The old man is shuffling back and forth, murmuring under his breath. He seems to be working his way closer to the edge.

"Well...no." The woman looks uncertain and tugs at the side of her pants. "I'm a Wonju Systems enforcer."

"And?"

"He's Hauser. And we're in a Hauser facility, so... I have no jurisdiction. It could be a liability if I do anything." Lin stares at her for a minute, then turns and approaches the man.

"Mr. Schell?" she says softly. The man doesn't acknowledge her. "John." Lin can make out a few words of his monologue.

"...On my own terms... whatever they say..."

"John," says Lin, "they told me that you don't believe your cancer can be cured." The man almost makes eye contact with her but pulls his gaze away.

"Not natural, it's not natural," he says. "I shouldn't have lived this long and so many died and now I pay."

"So many died? What do you mean? Who died?" Lin asks, trying to distract him from his goal.

"Before. Before there was all this." The man windmills his arms, seemingly gesturing to everything.

"Before... the Big Three?" Lin guesses. The report didn't tell her the man's age, only that he is "elderly." In appearance, he very much is. If he's a wealthy man who's had the best medical care and cosmetic procedures, he might be old enough to remember the early days of the corporations. If he's more like the people Lin and Sabohat associate with in Beijing, he might be as young as eighty.

"Ah, the Big Three," the man laments, finally stopping his pacing and looking at Lin. "Now we're supposed to pretend they were there for us then, in the dark times, just because they inject me with tiny computers to save me now."

"So you do understand about the nanotech," says Lin.

"My terms. My time," says the man. He turns and sprints for the edge of the roof. Luckily, his sprint is not much faster than his shuffle, and Lin catches his arm in a firm grip before he's halfway there. He sighs but doesn't put up much resistance as Lin guides him back to the stairs. She's startled to notice a news drone hovering nearby.

"Where did that come from?" Lin asks the Wonju enforcer.

"It showed up as soon as I called this into our Internal Security," the other enforcer says. "Didn't you see it when you got here?"

The next morning, video of Lin is all over the Hauser news feeds. It's not a big story, just a bit of fluff to show a Hauser "hero" in action. The video doesn't include any of her exchange with Mr. Schell—it's just a clip of her grabbing his arm before he dives off the roof as dramatic music plays in the video's background. It makes it look like he was harder to stop than he really was.

Lin's training mates and a few other people recognize her and call to congratulate her. Even Abena comments, "I guess I got one of the good ones," before sending her away again.

Within two days, the news feeds have moved on to other stories.

***

After the rooftop incident, Lin's life returns to its predictable routine. By day, she watches feeds and cruises the streets. At night, she returns to her apartment and runs training simulations until she burns off enough energy to sleep.

As she patrols the city, Sabohat's star sometimes hangs in the air beside her. Often, they say nothing to each other—if her mother is awake so late in Beijing, she's probably working. But they keep the direct line open and take comfort in the presence of each other's avatars.

Lin tries to feel her mother's warmth radiate from the star. She knows that a representation of Sabohat's actual physical features would be as artificial as any abstract shape, but still, she would prefer to see something resembling a familiar face. Lin can't help but wish that, after so many years on this planet, Sabohat could be a little more Earthly.

One especially humid afternoon, Lin stops at an outdoor cafe near the medical center for a cool drink. She sips it with her eyes closed, scrolling through the security feeds for the hospital and other Internal Security reports that might alert her to any local crime reports from Hauser citizens. She's desperate to feel useful despite her meaningless assignment.

"Yang Lin, right?" Lin's eyes fly open at the sound of her name. Dr. Singh from the Beijing Hauser Medical Center is standing at her table. He raises a hand in greeting.

"That's me," she says. Lin is surprised he remembers her.

"It's good to see a familiar face!" he says, and she is not displeased to see his handsome smile either. "I just transferred to the medical center here from Beijing a week ago."

"I've only been here for a few weeks," she says.

"I actually already knew you were here," he says. "I saw that news story of you and the man on the roof. It didn't say your name, but I realized you looked familiar. Really fantastic work."

"Oh," says Lin. "Well, that's my job."

"Are you here on some kind of official business, or can we have a drink together?" He gestures to the cup already in his hand. Lin hesitates.

"As long as I don't get called away," she says.

He slides into the seat across from her. Lin squints at her companion's face in the sun. Dr. Singh could be an advertisement for Hauser success. She's never personally been friends with anyone like that—even Kirs and Bogdan and Boyu are newly recruited to Tier One like her—but she suspects from his understated but perfectly tailored clothes and his polished way of speaking that Dr. Singh was groomed for the upper echelon from the start.

"So that implant is working out for you now?" he asks.

"Yes, I've gotten used to it. Thank you for helping me out that day, Dr. Singh."

"Please, just call me Rajan," he says. "You know, I almost didn't recognize you. I can tell the nanotech is working." Lin touches her newly strengthened forearm self-consciously. "Sorry, is that a strange thing to say? I spend too much time diagnosing diseases and not enough making small talk with beautiful women." His wide smile makes her want to laugh at things that aren't funny.

"Um, it's OK," says Lin. "Just a lot of new things to get used to lately."

"Of course. So how long will you be here in San Antonio? Is this a long-term assignment?"

"It's not an assignment to San Antonio," Lin says. She gazes out at the San Antonio streets, which are just starting to feel a bit familiar to her. "Just a short-term bodyguard assignment for a VIP. Then I'll be reassigned."

"So you have no idea where you'll land next," Rajan says.

"That's right."

"Well, I hope you end up someplace you love. Where would you most like to go?" Lin thinks of the various cities of the world and tries to imagine which ones would excite her, but can only come up with a single true answer.

"Back to Beijing, if I could," she admits.

"I get it," says Rajan. "Doctors don't get much say in where we go either. Our assignments are long-term, but it's still not like a typical job—we rarely stay in the home where we grew up. Is your family still back in Beijing?" As Lin is contemplating how to answer this, Moll Mackenzie's name flashes on her implant.

"Excuse me, I have a message," she tells Rajan. The message wasn't sent to her personally, but to all of Internal Security. As Lin listens, her skin goes clammy.

Hauser enforcers, be advised: all four Wonju representatives to the Directorate have been poisoned. Two second tier Wonju citizens who shared their meal are also dead. Our sources are saying that the attack was carried out by illegal aliens from Rogov colony. These offworlders are still at large—please be on highest alert.

Lin turns to Rajan. She can see from his unfocused stare and tense expression that he's received the news, too. She scans the cafe. At every table, customers are tuned into Mindlink and tuned out of real life. The story must already be all over the news feeds.

Lin flips through the news channels on her implant. The drones must have arrived on the scene before the Wonju reps' corpses were even cold. The most popular Hauser news feed is showing footage of the gruesome aftermath—three bodies slumped over a table, faces pressed into their food. The other three have fallen off their chairs into awkward heaps on the floor. Lin notices a line of foamy pink drool coming from the face of a young woman. She's not one of the Wonju reps—she's too young and her clothes aren't expensive enough.

On another feed, a man is yelling. The news drone has zoomed in so close to his face that you can see spit flying as he shouts, "Kill the Rogovan scum! Take earth back for the Big Three!" Lin stands abruptly, rattling the table.

"I'm sorry," she says, to Rajan, who blinks away his own feeds at the sound of her voice. "I have to get back to work."

Lin goes to the medical center, marching purposefully through the halls to Abena's room. She punches the door open, prepared to meet the entire gaggle of her charge's entourage, but it's only Abena and the woman she calls cousin.

Despite the familiarity of the title, Lin has never gotten the impression that the woman and Abena are close. She seems to be only a lower-level posse member. But today the two of them are almost forehead to forehead, talking softly. Abena's face, usually youthful in skin tone but old and jaded in expression, is suddenly young with worry.

Lin softens her own countenance a bit. "I see you've heard," she says. Abena's usual haughty mask slips back on.

"Of course," she says. "Everyone has."

"I'm not going to leave you unprotected any longer," says Lin. "I know you have your own team, but things are getting dangerous and this is a very public place. I can't in good conscience leave you alone anymore." To her surprise, Abena's protest is muted.

"You may stand outside the door if you think it's best," she says. "But if I'm dealing with any important business, you can't be in the room."

"That's fine," Lin agrees.

Later, as she guards her post, she calls Emas on Mindlink. It takes him so long to answer that she almost gives up, but finally, his avatar appears before her.

"Emas, there was an attack." She doesn't know how connected he is to the world of the Big Three. "The Wonju representatives are dead."

"I know."

"They're blaming it on colonists! This is so bad for us. Why do we always take the fall for things we would never do? Why can't they just leave us in peace?" It's a struggle to keep her words in her head and not yell them into the empty hallway.

"Lin. It was us."

Lin freezes.

"It was you?" she whispers, aloud this time.

"No, not me. And not my friends. I mean, it really was colonists. Ro-govans. It's a resistance group I'm familiar with. There's someone in the Mindlink group who worked with them before. Javi. He's Rogovan, too."

"How can you associate with people who do things like this?" Lin demands.

"He worked with them years ago," says Emas. "He isn't involved now."

"Good!" says Lin. "Because as an enforcer, I would turn him—or you—in immediately."

"It's a group called the Fourth Power. They fight against the unfair treatment of colonists." Emas's wide brown eyes on his avatar are filled with reproach. "It's not a bad thing."

"Of course it is." Lin wants to scream and punch something, but she maintains a neutral expression and a straight back in front of Abena's door. "They're supposed to be the ones who hurt innocent people, not us. That's why we hate them. We're supposed to be the good guys."

"They weren't innocent people, Lin. They were members of the Direc-torate. They're responsible for the atrocities you're talking about."

"What about the two who were Tier Two citizens? They didn't hurt us."

"For someone so smart, you're an idiot," Emas sighs. "So there were two Wonju casualties in this battle. How many of ours have died?"

"Theirs, ours, why do we have to look at it—" Emas interrupts her.

"I get it. You got a good gig at Hauser, and you've made friends with some of them. You have that luxury with your citizenship and your..." He gestures to his face again.

"You could get that fixed," Lin says, knowing instantly it was the wrong thing to say.

"Sure, I'll come down to your Hauser medical center right now then," he says angrily. Lin is silent. "Look, just ask your friends a question, OK?

What do they think should be done with non-violent colonists living on Earth? Let me know what you find out." He ends the call.

Immediately, Lin goes to call Kirs, then hesitates. She doesn't want to confront her friend just because Emas asked it of her. Still, it would be nice to see a kind face. She makes the call.

Kirs answers with her personal avatar rather than her official portrait. In it she wears thick metal armor and her hair, as blazing red as Moll Mackenzie's, falls down her back in waves that seem to be subject to a lighter gravity than her body is.

"It's terrible, isn't it?" says Kirs. "Wonju must be panicking."

"Do you think it was really Rogovans?" asks Lin.

"It sounds like they know that for sure," says Kirs. "Honestly, it's surprising that something like this didn't happen sooner, with all the tension between us and the offworlders." Lin looks into the avatar's heavily lined eyes, looking for a hint of compassion in their artificial expression.

"Kirs," she asks, "what about the non-violent colonists on Earth? What should be done to them?"

"They shouldn't be here," says Kirs. "People are getting more sympathetic these days because they've forgotten what it was like during the dark years. Food shortages, lawlessness, fighting over the water supply. And then millions of people left Earth. That migration is the only reason we can sustain this quality of life now, especially given our longer life spans. If we let offworlders live here, they're taking natural resources that we've worked hard to replenish."

"I get that." Lin hopes her tone sounds casual. "But is that really the fault of individual colonists on Earth? The colonies are harder to survive than the dark years on Earth were."

"They're a security liability, Lin," says Kirs, starting to sound a little annoyed. "As enforcers, that's how we have to think of them."

"You're right," she agrees, not wanting to argue. "Hey, I have to go." She hangs up the call abruptly, ignoring Kirs's surprised look. Then she enters Emas's virtual club. It's more crowded than before, and the round table has expanded to include over a dozen avatars. Lin recognizes a few members from her last visit, including David the purple spiral.

"Are any of you a part of the Fourth Power?" Lin asks. Her simulated voice rings with all the accusation that she feels. The room falls silent.

"Of course not," says David, and a few others murmur agreement.

"That's good. Because I'm an enforcer and I will hunt these people down. I don't care if we're all Rogovan. I won't let them just get away with poisoning innocent people." The avatars, a mixed group of human forms and inanimate objects, don't move.

"You might want to be careful about revealing the group's name, even in here," a female animal avatar says timidly. "We don't all know each other that well."

"It's all right," says David. "We're among friends. Or we were." Lin gets the impression that if a spiral could glare, he would.

"None of us want this, Lin," says the silver-haired moderator from Lin's last visit. "But aren't you tired of hiding?" Lin sighs and looks at the simulated ceiling.

"Very tired," she says.

Chapter Nine

CENRIC'S WORK IS PROGRESSING too slowly. It isn't his fault; he's mired in endless queues of meaningless tasks assigned by that dimwit Bao Ding. His real work, his fight against the offworlder threat to Hauser, he's forced to do furtively when Bao isn't paying attention. Sometimes, like tonight, he works long into the night. Cenric's head feels heavy, but he can't stop now. The Wonju murders proved that.

At least he's back on Mars now. The two months between Congresses were long and dull.

"Arthur," he says to that goddamned smiling avatar in front of his desk. "I have a question for Mo."

"You could ask him yourself, you know," says Arthur, but there's no hint of reproach in his avatar's grin.

"I'm asking you." Mo doesn't like Cenric. That's always been obvious—Arthur's lover and his avatar look at Cenric with the same curdled distaste. Mo is only a viable resource for Cenric because of Arthur's goodwill.

"No problem. What do you need to know?"

"It's about the dead Wonju representatives."

"Hey, I heard that they identified the group that did that. The Fourth something or other." Cenric shrugs noncommittally. He only learned the name of the group after the crime was committed. It's not good enough. He needs to be a step ahead of the colonists.

"I want to know what they were poisoned with," says Cenric.

"Ok, let me ask Mo." Arthur doesn't bother to turn off the call. Instead, his avatar's expression grows tender as he talks to Mo, who has probably been beside him in their shared suite the whole time.

"Yeah, it's another question from Cenric. I know, I know, just check with your contact about this one last thing. Please?" There's a pause. Arthur's avatar laughs. "He won't get you in trouble... Ok... I'll wait." Cenric is starting to feel awkward staring into Arthur's deep brown eyes. He looks at the floor.

The avatar loses its dreamy countenance.

"My god, Cenric. You knew about this?"

"Tell me."

"They were poisoned with the same unidentified substance that killed James Lyon. Does that mean..."

"Lyon was killed by Rogovans," says Cenric. He exits the conversation and cracks his knuckles.

He won't sleep tonight.

***

Cenric has a system. As he scans satellite footage for Bao's beloved warehouses and tunnels, he also looks for dark spots—buildings where things don't seem to add up. No Big Three ads are being piped in, they aren't receiving Big Three delivery services, no Big Three maintenance divisions contract there.

Finding the dark spots is difficult, tedious work. He can't see delivery drone contracts on the satellite images, after all, so if he spots something suspicious, he has to look through various Hauser directories and files and then request the same information from Xinqi and Wonju. Even if he confirms that the building is suspicious, it's hard to find a record of who lives or works there.

Cenric could simply report these dark spots to his father and hope the Directorate looked into them, but he doesn't trust the Directorate to care about what's right and just. Not like Lyon did and not like he does.

And now, finally, he's found something. In one of the dark buildings of Bangkok, a large billboard is visible from the satellite image. It advertises a tailoring business belonging to Dirk Kane. There's no Bangkok tailor named Dirk Kane in the Hauser directory, and Xinqi and Wonju liaisons have confirmed he isn't theirs either. Of course he isn't. But Cenric has a source from his work with Bao Ding, a file some other intelligence analyst put together of unsanctioned businesses in Bangkok. Dirk Kane is listed third under tailors and a contact number is provided. Cenric makes the call, pretending to be a colonist himself.

"How can I help you?" says Dirk when he answers the Mindlink call. He doesn't provide any avatar; he is a disembodied voice.

"A friend gave me your name," says Cenric. He's currently using an avatar whose clothes flash bright, humorous slogans—the tacky look of a Tier Three man. "He thinks we have something in common."

"Who is this friend?" Dirk asks, sharp suspicion clear in his voice. Cenric winces. He came on too strong.

"Someone who thinks you're the best tailor in Bangkok," he says. "And that you still know all the old techniques and don't use a fabric printer."

"That's true," says Dirk, the distrust in his words only slightly diluted by pride.

"Where did you learn that?"

Dirk is silent for a moment, then he says, "You said we have something in common."

"I heard we do," says Cenric.

"What's that?"

"A homeworld."

The tailor cuts off the call immediately. Cenric curses. It burns him to know that they're out there, blatantly breaking the rules that keep the world prosperous. He can't give up. He can't let impotent men like his father and Bao Ding control the governance of Earth. These criminals deserve what he'll bring down on them.

Chapter Ten

IN THE AFTERMATH OF the Wonju attacks, Lin gets to work. She examines each security feed in the hospital and convinces Dr. Zebulon, the medical center director, to install a few extra cameras in blind spots. She interviews any hospital personnel with access to Abena. On the rare occasions when Abena leaves her room, Lin escorts her around the medical center grounds, eyes vigilant and weapon in hand.

She still almost misses the intruder.

It's a sunny afternoon and Lin is waiting for Rajan to go on his break so they can go to the cafe again. They've been in touch since their last meeting, sending friendly messages and jokes back and forth, but they haven't had a chance to meet in person again. Abena is safely back in her room with at least seven of her friends and employees, so Lin feels justified in grabbing a quick drink. The woman walks right past Lin with a friendly smile.

Although the VIP wing is designed for privacy, it's not uncommon for patients' family members or other visitors to wander through the halls. Still, Lin knows immediately that the woman isn't a typical guest. There's something strange about the sense of purpose in her walk and the way her smile seems to know something.

"Hi!" Lin calls out. "May I ask who you're here to see?" The woman turns and smiles politely, her hands behind her back.

"My sister," she says.

"What's your sister's name?"

"Gulya Ito." Lin tenses. It's a Rogovan name if ever she heard one. She begins to search hospital records on her implant, but the woman turns and keeps walking.

"Stop!" commands Lin. The woman stumbles at the sound of Lin's voice, and something clatters to the floor. It's a gun. Not just any gun, one that wraps around the hand in the Rogovan style. The woman grabs for the gun, and the wrist darting out of her sleeve shows a geometric pattern typical of Rogovan tattoos.

Lin raises her own weapon.

"Stop!" she orders again. "Leave the gun on the ground and turn around slowly." The woman complies, but Lin is startled to see the mirth on her face, as if Lin's demand amuses her. Lin examines the woman. She's average height for an Earth-born woman—but then, so is Lin. The woman's hair is braided like a Rogovan, but lighter in color than is typical on Sabohat's planet. Of course, that's not exactly evidence of Big Three citizenship. And she does have the tattoo and the gun.

"What's your business here?" Lin asks.

The woman gives an exaggerated shrug. "No business at all," she says. Lin waits for more, but it doesn't come.

"What's your name?" The woman stays silent, so Lin speaks the words she hates. "Can I scan your Identification?"

Lin's implant isn't capable of checking Identifications, but the woman probably won't know that; most people believe that enforcers have more authority than a new recruit like Lin actually possesses.

The woman smiles wider. Then she turns and walks for the exit again. She doesn't hurry, and catching her feels too easy. When Lin grabs the woman and pulls her arms behind her back, she's sure it was the intruder's plan all along.

The woman willingly goes with Lin to an empty patient room, where Lin locks the door behind her and calls Dr. Zebulon on his implant.

"I need an Identification scanner," she says. "Does the medical center have one?"

"Sure," says Dr. Zebulon. "What's going on? Do we have trouble?"

Lin briefly explains the incident.

"I'll hold her here for Internal Security to pick up and bring to a holding cell," she says. "It's not my job to figure out who she is or question her. But I just need to know. For Abena's safety, I mean."

The director arrives with a portable scanner and stands behind Lin as she points it at the strange woman.

Nothing appears on the screen. Lin tries again. A strange weight settles on her chest.

"She's not a citizen," says Dr. Zebulon, in a voice filled with surprise and revulsion. The alleged non-citizen doesn't change her smiling expression.

"What do we do with her?" Lin already knows her protocol, but she hopes the director will give her a different answer. He doesn't.

"I'll call the Hauser emergency reporting number. They'll call it in to the Directorate." Lin watches the woman, questions swirling in her mind that she can't ask with the Director's nervous supervision.

"Do you mind if I talk to her alone?" says Lin. She braces for questions or disapproval, but Dr. Zebulon knows Lin from the rooftop affair and trusts her.

"That's fine," he says as he exits, leaving Lin alone with the woman. "Just let me know when I need to call the military."

"Where are you from?" she asks the intruder. The woman leans back in her chair and regards Lin calmly. She says nothing. Lin wishes she could yell into the woman's implant, but without having any name or alias to contact her by, she has to speak aloud.

"Did you lose citizenship because you committed a crime?" asks Lin, but she knows that can't be right. If her citizenship had been revoked, there would still be a record to appear on the scanner. "Or your parents committed a crime, so you were born without citizenship," amends Lin. The woman is still silent.

"Are you from New Palu?" she asks quietly. Though she wants to find out if the woman is an offworlder, she also needs to sound ignorant of such things. Refugees from New Palu are usually wan and dark-haired, like Emas. They often have scars. This woman has none of those traits.

"I think you know where I'm from." The woman leans in closer to Lin, who freezes, trying to figure out what she could mean. Is she simply referring to her tattoos and Rogovan weapon, or does she somehow know about Lin's background? Could she be someone from the online group? Lin and the intruder stare each other down, the criminal's lighthearted expression mocking Lin's shocked one.

Dr. Zebulon is waiting outside when Lin storms out the door.

"Call the Directorate to take her," says Lin. "She won't talk."

"Thank you for taking care of the problem," he says with a nod.

"I'm not sure I did," says Lin. "She was here for some reason. I'm afraid whatever she came to do is already done."

"Don't worry about it, enforcer," he says. "We would know if someone had been shot here, wouldn't we? You stopped her in time." But Lin still has a sinking feeling. She goes back to the place where she first saw the woman and eyes the nondescript hallway. Where had she come from? Lin contacts the director on the neural web.

"Dr. Zebulon, may I have access to the medical center's security feeds? Just the wing where I saw the woman, starting at..." Lin calculates, "14:20." The director agrees, and within seconds, the scene is playing in her field of vision. She closes her eyes to avoid confusing the recording with reality. Lin watches the woman stroll down the hall. Next, she sees herself call out to the woman, then their brief conversation and the arrest. Nothing there that she hasn't seen already.

"Was that really starting at 14:20?" Lin asks Dr. Zebulon. "I'd like to see what she was doing before I ran into her." Dr. Zebulon is silent for a few minutes.

"There seems to be a problem with the feed before that," he says.

"What kind of problem?"

"It's... not here. But that's impossible. We have a top-of-the-line security system, there's no way some... alien woman..."

"Never mind," says Lin. She makes her best guess at the direction the intruder was coming from and walks back in that direction, looking for any sign of something amiss. Everything appears standard.

Without her enhanced hearing from the nanotech, Lin wouldn't have heard the small, raspy voice calling to her.

"Hello? Enforcer?" The weak voice comes from one of the patient rooms and belongs to a young girl with a sickly pallor and emaciated face. The girl's mother sits by her bedside, stroking the girl's hair back from her sweaty forehead and murmuring calming words.

"Did you want to talk to me?" asks Lin from the doorway. The mother shakes her head.

"My daughter is confused," she says. "The medication makes her worry about small things."

"Did you see something?" Lin comes closer to the girl to hear her soft rasp.

"There's a door across the hall," the girl says. "No one ever goes in except the fat man in the morning. Today someone else went inside. She looked mean." The mother gives Lin a look.

"You see? It's nothing." Lin smiles at the girl.

"Thank you for telling me," she says. She calls Dr. Zebulon's implant. "What's behind this door?" She sends him a layout of the medical center with the door marked. There's no number or label on the door, only a keypad beside it.

"That's access to the pharmacy system," says Dr. Zebulon. "It automatically delivers the correct dose of medicine to each patient in their room." Lin blanches and takes off at a sprint for the room of the most likely target.

"Have you taken your medicine yet?" she yells at Abena as she flies through the door.

"No," says Abena. "I just heard it arrive." She indicates a small compartment in the wall where a liquid-filled cup sits. "Sia, will you hand it to me?" One of Abena's entourage moves for the cup, but Lin grabs it first and carries it swiftly out the door.

"How am I supposed to get my longevity treatments when you do that?" Abena calls after her.

***

Lin goes outside and takes long breaths of fresh air. A pharmacy tech confirmed that the medicine sent to Abena was incorrect. He didn't know what the new medicine was. None of the other patients were affected.

Hoping to calm her buzzing nerves, Lin wanders to the cafe and orders her favorite tea. The sun hasn't reached its noon peak in San Antonio, so Sabohat may still be awake in Beijing. Lin speaks into her mind, conjuring the gray star.

"I don't know if I should be doing this job, Mom," she admits. She isn't really expecting an answer—Sabohat hasn't responded to many of her calls lately—but this time she replies.

"I thought it was going well," Sabohat says.

"It's too much responsibility." Lin considers telling her mother how she's starting to realize her offworlder background is a liability in her new line of work, but she doesn't want to cause Sabohat any guilt. Or anger. "Someone would have died today if I hadn't saved her," she says.

"Who?" asks Sabohat.

"A high-ranking person here at Hauser. Abena Owusu." The gray star hovers silently for a moment.

"I know of her," says Sabohat. "She's famous. She'll probably be on the Directorate soon."

"I'm just glad I got to her in time," says Lin. She wraps her hands tightly around the teacup.

"Why?" asks Sabohat. Lin regards the avatar. If she could see her mother's projected image, would it seem less cold than the gray star?

"What do you mean, why? It was my job to protect her, and she almost died."

"If she had, I'm sure they wouldn't have blamed you. You're good at what you do."

"That's true," says Lin, disturbed. She dislikes Abena. She dislikes her extravagance and the callous inflection of her voice and everything she represents. She feels nauseous at the thought of Abena on the Directorate. And yet... "It doesn't seem right that she should be hurt while she's helpless at the hospital."

Sabohat clucks her tongue. "You're too kind, as usual, Lin. Like with Fan Fan. It's good to be compassionate, but as your mother, I have to tell you to worry about yourself, too."

"Why is it that so many nice people turn out to have such horrible thoughts?" Lin watches a young man help an older one get into a taxi. She thinks of Kirs calling offworlders a security liability, of Emas siding with the murderers in the Fourth Power. The question is rhetorical, but Lin is a bit surprised when Sabohat doesn't offer her input. "Mom?"

Maybe Sabohat has fallen asleep or gotten distracted. Then her mother's voice says lowly, "They're here again," and the star disappears.

The connection has been severed.

Chapter Eleven

DIRK KANE ISN'T ANSWERING Cenric's calls anymore, from any alias. He must be scared.

He should be. Cenric is coming for him.

Spots on the transport from Mars to Earth during the Congress are limited to encourage the elite to stay for the entire session. If the tickets are needed for personal reasons, they must be applied for well in advance. Luckily for Cenric, a mistake was made and the ticket issued to him when he was demoted after the shav incident was never revoked, and it doesn't expire. It means leaving the Congress early, which he regrets, but completing this mission successfully will make the long wait until the next Congress worthwhile.

As one of the first cities to take advantage of Xinqi's innovations, back when Xinqi was merely a fresh startup from the nation-state of China, Bangkok is now among the richest and most advanced cities in the world. But Cenric has no time to spend in the thriving downtown—he has to track down Dirk Kane in one of the seedy villages on the city outskirts.

To Cenric's distaste, the only way to find the offworlder tailor is to ask people. It's not ideal, since Cenric has no way to know who he can trust, and most of the people Dirk might associate with are surely degenerates themselves. But if he wants to right the wrongs that offworlders have committed, he has no choice but to question the locals. Cenric chooses to focus first on the most trustworthy group—his own people. Most of the small businesses in Dirk Kane's neighborhood don't list their corporate affiliation on their Mindlink advertisements, and of those that do, most proudly bear the Xinqi label. Three, however, claim to be subsidiaries of Hauser.

Cenric strikes out with the first two. One is closed and the other is run by a man who goes on a long tirade about low-quality printed goods undercutting his prices. By the time Cenric reaches the third Hauser subsidiary on his list, a bakery, he's feeling the familiar shaking of his hands and twisting of his emotions that can only be tamed with drugs or getting his way. The proprietor of the bakery is a petite woman with brunette curls and hard lines chiseled beside her mouth in a permanent frown.

"Why should I tell you where to find Dirk?" she asks.

"You know him."

"I didn't say that." Cenric narrows his eyes and steps closer to the woman with a snarl. At his height, he towers over her, and his shadow behind her looms taller. The woman remains calm.

"What's in it for me?" she asks. Cenric fingers the weapon in his holster. But this woman is a Hauser citizen, not offworlder trash.

"What do you want?" he asks. She tilts her head back to look him in the eyes. "My sister helps me in the shop here," she says. "But she's hoping to move into Tier Two. Doesn't matter what kind of job." Cenric pulls up the woman's sister's file. *Delta Charrat, Hauser Tier Three, Bakery Assistant*. She appears to be a hardworking and law-abiding citizen, one who deserves good things. In fact, the more Cenric thinks about it, the more he realizes that people like Delta Charrat are exactly who he's trying to protect. Why should a good Hauser employee like Delta Charrat toil in the obscurity of Tier Three while treacherous, lawless offworlders plot to usurp her way of life?

"Done," says Cenric. "I've recommended her for an open sales position. Now tell me, where is Dirk Kane?"

***

The offworlder works out of a crumbling residential complex. The entrance to his shop is a simple wood door that doesn't announce Cenric's arrival. Cenric stands in the doorway, the top of his hair brushing the low doorframe. A man sits sewing an old-style pair of pants at a table.

The man is old, centuries old by the looks of him, but his wrinkled face is probably just the result of a harsh upbringing and a lack of longevity treatments. He looks up as Cenric enters his small shop.

"Dirk Kane?" Cenric asks.

"What can I do for you?" Cenric takes two long steps toward the shriveled creature, who seems to shrink further into his chair.

"You can leave Earth for those of us meant to be here," he says. "And you can tell me about the Fourth Power."

"I don't know anything about that," he says. "I'm just a tailor."

"For which corporation?" Cenric demands, unholstering his weapon and leveling it at the alien. The old man's crinkled eyes sag, defeated but unsurprised. "Tell me about the Rogovans. Tell me who murdered James Lyon and the Wonju representatives."

Suddenly, strong arms grab him from behind, wrenching his weapon arm upwards. Cenric twists against the hold, slamming his elbow into his assailant until their grip loosens, allowing Cenric to spin and see the attacker. It's a younger man, lean and wiry. He lunges for Cenric again but Cenric shoots him in the stomach first. The young man falls to his knees, choking on one last word that might have been "Dirk," then he topples to the side and lies unmoving.

Cenric turns back to Dirk Kane and is startled to see Kane rushing at him with unexpected speed, wielding only a pair of scissors. Cenric raises his weapon again and splatters justice for Hauser and James Lyon across the back wall.

Chapter Twelve

LIN GULPS HER BITTER tea and tries to get her thoughts under control. She makes a call to Sammy Chen. After thirty seconds that masquerade as hours, Sammy appears. His avatar has changed, now approximating Kiki Kinubi, a celebrity animated performer. The frivolity of it makes her want to punch his incorporeal face. Instead, she goes straight to the point.

"Are the Directorate soldiers there again?"

"Yes, they came about an hour ago," Sammy says.

"Did you warn my mom?" asks Lin. Kiki looks sideways with an uncomfortable expression. "Well?" She hopes her voice is shouting in his head.

"Lin, it's one thing to warn you. But, you know... we sell some shav out of the restaurant." Lin hadn't known. "So we can't take any risks, and your mom... she's obviously..." From the look on the avatar's face, Sammy's real head must be about to explode from embarrassment. Lin turns the call off.

She has to go to Beijing.

She starts to contact the Internal Security dispatcher to let him know she's leaving to take care of a family emergency, then decides she can't risk him saying no. Or asking questions. San Antonio will remain safe and boring without her. Lin orders a taxi to the Hyperrail.

Sabohat has never traveled by Hyperrail, but she admires its groundbreaking engineering and Lin always hoped to show it to her someday.

She's suddenly gripped by the fear that she'll never again hear her mother marvel at the train's impressive speed. Today, the Hyperrail's blistering pace seems impossibly leisurely—the delay between the mechanical voice announcing the train's destination in each Big Three language and the doors sliding shut must be at least three minutes longer than usual. The crowd meandering through the cars is also composed of slow people and unworried people. People whose languid actions can't keep pace with Lin's heartbeat. People who are not vigilant and don't know how to be. One short man flirts with another. The woman who claims the seat next to Lin's immediately goes slack-faced and dead-eyed. As the train finally churns forward, Lin puts her head in her hands and leans against the seat in front of her.

***

Sabohat was wrong about Lin being kind, wrong about the incident with Fan Fan.

It happened when Lin was ten, just overcoming her fears of the streets around Hanting Community and just starting to get used to her new name. There was a gang of kids in the neighborhood—not the ones from buildings like Hanting, but rich kids who got a thrill from haunting the slums and acting like junior thugs when their parents weren't watching. Lin first spotted them from the apartment window. They were mostly around her age or a little older, all of them larger. They stood in a circle in the alley, sending mirthful giggles up to where Lin observed silently, and for the first time she could remember, Lin wanted to go outside.

Sabohat encouraged her new association with the gang. At the time, Lin thought her mother didn't understand that the kids were bad—something she herself knew immediately without any specific proof. Later, she realized that Sabohat missed nothing. She pushed Lin out of the door into the hands of ruffians because she had calculated that it would help Lin fit in with these offspring of higher-tier citizens.

The kids didn't know she was an offworlder. They probably didn't even know why they found her strange—they simply absorbed the attitudes of their parents towards lower-class people like her. Or maybe it's instinct for those on top to know who isn't. Still, for some reason, they took a liking to Lin. They started bringing her to their homes where seven generations lived under one opulent roof. Sabohat was thrilled, although even as she encouraged Lin to accept the gang's invitations, she couldn't help taking a few jabs at their parents' intelligence or morals. Maybe it was just habit, or maybe it's instinct for those on the bottom.

When the kids got a little older, they got meaner. Where before their miscreant behavior was limited to some taunting and a few rocks badly thrown at windows, now they turned to physical intimidation, targeting the kids from Lin's neighborhood—poor kids, kids that would grow into Sammy Chens, selling shav from dead-end jobs and dreaming about being musclemen or pop stars.

And then they met Fan Fan.

Just eleven, like Lin, and an orphan, maybe. Or at least she wouldn't admit to having any family. The gang started tracking down Fan Fan every day, surrounding her, shoving her around, though Lin never knew why. Eventually, they decided she needed to be beaten, and they decided that Lin would do it. Like their parents in the upper echelon of the Big Three, these children knew how to delegate.

Lin didn't want to hurt Fan Fan and quit hanging around with the gang, or so she told Sabohat. In reality, she threw one punch to Fan Fan's face and one to her stomach before she turned back to the gang leader, kicked him to the pavement, and ran back home to Hanting. Sabohat was tight-lipped about the incident. She didn't care about Earth kids, poor or otherwise, and felt that Lin should have done what the gang wanted.

"The girl would have gotten over it," she said, "and learned a lesson in the process. But what now? What if you've made those Earth families angry and they call the Directorate on us?"

***

The Hyperrail's deceleration always leaves Lin a bit queasy. She chokes back the nausea, pushing her way through the dawdling crowds on the platform and running out of the station. Mindlink shows a seven-minute wait for an automobile taxi, so she orders up a small scooter, which whips around the corner in less than a minute. She leans low as it races toward Hanting Community, hugging the handlebars and covering her face against the biting air. Running up the stairs of her building reminds her of fleeing with Sabohat the first night the soldiers came. She can almost hear their footsteps behind her.

Hanting Community is the same as ever. Still and dark. A neighbor sees Lin rush down the hallway and turns away with an expression Lin recognizes. Pity for Lin's fate and relief that it's not his own.

Lin bursts into the apartment, still screaming Sabohat's name in her mind. Had she ever stopped screaming it? Inside the familiar kitchen, she calls the name aloud, but softer than she wants to. It has been drilled into her for too many years that she shouldn't broadcast their existence. Lin checks the bedroom—also empty. She looks back and forth between the two rooms of their tiny home until the last bit of hope is squeezed out of her chest.

Lin's mother is gone.

She sits at Sabohat's desk and lays her hands on its surface. As the desk comes to life, pale blue light spreads across Lin's fingers, and tears pool in her eyes remembering countless nights falling asleep beside her mother's face bathed in the same hue. She scans the files on the desk. The usual encrypted work files—weapons and other illegal designs for illegal residents of Earth. Nothing seems out of the ordinary. Then she notices a slight variation in the shade of blue emanating from the desk in the left corner. She runs her hand across the spot and comes away with a scrap of paper.

Sabohat never wrote on paper. Neither she nor Lin had any interest in artistic endeavors, and until Emas handed her the group invitation, Lin can't remember ever having any paper in the house. This scrap looks a lot like that one, but the series of numbers scrawled across it appears to be someone's personal ID rather than a virtual room address. But whose? Was Sabohat involved in a network similar to Emas's virtual room? Lin doesn't dare make the call. She slips the paper into her pocket and goes back into the kitchen, staring at the table, letting the emptiness sink in, imagining that Sabohat will appear at any moment and dreading that she won't. Lin calls Jul on Mindlink and gets through on the third try. Jul's avatar appears before her, an ancient bow and arrow aimed angrily upward. The quivering tension in the string makes Lin cringe backward. The avatar leans with her.

"Jul," she says. "My mom isn't here. I can't find her." Icy silence.

"I know," says Jul's voice, taut like the bowstring. "The Directorate came again last night."

"Did they take her? What do we do? We have to do something."

"I would do anything for Sabohat," says Jul. "I care for her more than you can understand. But I can't help her, so you need to think about what you can do from your own position, enforcer." And then she's gone. Lin calls a few more times with no success.

She runs downstairs and hails a Quickcab, an expensive race over the uppermost express lanes of the highway to Jul's home in Fangshan district.

Jul's apartment complex makes Hanting Community look like a palace. It cowers low to the ground, a mere five stories of cracked windows and peeling paint. Lin's hand on the stair rail comes away greasy. It's inexplicable why Jul lives here when there are unaffiliated buildings with clean walls and a tolerable aroma, but Jul boasts that she pays no one here, unlike in Hanting, where Lin and Sabohat must trust an Earth-born landlord. Sabohat promises the landlord was heavily vetted, and he's a criminal, not a citizen.

"That makes it much better," Jul always says sarcastically before leaving the topic alone again.

Lin pounds on Jul's door. She senses the apartment behind the door become still. "Jul!" she yells into Jul's neural implant. "I want to talk to you!" There's no answer, so she yells aloud.

"Open the door, Jul! I don't have time for this. My mother was taken and we need to find her!" Jul flings the door open.

"Are you crazy? Do you want everyone to hear you? If you don't care what happens to me, at least remember that they could strip your citizenship at any moment, too."

"I just want my mom back."

"Of course you do." Jul's expression betrays no sympathy. "Just get inside before someone comes to see what you were screaming about." The apartment itself is as dingy as the building's exterior. Jul's apartment is smaller than Lin and Sabohat's, but it feels wider due to the sparse furnishings. A dented metal table stands in one corner, two cots in another. Next to the table stands a dark-haired Rogovan woman with wrinkles that prove she is old and an innocence in her gaze that renders her youthful.

"Hello, Kaori," Lin greets her. Kaori doesn't acknowledge her. In all the time that she has known Jul and her ghostly roommate, Lin has never been sure if she can't speak or simply doesn't, has never heard her say anything even over Mindlink. Perhaps she doesn't have an implant. Lin also doesn't know who Kaori is to Jul—sister, lover, charity case—but they've been a pair for as long as Lin has known them.

"What do you expect from me, Lin?" says Jul. Lin doesn't think she deserves the anger in Jul's tone.

"I don't know. There has to be something we can do to find her," says Lin. "I'm here because you know more about these things than I do."

"Yes, I do. And that's Sabohat's fault—it's the way she raised you. But it's time to grow up."

"And do what?" says Lin. "I just want answers." She tries to ignore Kaori's staring eyes.

"What is the point?" Jul's lip twitches in a brief sneer.

"The point of what?" says Lin.

"The point of you. The point of having one of us a Tier One citizen. Do you know Mr. Tomasy's niece?"

"Of course. Erna."

"She's like us, like me and Sabohat. She has no resources, no security herself. Poor thing, there's truly nothing she can do for her uncle. But still, she won't stop looking for him. And you! You have authority that we won't ever have. What are you using it for?" The situation comes into focus and she finally sees the source of Jul's fury—she misunderstands the amount of power granted to a fledgling enforcer. It was often this way with Sabohat too—she comprehended the basics of Earth customs, but not the details.

"Jul," Lin says, as calmly as her inner panic will allow. "I don't think you understand how Big Three positions work. I don't have access—" Jul cuts her off.

"No. You don't understand. You miserable, sheltered child. Get out of my home." Lin opens her mouth to try again. "I said, leave," says Jul.

Lin turns and walks away, nodding awkwardly over her shoulder at Kaori as she goes.

***

The Tomasy apartment has the same floorplan as the one Lin shares with Sabohat, but it's more colorful and lively than Sabohat's clean and practical décor. A few wood sculptures stand in the corners, and there's a tapestry on the wall, slightly singed. Erna lets Lin enter but slams the door closed behind her. She's angry. Lin knows that Erna was living in Beijing for years before her uncle arrived from New Palu, and unlike Mr. Tomasy and Emas, she shows no hint of the characteristic scarring from New Palu's toxins. Maybe she was just lucky, or maybe she found a way to have it fixed.

"How can you help find Uncle Bejo?" she asks.

"I don't know yet," says Lin. "My mother is missing, too. I just thought we could help each other. Do you know anything at all?" Erna clenches her fists and looks away.

"You do, I can see it," Lin says.

"I don't," says Erna firmly. "And you should be helping me, not the other way around." Lin sighs. She doesn't want a repeat of her conversation with Jul.

"Look, I'm sorry I don't know anything about your uncle. I don't have any inside information. But if you tell me what you know, it could help both of us. You're not a citizen either, are you? How did you escape when they took your uncle?" Erna eyes her warily.

"I was at my boyfriend's house. What are you going to do, turn me in?" Lin is startled.

"Of course not, why would you think that?"

"You've always kept yourself apart from us," Erna says. "As if your citizenship wasn't bought and paid for by your mother. I don't know where your loyalties really lie." Lin never knew Erna felt this way. Jul always had a hostile streak, but in Lin's limited interactions with Erna, she has been sweet and polite. Still, her mother's friends should be helping her, not airing old grudges.

"I'm on your side," says Lin. "But I can't do anything without more information." Erna's expression is still cold, but she relents.

"I think he tried to contact me a few days after he was taken," she says.

"So you know he's alive? What did he say?"

"He didn't say anything... I just saw his avatar flash for a moment. But that could only happen if he were alive and reaching out to me, right?" Lin sags. It's nothing, a tiny scrap of delusion that Erna is clinging to like it's the last thing keeping her from drowning. Erna stares at her, breathless, waiting for Lin to manifest a miracle out of her powerful Big Three citizenship.

"I'll look into it," Lin offers lamely. "Thank you, Erna."

Alone again in her own apartment, Lin sits on Sabohat's bed, drawing her knees up to her chest. In her life, of all the people who have crossed her path—classmates, coworkers, family friends—only two souls ever mattered. Hayato was the memory of naivety and childhood, and then of fear and death. Sabohat was all the love Lin ever knew.

Was. Lin is already starting to think of her mother as a memory. What is she supposed to do with both of them gone?

She sends a message to Emas, the only other person she can think of who might be able to help, if by any chance he doesn't resent her as much as Jul or Erna. She wonders if the tears stinging her eyes are translated into the voice playing in his head.

"They took her," she says to his concerned-looking avatar. "My mother is gone, and apparently none of you trust me or want to help me."

"Give me ten minutes," says Emas, and in eight he's at her door in the flesh, pulling her into his arms and pressing the red skin of his cheek against her hair. She lets herself melt into him for a moment, lets his caring touch smooth away the sting of how Jul and Erna treated her. Then she straightens and breaks from his embrace.

"You said before that we should be doing something," she says, pleased to hear her voice sounding calm and measured. "What can we do?" Emas looks like he wants to reach for her again, but doesn't.

"I don't know," he says, "But I asked in the Mindlink group, and Javi is working on it. His information is usually good. He says he's been looking into the disappearances for a while now with no luck, but maybe with some specific information about Sabohat, he'll have a breakthrough."

"Javi is the guy who used to work with the Fourth Power, right?" says Lin.

"It's not the time to judge, Lin. He can help us." Emas calls up Javi's avatar, a gold scale, on a group call with Lin.

"Javi, the Directorate came to Beijing again," says Emas. "And they took my friend Lin's mother. I know the group hasn't had success finding missing people before, but I want you to put everything you have into this one."

"Your mother is Rogovan?" Javi asks Lin.

"Yes," says Lin. "Can you help me?"

"What's her name?"

"Sabohat Iskakova."

"And you're from Rogov too?"

"I'm a citizen. This is about my mother. Can you get any information?"

"I'll look into it," says Javi, and Lin cringes, recognizing the words she used to pacify Erna.

After Emas departs, leaving her with a heap of heartfelt but useless promises to "keep trying" and "do whatever it takes," Lin takes the scrap of paper from her pocket.

Every instinct tells her to stay away from the unknown number, but if she's too cautious, she may never find Sabohat. And every other avenue she's tried has been a dead end. She tries searching the number in the official Hauser directory on Mindlink, but isn't surprised when nothing comes up.

It could be listed in the Wonju or Xinqi directories, but she doesn't dare submit a request for that information.

Lin calls the number. Her call is acknowledged immediately, but no avatar appears.

"Who is this?" says a voice, deep and masculine.

"Your number was by my mother's desk," says Lin. "Who are you?"

"Do I know your mother?" asks the voice. Lin hesitates. She has always been taught to guard her mother's identity, but what is left to lose at this point?

"Maybe," says Lin. "Her name is Sabohat."

"Ah," says the voice, "Ms. Iskakova."

"You do know her!"

"I had been talking to Sabohat. Why are you calling instead of her?"

"She's missing," says Lin. She's not ready to talk to this stranger about Directorate roundups quite yet. "I'm just looking for someone who can help get her back."

"I might be able to help you," says the voice. "I don't—"

The mystery voice is suddenly garbled. Lin just picks up a few words: Rogov, soldiers, and alive.

"I can't hear you," she tells the voice. "Is there a problem with our connection?" There's no answer. Lin disconnects and tries to call the number again, but doesn't get through.

She puts the paper carefully into her pocket. She'll try again tomorrow. In the meantime, she holds tight to just one word the mysterious voice said.

Alive.

Chapter Thirteen

For her crimes against Earth, the offworlder will pay.

She cowers on elbows and knees, her forehead almost touching the muddy street. Her braid has come undone and long dark hair sticks to her tear-streaked face. Cenric kicks her in the ribs and she collapses in a bloody pile.

Cenric fingers his gun, considering. The woman moans, rolling onto her side, letting Cenric see her face. She's young, under forty probably, with the tan complexion and stout body of a Rogovan. He doesn't need to kill her. She doesn't belong to any corporation, so who would she tell? But she's an offworlder, destroying the Big Three way of life, so Cenric fires his weapon. Justice for Hauser.

He aches to reveal to Hauser leadership the work he has done for them, but for now, he merely revels in the execution of justice. These Rogovans killed a good Hauser man and he will not let that stand.

Of course, as usual, he was only half successful. Eliminating one off-worlder at a time, although satisfying, won't fix the larger problem. The link between Lyon's death and the Wonju killings makes it clear—these aliens have some kind of organized plot against lawful Big Three citizens. He will uncover it, no matter how many offworlders he has to interrogate.

He needs to work fast now. Bao Ding told him last week the team is being dissolved. "A long time coming," Bao phrased it with a yawn. "It's incredibly inefficient to have top Hauser employees, all of whom spend a quarter of their time on Mars, looking at satellite images all day. A Tier Two could do it. Maybe even Tier Three."

When Cenric raised objections ("My work is important! Don't they know that?"), Bao seemed almost disbelieving.

"Cenric, you're a finance guy," he says. "I have no idea why your dad dropped you into the intelligence department to begin with, but you're not doing anything groundbreaking."

Cenric doesn't dare ask Cormand for another Mars Congress-worthy assignment, and he doesn't know what he'll get without family help. A demotion would bring a smirk to his father's face, Cenric is sure. Cormand doesn't know the contribution that Cenric is making. No one does, not his father or his boss or Arthur, who recently made a joke about Cenric's mysterious behavior being a sign he was "going rogue." He said it with a laugh but his eyes were concerned.

Cenric realizes more every day that he is following the path the Hauser founders envisioned. He's ensuring that Hauser citizens are protected and prosperous. It's not him but the others—his father, the Directorate, regular employees like Arthur—who have lost their way. If he's going rogue now, history will thank him for it.

Meanwhile, Cenric has other business in São Paulo. This time, he didn't have a voucher on hand for his trip to Earth—especially one that would allow him to return to Mars for the rest of the Congress—so he had to get creative. He combed through his department's files until he found one related to São Paulo: a few weeks of satellite surveillance on an unaffiliated building believed to be some kind of illegal medical clinic. Bao Ding hadn't followed through on shutting the clinic down, so Cenric went to his boss and presented the files.

"I want to go to Earth and investigate this," he said. Bao squinted at Cenric.

"You what? Why would you do that?"

"Medical center means pharmaceuticals. You always say we should be looking for drugs."

"Well sure, but not... and anyway, why would you go yourself? We'll just send in some Hauser enforcer, say we're looking for a missing Hauser citizen and whatnot. If anything is amiss, the enforcer tells us, we tell the Directorate, and boom. Nice commissions for us."

Cenric swallowed back the dirty taste in his mouth and suggested to Bao Ding that he might ask his father for a second opinion. Bao relented to the coercion with a roll of his eyes. All for the greater good, Cenric told himself.

* * *

São Paulo is too loud. The architecture is chaotic—no building matches the one next to it, there's no art to the skyline, and most skyscrapers lurch three times higher than anything on the elegant Martian campuses. People are everywhere, shouting to friends and hopping in and out of vehicles of all classifications. On one street corner, a musician strums a stringed instrument and sings an awful racket. Cenric can't wait to be back on Mars.

The supposed illegal clinic is under a Wonju office building. The office building itself only houses Wonju departments, Cenric confirmed with a Wonju liaison, but no one knows what's on the basement levels. At least that's what the liaison said.

"Undoubtedly not a single Wonju citizen thought to check," Cenric told the liaison drily.

Cenric enters the front doors of the office building and takes the stairs to the basement. No one pays him much mind when he strolls out of the stairwell into what's clearly a medical center—and a surprisingly upscale one. Cenric assumed he would find criminals and offworlders, but these people look like citizens. If he didn't know better, he would think he was in a legitimate Wonju hospital.

He chooses a hallway at random and walks down it with feigned purpose. Ahead of him, a nurse exits one of the rooms, pushing a cart ahead of her. On the cart are boxes of synthetic patches, the unmarked blue boxes familiar immediately to Cenric. Shav. The medical center is a front for drug production. Cenric follows the nurse and sees her leave the patches on a shelf with a variety of vials, pills, and other patches.

Cenric sends a message back to Bao Ding that he's uncovered an illegal operation, then quickly snaps a few stills from his implant to send his boss before turning to leave. His next item of business is the most important, his true purpose.

But suddenly he finds his arm is out of his own control. He watches it, detached, as it reaches out and takes a shav patch.

He won't actually use the shav, Cenric tells himself. He's not the type to get distracted from important work, he tells himself. He is strength in a sea of weakness. And as he tells himself these truths, his possessed hand places the shav patch on his arm. Cenric exits the fake clinic and leans up against the back wall of the office building as the edges of his world blur and numbness sets in.

Dark blue vines grow up from the ground around him. Strange, Cenric thinks, how evenly spaced they are. The blue vines creep to him like snakes. They scale the skyscraper walls, hissing. They wrap around Cenric's throat and chest. Cenric closes his eyes. Then blue peace and nothing matters.

***

Four hours later, the shav haze makes way for the usual angry shame. Why is he wasting his limited time here? Cenric has another lead in the area, more important than the lone woman alien or the basement shav clinic. He has to travel hundreds of kilometers and back before it's time to return to the Mars transport.

But if he brings justice to Hauser, what's a little shav high along the way?

Cenric's destination is a small town on the coast. At least, there used to be a town there; he's seen the town's name on an old map, seen its buildings on satellite imagery from fifty years ago, but the mark has disappeared from modern cartography and no satellite images exist from Cenric's lifetime.

Cenric hails a standard Hauser cab on Mindlink. He provides the name of the town and receives the reply that his destination is unrecognizable, so he sends coordinates instead and receives a message he's never seen from a Hauser cab: "Request Denied." Blood rushes in his ears. It's the confirmation he's been seeking—this town isn't what it seems.

He charters a manual plane instead. He's only flown with a human pilot a few times in his life, and he eyes the gaunt, leathery-skinned man warily.

"You're from Hauser?" asks Cenric.

"Sure," says the pilot. "Where you headed?" Cenric gives him the coordinates. The man smacks his blistered lips a few times.

"Well, that's a new one, isn't it," he says. "What you doing there?"

"Classified," says Cenric.

"Mmmhmm," says the pilot.

Cenric closes his eyes for most of the flight so the pilot will think he's busy on his implant and refrain from making conversation. In fact, his mind is racing with possibilities of what he might find when he reaches the small town. Why would an area be intentionally kept off the official record? He's certain that the Big Three and the Directorate are meticulous about surveying property they own, so this town must have somehow fallen completely out of their hands. Cenric has a strong suspicion whose hands it belongs to. Who else but illegal aliens would create such a large dark spot?

The excitement makes Cenric's breath short. He wonders if anyone besides him has discovered this anomaly.

"Well, that's irregular," says the pilot.

"What now?"

"I'm, um, I'm getting a message. I'm going to have to set you down here."

"Here?" Cenric looks out the window at the ground below. He sees only grass and trees. For a moment, his conviction wavers. It seems suspicious that offworlders could command enough power to reroute airplanes and erase maps. But he brushes off his doubts.

Never underestimate the enemy.

"Don't worry, it's only a few kilometers to where you're going. I'll be waiting here when you get back."

After the plane descends into a clearing in the Terratech forest, Cenric marches in the direction the pilot indicates, scowling at the brush snapping against his legs. The ground is muddy and pulls irritatingly at his shoes with each step. But it's not long before he smells saltwater in the air and sees a tan strip of beach in the distance. Small houses emerge on the horizon and Cenric picks up the pace.

The first house he reaches is small and understated with white walls and a flat roof. It seems to be a single-family dwelling with no visible smart features. Cenric catches sight of a shadow around the back of the house and creeps nearer to investigate, slinking close to the wall.

A woman in a colorful silk tunic and dark curls that reflect the sun is on her knees, her back to Cenric. She's working in a small garden, and the plants she's pruning are exotic, maybe not even Terratech. The whole setting is bizarre and antiquated. Surely, this woman is an alien.

She stands, brushes the dirt off her knees, and heads for her house. Cenric unholsters his gun and moves to follow her inside. A little intimidation should go a long way toward getting him an explanation for this place. When the woman gets to her door she turns around and smiles at him.

"Welcome to our village," she says warmly. Cenric manages not to look surprised that she noticed him.

"What is this place? Why are there no satellite images? Are you a citizen?" He steps closer with each question. When he reaches her, the woman places a gentle hand on his arm and smiles wider. He doesn't realize that something in her palm has pricked his skin until he's pitching forward into her friendly, blurring face.

***

When Cenric wakes, he thinks for a moment that he's back on Mars. The room and the sofa he's lying on are so neat, so crisp, and so modern that he assumes he's no longer in São Paulo or the mysterious beach village. His relief fades when he pushes himself into a sitting position and feels the heavy Earth gravity push back.

A young man sits in a chair across from Cenric, leaning just a little too close. Cenric notices the man's eager eyes before he notices the Directorate red of his uniform.

"You're Directorate military," he says in surprise. His own voice makes his head throb.

"Mr. Smith," says the man in red, "I am so incredibly sorry that Valeria gave you our treatment." He indicates Cenric's arm. "It's standard policy for unauthorized guests, but she should have recognized you." *Recognized me? I don't know this Valeria*, Cenric might have said on another day, but he knows the look on the Directorate man's face. For once, it might work in his favor.

"You know my father?" asks Cenric, but doubts the man does. People who actually know Cormand are far less sycophantic.

"Cormand Smith! Well, of course I know of him. He's been here before, naturally." This does surprise Cenric, especially since he's still not certain where "here" is. "I never actually saw him, but we've been here at the same time," the man continues. Not a man, Cenric thinks, just a boy, and one who worships Big Three royalty.

"Do all the members of the Directorate come to... this place?" Cenric asks.

"Yes! Yes, I often see very high-ranking individuals here. Not just from Hauser, either. One of the poor Wonju representatives who was killed was actually here at the base only a few weeks earlier. I was part of the group that greeted him." The base. Cenric is at a Directorate military facility of some sort then. There are only a few in the world. Cenric has never been to one before, but he thought he knew their locations. This one must be something unique. Secret. "And one of my friends here is actually the cousin of Di Wei." He pauses to make sure Cenric knows who he means. "You know, the Xinqi rep? My friend even introduced me to Di Wei."

Cenric smiles.

Half an hour later, he's getting a tour of a secret Directorate military base. The soldier, whose name is Mitt, blithers on about the important people he's seen in each room, occasionally throwing in a tidbit that's actually interesting to Cenric.

"This place is almost exclusively used for the most important meetings and summits," he says. "We're just here to keep it secure. But no one knows about it from the surface anyway—the whole thing is underground. Up there, it just looks like a little town."

A woman approaches them. Her long hair is now tied above her head and she's exchanged the skirt for pants, but Cenric recognizes her as the woman he first saw when he entered the village.

"I think the two of you have already met," says Mitt. "Valeria, you should really apologize to Cenric. His father is—"

"I know," says Valeria. She doesn't apologize.

"You're military too?" Cenric asks. She isn't wearing the red uniform.

"Yes," she says. "I work with TEDI."

"TEDI?" Cenric asks. "The system that keeps the offworlders out?"

"It's an AI," Valeria says reproachfully. "A being, not a system. And it protects us. It learns and it makes decisions. Otherwise, its methods of detecting threats would be long since outdated. But we can give it some input."

"How do you talk to it?" asks Cenric. Valeria gives him the same smile she flashed before she drugged him.

"Not even your father knows that," she says.

Chapter Fourteen

WITHOUT SABOHAT, LIN IS untethered. She's still connected to the neural web, to her training-mates with whom she chats regularly, to the news, and to her Internal Security superiors. But the strongest line, the one that has always felt like a physical object binding her to Hanting Community and Sabohat, has been slashed.

Lin returns to work. She watches the feeds and checks on Abena and sips tea at the teahouse, because what else can she do? But the pain of the severed connection doesn't relent.

Emas calls her often, and she answers, eager to connect with someone who knows what she's going through, eager to disconnect when she realizes he's mostly interested in the approaching Rogovan ship and the plotting of various resistance groups.

Her scattered mind betrays her and she fails to file documentation on the assassination attempt. As a result of her carelessness, Abena's departure from the San Antonio Hauser Medical Center is delayed.

"I'm sorry," says Lin, when the Internal Security manager calls her implant to let her know about the mistake. She is sorry, somewhere under the haze.

"Don't apologize to me," says the manager. "Just make sure Abena Owusu knows it was your fault, not Hauser Internal Enforcement's."

"Of course," says Lin. Then she remembers what day it is. "My assignment is ending," she says. "Where will I go next?" She hopes it's somewhere where she can be more useful.

"Let me check," says the manager. There's a brief pause. "You haven't been reassigned." Lin stiffens.

"I promise I won't forget the documentation again—" she starts.

"Relax," says the manager. "It's not a punishment. I don't know what it is exactly. Politics as usual, probably."

***

Abena is having her failing eyes rejuvenated and is temporarily blind while the nanotech rebuilds her optic nerve. She raises her chin at the sound of Lin entering the room, staring blankly just over Lin's shoulder.

"Enforcer Yang Lin," announces a member of her entourage.

"Ah yes," says Abena. "A little nano told me you're the reason I'm stuck here an extra day."

"Yes. I'm very sorry for any inconvenience the delay has caused you. Feel free to file a complaint about my conduct with Hauser Internal Security."

"Relax, kid," says Abena. "I don't have any complaints. That's why I'm taking you to Mars with me."

"Me? Why would I go to Mars?" asks Lin.

"And that's why I like you," Abena cackles. "Everyone else is dying for a ticket to the Congress."

Lin sighs. Secretly, she's been hoping to return to Fort Omar while Kirs, Bogdan, and Boyu are still there. Even if she can't actually tell them what happened to her mother, she would be comforted by their friendship.

"I've already put in the request to have you along as private security," says Abena. "They'll listen to me, they always do." She snaps her fingers and one of her attendants hands her a glass of water.

"Why me?" asks Lin.

"You have talent," says Abena, grinning as if she can see Lin's skeptical look. "Well, you don't say much, which is in fact a rare skill these days."

"So we'll be there for the rest of the Congress?" Lin doesn't think she can spend an entire month with Abena, and it will prevent her from searching for her mother.

"No, of course not. It's almost over anyway, and I don't have that kind of time. But the Directorate representatives will be chosen later this year, and everyone with a vote will be on Mars. If they haven't seen me recently, they'll have forgotten all about me. We'll go for just a few days. Maybe after that, I'll get you assigned to my home in Accra." Lin tries not to shudder, but Abena slaps her leg like it's hilarious.

"Well, anyway, Mars will be a fun trip—it's a magnificent planet. Maybe I can get you a vacation voucher to stay on for a while. Have you been?"

"No," says Lin, tired of repeating the lie. "I've never left Earth."

***

As she leaves Abena's wing, Lin runs into Rajan. He grins when he sees her and she gives him a shaky smile back.

"Is something wrong?" he asks. Lin attempts a laid-back shrug.

"Nothing serious," she says. "Just a little bureaucratic mess."

"Ah," he says. "So even our brave enforcers have to deal with red tape sometimes."

"They forgot to tell me about that part when I agreed to change citizenship." Lin feels some of the weight on her shoulders begin to lift in Rajan's jovial presence.

"I'm starting my own corporation," he says. "Founded on strict anti-paperwork principles. Want to be my first citizen?" Lin laughs, just a short chuckle, but it's the first time since Sabohat disappeared that she's felt this light-hearted. Then she frowns.

"I'm leaving soon," she tells Rajan. "Abena is taking me to Mars, and then I don't know where I'll go." Rajan doesn't lose his trademark wide smile, but some of the shine leaves his eyes. He touches Lin's arm lightly.

"We knew it was coming," he says. "But hey, Mars! That's amazing, isn't it?" Lin shrugs noncommittally. "Well, as long as you still have that super implant I put in we can still have our occasional afternoon tea, can't we?" says Rajan.

"Sure, that would be nice," says Lin, and wonders why it doesn't sound all that nice to chat with Rajan's official portrait from some other city. They stand in silence for a moment.

"I have to get to my patients," he says, not moving.

"Yeah, me too," says Lin. "I have to get back to Abena, I mean." She doesn't move either. Rajan cups her face in his hand and kisses her. Lin steps back, startled, and looks behind her to see if anyone saw.

"I'm sorry," says Rajan. "Was that inappropriate?" A hot flush creeps up Lin's face, and for a minute, she can't breathe. But Rajan is smiling again and it loosens her tongue.

"No," she says. "It was nice."

"I do have to go to my patient," Rajan says. "But if you'd like, we could have dinner together later. Not here in San Antonio. There's a little place I know in Guadalajara—we can catch the train after your shift and be there in thirty minutes." Lin agrees and walks away from him, her heart fluttering in happy anxiety. She reaches out to her mother to convey her excitement and confusion and her chest contracts painfully when she feels Sabohat's absence. The fog swirls down around her again.

Lin reminds herself that her mother wouldn't have approved of any intimacy with an Earth-born citizen, anyway. She doesn't know if that makes her feel better or worse.

***

The Guadalajara restaurant features a lounge singer with a throaty voice and a gown like a rushing waterfall. Chains of lights dance across the ceiling, forming mesmerizing patterns in time with the music. Rajan is also dazzling in a trendy jacket and slicked-back hair. Lin feels she's made the wrong choice by wearing her Hauser dress uniform.

"It's a Xinqi establishment," says Rajan. "I thought maybe you would feel more at home." Lin scans the lavish place settings and glittering lights until her eyes land on a skinny young man clearing the table whose clumsy demeanor reminds her of Sammy Chen. A server with smooth, dark hair like Lin's hisses at him, probably telling him to hurry up, while looking over her shoulder at the glaring hostess.

"You're right, it's very familiar," she says, and Rajan smiles with satisfaction. They sit, and Rajan orders a wine.

"This is not just any wine," he tells her. "The fruit isn't Terratech. It's an original, non-engineered species grown in an isolated greenhouse near here."

Lin takes one careful sip from her glass and sets it aside. She dislikes alcohol and the way it weakens her control over body and mind.

"You look stunning, even dressed up as a Hauser exec," Rajan says, leaning forward and placing his hands in the middle of the table. Lin mirrors his movement with a smile.

Their fingers, teasingly, almost touch.

They talk about family. Lin is better prepared this time. When she tells him about Sabohat, she uses her adopted mother's name and throws in a few mentions of siblings for good measure. He tells her about growing up in Mumbai. After so many from India left for the stars in the ships that would later be dramatically portrayed across books and dramas as the Ganges Fleet, those who were left behind, including Rajan's family, made a fortune claiming the property left behind and selling it to the Big Three.

"My grandparents were especially smart," he says. "When they sold their hotel properties, they negotiated a clause that they would always get a cut of the profits. So we were set for life. We had an 'iron rice bowl,' as I believe you like to say in Xinqi."

"So how did you end up as a doctor instead of a hotelier?" Lin asks, and Rajan rewards her with that grin again.

"I suppose I ought to say I became a doctor because I wanted to help people. And I do, I do. But back when I was a kid I didn't care about that. My friend's dad was a doctor and he was just so... dignified. Like one of those gentleman scholars in the romance dramas from Xinqi's entertainment division."

"You watch those?" asks Lin.

"They're the best," laughs Rajan.

"Our neighborhood doctor when I was a kid was completely different," says Lin. "An absolute eccentric. She was Wonju, but she didn't work out of their Beijing medical center. She had this little one-room clinic. I don't even know if it was legal." Of course it wasn't. "She was always muttering to herself—you couldn't tell if she was listening to you—but I tell you, the woman could fix any problem."

"I wonder why she didn't work at the medical center," Rajan speculates, but Lin just shrugs.

"Like I said, she was a strange one."

"Maybe she was an offworlder," says Rajan. Lin's smile collapses and she leans back.

"Why would you say that?" she asks.

"Don't you ever think about that?" Rajan asks. "You always hear on the news that the offworlders are everywhere, just blending in, so maybe you've met one and you don't even know it." Lin studies his face. It's as relaxed and friendly as ever.

"I doubt it," she says. "I think I would know."

"Don't be so sure." Rajan lowers his voice to a stage whisper. "They walk among us, watching our every move, plotting our demise." He switches back to his normal voice. "Or at least, that's what some of the fearmongers on the Directorate would have us believe."

"But you don't think so," says Lin, grasping at a sliver of hope.

"I don't know. I always thought we should just leave the colonists alone. We're lucky to be Big Three citizens, right? The Ganges Fleet disappeared, but what if my distant family members appeared again someday and wanted to come back to Mumbai? I used to think that would be fine. But then..."

"The Wonju poisonings," guesses Lin.

"Right. It made me think. We can't get too lenient. I might be friendly to aliens but they're not friendly to me."

"How would you know?" she asks. "It's like you said, anyone could be an alien." She looks down at her plate and swallows, then flashes him the most flirtatious smile she can muster. "Maybe I'm from the colonies." He laughs and she laughs with him. Thankfully, it comes out sounding natural.

"No way," he says. "You're all Earth."

"How do you know?" she asks, hoping she can maintain her teasing tone.

"Well let's see..." He leans across the table and grabs her hand. "You're tough, so there's that. But not scary tough, so you can't be from our own solar system, like Ganymede or an asteroid mine. You don't want to mess with those people. As for the outer colonies... well, Rogov is out."

"Why?"

"Too tall," says Rajan. "No one from Rogov ever had legs like yours." His foot brushes hers under the table. "And your eye makeup is way too normal for New Palu." Lin's laughter is increasingly forced.

"Britton?" she asks.

"Too nice," Rajan says. "Brittons are all jerks." Lin starts to lift her wine glass, then sets it down.

"Do you know anyone from Britton?" she asks, her voice holding a sharp edge now. Rajan hears it and quickly drops his smile.

"No, of course not," he says.

"Because if you found out someone was from Britton, you'd call the Directorate."

"I guess so. I've just heard they're very hotheaded."

"They have to be," says Lin. "The two groups that tried to colonize Britton have been at war for two hundred years. And the ones who don't want to fight have no choice because their original home planet won't take them back. Can you imagine that?" She takes a large drink of her wine. Then a few more. Rajan speaks in a measured tone.

"It was just a joke, Lin. I didn't mean anything about it." Lin laughs, and it doesn't sound at all normal.

"I know," she says. "It was funny."

They are silent on the train ride home. Rajan leans back and closes his eyes, seemingly content, their awkward talk of colonists forgotten. He slides his fingers around Lin's. She turns her head to look at him. Despite a few tense moments at dinner, the sight of him still makes her fears more distant. She slides over and presses her body into his.

"I'm sorry, Mom." Lin sends the unspoken words across the severed line to nowhere.

***

"Hey. Hey you." Lin stands in her apartment back in San Antonio. The lights are turned off, but she sees the tiled walls and low cot in sharp detail. Now that her night vision is almost perfect, Lin finds that she feels more comfortable in the dark, more alone, more safe.

She subvocalizes at the mystery man from Sabohat's handwritten paper. She still doesn't know his name or origin.

"Hello, young Iskakova," says the deep voice in her head. Still no avatar. It makes her angry that he won't send it.

"What do you know about my mother?" asks Lin. "Is she alive?"

"I need some more information from you before I tell you anything."

"Fine. What?"

"The ship coming from Rogov. I need to know what you know about it. Tell me everything." Lin mulls over his request, letting the silence stew between them. She has no reason to trust this stranger whose avatar she hasn't even seen. But she has no clues and no help. If she has to trust someone, why not the person Sabohat led her to with a handwritten note?

She hears distortion rising, and she's afraid they'll be cut off again soon.

"I'll tell you what I know," she says.

Chapter Fifteen

THE SHIP DIES, OF course. Because if there's one constant in the universe, it's that nothing goes smoothly for Vedra. Her family didn't keep her fed, her husband was a lout, and the probably-empire man who saved her has a piece of junk for a ship.

"How soon can you fix it?" asks Vedra.

"I can't," answers Myat.

"Can we take the flier?" asks Vedra.

"There's no place to take it to," answers Myat.

"What are we going to do?" asks Vedra.

"There's nothing we can do," answers Myat.

"So we're going to die out here?" asks Vedra.

"Eventually," answers Myat. She is trying to sound matter-of-fact, but her face is angry.

"How long do we have?" asks Vedra.

"Not long," answers Myat. "We were never equipped for more than a few weeks travel. Rations and life support will both run out."

"Of course they will," says Vedra.

***

Myat gives the last rations to Temar, who is bundled tightly in one of the sleeping sacks. He started acting weak and sleepy almost immediately when the ship's engine stopped working, as if he knew what was coming and was content to go along with it.

They've been adrift for three days. Vedra isn't tired—in fact, she's restless with hunger and anger, but she won't risk Temar spending any of his last moments alone, so she floats by his side. Myat flies around the ship, tinkering uselessly with the equipment, but eventually gives up. She hovers in the hatch between the sleeping space and the larger room, watching Vedra and Temar. If gravity were such that Vedra were lying on her back, Myat would be looking down on her from above.

"We're almost dead, then?" asks Vedra.

"We'll lose oxygen within five hours," says Myat. Vedra thinks suddenly that she looks quite vulnerable, maybe even a little scared.

"It's weird to have you just staring at us," she says. "Come here." She pats the space next to her, on the opposite side of Temar. Myat hesitates a moment, then glides down beside her, stopping a careful meter away.

"If we're going to die together, I might as well know a little more about you," says Vedra. "Tell me about growing up on Pluto." Myat shakes her head.

"I don't want to talk about that."

"Why?" asks Vedra. "Because it's a painful memory, or because that's not really where you're from?" Myat is silent, and Vedra pushes a little further. "We only have a few more hours to live. You might as well tell me the truth." But Vedra doesn't really want to spend those hours pestering the person who tried to save her.

"I'm sorry it turned out this way," says Myat.

"Me too," says Vedra. Temar is asleep, or unconscious, and Vedra strokes his hair and then moves closer to Myat.

"OK, tell me this," she says. "How does a woman end up as one of Fenton's men? Rather than serving the food and sleeping in the women's quarters with the rest of us."

"Where I come from, I'm not considered so unusual."

"Pluto, you mean?" Myat doesn't respond, but she keeps a straight face.

"I've admired you since I first saw you, you know," says Myat after a moment. "You're very strong."

"That's true," Vedra agrees with a sigh. The thought of Myat watching her in the compound warms her a bit. "I always had to be."

"I really thought I could rescue you," says Myat. "I'm sorry I failed."

Vedra shrugs. "You tried." They rest in silence for a while, the air around them slowly thinning. Vedra feels normal, not like she's a few hours from death.

"Will it be painful in the end?" she asks.

"No," says Myat. "I think we'll just fall asleep."

"Oh. Good," Vedra says. And then a few minutes later, "I suppose it's better than burning at the compound."

"Yes," says Myat.

Vedra thinks about her life in the compound, slaving for a man she felt nothing for. She remembers her boredom and disgust when Fenton chose to spend the night in her bed instead of passing out drunk in the banquet hall or sleeping with one of his employee's women. She remembers his smelly, hard belly pushing into hers. Vedra's lip curls at the unwanted memory.

If Vedra is going to die, she doesn't want her late husband to be the last one she loved.

She grabs the shoulders of Myat's coveralls, pulling their bodies close together and wrapping her legs around Myat. The momentum causes them to spin lightly in the low gravity, locked together, Vedra's long hair swirling around them both. Myat's hands are reacting well before her face loses its startled expression, running her fingers down Vedra's cheek. Vedra slowly lowers the zipper on Myat's coveralls and slides her hands under her light undershirt, finding the breasts hidden under Myat's shapeless attire. Myat gasps softly, and Vedra glances at Temar. He's out cold. She kisses along the side of Myat's neck down to the curve of her shoulder.

Myat grips her waist and pushes her out to arm's length.

"Damnit," she says. "I always wanted... I want this. But not under these circumstances. Not just because we're dying."

"Don't be so depressing," says Vedra, pulling them back together and planting her lips on Myat's. They bounce off the opposite wall without flinching, intertwined. Suddenly, Myat stiffens and stops responding. She pushes Vedra away. Vedra floats until she grabs a strap on Temar's sleeping sack and pulls herself back in.

"What is it?" she asks, indignant.

"The ship's scanners have detected another vessel," says Myat. "A very large one. It's close enough that we could intercept it in the flier." Her eyes are wide.

"How can you tell?" asks Vedra.

"When the ship's system discovered the vessel, it contacted my implant," Myat says. "Told me in my mind, I mean," she explains at Vedra's confused look.

"So what are you going to do?"

"Send a message, of course. Let them know we need help." Her eyes go blank as she composes the message. Vedra has seen this mind-to-mind communication before, often between Fenton and his men and sometimes between visitors to the station when she was young. Temar shifts slightly in his sleep.

"What if they're Empire? Or pirates?" Vedra straightens out her tousled clothing and hair.

"When you run out of options, you might as well trust somebody." Myat shrugs. A few moments later, a corner of her mouth turns up. "They're going to let us on board,"

"Oh, perfect, we're walking straight into their trap," says Vedra, but she's happy too. She looks at Myat's open coveralls, contemplates continuing where she left off, then reaches over and gently zips them up. The moment has passed. Myat looks down, swallows, and looks back up at Vedra.

"Get to the flier," she says. "I have to grab some things." Vedra narrows her eyes.

"What do you need? Can I help you carry it, or is it Empire stuff you don't want me to see?" A flicker of annoyance passes over Myat's face before it returns to its usually calm expression.

"You have to bring your son," she says. "Get in the flier quickly or we'll lose our window to transfer to the other ship." She pushes off the wall and sails past Vedra to the hatch. Vedra returns to Temar's side and shakes him gently.

"Temar, baby? Are you awake?" Temar wheezes slightly and tries to curl into a ball inside the sleeping sack. Vedra unbuckles him and pulls him out of the sack and into her arms. His frame already seems bulkier thanks to the medication Myat has been giving him; if Vedra had to carry him in high gravity now, she'd be in trouble.

"Come on, baby, put your arms around Mama," she says, but he only snuggles into her. She sighs and begins pulling him to the belly of the ship where the flier is kept. She places Temar in the seat, then crawls in behind him and maneuvers him into her lap. Temar's eyelids flutter.

"Oh, now you wake up," she says, but she's relieved. For a moment there she worried he wasn't going to last as long as the oxygen.

"I'm so hungry," he says.

"I know," she says. "We're going to fly on over to another ship now. They'll have some food for you."

"Is Myat coming?" asks Temar.

"Yes," says Vedra, and Temar looks relieved.

"I'm glad," he says.

"Me too," says Vedra. She thinks of Myat and how her unzipped cover-alls were the most exciting thing Vedra's seen since she used to sneak away and lie naked in the growing room with her friend Aria when they were teenagers, their bodies tangled lazily together, tracing each other's youthful curves and talking about everything except the thing they couldn't have. Aria, like Myat, protected Vedra when she was in trouble, like the time Vedra's father punished her for some cheeky remark by forcing her to work extra shifts packing product with no food or sleep. Aria sneaked into the processing hub and helped finish the work while Vedra laid her head on the table and dreamt.

Myat is there a few minutes later, loading equipment into the flier word-lessly. Then she jumps into the driver's seat, checks Vedra's safety harness with a quick tug, and fires up the engine.

"Do you really think these people will be friendly?" asks Vedra quietly, laying her hands over Temar's ears. Myat doesn't answer, just taps the flier controls to open the bay doors and they shoot out into space.

This time Vedra stays conscious long enough to see the deep black of open space fill the view screen. If not for the shaking of the little flier and the pressure pounding Vedra into the seat and Temar into Vedra, she wouldn't be able to tell that they were moving. She squints into the dark, looking for anything that resembles an asteroid or a space station, and sees nothing. Perfect.

The ship is almost as black as the universe, and Vedra doesn't realize they're approaching it until they are almost upon it. When she begins to make out the outline of the ship, it reminds her of a falling barrel at first, rotating endlessly through the air. Then its jaw drops open and it becomes the head of a snake, swallowing them into its deep throat. Myat lands the flier in a large room. Vedra feels the higher gravity sink into her bones.

"Let me go first," says Myat, and jumps out of the flier.

"Stay here," says Vedra to Temar, and follows her.

A semi-circle of five men have their guns trained on Vedra and Myat. The men have a different look than the ones from Fenton's compound or the station where Vedra was born, all shorter than average, but burly and strong.

"Get the other one," says the largest of the men, who has a pattern of geometric tattoos running from his collar up both cheeks. Vedra doesn't move.

"We know there are three of you," he says and aims his weapon up at the flier. Vedra raises her arms.

"He's just a kid!" she says. When there's no response she concedes, "I'll get him." She goes back to the flier and tries to get Temar to his feet. Her arms feel too weak to carry him. Suddenly Myat is beside her.

"I have him," she says, scooping Temar effortlessly into her arms. Vedra walks in front of both of them, trying to keep her body between the guns and her son.

"Come with us to the bridge," says tattoo face.

The bridge is a serious upgrade from the cockpit of Myat's sorry ship. Lights flash and monitors show a dizzying stream of information in a semi-circle around two chairs in the center. One is empty, the other one is occupied by a dark-haired man. Like the others they've seen so far, he's stocky and muscular. He stands ramrod straight when he sees them.

When they're face to face, he bows very slightly, first at Myat and then Vedra, and speaks to them in a language that Vedra doesn't understand but Myat seems to.

"Hello?" she says.

"Sorry," says the man. "We'll speak English." Nothing ever goes smoothly for Vedra, but she supposes she can't expect people so far from the asteroid belt to speak Anglian. English is intelligible to her, just a variation on Anglian, but its twisted vowels grate on her nerves.

"We're from an asteroid colony," says Myat.

"Recently deceased," adds Vedra.

"You're going to Earth?" says the man, and Vedra still holds out some hope that Myat will suggest an alternative plan. No such luck.

"We are," Myat says. "And based on your trajectory, so are you. We'll be there in what, five days?" The man jerks his head noncommittally.

"Are you in contact with anyone there?" asks Myat.

"Is that a trick question?" asks the man. "We're still out of range for the neural web, in case you were hoping to let someone know we're coming."

"I wasn't."

"Right. Well, as I'm sure you know, those of us outside the dominion of the Big Three can't be too careful."

"The neural web?" asks Vedra, but no one fills her in on the unknown English term.

"There must be thousands of people on this ship," says Myat. "At least two thousand on the larger deck, if you have them packed in tight like I think you do. And maybe a thousand on the smaller deck. You almost never see ships like this anymore, at least this close to Earth. A rig like this hasn't been typical since the days of emigration to the colonies. And in the hangar where we came in, you have six shuttles. I don't think it's an 'in case of emergency' situation. You plan to take the entire group of you to Earth."

The man seems a bit taken aback, but nods. "You're not incorrect," he says.

"You have a way to get past TEDI undetected," says Myat. "You wouldn't be risking all these lives if you didn't." They stare at each other, the man looking up at Myat's tall frame. Vedra swallows back her questions in the silence. The man shrugs.

"That's right," he says. "I'm Captain Nakamura Yusuke"

"Myat," says Myat. "Where are you coming from?"

"Rogov," says the captain.

Chapter Sixteen

LIN TAKES A LATE-NIGHT walk, soothed by the cool autumn air. Her nanotech-enhanced senses are hyper-aware—she sees sharply in the darkness, hears quiet conversations flowing from apartment windows above her, smells fried appetizers sizzling at a pub two blocks over. Focusing on these details clears her mind of heavier thoughts.

She's almost back to her apartment when she hears footsteps behind her. She takes two random turns and listens to the footsteps turn as well. Someone is following her—no, two people. Her stalkers aren't even trying to be quiet—their footsteps scuff along on the pavement, and one of them breathes with a wheeze. Lin turns into an alley and waits, her back to the wall.

"Where'd she go now?" The voice is only halfway to a whisper.

"This way." Lin leans out slightly to scout out her pursuers. She sees two men bumbling down the road without confidence. One is large and flabby, the other skinny with poor posture. Not fighters.

She jumps the bigger one and quickly knocks him unconscious. The smaller man tries to scuttle away, but she kicks his knees out from under him and draws the weapon from her belt. As she walks toward him, driving her gun toward his forehead, she's hailed by a name she doesn't recognize. She ignores it. The larger man comes to with a groan and she points the weapon at him for a second before swinging it back to the skinny one.

"Don't think I'm not fast enough to take down both of you," she says.

"Just wait!" says the smaller man. "That's me calling your implant. Please answer."

"Why?" asks Lin.

"Just do it." He's trying to distract her maybe, as if he could get a jump on a woman who can hear the terror in every breath he inhales.

"Fine," she says and answers the call. A purple spiral bursts into her mind. Lin remembers the avatar.

"David?" she asks cautiously, without lowering her weapon. The man from Emas's virtual room nods and very slowly gets to his feet, hands raised.

"If you have my Mindlink number, why didn't you just contact me over the network?" Lin's voice comes out louder than she meant it to. Her hands and breath are steady, but inside she's shaking. She should be able to walk in her own neighborhood in peace.

"We wanted to make sure that you are who you say you are," says the spiral. He switches back to speaking aloud. "Emas is our friend, and he said you were a Tier One enforcement officer, but we weren't sure we could believe it."

"We believe it now," says the friend, holding his injured arm.

"What do you want from me?" Lin asks. She holsters her gun and the two friends slump visibly.

"We need your help," says David. "Rogov needs your help."

"I keep hearing that." Lin looks up at the stars and lets out a breath and says, "How can I make this more clear? There's nothing I can do. I'm not important, I'm just an enforcer and a brand new one. I'm just trying not to get caught myself."

"There is something you can do," says David's pudgy friend.

"Who's this guy?" asks Lin, jerking her head at the friend.

"His name is Jimmel," says David. "You can trust him too."

"I'm sure," says Lin.

"You know about the Rogovan ship coming," says Jimmel.

"I've heard about it a few times," Lin says.

"We have a plan to get it here safely."

"Impossible," says Lin. "The Directorate shoots at anything it sees."

"No, not the Directorate," says Jimmel.

"The AI that's owned by the Directorate. Same thing."

"It's called TEDI—it destroys anything it thinks is a threat. So we just have to take TEDI off the board for a little while." Jimmel seems overly smug about having had this idea.

"You're crazy. Messing with TEDI will certainly require access to the most heavily guarded facilities we have." The friends look at each other. Lin sighs. "That the Directorate has, I mean," Jimmel continues.

"Rogov is scientifically ahead of Earth, and new developments have been made just for this voyage. The ship will be able to get very close undetected. But eventually, TEDI will find it."

"And kill them all," Lin points out.

"Not if we protect them."

"How do you plan to do that?"

David and Jimmel look at each other. "Not us," says Jimmel. Lin's lip curls involuntarily. Of course not.

***

The enforcer position at Hauser wasn't Lin's first attempt to move on from her low-paying, dead-end job at the noodle house. Near the end of her university studies, she began to feel a desperation to do something bigger than wait tables. She excelled in her Xinqi University classes on the network and was grouped in a cohort with others of the same capabilities. Her classmates lived on all continents and had skin and hair of every shade, but they all had one thing in common: they were going places.

Lin didn't lack for offers. Her performance in secondary school and university was a matter of public record for Xinqi department heads and she had been approached more than once about joining product teams or administrative fields. She held back, waiting for Sabohat to get healthier so they could talk about it. The chronic pain had been making her short-tempered and Lin hardly wanted to broach the subject. Sabohat loved to talk to her friends about Lin's bright future, but the specifics of what Lin might be allowed to do were not forthcoming.

One day when Lin opened her eyes after her virtual classes ended, her mother was sitting in front of her, chin on her cane, peering into Lin's face.

"Something has been bothering you," said Sabohat. Lin started to deny it, but Sabohat just raised her eyebrows.

"What should I do after university?" said Lin finally. Sabohat smiled.

"The fact that you can ask that question is why I brought you to Earth. I'm sure you'll have offers."

"Well, I do, actually," said Lin. "Several." She shared a few of the files with Sabohat and they read through them together.

"Which one appeals to you the most?" asked Sabohat.

"This administrative assistant job in Xinqi's transportation sector. It's similar to what several of my classmates are doing. I think I could do it well."

"Hmmm. Tier Three?" asked Sabohat.

"Two."

"Tier Two, right out of school! Not bad at all," said Sabohat. "Do it, Lin." Lin sighed with relief.

But as soon as the paperwork was complete, an obstacle arose. Like most white-collar positions, the transportation job was meant to be done from home over the network. However, Xinqi wanted reassurance that she was who she claimed to be, so a human resources inspector made an unexpected visit to her home.

The man was classic upper-crust Beijing, with a round face, dark hair, and northern accented Mandarin.

"I am Hu Shuyu," he announced, transmitting his credentials to her with a slight dip of the head. "But you may call me Mr. Hu."

Ignoring the stuffiness, Lin smiled and tried to be pleasant, but Mr. Hu was suspicious from the start. He walked around the kitchen, pulling open drawers and cupboards, until Sabohat stumped out from her bedroom, leaning heavily on her cane but smiling widely.

"We're so excited for Lin to get this position," she said. Mr. Hu turned his narrowed eyes on her.

"This is my mother—" At the last minute Lin realized that Mr. Hu would have her file and the identities of her adoptive parents. "My mother's friend, Sabohat," she said.

"I see," said Mr. Hu. And then Lin did see, suddenly, how Sabohat would look through his eyes. Her stocky body didn't preclude her from being a regular Earth-born citizen, but her accent was suspicious, and something was always just a bit off about her style and mannerisms. Did Mr. Hu have the background to realize why? Sabohat lowered herself into a chair.

"What happened to your legs?" asked Mr. Hu. No time for pleasantries, apparently.

"Old work accident," said Sabohat. "And arthritis besides. Good thing I have Lin here to help me out, huh?" Mr. Hu's eyes got even narrower.

"I suggest you go to the Xinqi Medical Center on the Third Ring Road," he said. "This is a thing they could fix, I believe," and Lin could feel her future crashing down. Sabohat was too alien, too suspicious. Lin couldn't take this job and she couldn't let anyone else visit their home.

"Mr. Hu," she said. "I'm so sorry, but I've decided not to accept the position after all. Something else has come up." Mr. Hu didn't bother to act surprised as she ushered him out the door.

When Lin turned back into the apartment, Sabohat had a devastated expression on her face.

"It's OK, Mom. I'm a citizen of the corporation, so I'm guaranteed some sort of work. Tier Three is fine. There's a restaurant not far from here that's hiring."

"Chen's," said Sabohat sadly. "You could do better than that."

"It's fine." Lin forced a smile. But it wasn't, because in that moment Lin understood her fate. This incident would only be the first of many sacrifices made for Sabohat's safety. She continued this way for years, not daring to dream of more. Only when she learned that the Hauser enforcer role was based on merit tests rather than interviews had she finally decided to take a chance and pursue her own prosperity.

And look what happened.

"Okay," says Lin to Jimmel. "What do I have to do?"

***

When she's sent David and Jimmel on their way—with a little more physical intimidation for good measure—she gets a call from Emas.

"I'm so sorry about those guys," he says. "I didn't know they were going to do that. Honestly, the group has been going a little crazy lately not knowing who to trust. At first, it was only a few of us who met regularly, and our in-person verification system worked great. But then we all brought in friends and the paper handoffs got complicated. Now who knows who's the real thing? I hope they didn't scare you."

"I can handle myself," Lin says with annoyance.

"Yeah, Jimmel says you handled yourself real well," says Emas with a chuckle. There's a moment of silence when Emas looks like he's working up to saying something. For a moment she hopes it's romantic, then chides herself.

"Are you going to help us take down TEDI?" he says. Lin sighs.

"I don't know. It will ruin my career if they found out," she says. Emas's avatar's face twitches.

"Your Hauser career."

"Yes, my Hauser career. I've worked hard to get where I am. I haven't had as many opportunities as most people in my position, and I don't want to lose this one."

"Lin, think of your mother."

"What are you talking about? I think of my mother every minute of every day, but what does she have to do with this?"

"This was her plan. David and Jimmel are running point, but Sabohat designed the technology that's going to help us do it. She's brilliant, Lin."

"I know." Lin thinks about the implications of what he's telling her. "If this is her plan, then she planned all along to have me be a part of it, didn't she?"

"Yes." Lin hopes that her avatar is giving Emas a particularly powerful glare right now.

"How can that be? She always wanted me to be safe from that part of her life. She barely even let me meet most of her friends." *Present tense, Lin, present tense.*

"Maybe she just thought that this was more important than you rising in the Hauser ranks." If only Lin could actually ask her mother what to do instead of listening to Emas's biased interpretation. A thought occurs to her.

"Is the guy my mom was talking to also a part of this?" she asks.

"What guy?" Emas looks confused so Lin describes the paper she found and her conversations with the mystery man. As she explains, Emas's expression grows angrier.

"You've been trusting this person just because you found his number at the crime scene?" Lin puts a hand to her head at the volume of his voice in her implant. "It was probably planted there for you."

"By whom?" asks Lin. "Has the Directorate ever left slips of paper during purges before? The only time I've seen anything like it is the papers from your group."

"I don't know! Look, what's done is done, but from now on, don't talk to anyone about the plan other than the people I've already introduced you to." Lin rolls her eyes.

"How do I know I can trust them? Maybe Jimmel would have actually killed me tonight if I hadn't stopped him." She thinks of Jimmel's puny defense against her and almost laughs.

"Jimmel and David are my friends," says Emas.

"Well, I don't know them," says Lin. "I barely know you. Why trust one stranger and not another?" She could almost imagine Emas's avatar looks a bit hurt, but she pushes on. "Who are you to talk about caution? You've apparently been handing out my information and my personal ID left and right. David and Jimmel were able to track me down, so others could, too. You could have put me in real danger and you're telling me to be less trusting?"

"You should know by now I'm on your side," says Emas. "I've told people I trust about you, but I care about your safety." Lin thinks if that were true, he wouldn't be pushing her to accept the mission at all.

"Are you on my side?" asks Lin. "I'm about to risk everything because you asked me to. But there's only one thing I really want, and that's to get my mom back. And there's only one person who might know something about how to find her. If you were on my side, you wouldn't stand in my way."

She expects him to argue, but he doesn't.

"You're right." He looks at her long and hard. "I haven't been thinking about how worried you must be. But I am on your side. This is for your own safety. If you get caught—" He stops talking and shakes his head. Is he upset thinking of the fate that would befall her, or is he thinking only of the Rogovans?

"Just do me a favor," he says. "And don't tell this guy anything more until I have Javi look into him. He's great at tracing this kind of thing." Emas looks at her imploringly, and she wishes she could see the real him and wonders where he is. This unscarred, short-haired avatar version is as bad as a gray star.

"I won't tell him the details of the plan just yet," she concedes. "But I need Javi to work fast."

***

In her time off before the Mars mission, Lin crashes in her old room with Kirs. Kirs, like Lin, has lost some of her willowy look and packed on solid muscle. Her physical stature is intimidating, but she smiles in the same cheery way and hugs Lin and giggles. Lin wonders if Kirs also finds comfort in darkness these days with her superior vision, or if that's only something felt by people with something to hide. They stay up late into the night, and Lin tells Kirs about Abena's eccentricities, their upcoming trip to Mars, and Lin's relationship with Rajan.

"So you're going to stay in touch with him?" asks Kirs, a twinkle in her eye.

"Yeah," says Lin. "We'll see each other in person when we can." Kirs reveals she's fallen into similar patterns with Bogdan.

"Boyu is always tagging along, though," she says. She looks thoughtful for a moment.

"Actually, Bogdan has been strange lately," she says. "I don't hear from him much. And now that we can't see each other in person, I've started wondering how well we really know each other."

They turn in for the night. Lin is dying to reach out to her friend with something real. To talk about her desperate grief for her mother, her paranoia about who to trust, and her confusing feelings for Emas, not Rajan. But it's Kirs who speaks a thought uncannily similar to what is happening in Lin's mind. She uses the neural implants to do it, possibly feeling her fiery-haired and armored avatar more equipped to speak her fears.

"Do you ever feel like an imposter?" The avatar stands next to her bed. Across the room, Kirs has her back to Lin, but Lin knows she's looking at Lin's projected face as well. Neither of them speaks aloud.

"What do you mean?" Lin subvocalizes.

"Nothing," answers Kirs, but she keeps the line open, her avatar standing watchfully beside Lin's bed. Lin fights panic about how to respond. Eventually, Kirs speaks again.

"I just mean, I'm a Tier One enforcer now. Supposedly the best of the best—tough, skilled, smart... But I don't feel that way. I felt like a good security officer back in Calgary, but I never actually felt like I was meant for something like this. It feels like someone's going to figure out any minute that I don't belong here."

Lin lets out a breath. "You belong here," she says. "Trust me." Kirs's avatar smiles. Lin says goodnight and ends the connection. The red-haired warrior fades.

Lin closes her eyes and speaks in her mind again, this time to Sabohat. She has no expectation of anyone hearing her; her subvocalizations are pure prayer.

"These people aren't so bad, Mom," she says. "They just want the same things I want: to get a good job, to do something useful. Why is it always my job to protect someone?" The next thought makes her guilty, but then, it isn't a real conversation anyway.

"Why is it my job to save the Rogovans? Why was it always my job to save you?"

Lin's heart is pounding and her skin feels sweaty. To calm her nerves and fall asleep, she practices a Guardian meditation that Kirs taught her before, whispering the words under her breath and relaxing her body, clearing her mind and latching onto the first image that comes to mind as a possible representation of her personal Guardian. She tries the words, but all she sees in her mind's eye are people from her life: Sabohat walking away into a shadow, her back to Lin. Emas, who looks into her eyes with an understanding of who she is and then raises one of Sabohat's weapons. Rajan smiling and laughing about people from Britton. Kirs, wearing the armor from her avatar and offering a hand to Lin. Are they just useless amalgamations of her imagination, or is she supposed to follow one of them? And which one?

A call interrupts her. The name that flashes is Javi Garcia. Lin keeps her eyes closed so Kirs can't see she's awake and talking, but she can still see Javi's gold scale avatar in front of her.

"I may have a lead on your guy," he says. "The one Emas said you've been talking to. I should know the stranger's identity soon. Until then, just try to find out what he wants. By the way," the avatar has a concerned look, "Emas is acting strange. Do you know what's bothering him?" Lin rubs her temples, wanting to go back to her meditation.

"The same thing that's bothering everyone in your little group," she says. As if he doesn't know. "This damn Rogovan ship coming to Earth."

Chapter Seventeen

HE'S GOT HER.

Cenric raises his arms and shouts in triumph.

For his first few weeks on the job, Cenric had failed to uncover even the faintest scent of an alien plot. He'd even had a few minutes here and there in which he doubted that the Rogovans were as organized in their criminal activity as he had believed.

And then he was attacked by Dirk Kane's associate. Javi Garcia. After doing away with Dirk, Cenric turned back to Javi, breathing his last on the floor. He searched the man's pockets, determined to be thorough in his quest for information about the conspiracy, and discovered a crumpled paper—the information for an unlisted chat group for offworlders. The idiot had actually written the number down.

Cenric flashed his gun at a few people around town and learned Javi's name and that his avatar was a gold scale. When he contacted the alien group, they recognized him as "Javi."

However, although they'd allowed him into their midst, the group members weren't a trusting bunch. They hadn't been quick to befriend him or give up personal information. Except for stupid, naïve, Emas Day.

Cenric can't help but congratulate himself on choosing this indirect route. It had been tempting to go after Emas immediately—stick a gun in his face, insist that he talk—but some ingenious instinct kept him from it.

His plan had been so brilliant, he now truly knows how Tiana Williams must have felt when she launched Hauser's first innovations.

Emas isn't from Rogov, that most dangerous of colonies, but he turned out to be deeply connected to the Rogovan network. And, as much as he claimed that secrecy was important, that no one could be trusted, he was quick to start mentioning "something big" to Javi. He didn't give details, but Cenric persevered, meeting Emas's friends on Mindlink, picking up clues wherever he could.

And finally, Emas introduced Cenric to Lin. She didn't seem important at first. Just some girl Emas was hung up on. But Lin turned out to be the most valuable source of all. When the plot is foiled, when Hauser is saved, when Cenric's victory is known far and wide, it will be because he found Lin.

He can't make any mistakes now. A Rogovan ship coming—it could be an attack on an unprecedented scale. His interactions with her must be flawless. He will get close to her, learn every detail about her, find out who she is and what she does every minute of every day.

Like Dirk Kane in Bangkok and Renata Luca in São Paulo, he'll one day bring justice down on Lin. But simply killing her would be shortsighted. This is a time for strategy. Lin isn't just another criminal, she's the key to destroying the entire Rogovan plot.

Chapter Eighteen

THE ROGOVAN BOY WHO picks a fight with Temar is a head shorter and a couple of years younger than he is. Vedra wakes to the sound of their scuffling outside her room. She rubs her eyes and tries to get her bearings. She's on a narrow top bunk with no blankets or pillow. On one side is a wall, on the other is the neighboring set of beds, occupied by snoring Rogovans.

The occupants are not the same people who were there when Vedra fell asleep the previous night. She was told that on the ship they sleep in shifts, sharing beds.

"How do you have the space for us to take these two spots, then?" she asked Captain Nakamura.

"We've lost a few," he said.

Vedra fell asleep clinging close to Temar beside her and taking comfort in the rhythm of Myat's deep breaths from the bunk below.

Now Vedra leans over the edge of her bed. Myat is already gone, leaving crisp hospital corners behind. Vedra's own bedding has fallen in a heap on the floor.

"Let go of me!" Vedra hears Temar say, followed by a thump and a quick shuffle of feet. She scrambles down the bunk bed's ladder and runs out into the hall. The Rogovan boy, practically an infant compared to her son, has Temar pinned to the floor and is pulling his hair back.

"Hey!" says Vedra. "Both of you, on your feet!" The boys leap up and stand at attention, side by side. While the Rogovan boy is still shorter than Temar, he's tall and thin for his age, and will probably be taller than any Rogovan adult on the ship before he hits puberty. He's handsome, strong, and healthy—a look Vedra saw on many of the Empire men who visited her station. The kid is fortunate that he'll grow up on Earth.

"What do you think you were doing?" Vedra prepares to give the boy the kind of lecture that will leave him terrified to bother her son again, but then she catches a glance of something out of the corner of her eye. Temar is grinning ear to ear.

"You were having fun," she says incredulously. She's never seen him willingly engage in anything physical in his life. On good days at the compound, Temar was allowed to hang around the women's quarters, reading, listening to music, and telling rambling stories to whatever poor woman was finished with her duties and trying to get a bit of rest. On bad days, Fenton would force him to participate in a show of archery or shooting for his men, then get angry at Temar's inevitable clumsiness.

"Uli was showing me how to fight," says Temar. "It's a thing called Sombo."

"Well..." says Uli sheepishly, "I made up my own version."

"Right." Vedra looks at the two boys and grins. "Carry on, then. I'm going to go see if I can find Myat."

"OK, Mom," says Temar. Vedra leans over and whispers in his ear.

"Let me know if you ever want me to show you some real moves." Then she heads off down the walkway, still smiling.

Vedra marvels to think of the choices she has. Right this moment, she could do anything—wander down any walkway, pass through any open door. Or stay in bed, for that matter. She hasn't had such freedom in her whole life. She never controlled her own movements on the space station until the day she chose to leave with Fenton. Her days on the compound were filled with work she was obligated to perform, and even if her duties were finished for the day, god forbid that Fenton didn't know where to find her. She was free on Myat's junker of a ship, of course, but then there was nowhere to go.

This ship, though, is a different class of vessel altogether. Just thinking about how big it must be excites her. Bigger than the station, bigger than the compound. If only these crazy people weren't so intent on getting to Earth, maybe they would let her stay and live here forever.

For now, she'll just try to figure out where Myat ran off to.

"Vedra Ols?" says a female voice behind her. Vedra spins, half expecting to be reprimanded for leaving her quarters. The Rogovan woman who called her name is old, a gray braid falling down her back almost to the floor. Behind her wrinkled skin are exquisite cheekbones and dark eyes.

"I'm First Officer Seki," says the woman. "I wanted to welcome you to our crew, and also to let you know that Captain Nakamura would like to talk to you. I can take you to his quarters."

Vedra tenses. "Do I have to?"

"No," says First Officer Seki with a small smile. "But he would like your help with something if you're willing."

"Sure, I can help out."

"Come this way," says Seki.

"I should let my son know," Vedra says with some hesitation. "Or he'll probably get himself into some kind of mess while I'm gone." Actually, Vedra likes the idea of Temar as a troublemaker.

"Don't worry too much about him," says Seki with a smile. "Out of the three thousand of us on board, there are only twelve children." Her face darkens a bit. "Surviving children. Anyway, everyone on the ship looks out for all the kids. They're horribly spoiled."

Vedra follows Seki down the hall to a set of double doors. They slide open to reveal the tiniest room Vedra has seen on the huge ship. The doors close for a few moments, then open. The walkway in front of Vedra is different than the one she was on before. She looks at Seki, startled.

"What happened?" she asks.

Seki seems confused for a minute, then laughs.

"It's an elevator," she says. "It took us from the third deck to the first. You haven't been on one before?"

Vedra shakes her head. "I guess that's easier than climbing a ladder," she says.

Seki leads her down the new walkway to a blue door. "This is Captain Nakamura's office," she says, and the door slides open on cue. The room behind the door is nothing like the lavish space Vedra imagined the captain occupying. In fact, it's only a little bigger than the elevator, but more claustrophobic, with a desk and two chairs jammed inside. The air above the desk flows with animated words and diagrams. Vedra gasps at the sight. Nakamura is standing behind the desk, and he bows when she comes in.

"Thank you, Officer Seki," he says, and Seki bows in return and leaves, the door closing behind her. Nakamura turns back to Vedra. "Have a seat."

Vedra sits.

"Let me get straight to it," says Captain Nakamura. "You are obviously not from Earth."

"Same to you," she says, straightening in her seat. Nakamura laughs and puts his hands up.

"It's not an accusation," he says. "I'm saying I trust your story. You have the look and the dialect and the attitude of an offworlder."

"But?" prompts Vedra.

"Your friend," says Nakamura. "Are you sure about who Myat is?" Vedra hesitates.

"Myat saved my life," she says.

"Of course," says Nakamura. "But I'm talking about before that. Do you know anything about Myat's life before the asteroid colony?"

"She was born on Pluto," says Vedra, but she says it without confidence.

"Are you certain about that?" asks Nakamura. Vedra doesn't answer. "The way they speak Anglian on Pluto is barely understandable to people like you and me. And Myat is a bit tan for the Plutonian climate."

"I wouldn't know about that," says Vedra. "I've never been to Pluto or any planet." Captain Nakamura reaches into his pocket and pulls out a small, square device that he hands to Vedra. "What's that?" she asks without touching it.

"You've probably noticed how most of us have neural implants to help us communicate," says the Captain.

"Sure. You can send messages in your heads."

"Yes. That means Seki or the other officers or even little Uli could send me a message instantly, at any time."

"I get the concept," says Vedra. He's talking to her like she's an idiot.

"Even Myat could talk to me anytime," he says. "And I want to make sure that you can, too. Take this, and if you ever want to tell me something, you just press that round button and talk into it." Vedra takes the little box and turns it over in her hands. Of course, the box is old-fashioned technology, even she knows that, but she likes the idea that she has the captain's ear as much as anyone on the ship.

"Thanks," she says. "Now I really have to go find my son."

***

Temar is not far from where she left him, but now he's sitting against the wall, arms around his gangly legs, looking dejected. Vedra sits down beside him.

"Where's Uli?" she asks.

"He wanted to play a game called basketball in the common area," says Temar. "But then he told me I couldn't play anymore because I wasn't any good at it." Vedra goes to stroke his hair, but he pulls away.

"Oh honey," she says, "you'll learn all these games, eventually. Do you want to play basketball with me?" Temar somehow looks even sadder.

"Maybe I could play it with Myat," he says.

"Well, we can ask her," says Vedra. "I don't know where she is, though."

"I saw her earlier," says Temar. "She went in some doors with numbers on top. When she got in, the number was three. And then it said two, and then one, and then zero. And then it stayed at zero, and I waited, but Myat didn't come back."

Vedra considers this. "Come with me." She leads Temar back to the elevator. There is indeed a number zero above the door.

"Is this where Myat went?" Vedra asks. Temar nods.

"Perfect. I'm going to go find Myat and let her know about the basketball. Why don't you wait back in our room." Temar shuffles away, looking like the slow-moving, unhappy kid he was at the compound. Vedra hopes Myat really will play a game with him. She imagines that Myat is good at lots of games.

Vedra looks around to see if anyone is watching and then reaches out and touches the elevator doors, grasping for some kind of handle. She doesn't feel one, but the numbers above the door start to count up anyway—one, two, three. Then the doors open. Vedra steps inside. She still doesn't see any way to control the thing.

"Take me to zero," she says aloud, feeling foolish, but the doors close behind her and open again a moment later to a completely new space.

Unlike the smooth design of decks one and three, the walls of deck zero give the impression of being unfinished. They're taller than the walls of the other decks, with wires and tubes still visible, and they remind Vedra of the cold metal aesthetic of her station. Rather than a single curved hallway with intermittent doors, deck zero is a grid of small dark passageways reaching inward from the outside. It would be easy to get lost.

Vedra doesn't know where to begin searching for Myat so she stands perfectly still and listens for footsteps.

Instead, she hears a voice. The timbre is recognizably Myat's, but Vedra can't make out any words. She slowly follows the sound, taking care to note the turns she takes—left, right, two more left, another right.

On the space station, walking quietly undetected was a survival skill that every unfortunate resident child mastered. In a metal chamber where even breath can echo, Vedra glides down the dark hallways as silently as the ship through space. She finds Myat crouched on her heels, leaning over a blue metal box embedded in the wall. She holds two wires in her hands, pressed against whatever is inside the box. Myat speaks into the box in a language Vedra doesn't understand, but recognizes.

It's an Empire language. She knows that much. She even recognizes a word that Myat says into the box three times: *Dongshihui*. It's a word that Vedra heard spoken by fat Empire men who visited her station or shady suspects who came to do business with Fenton. Vedra doesn't know what it means, but the word is always spoken with importance. Slowly, silently, Vedra backs away.

When the elevator doors open to reveal the reassuringly smooth walls of deck three, Vedra reaches into her pocket and retrieves the little box from Captain Nakamura. She pauses with her thumb on the button. Talking to the Captain feels like betraying Myat, who saved her life and who is her friend and maybe something more, but she needs to understand what she saw and she doesn't know who else to ask.

She pushes the button.

"Captain?" she says, feeling ridiculous for talking to the tiny contraption.

"Vedra? Hello. Do you have something to tell me?"

"Yes," says Vedra. "I was wondering. What does Dongshihui mean?"

"Why do you want to know?" asks Nakamura.

"Well, I saw Myat on deck zero, and—" before she can continue the story, the captain interrupts.

"Deck zero? What was she doing there?"

"That's what I was about to tell you," says Vedra.

"You better come back to my office," says the captain. "I'll meet you there."

***

Both the captain and First Officer Seki are waiting for her, standing, when she arrives. They maintain neutral expressions as Vedra describes how she followed Myat and found her leaning over the box and talking.

"What was she saying?" asks Seki.

"I don't know," says Vedra. "It was a language that I didn't understand. But definitely an Empire language."

"How do you know?" asks the Captain.

"Because of the word, 'Dongshihui.' I heard her say it." Vedra is starting to get annoyed at the way the Captain isn't listening to her. He and Seki look at each other.

"It doesn't mean Myat's Earth-born," says Seki. "It just means she's attempted some kind of communication."

"But where else? And why else?"

The two of them continue to talk, their voices almost falling to a whisper, completely ignoring Vedra. Typical—the people in charge are always like that. Vedra sighs and tunes out their strange accents. She wonders what basketball is exactly, and if Temar and Uli might still play it together on Earth when they're older.

"I've asked Loui Fatkullin to bring Myat in," the captain says. The statement seems to be aimed at Vedra, who just nods. It's only in the waiting silence, looking at the stony expressions on the two stout Rogovan faces, that Vedra feels how grave the situation is. Myat is in trouble, and it's because of her. Vedra's heart suddenly races.

The door slides open, and Myat appears, accompanied by a young Rogovan man. Myat arrives with her usual unreadable expression, but as soon as she sees Vedra, a trace of worry twitches across her lips.

She knows.

"Vedra witnessed you contacting the authorities on Earth. Your home planet," says the Captain.

"I didn't say that," says Vedra. "I only said she was talking into a box." She doesn't meet Myat's eyes.

"I'm from Pluto," says Myat. They all wait for her to address the other accusations, but she doesn't.

"Are you a part of Directorate Special Operations?" Nakamura's voice booms. Vedra jumps. The accusation seems to come from nowhere. Vedra doesn't even know what Directorate Special Operations are, although she's heard the word 'Directorate' spoken by the same type of people who said 'Dongshihui.' She doesn't see how Nakamura could possibly have reached any conclusions based on her story.

"No," says Myat. "I'm not."

"Why are you wasting time on interrogation?" Seki turns to Myat.

"If you're Special Ops, you'll have an implant that shows it." Myat's eyes have gone a little wild and she laughs loudly. Vedra wonders if anyone else hears the fear in the sound.

"You're bluffing," Myat says. "If I were Directorate Special Ops, which I'm not, you know you wouldn't be able to see any chip I was carrying. Directorate implant technology is undetectable."

"Not on Rogov," says the captain.

Chapter Nineteen

"How can I take down TEDI?" Lin is at the colonists' virtual meeting room with Emas, David, and Jimmel. If she opens her eyes—and she doesn't care to—she has just taken her seat on the transport to Mars with Abena Owusu and is pretending to listen to Abena's complaints about Martian building restrictions.

"A whole planet's worth of space, and we're holed up in public dormitories like University students in a period drama," she keeps saying to Lin, as if it's a new insight.

"You can't destroy TEDI," says Emas. "Or even damage it. No one can, not even the people who created it. The Directorate hates to admit it, but TEDI is outside of their control. They built it to protect Earth from outside threats, and it does. But its thought process is all its own."

"So it's actually TEDI deciding that Rogovans should be shot down?" Lin asks. That doesn't seem right.

"No," says Emas. "TEDI is on its own system. It doesn't have access to any data other than what the Directorate gives it."

"And what it observes itself," Jimmel interjects.

"Sure. But the point is, the Directorate can give TEDI information that leads it to believe that ships from Rogov are a threat and ships from Mars are not. But how TEDI acts on that information is totally up to TEDI, and the Directorate can't do anything about it."

"Okay," says Lin, "So I have to tell TEDI that Rogov is no longer a threat."

"Yes. Basically. Sort of," says Emas. "The problem is that you can't make TEDI forget anything that it already knows. And it knows all sorts of sinister things about Rogov and the other colonies."

"Lies," says Lin.

"Obviously. But you can confuse it for a while. We have a device, designed by your mother, that will feed the AI a steady stream of data about Rogov no longer being a threat. But TEDI is smart. Smarter than any of us can hope to be. Your mom and her team predicted that it will only take a few hours to figure out what's happening, disregard the new data, and attack any Rogovan vessels in sight."

"Where do I get the device?"

"I have it. Let's meet in person when you get back to Earth so I can give it to you."

"I'd like that," says Lin, and they're silent for a moment. She thinks the eyes on Emas's avatar are nice. They look kind. Is that real, or just the artist's rendition? She can't remember.

"Anyway," says David, in a voice that indicates that if his purple spiral avatar had eyes, they would be rolling, "there are only a few locations where you can communicate with TEDI, all at Directorate facilities. These places are off the grid. To plant the device, you're going to have to get inside one of them."

"Which Directorate facilities?" asks Lin. "I know where a couple of the bases are."

"You won't have heard of this one," says David. "We only know it exists because of some serious deep intel. You'll have to go to São Paulo and charter a plane from there. Sabohat had some recommendations for what kind of weapons to take. Her notes don't mean anything to me, but I'll transfer them to you. Whatever you carry will have to be sanctioned for use by enforcers, of course, since you're entering the base legally. Nothing using Rogovan tech."

"Weapons?" asks Lin. "Do you think I'll need to use one?" The purple spiral is silent. "I think I should just get in, get out, and try not to get caught."

"Ideally, yes," says Emas. "But we expect very rigid security at a place like this. If something goes wrong... well, better to take out a few of theirs than fail in the mission or get caught."

"I don't want to kill anyone," says Lin.

"TEDI does," says Emas. "Thousands of people." They're all silent for a moment.

"Aren't you a Big Three enforcer?" says Jimmel. "I thought you were a killing machine."

"I'm more of an arm breaker," Lin reminds him. Jimmel is quiet.

"What do I do until then?" asks Lin. There are only a few days left until the Rogovans arrive.

"Just don't arouse suspicions," says Jimmel. "Try to act like a normal Earth-born person."

"It's what you do best," says Emas.

***

The people on Mars, like the ornate basalt buildings and neatly trimmed trees on Hauser's Martian campus, are highly decorative. Lin has never seen so many Hauser dress uniforms in casual use, and many of the people have clearly undergone cosmetic rejuvenation and enhancement like Abena. She watches them out the window of the bus that shuttles Mars Congress members from the transport to the campus. The bus ride was long and seemed longer because Lin was subjected to the inane chatter of Abena's entourage, but Lin has to admit that she feels a bit of pride about getting the chance to come to Mars. For just a moment, she allows herself to put aside reality and imagine that someday she could come here as a member of the Congress. She quickly chastens herself for the thought. How could she dream of hobnobbing with the very people responsible for her mother's disappearance? Then again, if she achieved that kind of position, she wouldn't waste the opportunity. As an influential Mars Congress member—not just a brand new enforcer—she would put her power to use to help other refugees.

The group disembarks from the bus and strolls onto the lush green campus. Lin loves the low Mars gravity. It seems to lighten the anxiety that began piling onto her shoulders after the Fourth Power murders and grew exponentially with Sabohat's disappearance and all the planning around the Rogovan arrival. When Abena's group is distracted bickering over which influential Congress attendee to visit first, Lin leaps two meters into the air with a flying kick. Abena glances back at her as she lands and Lin stifles a grin. She thinks about Sabohat, coming of age bent under the pressure of Rogovan gravity, and wonders if it made her burdens feel heavier, or if never knowing an easier atmosphere made her stronger.

They stop near a fountain that seems to serve as the center of the extravagant campus. Lin stares at the water lapping at the toes of the four sculpted figures. The extravagance of it astounds her. On Rogov, water is the greatest luxury. Despite being a colony founded by some of Earth's top scientific minds, development and even basic survival has always been limited by water scarcity.

Standing here on Mars, Lin can understand for the first time why her colonist ancestors believed Rogov could become a utopia of science and discovery. Mars, too, was once lifeless and uninhabitable until the technology to thicken the atmosphere was developed and Terratech worked its miracle. Now it's a paradise beyond even Earth. Early colonists thought that if Mars could be tamed, surely exoplanets with more Earth-like atmospheres were humanity's for the taking. How could Nadya Rogova and her band of eager followers know that after eighteen years of space travel, they would discover that their new home was an even harsher world than the red planet? Terratech withered again and again in the dry Rogovan heat.

One of Abena's assistants jabs Lin in the arm and points at an approaching man.

"That's the VP of Hauser Internal Affairs himself," whispers the assistant, awestruck. "He wants to meet with her in person." The VP is an odd snake of a man, with the sleek look of one who has gone beyond the usual anti-aging treatments and become slightly inhuman. The bone structure of his face is smoothed over like a rock in the ocean tide and his skin tone, probably once a light brown, has an almost red sheen. When he smiles at Abena, no lines appear around his mouth—his lips simply slide back to bare his teeth. Lin tries not to stare. Abena doesn't introduce the VP to Lin or any of her entourage. The VP doesn't introduce his bodyguard either, an older man with a shaved head. They all follow Abena and the VP into a nearby building, where the two of them enter his suite and close the door behind them. The entourage dissipates and Lin stays behind to guard the door. She stands on the right side, the VP's man on the left. With her enhanced hearing, she can pick up much of the conversation.

"Fia Bernardo is another top choice for Directorate in the next round. But I don't trust that she'll speak up for Hauser's interests. Do you have a plan to beat her?"

"Fia Bernardo? Please. She's a mouse. What has she ever done besides fawn over all the right people?"

Lin does her best to ignore the political talk. From the corner of her eye, she looks at the VP's man. He doesn't make any indication that he's listening either. After almost an hour has passed, Lin opens up a weapons training program on her implant. It's the kind that works her mental acuity and reflexes only—no physical movement required. She pretends the silhouettes she needs to shoot in the game are soldiers at the Directorate base; every time she "kills" one, it puffs into smoke. *That's for the Rogovans*, she thinks at the advancing figures. *That's for my mother. That's for Mr. Tomasy.*

Suddenly, a siren pulses and all the walls flash red. Lin jumps. Her first thought is that someone saw her in the game and knows what she's planning, but that's obviously not right. She readies her weapon, swinging it a bit too far in the low gravity. She notices the VP's man smirk. Together, they enter the conference room. The VP is standing with a worried expression on his serpentine face. Abena is still sitting calmly, legs crossed, leaning back.

"The siren indicates a threat in this building," says the VP's man. "We're here to evacuate you safely. Stay behind us." The VP hurries to stand behind his bodyguard, but Abena doesn't move.

"I'm sure Lin and your handsome friend can take care of whatever's going on," she says. "We were making so much progress."

"We should at least evacuate until we know the nature of the threat," says Lin. "If it's nothing, you can come right back here. Or we'll find you another room." She feels oddly embarrassed by Abena's behavior.

"Rubbish," says Abena. "Sit back down, Arden, and I'll have Lin bring us some tea." Lin grits her teeth and doesn't mention that she can't make tea and "take care of whatever's going on" at the same time. At that moment, the sirens stop and the walls return to their regular hue.

"See? No reason for concern," says Abena. "Now sit back down." If one of the most powerful executives of Hauser Corporation has any objection to being ordered around by Abena Owusu, he doesn't show it. He slides back into the seat across from her. "Why don't you have your guy go see what that was all about," Abena says, "and Lin will stay here to make sure we're safe from any future loud noises and flashing lights." The VP's bodyguard is gone by the time the VP has finished nodding. Lin goes back into the hallway. She feels too on edge to go back to her game, so she shifts her weight from foot to foot, one hand still on her gun. She grips it harder when she hears footsteps coming down the hall.

The man that appears is young and handsome, with deep brown curls that bounce lightly in the low gravity. From his muscular form and regulation weapon, Lin knows that he's Hauser Internal Security like her. He raises a hand in a wave. Lin smiles slightly but keeps her hand on her weapon.

"I'm so sorry about all the excitement," says the man. "Turns out it was just a recently demoted employee committing a little harmless vandalism. Wasn't even armed."

"That's good," says Lin, relaxing her hand.

"Looks like we're colleagues, eh? I work in the investigations division, and I'm pretty sure I'm the only detective actually on Mars at the moment, so they sent for me. Wasn't much to investigate this time, though. Luckily, my suite is in this building, so I didn't have to go far, eh?" Lin doesn't know how to respond to the chatty stranger.

"That's good," she says.

"Mohammed Al Jaber," he says. "Call me Mo. Everyone does."

"Yang Lin," says Lin.

"Call you Yang? Or Lin?"

"Lin."

"Pleased to make your acquaintance, Lin." Lin wonders if she could shoot this charming man if he were coming at her in São Paulo. She imagines him poofing into smoke like in the game. *This is for my mother.*

"You too," she says.

"Mo?" a voice calls from down the hall and another man comes scurrying along. This one is clearly not security—his body is so scrawny beneath his wide head that he looks like a dark brown lollipop. A lollipop with very worried eyes. "Is everything alright? I went out for a bit, and when I came back I couldn't get back in because of some kind of evacuation, and I didn't even know where you were!" Mo smiles and Lin can't help but smile too at the obvious love and concern in the lollipop's voice.

"Like I said, we have our suite in this building," Mo says. "Don't worry, Arthur, it was no big deal. We already got the guy."

"Who was it?" asks Arthur. Mo looks at him solemnly.

"It was an offworlder," he says. Lin jerks, but it thankfully goes unnoticed.

"Really?" asks Arthur.

"Yeah..." says Mo. "A Martian." They both laugh. Lin doesn't.

"It was a joke," Mo tells her.

"Not a very good one," says Arthur.

"Right. I get it," says Lin.

"Mo doesn't take offworlders seriously," says Arthur. "But don't get him started on that topic."

"I don't take the hype seriously," says Mo. "The fearmongers want you to believe that aliens are a bigger threat than they are. But I think public sentiment is changing. Most people don't have any real ill will towards colonists. Well, certain friends of yours notwithstanding, Arthur." Arthur shrugs.

"Certain friends of mine are losing it a bit, I admit." Lin doesn't want to let them get sidetracked. She remembers the question Emas told her to ask.

"What should be done about non-violent colonists already living on Earth?" Mo laughs.

"Give them Hauser citizenship! It's probably the only way we'll manage to keep up with the other corporations. But seriously, I don't have a good answer. I know it's complicated. But I don't wish them any harm. Eventually, I think we should allow legal immigration."

"You do?" Lin is amazed to hear such a sentiment from a Tier One Hauser citizen. She almost wants to hug the smiley stranger.

"Well yeah, but it won't happen for a long time, and I'd highly recommend the colonists stay colonists until then. Probably better to just stick it out at home."

Lin takes a big chance. "Popular opinion may be changing, but refugees are still targeted by the Directorate."

Mo, more somber now, nods.

"I know life is dangerous for offworlders who come here. I had an informant once who was Rogovan. I think. I mean, I'm pretty sure. I never asked for his Identification because I didn't want to scare him off. But it was pretty obvious he wasn't a citizen. He had some really outdated implant. I was actually able to track it—no security on the thing whatsoever, I hadn't seen anything like it in years. Anyway, he disappeared and I tracked him to Europe."

"What was he doing?" asks Lin.

"No idea. One day, the implant just stopped moving. Forever."

"He died," says Lin.

"Or had the implant removed. But I'm going to go with died. And Arthur may think I'm a little crazy, but I think he died at the hands of the Directorate. Who else would bother? Hauser doesn't want them in our jobs or our property, but other than that, we don't care. Using the term 'we' loosely."

Lin feels sick. She tries to remind her head to nod.

"Don't tell the Hauser enforcer bosses that one of their top investigators is a conspiracy theorist," says Arthur, not quite joking.

"Like I said," says Mo. "I think sentiment is changing. People will start asking questions. But groups like the Fourth Power should tone it down or they'll turn us against all offworlders. Again, using 'us' loosely, of course."

"Of course," says Lin.

***

"Javi, are you there?" Lin subvocalizes as Mo and Arthur disappear together down the hall.

"What can I do for you?"

"Emas keeps saying you'll be able to help me find my mother. Don't you have anything yet?"

Chapter Twenty

"I CAN'T WAIT MUCH longer."

Cenric barely hears the Rogovan girl's voice in his head through the rushing in his ears.

She's here on this planet.

A Trojan horse in Sparta.

An offworlder on Mars.

Communication between Mars and Earth always has a delay of at least a few minutes due to the limitations of lightspeed, but now she's answering his questions in real-time. There's no doubt. She's here. Cenric rummages in his desk for a device he procured for his missions. A handheld Identification scanner. Cenric doesn't have authorization to use it, but it's been invaluable in his missions, so he's sure Hauser would approve.

For once, the light gravity doesn't feel silly as Cenric crosses the campus. He is floating, he is elated. A Rogovan has infiltrated his own territory.

He frowns. She could be on the Wonju or Xinqi campuses—there's no reason to assume she came to Hauser. But no, somehow he knows she'll be here. She has come to him. She is teasing him.

He waits a few minutes before responding to her. She can't realize that "Javi" is on Mars. Hopefully, she won't notice how quickly he replied to her initial call.

"Where are you?" he finally asks.

"It's not important." Cenric silently curses.

"Emas told me you were on Mars," he hazards. Emas is probably stupid enough to tell him that. Lin's sigh sounds irritated.

"I am. I'm not a member of the Congress, obviously, but I'm here with Abena Owusu."

Cenric taps his fingers on his desk impatiently as he waits for a few more minutes to pass. Abena Owusu is a Hauser Directorate hopeful—how can Lin be associated with her?

"What are you doing with Abena Owusu?"

"She brought me here as personal security. Tell me about my mother. Do you have any new information?"

"Wow, the Mars Congress? I've seen pictures of the Hauser campus. Which building are you in?" Lin is angry now.

"Are you some kind of Big Three fan? Who cares which of these over-the-top mansions I'm in? Do you know anything, Javi?" Cenric waits. "OK, fine. I'm in the building where the VP of Internal Affairs has his suite. Abena is meeting with him." Cenric's eyes widen. The danger is imminent—the offworlder girl is with the VP right now.

Cenric bolts out the door and sprints across campus, flying with each step like he's high on shav. Was it only a few months ago that he was storming towards the VP's suite in shame? Now he will go as the VP's savior.

Cenric turns the corner into the hallway where the VP has his suite, and he sees her. She's alert and armed. Her short, dark hair is pulled back in a ponytail, not the long braid of a Rogovan woman. Her fine features could be descended from the heritage of Rogov, whose original mission had a large Asian contingent, but she's too tall and slim to look the part. Cenric backtracks and peers at the girl from around the corner. Presumably, two of the most powerful members of Hauser are behind the door at her back, but she doesn't seem to be making her move against them. What is her plan?

Cenric searches the directory for Abena Owusu's number and tries to contact her, but she isn't answering. He already knows that the VP won't bother with him.

"What are you doing, lurking around our building?" says a voice behind him. Cenric turns around. Mo is eyeing him, arms crossed.

"Do you have a thing for Lin? Aw, she's way too nice for you."

"You know her?"

"I talked to her a bit."

"What about?"

"Oh, I don't know. Colonists."

"Colonists? She asked about offworlders?" How dense could Mo be? One of Hauser's so-called top investigators had this criminal right under his nose and didn't even know it. Cenric really is the only one who can save Hauser now.

"We were just making normal conversation. You should try it some-time." Mo leaves with a shake of his head.

Cenric turns back to Lin. He can't just let her stand there, that smug look on her face like she has some kind of authority, like she belongs here at the Mars Congress. He storms towards her, Identification reader raised.

"You!" he says.

The Rogovan girl turns, hand on her weapon. The Identification reader in Cenric's hand beeps. He stumbles and looks down at it.

Yang Lin, Hauser Internal Security Enforcement Officer, it says, with an obnoxiously happy-looking official portrait of the offworlder. Cenric blinks, uncomprehending. An Identification can't be faked. How has she done it?

"I thought you were someone else," he says, backing away. She keeps her wary eyes locked on him until he stumbles back around the corner.

An icy uncertainty wraps itself around Cenric. He leans against the wall, struggling to suck air into lungs that refuse to expand. Then a new realization comes over him, and he breathes deeply with relief.

It doesn't matter how Lin faked her Identification or what she's doing here on Mars. What's important is that he knows who she is now, because there's no doubt that she will be the one executing the Rogovan plot. If the offworlders have a Tier One insider, they won't waste her on Abena Owusu and that slimy VP.

Cenric only has to wait and listen. She'll reveal everything to him. And when she does, he'll take her down.

Chapter Twenty-One

MYAT DISAPPEARS FOR THREE days.

On the first day, Vedra talks to the captain through the device he gave her.

"Where is Myat?" she asks.

"Myat's fine," answers the captain. His voice coming out of the tiny contraption sounds thin and distant. "I'll let you know more when the information is available."

On the second day, Vedra talks into the device again.

"Have you done something to her?" she demands. "Tell me where she is." This time, the captain doesn't answer.

On the third day, Vedra uses the device again, a little more desperately. She can't stop replaying that day in Nakamura's office when she told him about the box on deck zero. She betrayed Myat, and now Myat is nowhere to be found. Vedra should never have trusted the captain.

"I didn't know what I was seeing," she says into the device. "I was wrong. I'm sure Myat isn't... whatever you think she is." For several hours, she gets no answer. She goes to the captain's quarters, but the door is closed and no one responds when she pounds her hands against it. Finally, Nakamura's tinny voice rises from the device.

"Come to deck zero." Vedra rushes to the elevator.

She finds the captain, First Officer Seki, and two others in the same corridor where she first caught Myat with the box. The Rogovans surround Myat. Myat's hands are chained to the wall behind her and blood is crusted on her face. She's standing on her own feet, but her back is stooped, her eyes staring vacantly at her boots.

"What have you done!" yells Vedra, running towards them. Myat turns her head slightly to see Vedra and loses her balance, falling to one knee, her bound arms wrenched upward. One of the Rogovans grabs Vedra before she reaches Myat, and she twists uselessly in his thick arms.

"I'm sorry, Vedra," says Nakamura. "I know Myat is your friend, but Rogov has a long tradition of trusting science and technology. It doesn't lie like people do. Seki." He nods at the first officer who holds a palm device in front of Vedra's face. The screen is washed in waves of color.

"This is Myat's brain," says Seki. "And this," she points at a small blue spot, "is a Directorate implant."

"Top of the line," adds Nakamura. "Indistinguishable from organic matter in most parts of the galaxy. But Rogovan technology is more advanced than in the rest of the galaxy."

"That little thing means she's from Earth?" asks Vedra.

"And not just a regular Big Three employee," Nakamura explains. "Myat is Directorate Special Operations." There's that word again. Directorate. Vedra is starting to have an inkling what it means.

"She's Empire," Vedra says. She thinks she sees a flash of annoyance in Nakamura's eyes.

"Special Ops agents are the eyes of the Directorate—the Empire, as you would say—outside of Earth and Mars. They keep tabs on activity around Earth's solar system and sometimes farther away. Ostensibly for security purposes, but usually there's an economic reason. What kind of business did you do on that asteroid of yours?"

"Imports and exports," says Vedra. Nakamura laughs, and it's cruel. He takes a small bag from one of the other Rogovans and pulls out a syringe. Vedra's chest tightens.

"What are you going to do to her?" she asks. But Myat already knows.

"That would be a very bad idea," Myat says. She struggles back onto her feet.

"I'm sure you think so," says Nakamura.

"I have an implant programmed to send out a beacon if I'm killed. Someone on Earth will see it and investigate where it's coming from." She raises her chin and a note of defiance enters her voice. "That's how us Empire folk know where the dangerous parts of the galaxy are. When some rogue gang or terrorist cell gets us, everyone back home finds out."

"We removed your implant."

"There's another. It's not neural, and you can't remove it without setting it off. TEDI will figure out what it means and know you're coming." Nakamura gives Myat a slow, patient smile.

"You're bluffing," he says, but Myat's calm expression doesn't waver.

"I'm not," she says. "But it's your decision. Do you want to risk everyone on this ship?" Vedra feels tears welling in her eyes. She hasn't cried since she was barely grown and Aria overdosed on their station's own product. Nothing seemed to matter enough for tears after that.

She breaks from the grasp of the Rogovan and runs to Myat, flinging her arms around her friend.

"You can't do this to her," she says, her voice thick with tears. She closes her eyes and plants a kiss on Myat's cheek before she's dragged away again. "I was wrong," she says. "I take it back. I was wrong about everything."

"It's OK, Vedra." Myat smiles broadly, a rare sight, and the saddest thing Vedra has ever seen.

Captain Nakamura slides the syringe into her neck and Myat falls to the floor.

Chapter Twenty-Two

CENRIC IS CLOSE NOW. Close to unraveling the secrets of the Rogovan insurgency, close to his corporation and his father finally recognizing what he's done for them, and so, so close to Yang Lin. He has the address of her family in Beijing saved to his implant and it's the first place he goes to after the end of the Mars Congress.

He doesn't know what to expect, and the anticipation throbs inside him. Are these people who are listed as her parents also Rogovans? Could they also have somehow obtained illegal Identifications? The very house he's headed to could be a hub for offworlder criminals! Or perhaps it's not her real home at all and the citizens living there will say they've never heard of a Yang Lin. Cenric can't wait.

Cenric is loyal to Hauser. Before he resorted to taking matters into his own hands, he made sure to exhaust the official channels. As soon as he saw Yang Lin on Mars, he went to Bao Ding's suite and informed his supervisor that an undercover colonist had been discovered in their own ranks.

Bao Ding sighed as if he had already been shouldering all of the world's problems, and Cenric's good deed was the straw that broke his back.

"Cenric, you haven't finished half of the work I gave you a month ago."

"All insignificant compared to this."

"You're the least productive member of this team. It's amazing you're employed above Tier Three, much less here as a Mars Congress member. If it weren't for your family connections, I would have rebalanced the corporate workflow and gotten rid of you weeks ago."

"I haven't been unproductive," Cenric insisted. "This is what I'm here to do! What James Lyon wanted." Bao Ding sighed again.

"Cenric, you haven't found any illegal drugs and you've taken more vacation days than you're allowed. We still have a few more weeks before the team is dissolved and I need you to do your job. The one I gave you, not the one you invented. If this woman is Tier One Hauser, she's obviously not a colonist. Now get back to work."

Cenric returned to his own suite, shaking with fury at Hauser's downfall into feeble bureaucracy. A good Hauser man died and the idiot Bao Ding couldn't care less about justice. Only Cenric cares.

***

All around Cenric, citizens on the Hyperrail go about their day, unaware of the danger they face from imminent Rogovan attack.

"Are you all right?" asks a fat man seated next to him. Cenric realizes he's been punching a hand into his thigh repeatedly.

"I will be," he says. As soon as he finds Yang Lin.

***

After Cenric was scolded by that layabout Bao Ding, he took his case to the VP of Internal Affairs himself. For the third time in a matter of months, he strode across the Mars campus, by the fountain dedicated to his ancestor, to the suite of the most powerful Hauser man on the planet. The first time he went to beg for his Mars Congress membership back, and the VP wouldn't see him. The second time, he went to save the VP's life, but still never laid eyes on the man. On the third trip, he knew he would finally prove his worth to Hauser and the VP. Also, he set an appointment in advance this time.

The VP reminded Cenric of a poor man's version of Cormand Smith, although they looked nothing alike. Both men had sculpted their bodies and personalities to best cultivate power, but where Cormand had taken likability to an art form, the VP lacked such sophistication. His stretched skin and exaggerated charm revealed him as the simple bureaucrat he was.

"Please, Cenric, sit down. I haven't seen you in ages. I believe you were trying to connect with me at the last congress, am I right? I apologize for never getting to your messages. I have a lot on my plate. But I see you got your problems all sorted." The VP was hardly subtle about reminding Cenric of his failure, but he ignored the jab.

"I've uncovered something important, sir," he said. Cenric once again described his discovery of Yang Lin and her assumed role in the Rogovan plot. "We just need to put some surveillance on her and I'm sure she'll lead us to others involved." The VP flipped through a few files on his desk display.

"You should go to your supervisor about this," he said. "Bao Ding, isn't it?"

"I already told Bao Ding about it," said Cenric. "He didn't appreciate the gravity of the situation."

"Mr. Smith," said the VP. "As a Smith, I'm sure you're accustomed to people listening to whatever pigshit comes out of your mouth. But frankly, I'm trying to run a company here, not catch aliens. Come back and see me if you have something to contribute."

***

And so by the time Cenric arrives in Beijing, his future with Hauser seems uncertain. Being a part of the Mars Congress has always been his dream—it's everyone's dream—but he can't quite see the point of lounging on the red planet with people like the VP, who climb the ranks without understanding the vision of the founders.

In Tiana Williams's day, Mars was the ambition of a small group of dreamers. No one had been there yet, and almost no one believed that within a century, it could be beautiful and habitable. Almost no one believed in science at all—innovation had lost its popularity amidst nation-state squabbles and resource scarcity. But Tiana and her ilk knew what the future required and gave birth to it.

If Tiana Williams were alive today, what would she think? Cenric's era is different than hers was. Today's Big Three citizens love tech, but they no longer respect law and order. She and the other founders had led the revolution of their time. Perhaps it is up to Cenric to lead the revolution in his.

***

The home of Yang Zirong and Wang Qing is stately beyond what Cenric imagined for probable offworlders. Through the fence around the property, he can see Terratech bushes carved to look like animals from an older time. A decorative bridge spans a small pond in front of the house. The front gate is constructed with an ornate latticework that Cenric originally takes for a traditional Chinese design, but as he gets closer, he sees each vertical metal bar consists of small human figures stacked on top of each other, dressed in modern garb and bearing the logos of the Big Three corporations. The horizontal beams are shaped like strange, distorted creatures that Cenric is fairly sure never existed on Earth.

He has a strong suspicion that the message of the gate design is a nefarious one, but he can't quite figure out the interpretation.

Cenric didn't expect the heavy metal gate to be smart, but if it's not, Yang Zirong is prescient, because she emerges from the house and raises a hand to greet Cenric, ruining his plan to observe the family from afar. The gate swings open.

Zirong is tall and angular with a nose like a downward-facing arrow. She's dressed entirely in black and her hair hangs long and sleek. Her wife, Wang Qing, joins her on the front step as Cenric approaches. Wang Qing is a shapely woman who hardly looks the hundred years old Cenric knows her to be. Only a few lines and two symmetrical white streaks in her hair give away that she is older than her daughter.

These people are even less Rogovan-looking than Yang Lin. They run a Xinqi art gallery, and although Cenric doesn't have an Identification scanner anymore, he couldn't find any evidence that they're offworlders. Cenric stands in front of the step and looks up at them.

"Hi there," says Zirong. "Are you looking for one of us?"

"I'm a friend of your daughter's," Cenric improvises. "Is she here?"

"Which one?" asks Wang Qing with a smile. "We have four. And three sons." Cenric raises his eyebrows.

"That must be incredibly costly. I've heard that Xinqi has the highest taxes for excess children." Yang Zirong and Wang Qing look at each other briefly.

"They're all adopted," says Zirong. "Neither of us have any biological children, so the taxes don't apply." Everything is suddenly clear to Cenric.

"That's how she got the Identification!" he says, forgetting the pretense of being Lin's friend. He tries to peer past the women into their mansion, but they block his way.

"I have to give you credit," says Cenric. "It's a flaw in the system I never thought of. An offworlder gives you their child for adoption and the next thing you know, she's Tier One Internal Security."

"You mean Lin, then," says Qing. "Lin was abandoned as a child. We don't know where she came from." Cenric reaches into his waistband and pulls out the small handgun he's been concealing.

"Tell me where she is," he demands. Neither of the women flinch.

"You're not going to shoot us," says Zirong calmly. "I hate to think about what kind of unfortunate people you usually wave that thing around at, but our gallery is frequented by Xinqi elite. Hurting us won't go unnoticed or unpunished." Cenric glances around the property again and puts away his weapon.

"You're not the first to come after our children," Qing says. "But they're all good citizens with flawless records. You can't touch them."

***

Cenric clenches his fists, furiously bumping shoulders with startled pedestrians as he storms back to the Hyperrail station. He's done everything right, he knows it. He hunted down dozens of illegals, he found out about the approaching ship, and he discovered who the Rogovan insider is. And yet, he's come up against a wall.

He can't touch Yang Lin. Her methods of obtaining citizenship were shifty, but she's a citizen, nonetheless. The only thing left to do is warn Hauser or the Directorate about the Rogovan ship. But who will listen? Not Bao Ding, not the VP, and certainly not his father.

Cenric thinks of Valeria in her garden and the way she smiled before she stuck him with the needle. Valeria knows TEDI better than anyone—she would want to know that a ship was attempting to get through. But he has no way to contact her over Mindlink.

He'll have to return to the Directorate base outside São Paulo to sound the alarm.

Chapter
Twenty-Three

THE FIRST DIRECTORATE SOLDIER Lin encounters at Urutu base bears a striking resemblance to Kirs Jonas. Lin doesn't acknowledge the soldier as they pass in the hallway, and to her relief, the soldier ignores her as well. Lin reaches the room labeled G-112 and looks over her shoulder to make sure no one is watching. She slips into the room, closes the door behind her, and locates a square panel in the floor. From her boot, Lin removes a narrow flashlight. She's not sure what's special about the flashlight, but when she points the beam at the floor panel, it reveals itself to be a smart door and springs open. Below the panel is a staircase leading to a room with several servers. This is the programming center, the place where TEDI can be fed new information. Lin takes out a second device from her waistband and attaches it to one of the servers.

"Good job," says Emas, standing in front of her suddenly. "Now you just have to get out." Lin blinks, and the simulation melts away, leaving her standing in a clearing with only a few tall trees and Emas's fresh-faced avatar in front of her.

"Something tells me it won't actually be that easy," she says.

"The simulation is realistic," says Emas. "We have great intel about the base, I promise. You'll get in and get out, just like that."

"Or I might get killed. Or lose my citizenship."

"Or you might be a hero to thousands of your fellow Rogovans."

Lin sighs.

"How will I know if they've identified me? Assuming I get out of the building OK. What if I go back to my job and think everything is alright and then they come the next day and arrest me?"

"It won't happen," says Emas. "The jammer in your uniform will prevent them from reading your Identification. Of course, if they scan you and don't get a reading, it will raise suspicion. But as long as you can get out of there without having your Identification scanned and without showing your face on camera, you'll be fine. Have you downloaded the map of where the cameras are?"

"Yes."

"Just keep your face away from those, and they'll never know it's you. They think no one knows about this base. In some ways, that means they're more relaxed about security once you're in. If you look like every other Directorate soldier, no one will question you." Lin is bothered by Emas's confidence. The colonists involved in this scheme all seem to think that they're smarter and better prepared than the entire Directorate military, but none of them have experience on the inside of the Big Three. Through Lin's eyes, or through the eyes of the woman in her official avatar, the eyes she's learned to have as an Earth citizen, they're a woefully naïve group of dreamers going up against Earth's strongest force.

"That's another thing," she says. "This plan seems a little too simple. Old-fashioned even. For all the technology you seem to have, isn't there some way to get to TEDI without actually sending me in? A drone, maybe, if the system can't be hacked." Emas shakes his head impatiently.

"Sometimes simple is best," he says. "TEDI isn't hackable from outside the base, I promise, and what do you think is more noticeable, a drone flying down the halls, or just one more woman in red?"

"Fine. Let's run the simulation again."

"No time," says Emas. "You have to go now."

"OK. I have to do this," she says, more to herself than Emas. "It's the right thing."

"It's the right thing," Emas echoes. "And Lin... don't be afraid to use your weapon."

"You're the one telling me everything will go smoothly," she says, but she runs a hand along the smooth side of her standard-issue Directorate firearm.

"Just remember what's at stake."

***

The next time Lin turns to Emas, his avatar has already vanished. She marches forward along the trail, beating back grasping Terratech vines, until she finally reaches the small village of Urutu. She wraps her hands tightly around the straps of her knapsack, which contains her weapon and Directorate military uniform.

The village is a sham—it serves only as a front for the base. Several of the buildings in the village allow access to the base. Lin has been told to enter through the local bar, which Emas assured her would be empty until later in the evening. He did warn her that it might be locked up, but she has good instructions on how to break and enter.

The friendly greeting of the bartender is Lin's first hint that Emas's intel might be flawed.

Hi there! You're not from around here, are you? Can I get you a drink?" The woman is leaning casually against the bar and smiling, but her eyes are mistrustful. Everyone above ground in Urutu keeps watch for strangers.

During her preparations, Lin asked Emas why she couldn't wear the Directorate soldier disguise into Urutu.

"Soldiers are never seen above ground there," he said. "At least, not dressed as soldiers. And if you claim to be a soldier dressed in civilian clothing, they'll check your Identification."

"So what do I say if I run into someone?"

"To tell the most convincing lie," said Emas, "make it as close to the truth as possible. Tell them you're an enforcer."

"Actually," says Lin to the bartender as she slides into a seat, "I'm not here for leisure. I'm a Hauser enforcer, and I tracked a suspect to this town. I didn't even know it was here—I thought he'd just disappeared into the jungle."

"Oh wow, a criminal, here?" says the bartender. She's not a talented actress. "I hope you find him!" She reaches her hand forward to pat Lin's shoulder.

Lin grabs her wrist and squeezes hard. Caught by surprise, the bartender drops the small round object that was clenched in her palm. It clatters to the bar, revealing a tiny spike on one side. Lin picks it up and drives it into the bartender's upper arm.

It takes about three seconds for the bartender to fall to the floor, unconscious. Was that enough time for her to call for help on her implant? Lin can only hope she was too startled to alert anyone else.

Access to the base is through a supply closet behind the bar. Lin throws open the closet doors to reveal a metal ladder attached to the back wall and disappearing into a hole in the floor. Lin shuts and locks the closet door behind her and begins to descend the ladder, stepping as quietly as she can on its metal rungs, into a long, vertical tunnel, dark and dusty. She looks down and sees a small opening, revealing a glimpse of a carpeted floor. She must be as high off the ground as her seventh-floor Hanting Community apartment.

Halfway down the ladder, a name flashes in Lin's peripheral vision. Rajan Singh. Lin almost doesn't answer, then changes her mind. She doesn't want to arouse any suspicion. She stops climbing.

"Hey, Rajan!" she subvocalizes, hoping it comes across as carefree. His avatar appears fuzzily from behind the ladder, hovering in mid-air with no need to grip the rungs.

"Hi, you!" says Rajan. "I hope you like surprises!"

Lin really doesn't.

"What do you mean?" she asks.

"Well, I know today is your day off," he says, and Lin mentally kicks herself for revealing too much information in their conversations. "So I took the day off too. Let's meet up! In person. Wherever you are in the world right now, I'm coming." Lin rests her forehead against a rung of the ladder.

"I'm sorry, Rajan, I'm really busy today," she says. His avatar's face falls.

"Are you sure? I took the day off for you."

"You didn't ask first, though, did you?" It comes out sharper than she wanted, then she sighs. "How about dinner in São Paulo?" she says. "That's where I am." The best lies are close to the truth, right? She hopes Emas was right about that. "Meet me in about three hours?"

"Sure, see you then!" Rajan's avatar disappears. Lin hopes she doesn't regret giving him a location so close to her real one, but if she actually makes it out alive, it might be nice to unwind tonight. She thinks Rajan's intentions are innocent. Although the timing of him asking her location is suspicious. Could he know more than he lets on?

She can't worry about that now. It's time to become a Directorate soldier. Her disguise is rolled tightly into her knapsack.

Changing into the red uniform is harder than Lin anticipated from the simulation, when her real feet never left the ground. Partway through struggling into the pants, the flashlight falls out of her boot and clatters to the floor, bouncing so loudly that Lin is sure it was heard throughout the base.

She can see it on the ground below her. What if someone finds it? Will they assume it's a regular flashlight, or will they be suspicious? Will they look up? Lin finishes changing as quickly as her awkward position on the ladder allows. She tucks her gun into its holster and leaves the knapsack and her enforcer clothes shoved behind the ladder for later. Then she climbs down the rest of the ladder and drops to the floor.

There's no one around, but Lin's heart thumps coldly. She pulls at her shirt where it sticks to her sweaty skin, then runs her hand down to her hip. A small patch of the fabric is thicker where the device is tucked inside. To anyone not observing closely, it looks like a regular pocket.

Lin looks around, getting her bearings. She's in a long corridor with a domed ceiling, smooth white walls, and Directorate red carpet. She knows from the simulation that all of the halls look the same. The East-West halls, like the one she's in, are lettered A-K. She's just dropped into B, but she needs to find G.

The lettered halls are connected by a single North-South hallway. Lin turns down that corridor, half expecting to see the Kirs-lookalike from the simulation. But although she can hear voices coming from some of the rooms, she's alone in the hall. She concentrates on making her walk look casual. Unless Directorate soldiers walk in some special way. Lin realizes she can't be sure. She wipes sweat from her forehead.

Two soldiers turn into the main hall, heading toward Lin. She panics and turns down hall E, ducking into an empty room.

"Damnit, Emas," she yells at him over the web, but Emas isn't answering. The room is set up for a presentation, with rows of chairs facing a large screen. Lin sinks into one of the chairs and rubs her temples.

She can't shoot the guards. Her personal opposition aside, killing any Directorate soldier will cause their implant to trigger an alert, and then the whole military will be on her in no time. If she's forced to kill anyone, she better be prepared to get out within a few minutes. Or not get out at all.

She'll have to try to talk her way past the soldiers and hope they accept her as a peer. But she knows nothing about the Directorate military. Lin kicks the chair in front of her and curses Emas's "intel."

"You're not supposed to be inside the room."

Lin jumps so hard that the chair jumps with her. A man is standing in the doorway, dressed in a suit. Not a soldier.

"Sorry," says Lin hoarsely, not knowing what else to say.

"Security always stands outside the door," the man continues slowly, speaking as if she's dense. "Our meeting is classified. You can't be in here listening, even before the presentation officially starts. Stand at your post outside."

"Ok," says Lin. Then amends her response, "Yes, sir." How do Directorate soldiers speak? At least she knows how to guard a room. She goes outside and stands to the side of the entrance, nodding slightly as a pinched-looking woman clutching a tablet to her chest glides past her into the room. Three more people in suits are coming down the hall.

Lin has twenty minutes left to plant the device.

Chapter
Twenty-Four

"WHAT'S SO SPECIAL ABOUT this place?" the charter plane pilot asks Cenric as they prepare for take-off. It's the same pilot that took him to the base before.

"Nothing," says Cenric. The pilot chuckles.

"Ok, then. But three months ago, when you flew with me, I didn't even know there was anything in that area. And now I've made two runs to Urutu in one day. Urutu's the name of the place, right? That's what the girl said." Cenric sits up straight.

"The girl," he says, and even without any more information, he knows. It's her. Yang Lin. He thought he was going to Urutu for help because he had run out of options to find her, but he's been hot on her trail all along. Cenric smiles slowly.

"Yeah, nice girl, said she was an enforcer. I don't know why an enforcer would go to this place. You're not an enforcer, are you?"

"No," says Cenric.

"Well, the two of you do have one thing in common," says the pilot. "You don't talk much."

***

"Valeria! Valeria!" Cenric stands outside the house where Valeria Hattori once gave him her special "treatment." "Valeria! I need to talk to you!" Valeria appears, leaning on the doorway. She's dressed in a black suit, very unlike the sunny outfit she was wearing the last time he saw her here.

"It's you," she says, expressionless. "What are you doing here? I need to get to a meeting."

"I've come to warn you," says Cenric. "I'm tracking a Rogovan, and she's here. I know she is." Valeria frowns.

"A Rogovan? She wouldn't even know that this village exists, much less what's underneath it."

"She knows. I don't know how. She's posing as a Hauser enforcer." Valeria shakes her head.

"Even if that were true, being an enforcer wouldn't give her access to the base. If she came to our village, we would get rid of her. Like we tried to get rid of you. I appreciate the concern, but an offworlder can't just walk into this base."

"There's a ship coming!" calls Cenric just as Valeria turns back into her house, and at that, she stops. "A Rogovan ship. She's trying to help it get past TEDI." Valeria has turned back to him, her face just slightly more concerned. "I don't know how being on this base can help her with that."

"I do," Valeria says.

"We have to stop her," says Cenric.

"Yes," says Valeria. "If she actually managed to get to the base somehow, we would have to stop her. But I can't sound the alarm until we know for sure. It will cause chaos, and I'll never set foot in Urutu again if I'm wrong. Let me check the cameras." Valeria's eyes lose focus as she looks at the security feeds on her implant. "I don't see anyone who doesn't belong," she says.

"The Rogovan is there," insists Cenric. "I know it."

"OK. I'll let the soldiers know and see if we can find how she got in. There are five entrances to the base." Valeria looks sideways at Cenric. "You shouldn't know this."

"You can trust me," says Cenric.

"I hope so," says Valeria. "One of the entrances is through my house. She didn't come this way."

"Where are the others?"

"Follow me."

She leads him first to a small store selling groceries and a handful of other items. A man in a brightly colored shirt lounges by the cash register. Another man, wearing no shirt, browses the aisles. Valeria nods to them both.

"Sam, Milo. Did anybody unexpected come through here today?"

"Just him," says either Sam or Milo, pointing at Cenric. Valeria thanks them, and she and Cenric continue to the next entrance point, a bar.

"Who are these people?" asks Cenric as they approach.

"Military, just like the ones in uniform," says Valeria. "We all are, although I haven't worn the red in ages. I just work with TEDI. The others here, like Sam and Milo and Jill, who we're about to meet, are lower-ranking soldiers. They enjoy the chance to come up here and act like civilians on vacation." They enter the bar. There's no one there.

"Jill?" calls Valeria. She looks at Cenric worriedly. "She would never leave her post." Cenric spots a curl of long hair peeking out from behind the bar.

"She didn't," he says. Valeria races around the bar and drops to her knees, feeling for Jill's pulse.

"She's alive," Valeria says with relief. "I'm calling for help."

"This means the offworlder is at the base," says Cenric.

"I know," says Valeria. "I'm sending out an alert. Everyone will be looking for her."

"I can help," says Cenric. "I know how to talk to her."

Chapter Twenty-Five

As soon as she's alone in the hall, Lin abandons her post and heads for the programming center. She walks quickly and purposefully, holding her breath and hoping the guards won't stop her on her way to hall G.

No such luck.

They grab her arms in unison and push her back a step. They aren't rough, but Lin can tell from their expressions that they're suspicious.

"Did you get turned around?" says the guard on the right, a stocky woman with a snub nose. "You're not cleared to go beyond hall F." Lin gives both guards her best disarming smile.

"I was ordered to get room G-110 ready for a meeting," she says, naming a room a few doors down from the one she needs. "Is that a problem?"

The other guard is staring at her. She realizes suddenly that he's the blond soldier she talked to at Hanting Community the night she and Sabohat hid. Could he possibly remember her after six months and significant physical changes? Lin tries not to look at him directly.

"Who gave you the order?" he asks.

"You know, maybe I got it wrong," she says a little breathlessly. "Give me a minute to check." She raises one finger to indicate the minute.

"Emas! Please be there. I need your help," she subvocalizes. To her relief, he answers.

"What's wrong?" he says.

"There are two soldiers guarding the way to hall G. I can't..." Lin trails off. Both guards are clearly receiving a message on their implants. With their attention off of her, Lin slowly reaches for her weapon. The guards simultaneously refocus on her and grab their guns.

Lin is faster. Both soldiers are dead before they fire a shot. Lin feels bile rise in her throat. She's downed hundreds of soldiers in games and training simulations. She's seen and heard and smelled the death of her victims on her hyper-realistic neural implant, but she's never sent a bullet into human flesh. The blond soldier has fallen on top of his colleague, his slack face pressed into her bloodstained uniform. Lin looks away and forces back her panic. They'll be onto her now and she can't waste a moment. She sprints for hall G.

Room G-112 isn't as bare as it appeared in the simulation. A long table of dark polished wood sits centered below a three-tiered chandelier. And there's carpet. Carpet that stretches to every wall, covering the panel in the floor that leads to the programming center.

Heavy footsteps approach. Lin leans around the door and surprises two of the four approaching soldiers with her fire. They slump to the floor as Lin dodges shots from the remaining two. She gets them on the second try. The hallway is silent.

Lin runs to the side of the room where the door appeared in the simulation and drops to her knees, feeling the carpet. Her fingers find a small dip where two separate pieces press together. She works her fingers into the space and pulls upward, ripping a large section of carpet away and revealing the door. Just like in the simulation, she pulls the flashlight from her boot and shines it at the door.

Nothing happens.

She tries standing on the other side of the door. Still nothing. She holds the flashlight higher, then lower. The door stays closed. Suddenly, Lin realizes more soldiers are approaching. They're treading more carefully than the last group, but Lin's enhanced hearing detects the shuffle of many boots in the hall. It's too late to shoot from the doorway this time, so she grabs one of the heavy chairs from the table and ducks behind it.

It's another group of four. She takes out the first one the moment he enters the room. The second manages to graze her arm, but she downs him along with the third soldier on her next round.

The fourth seems to stumble as he turns the corner. She kills him before she sees his face. Lin comes out from behind the table and cautiously checks the hallway—it's quiet. The thrill of surging adrenaline almost overtakes her terror. Then her eyes fall on the fourth soldier, the one who hesitated as he came into the room. Tall, bearded, staring vacantly at the wall as blood pours from his wound.

Bogdan.

Bogdan who raised a smile from her in training.

Bogdan who is one part of a comic duo with Boyu.

Bogdan who maybe loves Kirs; who she maybe loves too.

Lin's legs are weak as she kneels down beside him. How could she know that he was Directorate military now? No one told her. She thinks the same thought over and over: no one told her it would be Bogdan.

She should do something. She can't just leave him. That would make the worst thing she's ever done so much worse.

"Emas!" she yells helplessly, realizing belatedly she said it aloud.

A name flashes. It's not Emas.

"Javi," she says frantically. "It's all going wrong."

Chapter Twenty-Six

WITHIN A FEW HOURS, Vedra is certain, the landing shuttle she's boarding will go the way of Fenton's compound, obliterated by flames.

On the plus side, it has safety belts.

Vedra straps into a narrow seat between Temar and Uli. Uli's mother sits on the opposite side of Uli. She seems disoriented and mutters about something that sounds like danger or maybe daggers.

The shuttles are long and remind Vedra of the narrow corridors of the compound. Although it seems like an impossible number of people strapped to either side of the slender vessel—more people than Vedra has ever seen at once—there are supposedly five other shuttles just like it. As Captain Nakamura explained to her, all six will be expelled from the belly of the larger ship, which will simply stay in space. Each shuttle will land in a different part of Earth to spread the risk out between them.

Vedra is on the same shuttle as Captain Nakamura, which makes it the most important shuttle, she gathers. Being on it is an honor she was given for betraying Myat. This shuttle will land in the desert, a world made of sand, which is apparently similar to the dirt that covered every inch of the compound but also not at all like it.

Nakamura didn't explain it very well.

Vedra turns to Uli. "What are you going to do when we get to Earth?" she asks.

"Jump into a bowl of water so big that I can't see anything but water all around me." Vedra smiles at the earnest youth.

"They have that on Earth? I never knew."

Uli scoffs. "Everyone knows that." And at this, Vedra laughs out loud, which somehow makes Uli's mother go from muttering to wailing. Uli looks a little scared and digs his fingers into his mom's arm. Vedra keeps talking to try to distract him.

"I'm from a place called Ghiraz," she says, naming her station of birth. "We never talked about Earth. Never talked about other places at all."

"Is that why you talk funny?" Uli asks.

"I think you talk funny!" she says. But the boy is right. Over the weeks she's gotten a feel for how to shape her rough Anglian into Earth English, and she'd be wise to remember it when they land. If they land.

The shuttle starts to rumble, a low sound that rises to a roar that fills the air. Vedra can hardly hear her own voice as she yells to Temar that he should go swimming in this alleged water bowl, too. Then her stomach shifts a little higher in her abdomen and her hair and clothes lift from her skin. The shuttle has been launched from the ship and she's back in zero gravity. Temar is smiling at the weight lifted off his body, but Uli's face has lost its color. He looks like his mother when he's terrified.

"Enjoy it while you can!" Vedra yells, before realizing that the roar has quieted. "I hear living on Earth is very heavy." Uli looks a little less tense, so she continues to babble. "I believe that living there will make you very strong. Strong enough to swim across that entire bowl of water."

Uli brightens. "It's so big that it will take days," he says.

"I heard it will take years," says Temar, although he certainly has heard no such thing. Vedra closes her eyes contentedly, listening to the boys continue to bicker. Her mind drifts and she imagines herself back in the compound, except everyone is dead except for her and Myat.

She wakes to screaming and her skull crashing against the back of the seat. Before the pain clears there's another jolt, this time slamming her forward against the safety belt. Then the shuttle settles again, but all around Vedra, people are crying and yelling. Several moan in pain. Vedra looks at Temar, who is wide-eyed and pale, but quiet.

"Are you OK?" she yells over all the other shouting. Temar nods.

Six seats down from Vedra, a man unbuckles. To do what, she doesn't know. He seems to need more space just to yell and flail.

"Strap back in!" Vedra calls to him, but it's too late. Another hit, the biggest one yet, presses Vedra's thighs down into her seat hard and the man splatters onto the floor. Four round drops of his blood make their way past Vedra's face.

Temar is crying now but still unhurt, and as she grabs his hand, Vedra says a silent prayer of thanks to Myat for the bone-strengthening drugs. Uli, strong young thing that he is, is also still fine as he clings to his mother and wails.

Several minutes pass without incident. Vedra doesn't move or let go of Temar's hand, but others are taking advantage of the reprieve. They're massaging bruised limbs, trying to help their injured neighbors, and talking in frenzied tones about what's happening.

"They weren't supposed to know we were coming," says someone near Vedra, over and over. "They weren't supposed to know." More people are unbuckling now, some to help their friends, others simply to be free of constraints. Stupid. Vedra looks at the pool of blood and gore from the man who hit the floor earlier. Better to stay put. And yet, she can't just sit and wait for death.

Before she can finish her thought, she's slammed backward again. Several more are killed in a gruesome second, and Vedra begins to notice a burning smell from somewhere. Twice more, she's tossed violently against her restraints. Vedra knows she's lucky to not be seriously injured, but an ache is spreading throughout her entire body. It's getting hard to breathe.

"Are you OK?" she asks Temar again. He is, but he's crying harder than ever.

The next time the crashes stop, Vedra makes her move. She'll either save herself and her son, or it will all be over quickly. She unbuckles herself and Temar.

"Hold on to me," she says to him, as if there was any chance he would let go. Uli is clinging to her too, but she pries his little fingers off of her sleeve.

"Stay here and take care of your mama," she instructs, and without waiting for a response, propels herself and Temar toward the front of the vessel.

It's not just bruised ribs tightening Vedra's chest. Every second that goes by is another chance for her to be smashed against a wall or ceiling. They sail past rows of strapped-in Rogovans. Those closer to the front of the ship are higher ranking—maybe some kind of military from what Vedra can tell. They seem a bit dazed, but not as broken as the civilians near her assigned seat. All of them are still strapped in.

"You need to go back to your assigned area," says one, but Vedra doesn't give him a glance. At the end of the corridor, she comes up against a metal wall and a round door. She tries to open it, but it's locked.

"Only the captain and the pilots are allowed in there," says a man beside the door. Vedra turns to him. She doesn't recognize him. Seki and the other highest-ranking officers are commanding their own shuttles, so this guy must be the most important person not important enough to get his own ride.

"How do I get in?" Vedra asks.

"I said, only the captain—"

"Tell me how to get in!" Vedra yells. "Or tell him to open the door because he owes me this!"

"Let her in," says a woman across the aisle, her voice dark. "Does it matter at this point? Let Nakamura die looking at the faces of his victims."

"The captain didn't lie to us. He didn't expect this," says the man, but he looks unconvinced. Vedra has no time for this family drama.

"Tell me how to open the door," she says. The man sighs.

"See that little keypad above the lock?" he says. "Type A56N328B." Vedra does, and the door clicks twice. She shoves it open and goes inside, pulling Temar with her.

Four chairs face a row of monitors. The monitors display lines of words and numbers, not images of the space outside like when Myat showed Vedra the rock that housed the compound.

Oh, to have died with Myat on her junker, Vedra thinks.

"You should be in your assigned place," says Nakamura, with barely a glance back at Vedra. He's strapped in the center seat. Two of the chairs on either side of him are occupied by the pilots, but there's an extra chair behind Nakamura. Vedra straps Temar into it.

"People are dying back there," she says.

"If our person on the ground is on time, the attack should be stopped, according to the information we were given."

"If?" yells Vedra. "This is your plan? Hope that some Empire man down there saves us before we've all been battered to a pulp?"

"This was always the plan. You didn't have to join us," he says with infuriating calm.

"And what happens if this Earth friend of yours doesn't come through? And I mean really soon!"

Nakamura doesn't answer. Vedra doesn't need him to. They're going to die.

Chapter
Twenty-Seven

LIN IS FROZEN, HER eyes melded to Bogdan's lifeless ones. If she moves, she'll see the blood pour from the hole in his chest and be crushed by what she has done. If she moves, she might have to do it again.

She can't move. She can't even breathe.

Her vision turns hazy, and for a second, she thinks it's just a symptom of her shock. Then she realizes it's Javi's avatar appearing. Lin stays on the call but blocks his avatar. She doesn't release Bogdan's dead gaze. Javi's voice invades her mind, harsh and direct.

"Where are you?" he asks. Lin starts to answer, then hesitates. Something about the question seems off.

"You should know," she tells him, feeling a rising chill.

"At Urutu base," returns Javi. "But where exactly? How much progress have you made?" Lin's inner alarm overpowers her shock over Bogdan's death. She rocks back into a crouch and rubs her temples. Then she hangs up on Javi and tries Emas again. This time, he answers, and she blocks his avatar as well.

"What's happening?" he asks worriedly. "Has something gone wrong?"

"How long have you known Javi?" asks Lin.

"Um, I don't know. He's been in the group for a while."

"In the group. But he's been doing some work for you personally, right? You've had him look into things."

"Yeah, he reached out to me personally about a month ago."

"*He* contacted *you*? Just out of the blue?"

"No, he contacted me because he knew Druilla, who's friends with Nedwani. You met her in the room, right?" Lin digs her fingers deeper into the side of her head.

"Oh, Emas," she moans, "and you thought I was too trusting."

"What? What are you talking about? Why are you asking about—" Lin cuts him off.

"Never mind. Emas, I can't get the flashlight to work. I think it's broken."

"There's no beam?"

"There's a beam, but the door won't open."

"If there's a beam, it works. Try again."

"That's not helpful!" Lin says, but she ends the call and tries again, holding the flashlight at different heights and angles. Finally, sure that it's hopeless and a new batch of soldiers will be upon her in moments, she hits the flashlight hard against her palm.

The door pops open. She steps through it.

Just before she pulls the door back down over her head, she sees a tall, dark-skinned man with thick upright curls stalk into the room, hand on a weapon. Lin recognizes him. He's the one who awkwardly almost approached her on Mars, then disappeared. So that was Javi.

Lin races down the staircase. It's darker and dustier than it was in the simulation. Lin's enhanced eyes quickly adjust to the dim lighting, but the staircase is long and she can't see where it ends. She accepts another call from Javi, but she doesn't speak to him.

"Lin? Are you there?" comes his voice in her head. As she descends the stairs, Lin unzips the secret pocket in her waistband and readies the device.

"Are you OK?" asks the man she knew as Javi. "Do you need help navigating the base?" Lin doesn't answer. She's in the programming center now. She hears faint scuffling from the top of the stairs as Javi tries to open the panel in the floor and follow her. The next time she hears his voice, it has lost all its friendliness.

"I know what you are, Yang Lin," he says. Lin hears the door in the floor creak. He must be prying it open with something. She starts to loosen the screws on the side panel of the server.

"I'm a Tier One Hauser employee and a citizen," she replies, pulling the panel away.

"A Hauser citizen!" he says. Lin has never heard an avatar voice sound quite so riled. "Only by deceit and betrayal of everything that Hauser stands for! But don't worry, Yang Lin, justice is coming for you."

"What about justice for the Rogovans?" Lin scans the inside of the server, searching for a crucial red wire. She found it so many times in the simulation. But in the simulation, her hands weren't shaking and hot sweat wasn't falling in her eyes. Javi's laugh echoes meanly.

"Justice is coming for them too, don't worry! They've broken the law. They deserve even worse than what they'll get from TEDI."

A sudden calm comes over Lin. Her hands steady and her breathing slows. She pictures her father, dying in flames, and for the first time, instead of terrifying her, it galvanizes her. Hayato sacrificed everything to give her a new life. She can do the same for three thousand Rogovans. She finds the red wire and pulls it out.

"A new era is coming for Hauser," Javi rambles on. "One where the laws matter. One where weak men like my father, captive to public opinion, are nothing."

"What does your father have to do with anything?" she asks, trying to distract him. She doesn't listen to his answer as she readies the device. In her waistband it was rolled tight, no thicker than her finger, and it unfurls into something that looks like cloth, but when she attaches the corner to the red wire, it hums to life, flashing lights across its surface.

She hears a footstep behind her and spins with her gun raised. Javi raises his weapon as well, but neither of them shoot. As much as she hates him, whoever he is, she can't stomach killing anyone else today. They stare at each other without speaking. The device makes a whirring noise and continues flashing lights. Then everything explodes in a burst of white.

Chapter Twenty-Eight

IT'S SNOWING. BIG, THICK flakes drift from the sky and pile around Cenric. He's back in Denver at his childhood home. Cormand is away at the Mars Congress and Mama has let Cenric make snow angels outside instead of finishing schoolwork. He opens his mouth and sticks out his tongue to catch the largest flake.

And spits out the dry, sour clump of dust. Cenric opens his eyes.

He's still in the programming center of the Directorate base, lying on his back. One side of the room has caved in, but Cenric was spared from the rubble. He stands and brushes grit and debris from his clothing.

One of the dead Directorate soldiers from the room upstairs has somehow fallen down the stairs in the explosion. He'll have to tell someone that the soldiers weren't killed in the blast, but coldly gunned down by the Rogovan. Then Cenric sees her. Then he remembers staring into her defiant brown eyes the moment before everything rained down around them. She's on the floor between two fallen beams, curled on her side, framed in pooling blood. Her face is as white as snow.

Justice has been served to her by her own bomb. Maybe suicide was even part of the plan. Cenric shakes more dust from his hair and looks around. The exit is unblocked. He heads for the stairs. He stops.

Something isn't right.

He returns and surveys the scene again. The murdered Directorate soldier, the widening pool of blood around the Rogovan girl, and the bomb.

How can that be? The device he saw her attach to the server is still there, touched with dust but unharmed, making a soft whirring noise. He steps closer to examine it. It could be a bomb of some sort—just because it's still humming away after the blast doesn't mean that it didn't cause the explosion. And yet...

Something isn't right.

If anything, the blast came from above them. If he'd been at the center of it, he would be dead now.

Cenric looks back at the girl. Yang Lin. She'll be dead soon, if she isn't already. But when Cenric sees her broken body, he doesn't feel the endorphin rush of justice served. Not like when he destroyed Dirk Kane or the Rogovan in São Paulo. Cenric feels uncertain and weak, like the moment right after he pastes a shav patch to his arm but before it dissolves all his cares.

Maybe he hit his head in the blast.

He kneels by the girl, his boots sliding in her blood. It won't do to let her die before she gives up her accomplices, he decides. Having realized that she must live, temporarily of course, gives him a course of action and dissolves his dizzy uncertainty. He'll go for help, he'll save the girl bleeding out on the floor. He'll do it so she can give him information on other Rogovans. Then she can die. Cenric runs for the stairs.

The main level of the base is in worse disarray than the programming center in the basement. Bodies lay amidst the rubble, blood just barely visible on the deep red Directorate uniforms. Floating dust and debris is illuminated in the light pouring in from a blasted hole above the underground structure.

Fresh Directorate soldiers pour into the building, their uniforms un-stained but still, in their dark red glare, reminiscent of yawning wounds. They rush past Cenric, pushing him aside. He calls to them that someone is hurt, but they don't stop. So many are hurt. But Cenric can't let them forget the girl. It wouldn't be right.

Two people enter the building, a man and a woman, strapped with emergency medical packs bearing bright red insignias. The packs come from the Directorate military, but the doctors are dressed in civilian cloth-ing. They kneel by the dead, one by one, then move on.

"Hey!" Cenric calls to the man. "There's a person downstairs who needs help."

"Lots of people need help," says the man, placing a patch over his current patient's head wound. It molds to the skin and stops the bleeding.

"She's going to die!" Cenric yells, considering dragging this medic downstairs at gunpoint. But the doctor nods.

"Show me where," he says. They rush back down the stairs, and Cenric leads the doctor into the server room. He scans the dead soldiers first, looking a bit confused, then his eyes land on the Rogovan. The doctor's knees buckle slightly, then he rushes to her side, ignoring the blood seeping into his pants.

"Lin," he says, touching her hand. Cenric narrows his eyes. Is this alleged medic one of the offworlders as well? He's digging in his emergency pack and pulling out tools. Cenric will let him work, but he'll keep an eye on the doctor. "Lin," says the doctor again, as he pulls away her crusted uniform, "can you hear me?" The Rogovan girl is as good as a corpse.

Cenric goes back upstairs. Now, in addition to the rush of red shirts, drones from all the major Big Three news stations have found their way through the hole in the ground. They hover about, flying through the rubble, asking any survivors who are still conscious to talk about their experiences. One Directorate soldier with a bandaged hand uses his good arm and a piece of a shattered table to bat the drone to the floor.

"How's that for an experience?" he mutters. Cenric is confused by the speed at which the drones appeared. He would have expected the location of the base to be a secret from the media. He pushes farther into the fray.

Attention citizens of Hauser, Wonju, and Xinqi.

The voice in Cenric's head is sudden and invasive, an uninvited call answered without his permission. From the abrupt halt to movement and speech, Cenric knows that everyone is receiving the same message. Only the low moans of the wounded continue as background noise to the announcement.

A key Directorate facility has just been bombed. The attack was carried out by an old enemy, Rogov. Rogovan insurgents, having forgotten that they themselves were once from Earth, that they themselves once had humanity, have struck us in the place that matters most. The Directorate is what brings all the citizens of the world together, and Rogov will see that it cannot take that from us.

The voice signs off without identifying itself.

The announcement, wherever it came from, is even more startling than the fast arrival of the news drones. Moments ago, Cenric alone knew of the Rogovan plot, and no one would believe him. Now it seems to be common knowledge.

He allowed himself to feel sympathy for Yang Lin too easily. Apparently, this was the work of her people after all. Cenric grabs the arm of the nearest Directorate soldier, who stiffens and forcefully removes Cenric's hand.

"Do you need help, sir?" asks the soldier.

"No," says Cenric. "I have the bomber downstairs. I saw her plant the bomb. She's injured now, but alive. I think."

The soldier turns for the staircase, and five others immediately follow, responding to silent orders across the neural network.

"I'll show you where she is," says Cenric, but the soldiers are already far ahead of him. He runs after them. "Her name is Yang Lin. She's masquerading as an enforcer, but she's a Rogovan. She's in the programming center," he calls to the front soldier as they jog down hall G. They enter room G-112. The soldiers see the bullet holes in their comrades and raise their guns. Cenric follows them down the stairs to the programming center. All of them scan the demolished room.

The Rogovan and the doctor are gone.

Chapter Twenty-Nine

A GASH IN CAPTAIN Nakamura's forehead has spilled blood over one half of his face. The attacks have been coming for what feels like hours, although it has only been minutes.

They don't have much time left. Vedra knows this from the heat, the scorching waves obscuring her vision and blistering her skin. She knows it from the flashing lights and sirens. And she knows it from the muffled screams coming from the other passengers on the shuttle.

An explosion turned one of the pilot's consoles into a gaping hole, and one of the pilots is dead, tipped sideways, an arm mangled. Nakamura looks like he's ready to be dead too.

At least he was a gentleman in the end, showing Vedra how to unfold an extra chair from the wall. At least there's a safety belt. Temar has somehow held up better than the military men—he isn't even crying anymore.

The captain is yelling orders to his remaining pilot, but he keeps losing his train of thought, as if his ideas are pouring out of the cut on his head.

"Engage the... Maneuver! Maneuver..." Nakamura fumbles with the silver suit he's wearing, and Vedra sees that a shard of the blasted console has lodged itself in his side. He yanks it out, and the suit melds back together like magic.

"Now engage…" Nakamura tries again, then he stops yelling and his face slackens. Vedra thinks for a minute he's dead, but suddenly, he smiles.

"It's only us," he says. A fire is spreading from the console. Vedra watches it, remembering the fire that roasted Fenton. This time there's nowhere to run. "TEDI isn't attacking the other shuttles. Our soldier on the ground must have done her part before TEDI found them."

"Great," yells Vedra over the roar of the fire and sirens. "So what about us?" The captain takes several deep breaths.

"Two thousand Rogovans descending on Earth!" he booms. "Safe! Ready for a new life!" He turns to Vedra. "I'm full of peace, knowing this," he says.

"Well, stop being peaceful and do something!" shouts Vedra, although it's clear the captain is beyond doing anything. Vedra looks around for what she can do herself.

All the Rogovans, and even Vedra and Temar, are wearing the same silver suits as the captain. Vedra was told that when the suit is fully zipped, the wearer can survive out in space for several minutes. They zip down the middle of the face, leaving only a thin sliver the wearer can see out of. Vedra unbuckles and leaps to Temar's seat, helping him zip his suit. Nakamura and his pilot keep their hoods down. The captain catches Vedra looking pointedly at his.

"What do you think is going to happen if we end up outside?" he asks. "No one is coming to save us."

"What if they do?" says Vedra, zipping her own mask across her face. "I'm not dying before I have to."

***

The next thing Vedra knows, she's waking up. Her arms are wrapped around Temar, their bodies pressed together. She's relieved to feel his chest rising and falling against hers. Then she realizes the reason they're pressed so tight is not simply from love and fear—they're in a tiny, cramped space. She scrambles to unzip her hood, but it's still too dark to see anything. Vedra feels around with her hands. She and Temar are packed into a smooth cylinder. Like pickled vegetables stuffed in a can at the compound.

"Hello?" Vedra yells.

"Hello," a voice answers, but it isn't coming from outside the cylinder. The voice is in the tiny can with them, and it's not human. Vedra knows that right away, although she isn't sure why.

"Who are you?" asks Vedra.

"I am TEDI—Tactical Earth Defense Intelligence," says the voice. Vedra doesn't trust it. "My job is to keep Earth citizens safe from any outside threats."

"What about the others?" she asks, thinking of Uli and his mother. "Are they in cans too?"

"According to the data available, you were the only Earth citizens present," says TEDI.

"But I'm not—" Vedra catches herself. Wherever this lie came from, it seems to be what's keeping her alive.

"TEDI," she asks. "How did you know that we're Earth citizens?" Vedra wishes her eyes could focus on something, just a shape or a color in the darkness.

"TEDI uses many sources of data," says TEDI, as if it wasn't talking about itself. "The specific source of information on your citizenship was a message from Special Operations Agent Myat Shin."

Vedra pulls Temar closer against her and kisses his cheek.

"Thank you, Myat," she whispers.

Chapter Thirty

"EMAS... EMAS ARE YOU there?"

Lin calls out through the burning pain that radiates from her side through her whole body.

"I'm here, Lin," says an unexpected voice. She opens her eyes. Rajan's head looms over her, his face taut with worry. She tries to sit up, but something strapped tight across her chest pulls her back down. The pain sears through her side again and she moans. Rajan puts a calming hand on her arm. Lin cranes her neck to look around and realizes she's strapped to a metal stretcher, rattling noisily along in some kind of vehicle.

"Don't try to move yet," says Rajan. "You had some shrapnel in your side, but it didn't hit any vital organs, thankfully. I've stopped the bleeding and we're on a medical transport to the nearest Hauser medical center."

Lin pushes against the restraints again, but all she achieves is a new flash of pain.

"Careful," says Rajan. "Save your strength."

"What happened?" she asks him.

"There was a bomb," says Rajan. "But, Lin, what were you doing there? Why are you wearing a Directorate uniform?" Lin exhales. If he doesn't know why she was there, she hasn't been caught yet.

"It was an assignment," she says.

"For Abena? Was she at the base?" Lin shakes her head.

"No," she says simply. Better not to over-explain herself. "Do they know who set the bomb?"

"Rogovan terrorists," says Rajan. "A message went out to everyone about it. Not a regular message, though. Somehow it played to everyone on Mindlink without their permission. You were still unconscious." Lin stares at him.

"Rogovan?" This can't have been the work of other Rogovans. The Rogovans sent Lin and her device, not a bomb.

At least, she thinks so. But she's been wrong before.

"That's what the message said. Anyway, I was already at the scene when the message went out. As you know, I was in São Paulo, waiting for you. So when Hauser Medical Central put out a call for doctors in the area to respond to an emergency, I did. And then I found you. But Lin, what in the world were you doing on a Directorate base?"

"You saved me," says Lin

"I wasn't at all sure you were going to make it." Rajan grabs her hand.

"I have to get out of here," says Lin.

"Out of where? Out of the transport? Lin, you're not thinking clearly."

"I am. I can't go to the hospital. I have to get out of here." Rajan just rubs her hand soothingly.

"Who's Emas?" he asks.

Lin tenses. "What do you mean?"

"You were asking for Emas." Lin remembers calling out for him, but she thought she was subvocalizing.

"Someone I work with," she lies. Lin hears a groan and turns her head. She's been focused on Rajan and her own plight and didn't even see the other passenger. A Directorate soldier, a woman around her age, is strapped to a stretcher next to hers. A chunk of the soldier's skull is missing. Is she a victim of the Rogovans? Of Lin herself?

Lin closes her eyes. Let Rajan think she's sleeping or unconscious again.

"Emas!" she calls. This time, she does it silently. With her eyes still closed, she sees Emas's avatar appear. Its expression is ecstatic as it hovers above her stretcher.

"Lin! You're alive!"

"Last I checked," says Lin.

"Are you safe? How did you get out?"

"Not safe yet. I'm on a medical transport on my way to a Hauser hospital."

"A hospital! You're hurt?"

"I'll be fine," says Lin. "If I can get out of here without anyone realizing that I'm the one who infiltrated Urutu. But Emas, what happened? My device wasn't a bomb, right? Was it really Rogovans who bombed the base?" Emas is silent for a moment.

"I don't know. I promise you I'm not keeping anything from you. As far as I know—as far as anyone told me—you were supposed to be able to get in and get out safely. No explosions involved. You have to believe me." The avatar's eyes are pleading.

"I believe you," says Lin. Emas has always shared information readily—too readily, most of the time. She doesn't believe he was keeping secrets from her. She starts to sign off the call and then remembers.

"Emas, you can't trust Javi. I don't know if he survived the explosion or not, but he's not Rogovan. He's not on our side."

***

"We're almost there," says Rajan a few minutes later, squeezing her hand. Lin opens her eyes.

"Rajan, do you trust me?" She tries to sound confident. He has no reason to trust her—everything between them is a lie. But he doesn't know that.

"Sure," he says.

"I can't go to that hospital," she tells him. "I can't tell you why right now, but it's very important that I don't go yet." Even if no one has identified Lin, she's still wearing her Directorate uniform, the one that blocks Identification readers. She'll be pegged as a non-citizen in an instant. And some of the soldiers she encountered as she shot her way through the base could still be alive and at the hospital.

"Lin, your injury isn't as serious as I feared, and those enforcer nanobots in your blood will help a lot. But you're not out of the woods. I really want you to go to the hospital," says Rajan. He pauses. "But yes, I trust you. If you don't want to go to this medical center, we can go wherever you want instead."

We. So he plans to stay with her. She'll have to figure out how to ditch him later. But then where will she go? Not back to her own place—the Directorate will go there first. She could go back to Hanting Community, but what's left for her there without Sabohat?

Sabohat.

If she's honest with herself, there's only one thing she cares about now. She's done her duty to the offworlders and her enforcer career is surely over. All that's left is Sabohat. If it's the last thing she does before they lock her up or put her to death, she'll find her mother.

Lin calls the number from the paper in Sabohat's apartment. The first time she called, she could barely catch a few words before the connection was lost. The second time, she gave the mystery man details about the Rogovan ship, but again the call was cut off again before she could learn more. She hasn't been able to get through again, but this time she gets lucky.

The call begins with the same distortion that always interferes with their communication, but eventually the man's voice comes into focus.

"...ships on the way? Was your plan a success?"

"As far as I know," Lin subvocalizes. "But I can't tell you anymore about that until you tell me what you know about my mother."

"She's here with me," says the deep, faceless voice. "She's well."

"Where's here?" Lin's heart races. "How can I get there?" There's a long pause, and Lin is afraid she's lost the connection. But then the voice speaks.

"There's a Wonju spa. The name is Jade and Pearl." The man continues to talk but his voice is fading, overtaken by the distortion. Then it's gone. But at least Lin has a clue. She searches Jade and Pearl Spa on Mindlink and finds only one, in Europe.

The medical transport is arriving at the hospital. Rajan loosens Lin's restraints as the vehicle decelerates. She sits up on the stretcher, a new bolt of agony shooting through her body, and Rajan steadies her.

"I don't like this," he says as the transport comes to a stop. Lin grabs Rajan's shoulder for support as she steps off the stretcher.

"Get me to a Hyperrail station," she says.

***

Lin is worried about what the other Hyperrail passengers will think of her bloodied uniform and dusty hair, but her concern turns out to be misplaced. Most citizens pay her no mind, but those that do acknowledge her, do so with a smile or nod. One older man gives her a salute.

"I hope they get those alien bastards," he says. Lin realizes that everyone has heard about the Urutu bombing and can infer that she was there. They think she's a real Directorate soldier. A victim of the Rogovan attack. A Hero in Red.

She and Rajan take a taxi to the spa. Lin watches out the window as they approach, looking for any clue that might help her anticipate the situation she's walking into. The buildings in this area are old, and many look abandoned. Lin doesn't see any skyscrapers like the ones she's used to in Beijing and even San Antonio. Their taxi bumps and jolts on the crumbling cobblestones before pulling up in front of Jade and Pearl Spa.

The spa is in a brick building, short and old-fashioned, but better maintained than many of the structures Lin has seen in the area. A few other nearby buildings are barricaded closed, their doors obscured by metal bars and creeping Terratech.

Lin exits the taxi. The pain in her side still burns, but she's getting used to it and only lets out a slight grunt as she stands. She marches toward the green doors of Jade and Pearl, trying to mask her limp and wishing she had a weapon for whatever she finds inside. Rajan jogs up behind her and grabs her arm.

"Lin. Stop. Why are we going to this spa? I haven't asked many questions, but I need to know. I assume you're not going for a massage." Lin doesn't turn to face him.

"I'm going to meet my mother," she says, her eyes still locked on the spa doors. She hopes it's true. Rajan holds her arm a moment longer, then releases it and sighs.

"OK, I've come this far, I guess. Let's meet your mother." They walk through the doors.

The inside of the spa is surprisingly modern compared to the rough exterior, with smooth marble floors and screens on the walls that flash the prices of various treatments. A sign instructs visitors to remove their shoes before proceeding into the lobby. Rajan bends to slip his off, but when Lin strides forward without stopping, he follows suit. She can't afford to leave herself vulnerable.

On the other side of the room is a desk. A woman sits behind it, her long, immaculately painted nails twirling her glossy hair. Her name tag reads Eunha. As Lin approaches her, the woman appraises her with an expressionless gaze that drifts down her ash-covered shoulders to her bloody uniform and back up to her face.

"Do you have an appointment?" Eunha asks.

"No," says Lin. "I'm meeting someone here."

"What's their name?" asks Eunha. Lin doesn't answer. "What do they look like?" Eunha asks. When Lin stays silent, she sighs. "No one else is here. You're the only customers, if you are customers. The locker rooms are that way. You're welcome to get changed. Maybe your friend will come later."

Lin wonders if this is what she's supposed to do. She doesn't even know if this is a meeting, an ambush, or something else. She takes a closer look around the lobby of the spa. Besides the hallway to the locker rooms, there's only one other door.

"Where does that lead?" she asks, gesturing to the door behind the desk. Eunha glances back at it with disinterest. Then, so fast that even Lin with her enhanced reflexes can't dodge it, she pulls out a portable Identification scanner and aims it at Lin.

Lin steels herself for Eunha's reaction, for the woman to try to restrain her or to cower in fear of a non-citizen, but Eunha only gives her a polite smile.

"Oh, is that why you're here?" she asks.

"I don't know, is it?" Lin returns.

"You're welcome to take a look in the back room," Eunha says. "I'll show you." She stands and holds a hand out, indicating that Lin should go ahead of her. Lin cautiously walks to the door. Rajan follows her like a puppy.

"I'd rather do this alone," says Lin.

"Not a chance," he says. Eunha opens the door and Lin and Rajan step inside. Ahead of them is a long, dim hallway. Lin can't see the end of it.

"What is this?"

"Mostly storage," says Eunha. "But I think you'll find what you're looking for."

"This is weird, Lin," says Rajan.

"I know," she says, exasperated. "You didn't have to come with me." He's silent. Lin starts down the hall, the other two following behind. Her head is pounding, and she wonders if she hit it in the blast.

Rajan makes a small noise, and she turns to see him leaning against the wall and wincing.

"Are you all right?" Lin asks.

"Sure. I just felt lightheaded for a minute," he says, giving her a shaky smile. Lin continues forward, finally reaching an open door at the end of the hallway. She steps through. The room on the other side seems to hold nothing but stacks of boxes and some defunct electronics. Lin turns to ask Eunha what she's looking at, but flashing colors and images obscure her vision. She hears Rajan cry out and she grasps blindly, trying to push her way back into the hallway, but she can't find the door. She hears it lock just before she blacks out.

Chapter Thirty-One

CENRIC EXITS INTO THE store above the base, now partially collapsed, a muddy crater in its backyard. No sign of Sam or Milo. He steps into the sunlight. The little village is mostly intact, although considerably less peaceful due to a growing crowd of military transports, press vehicles and drones, and rubberneckers.

Inside Cenric is a gaping hole where once the drive for justice burned. He knows that not even shav would take it away. He had been so sure he was doing something important, something that would cement his place in the annals of history and in his family. And he did do something important—he found the Rogovan girl and turned her in. The soldiers said they'd send her identity out over Mindlink as soon as they confirmed what he told them about her position at Hauser.

But something isn't right.

"I'm here in person at the site of an attack by Rogovan militants," says a voice not far from Cenric, and the voice makes him cringe. He spots Cormand holding forth in the center of a clump of jostling news drones and gawking bystanders. Cenric wanders closer, but not too close. He has no interest in fighting the crowds for a glimpse of the man of every hour. He tunes into an audio news feed so he can better hear his father without close proximity.

"As per Section B of Directorate Clause 1816, the recently-formed Committee on Immigration will be temporarily assuming control of the Directorate. Decision-making power will be in our hands until we've determined that the Big Three are safe from external threat." Cenric isn't looking at his father's face, but he knows that this is the point where Cormand flashes his sheepish, I'm-just-a-regular-guy-like-you smile. "Now I know this all sounds very scary and official," he continues, "but here's what it means. Business for the Big Three will continue as usual. Nothing is going to change, except that my new committee will be in charge of looking after Earth security and keeping you safe."

As Cenric puzzles over this decisive action, so different from the political way his father talked about the committee a few months ago on Mars, he spots another familiar, more welcome face. Valeria Hattori, who introduced him to TEDI just last week. She isn't crowding in to listen to Cormand or trying to get closer to the site. Nor is she fleeing the carnage. She simply stares, alone.

"What do you think they were targeting?" he asks.

"Nothing that an explosion could destroy," she says. "I don't understand it. This part of the base is incredibly important to TEDI, but the blast won't hurt him at all. So many lives lost for nothing."

***

On the Hyperrail back to Denver, Cenric scans the news feeds. They've released Yang Lin's name and picture. She'll be caught soon, and it's thanks to his intelligence.

But he can't shake a feeling of heaviness. He also can't quite place a finger on the source of his melancholy. Several things keep coming to the front of his mind. The message, coming so soon after the attack, declaring that the bomb was Rogovan. The way that message was broadcast directly into his implant without permission. The news drones flying in before the dust had settled. His father's appearance at the site. The Rogovan, bleeding out while her bomb kept sputtering long after the attack.

It all means something. If only he knew what.

Chapter Thirty-Two

AROUND THE TIME THAT Vedra's cramped joints start feeling hotter than they had in the burning shuttle, and around the time that Temar's incessant questions—*where are we going, can I get out now, where's Myat*—are about to drive her mad, the can she's riding in stops moving. Vedra doesn't know exactly how she's sure that it's stopped, but it seems that the can, which had been sending a kind of vibration across her skin, is now motionless.

"Where are we now?" she asks in the darkness. Asks TEDI. She's not sure if it will answer, but it does. She wishes she had a face to talk to and wasn't just spouting words into nothingness.

"Latitude 33 degrees, 42 minutes, 2 seconds. Longitude 38 degrees, 33 minutes, 12 seconds," answers the voice.

"Latitude, longitude," Vedra whispers. She doesn't know the words, but she better get used to speaking Earth English right away.

"Latitude 33 degrees, 42 minutes, 2 seconds. Longitude 38 degrees, 33 minutes, 12 seconds," TEDI replies, thinking she was requesting the information. She slams the side of the can.

"I know!" she yells. "Now let us out!" The top of the can retracts so fast that Vedra doesn't see it disappear. She's still curled at the bottom, wrapped up with Temar. She throws a hand over her eyes against the bright white and Temar does the same with a whine. Then Vedra pushes herself to her feet, her arm still blocking the sun. She grips the side of the can and sways, overwhelmed by the vastness of the world around her. Not a single wall to be seen anywhere, just towering piles of something soft and tan. Sand. Vedra leans over the side of the can for a closer look. The sand is made up of tiny little granules. She imagines that every piece of it, every pebble, houses a compound with a Fenton. She could crush them all.

"Welcome back to Earth," says someone behind her. The word back is said with a peculiar emphasis. Vedra puts a protective hand on Temar and turns around. A woman is standing there, next to two vehicles with enormous wheels. The woman has long gray hair and is wrapped in a green robe.

"It's good to be back in the place where I was born," Vedra says, pronouncing each English syllable carefully. The woman gives her a sideways smirk.

"Well, come on out of that thing," she says. Vedra looks at the walls, almost up to her chest, too high for Temar.

"Does it have a door?" she asks. Is this the kind of thing she should know if she's pretending to be from Earth?

"Damned if I know," says the woman. "TEDI is evolving all the time. He makes his own weapons, equipment... whatever this thing is. He's long past the point where we even know what all the pieces are."

"TEDI," says Veda, "Can you please let us out?" The sides of the can break into four even pieces along invisible seams and fall flat on the ground.

"That's just creepy," says the woman. Vedra and Temar step onto the sand. Vedra's shoes sink deeper than she expected.

"Who is she?" whispers Temar to Vedra. The woman hears and smiles at him.

"My name is Si Rancourt," she says. "I'm in charge of estates in the Directorate." There's that word that got her in so much trouble, Directorate. Vedra doesn't say anything. Si approaches her and pulls a tablet from her robe.

"I'm here to inform you that after signing this, you will have officially inherited the estate of Myat Shin. That includes Myat Shin's home in Yangon, Myat Shin's seventeen fliers and four boats, Myat Shin's arsenal, and Myat Shin's accumulated wealth, which," Si raises her eyebrows as she meets Vedra's stunned look, "is considerable. Sign your name here, and the blue car will take you and your son to Myat's home, which is now your home."

"Why?" Vedra shouldn't question it, but the shock is too much. Si presses the tablet to her chest and sighs softly.

"This is what you get because you're Myat's spouse," she says.

"But-" Vedra stops and snaps her mouth closed. Si looks up into the bright sky, then back at Vedra.

"Let me tell you how I know you're Myat's spouse. Because my dear friend Myat, at great risk, sent me a message from an offworlder ship."

"The box..." says Vedra. "The box that Myat was talking into." The one that got her killed.

"This message said that you were Myat's spouse, from Earth, and you had lost your Identification chip and needed me to pull some strings with the Directorate to make sure you were recognized on Earth. And consequently, recognized by TEDI, who saved you.

"Of course, if it were anyone else except my dear friend Myat, who I once thought would be *my* spouse and who would never lie to me, I would have said that losing an Identification is technologically impossible. But I didn't say that."

"You're saying... you know I'm not..." Si grips Vedra's arm.

"Just go," Si says. "You've been saved. In Myat's honor, I couldn't possibly try to stop you."

"And no one else knows?"

"You're a citizen like any other. I'll make sure you get set up with a replacement Identification," says Si. She gets into the red car without looking back.

Vedra climbs into the blue car and pulls Temar closer to her.

"What are we going to do now, Mom?" he asks.

"I don't know." Then, seeing her fear echoed on her child's face, she straightens and slaps him on the back. "I'll figure it out," she says.

Vedra always figures it out.

Chapter Thirty-Three

THE WALLS ARE MELTING, decomposing into pools of color that make Lin's eyes ache. She tries to use her implant to call for Rajan, Emas, Sabohat, anyone, but instead, her actions cause a personnel file to flip open. Bogdan Lupescu, his new profile photo a clammy mask of death. Lin swallows and closes the file. She doesn't know where she is, can't remember how she got there, and can't see anything except walls that refuse to behave as solids.

She tries to move, or at least to feel where her body is, but now the liquid walls are spinning faster and faster. Lin closes her eyes to ward off dizziness, but the colors refuse to disappear. Bogdan's file opens again. And again, and again, an endless row of Bogdan, Bogdan, Bogdan stretching back into the spinning colors. She reaches out to the files with her arms, trying to brush them aside, and her arms are scorched and black.

The pain brings Lin back to reality.

Amidst the spinning and the colors and the endless face of her victim, a single point of pain in her core remains constant. It's real, Lin knows. The ache is her body, not another hallucination. She concentrates on the spot and works her way outward, acknowledging her hips, her shoulders, her face. Just like when Rajan touched her hands on that first day with her new implant, once Lin knows where her body is, it's surprisingly easy to turn the implant off and stop the vivid hallucinations it's creating. She relaxes in the comfort of darkness for a slow count of three, then opens her eyes.

She's still in the Jade and Pearl storage room, laying on the hard floor. She turns her head to the side. Rajan. She thinks for a panicked moment that he's dead, laid out on his back, but then she sees his chest twitch. She pushes herself onto her hands and knees, wincing against the renewed pain in her side, and crawls to him. His eyes behind his eyelids twitch wildly—she can only imagine that he's suffering through the same kind of implant malfunction that she experienced. She runs a hand through his hair.

"Rajan," she whispers. He starts. She thinks she's getting through to him, but he starts to twitch and moan again. "Rajan, it's OK. It's not real." She takes his hands, and gradually, his breathing slows and his eyes flutter open.

"Lin," he says with a genuine smile. She wonders what horrors he was seeing while she stared into the eyes of her victim. Rajan's hands are warm on hers. "What happened?" he asks, sitting up and rubbing his eyes.

"I'm not sure," she says. "We walked into the back room of that Wonju spa, and suddenly... well, your implant was on the fritz too, right?" Rajan nods.

"I saw some crazy stuff. I thought it was real until I heard your voice." He smiles slightly, but Lin doesn't feel like smiling back this time.

"Why would that happen?" she asks. "It's like what happened when you first put my implant in. But I've learned to control it." Rajan looks thoughtful.

"I've heard that there's technology out there that could mess with any implants in the vicinity. I've never seen it before though. Didn't know if it was a real thing. But I know that I don't dare try to access my implant again."

"Same." Lin's mind races. She remembers Eunha from the spa aiming a scanner at her. Maybe she's calling the Directorate right now. But Rajan is only here because he was worried about her; she hates to think that she's dragged him into danger.

Lin stands and appraises the room. There are two doors on opposite walls. She goes to the one they came through, the one that leads back into the hallway to the spa, and pounds on it.

"Hey!" she yells. "Let us out of here!" But she's almost glad when no one responds. Whoever Eunha really is, she trapped them there on purpose.

Lin goes to the other door. Like the one into the spa, it's not a smart door. She tries to turn the doorknob. "It's locked," she says, unsurprised, but Rajan's jaw drops.

"We're trapped in here? Who would do that?"

"I don't know," says Lin.

"We might be able to call for help on Mindlink," says Rajan. "We just have to work up to using our implants bit by bit, like you did when you first came to me," he says. "Maybe I could send a quick message out without letting the implant fully take over again."

"I don't know," says Lin. The faulty implant feels like a parasite lurking in her mind, ready to devour her whole.

"I'm going to give it a try." Rajan closes his eyes and Lin can tell that he's concentrating. He sways forward, and Lin thinks the implant has taken over again, but then he straightens and says, "OK, I'm into my messages. Everything is working slowly, but if I focus, I think I might be able to open a message. How about you?"

"Same for me," says Lin. She isn't actually trying to get online. She'd rather hold onto her wits than access the outside world, and she'd rather deal with the situation the old-fashioned way than see Bogdan's dead face again. Was that his real corpse's face in his updated personnel file, or was it only a manifestation of her guilt?

"I think I can do this," says Rajan. "I have a waiting message. I'm going to try to access it."

When he opens his eyes, they're steel cold.

"It was you," he says. They stare at each other silently for several minutes.

"Why would you say that?" she asks measuredly.

"The news came out while we were unconscious. The bomber has been identified as one Yang Lin, a Rogovan who's been posing as a Hauser enforcer."

"I had nothing to do with the bomb," says Lin. Rajan's expression remains hard. He slowly stands, raising his arms in front of him like he thinks she might attack.

"It says you're Rogovan. Is that true?" He recognizes her silence as an answer. Lin takes a deep breath against the pain in her core, gathering strength, then she wipes all emotion from her voice.

"Listen, we have to get out of here. Let's just deal with that. Once we're free, you never have to talk to me again."

"Yeah right," he says. "For all I know, you're the one holding me here. You could have knocked me out right after we walked through the door."

Anger surges through Lin. "Is that right?" She backs up and does a running kick at the door. It splinters easily. She doubles over, holding her side in pain for a minute, then straightens back up.

Rajan looks impressed for a moment before he remembers that he hates her. Lin shakes her head.

"I don't think whoever put us in this room meant for us to stay here," she says. It was too easy to get out. Lin walks out the door, Rajan following close behind.

Her first impression is of endless brown. The ground is flat and muddy, with only a few spare clumps of dying grass gasping through. All of the buildings nearby are similar to the one they have just emerged from—small, brick, slumped with the weight of time. Surely this was a charming village at some point in history, but Lin doubts it has been maintained in this century. A bit farther out, she can see fallen ruins of a larger building. Farther still, too distant to clearly distinguish the details, she can see much taller, more modern buildings.

And there are people. A few who see Lin duck quickly into doorways, but she catches a glimpse. Thin, dusty faces with wary eyes. She struggles out of her crusty Directorate military jacket, crumpling it into a ball and tossing it in the dirt so it won't intimidate these guarded people. Her once-white undershirt makes the blood from her wound look brighter.

"Let's ask one of these people where we are," says Lin. Rajan shakes his head.

"I don't trust them," he says. "Let's head to the outside." He gestures at the ring of tall buildings in the distance. Lin starts to walk, while Rajan waits a few seconds, then jogs to catch up with her.

"Is this some kind of squatter village?" he asks. Lin shrugs, then realizes he expects her to know the answer.

"I've never seen anything like this," she says. Rajan's expression remains doubtful but Lin resists the urge to try to convince him to trust her. He'll believe what he was told to believe. That's what good citizens like Rajan do.

From inside one of the houses, voices rise in a melody that Lin had forgotten she ever knew. She learned the song when she was very small, maybe even when she was still on the ship from Rogov. The words are Japanese, a language she doesn't speak and rarely hears used on Earth.

Lin stops.

"What now?" says Rajan. Lin looks around at a handful of people going about their business in the muddy town, and she knows. She's been seeing their look her whole life. Everyone here is a colonist.

Lin looks at the contemptuous expression on Rajan's face and feels a rising fury. He thinks he's better than these people—than *her* people. He wants to go back to the safety of Big Three skyscrapers. Of course he does.

As she starts walking again, she sings along to the Japanese song, not caring that she doesn't understand the lyrics. Rajan sighs heavily, but Lin only sings louder.

The village is walled in. Lin doesn't realize it at first, because the wall doesn't look like a wall, or at least not all of it does. The windowless backs of buildings butt against each other with no space to pass through. Here and there, a small gap between buildings is spanned by an actual section of high wall.

"There's no way out," says Rajan.

"There has to be," says Lin.

They keep walking along the patchwork wall until they see a gate ahead. It's guarded on either side by people whom Lin recognizes immediately as fellow enforcers. As they approach, Lin hesitates. Both enforcers carry very large guns.

Rajan sees her slow.

"I thought you didn't do anything wrong," he says.

"I didn't," says Lin. "But if you can't figure that out, they certainly can't."

Seeing the enforcers up close makes Lin think her own nanotech is inadequate. Both men are almost a meter wide in the shoulders with bulging chests. Rajan hurries ahead of Lin.

"Excuse me," he says to the enforcers. "I need to catch the Hyperrail back to San Antonio. Can I get through here?" The boulder of a man on the right pushes his chest out.

"You a citizen?" he asks. "If so, you can enter this Hauser hotel behind us. Go out the other side, and you'll be able to hail a taxi there."

"Yes, yes I am. Are you equipped to check?" The enforcer nods slightly. "Perfect," says Rajan.

"Checks out," says the enforcer. "You're welcome to enter the hotel." He turns to Lin.

"Citizen?" he asks. Lin lifts her chin.

"Yes," she says, to which Rajan scoffs. The enforcer stares at Lin for a second, then shakes his head.

"Doesn't look that way," he says. "No citizenship detected."

"Well, arrest her!" says Rajan. "This is the offworlder who blew up the Directorate base." The second enforcer, silent until now, spits on the ground, then goes back to looking straight ahead.

"Don't worry," he says. "We're not letting her into the hotel."

"You're just going to let her walk away?" asks Rajan. His voice is unattractively high-pitched.

"I'm not going anywhere," says Lin. "They keep us trapped in this... camp, or whatever it is."

"Not true," says the first enforcer. "We don't care what you do, you just can't come into the hotel."

"And the hotel is the only way out, right?" says Lin. At this point, the second enforcer can't contain his smirk.

"No," he says. "There's a Wonju spa back the way you came. And Xinqi has a shopping center just across from here. You're welcome to try to get past their enforcers." Lin is livid.

"What's the purpose of this?" she demands. "What are you doing with these people?"

"The people can do whatever they want, and I won't try to stop them," the first enforcer says. "Unless they try to come through this gate right here." Both men laugh.

***

Lin doesn't allow herself to look back at Rajan as she heads back into the camp. Back to her own people. In a strange way, it frees her to think of herself as one of them. To stop pretending.

It's time to meet her fellow prisoners. Lin's eyes land on a young man sitting cross-legged on the ground. His long hair and smudged blue eyeliner remind her of Emas, but he's less scarred and less handsome. The man is thumbing an old-fashioned paper book, broken at the seam and crumbling. She wonders if he found it here and how long it had been abandoned before he brought it into the light.

"Hello," Lin says. The man looks up without surprise. His eyes travel down her body and she follows his gaze to the torn undershirt and dried blood, which she covers self-consciously with her arms. He smiles serenely.

"A new arrival, I see," he says.

"I am, yes," says Lin. "Can you tell me about this place? How did you get here?" The man's calm smile doesn't waver.

"The same way we all got here, I suppose. I was living my old life, and then the soldiers came and I was brought here." Lin's heart flutters.

"So you were abducted by the Directorate and ended up here? Have you seen a woman by the name of Sabohat Iskakova? Is she here as well?" The man cocks his head.

"Sabohat," he says, and Lin holds her breath, waiting. "Sarah, Shakanoush, Silkie, Sandwich. Why be concerned with our names from before?" he asks. "They don't matter here." He thumbs his book more rapidly. Lin sags. This is not the right person to talk to. She needs to find someone who knows what's going on. She keeps walking.

If Lin were looking at the camp through a blurred lens, the view would be idyllic. She sees children chasing each other in circles and a couple of old men chatting in front of a house. But she also sees their gaunt faces and tired eyes. An approaching woman struggles under the weight of two water jugs.

Lin waves to her.

"Excuse me," she says. "I'm new here. Is someone in charge?" The woman looks at her like she's crazy.

"In charge of what?" she asks. "We're all just trapped here."

"Are you Rogovan?" Lin guesses. If Sabohat is here, she would have tried to befriend her own kind first.

"How can you tell?" The woman laughs harshly. "Is it the fact I'm hauling water back to my starving children? Just like my parents did for me back on Rogov? Look how much things have improved!" She lowers her head and quickens her pace, and Lin doesn't try to follow her.

One of the quaint little buildings has a crude sign that appears recently painted with the word cafe. Through the door, Lin sees someone inside standing behind a counter. Just what she's looking for—an industrious type who has taken initiative and set up shop in the camp.

The moment she steps inside, a plate flies at her face. Lin dodges it easily and stares at the middle-aged man behind the counter.

"What was that for?" she asks as she steps out of the way of a second plate.

"Get out!" cries the man. Lin approaches the counter instead. He raises another plate, but she pulls it from his hand before he can throw it.

"Don't waste these," she says. "Don't you need them for the cafe?" The man crosses his arms.

"This cafe isn't for your kind," he says. For a moment Lin, accustomed to masquerading as Earth-born, assumes that he's accusing her of being an offworlder. Then she realizes it's the other way around. The man has the undeniable stature and mannerisms of a Rogovan. He thinks she's from Earth.

"I'm like you," Lin says. "I'm from Rogov." Almost true. The man glowers.

"You're not," he says. "Don't take me for a fool. This cafe is an estab-lishment for my homeworlders." Lin glances around. There's no food to be seen, and the tables and chairs have been heaped with dust for ages.

"I am—" she starts, but he has her figured out after all.

"You may be Rogovan," he says, "but you're not from Rogov. Who did you lose in the famines? Who did you hurt to earn your ride to a better place?" Lin doesn't know how to respond. She backs out of the cafe.

"Is everyone here crazy?" she asks no one in particular.

"It happens to the best of us," says a voice behind her. Lin spins. The man who addressed her is clearly from Britton, with bracelets around his wrists and the straight back of a military man. Blond hair, bronzed skin, and a spark in his eye.

Lin takes a step back before she can help herself.

"It might have something to do with the malfunctioning implants when we arrive. Or maybe it's just a way that some people deal with a situation they don't understand. But many of us," the man continues, "are un-fortunately still living in the here and now." He extends a hand. "Devon Strassman," he says. Lin goes to shake but he takes her hand and raises it to his lips.

"You're from Britton?" she says.

Devon laughs. "Easy to tell, is it? But I can't say the same for you."

"Well, I..." Lin hesitates for a moment, thinking of the last conversation. "I'm Rogovan," she says cautiously.

"Huh. I never would have guessed it," says Devon.

"So, Devon," asks Lin. "How do we get out of this place?"

"You're asking the right question," says Devon with a smile. "And I'm going to give you an answer. Follow me."

They walk together without saying anything else for a while. Lin feels nervous next to the strange man. She hasn't known many from Britton in her life, and honestly, she has the same stereotypes as her Earth-born friends. That they're all warriors who spend their lives fighting each other in pointless wars and remain tough and unpleasant when they come to Earth. The journey takes twenty years, and they're not happy when they get here.

She looks up at Devon again. He sees it.

"What are you thinking?" he asks, which makes her blush.

"Well, you have the bracelets of a warrior. You have to fight in a war to get those, right?" At least that's what the dramas and the old gossips say.

"That's right."

"And it takes twenty years to get here from Britton, but you don't look old enough," she finishes and cringes, hoping she hasn't offended the large man. Devon just shakes his head.

"Well, Lin, on Britton, we don't exactly have to finish up our advanced degree in military strategy before they send us off to fight," he says.

"How old were you when you went to war?"

Devon shrugs. "About twelve, in Earth years, I think. That's when the Sons of Graham recruited me. Later, the Nikula Family captured me and I fought for them. Those are the most famous armies on Britton, of course, but I ended up with a smaller faction after that. I was probably sixteen then, and that's when I had the blessing to find out about Earth." Unlike the woman with the water jugs, he doesn't seem sarcastic about calling it a blessing.

"You fought for more than one side?" Lin thinks about what it would be like to fight against the army you had grown up in. She's heard of the Sons of Graham and the Nikula Family before. Sabohat always said the Nikulas were nicer; Jul said that at least the Sons of Graham were honest, not a bunch of backstabbers.

"So which side was the right one?" she asks. Devon snorts. "I never knew! How could I? It always seemed to be changing."

They walk in silence for a few minutes, then he says, "At least here, it's clear. I'm grateful for that. They're wrong to do this to us, and I'll fight against them with a clear conscience." Lin looks at a skinny man sleeping on a doorstep and doesn't respond.

They stop in front of the ruined building that Lin noticed when she first arrived. It must have once been huge, and its walls still stand many times her height, but end jaggedly and open to the sky. Fallen bricks lay all around.

Stairs at the front of the building lead to a doorway impassable with rubble and weeds. Beside the doorway is a large rusted metal cross.

"It was a church," says Devon. "Let's go around back."

On the back wall of the church is another door, this one smaller. Lin follows Devon through. He slides a large rock aside, revealing a dark hole tunneled in the dirt. Lin's legs go weak and she sits down hard.

"Are you alright?" asks Devon. For some reason, Lin is finding it harder to draw a breath.

"I'm not going down there," she says, alarmed to hear tears behind her voice.

"Hey, it's OK," says Devon. "This part is narrow and a little scary, but there's a big room down there and it even has lights. It used to be a bomb shelter, we think."

"You don't understand," says Lin. "This is what they do. The Directorate. They have these places underground..." She wipes at her eyes, embarrassed at her reaction but unable to stop the visions of her last foray into a tunnel system. Devon crouches down and puts a hand tentatively on her back.

"I'm sorry," he says. "But there are some people down there that you'll want to talk to. Smart people with a plan." Lin nods and takes a couple of deep breaths. Her pulse begins to slow.

"OK," she says. "Let's go." Devon helps her off the ground. Then he sits and slides into the hole. Lin hesitates for one last minute and does the same.

She slides on a dusty chute for a few meters before landing on a brick floor. Her eyes adjust enough to see a door with a white crank that Devon spins, and it swings open to let the light spill out. Lin barely has time to register the rounded metal walls and small group of people standing inside before someone flies into her arms.

"Lin! Darling!" Lin squeezes the familiar warmth of Sabohat's body in disbelief. She doesn't dare speak for fear the moment will disappear like the hallucinations of a malfunctioning implant.

"You're alive," she finally whispers.

"Of course I'm alive," says Sabohat. "I'm impossible to get rid of. But sweetheart, why are you here? How did they find you out?"

"How do you think?" asks Lin, a note of anger creeping into her voice. She wants to savor the joy of finding her mother again, but the question annoys her. "I was following through with your plan. Planting the device that you made. Trying to help the Rogovans. I don't even know if it worked." Sabohat holds Lin's face in both hands and looks her in the eyes.

"You really did it? Oh, I'm so proud of you. It did work, mostly. Details are hard to come by here, but we know that many of the Rogovans made it through. They were saved, thanks to you."

"But, Mom." Lin glances around, not sure what she should say in front of Devon and the six strangers in the room. All are watching her intently. "Something happened. I planted the device, and then a bomb went off. They said it was a Rogovan bomb. They blamed it on me. Now everyone knows my name and thinks I'm a terrorist. But the bomb wasn't mine. Right? The device you made for me had nothing to do with the explosion." Sabohat's face falls, and she sinks into a chair.

"Oh, darling," she says. "I'm so sorry."

"For what?"

"You're right, the device I made for you was harmless. But I think I made the bomb as well."

"What?"

"Lin, I'm new to this place myself. Some of the others have been here for months, but when I was first taken, they brought me somewhere else. I was kept by myself, locked in a room with a desk. I don't know who told the Directorate about me—maybe one of our friends or neighbors who was taken in the past—but they knew who I was. They knew my specialty, that I'm the best with weapons and that I know Rogovan technology. That's what they told me to do—make them a bomb that was undeniably Rogovan."

Lin sways slightly. She twists at her blood-crusted clothes while her mouth works with the appropriate response to Sabohat.

"Why did you agree to it?"

"What else could I do? Somehow they knew I had a daughter. They said they would kill you."

"You almost killed me yourself!" Sabohat rubs her hands along her face.

"I'm so sorry, Lin. I had no idea. But tell me, did it at least take some of those Directorate pigs out too?"

Bogdan's glazed face, splashed with blood, flashes in Lin's mind. But of course, he was Lin's victim, not Sabohat's.

"How can you say that? How can you be happy that you killed people?" demands Lin. Sabohat's steely expression doesn't waver. "And now I'm here! You almost killed me, and then because of you, here I am, wherever this is. Accused of being a traitor."

"Don't speak to me like that," Sabohat says angrily. "I didn't bring you here, they did. They used you for their own purpose and then dumped you here when you were no longer useful, just like they did to me."

"Who are they? Who put us here?"

"Them, them. I don't know who they are. Somebody who has a use for us. Does it matter who they are this time? It's always somebody."

"I don't know what you're talking about, Mom." Lin massages her head, desperately wanting to access her implant to find some answers.

An older man steps forward.

"What your mother is getting at, Lin, is that some of us have developed a theory. The soldiers don't take us from our homes to get rid of us or to protect Earth's resources like they always say. They do it because they have some purpose for us and they can simply take us if they want us. When they have a need, they come and get some offworlders. They can get away with it because no corporation will stand up for us."

"They had a use for me," says Sabohat. "Make the bomb. Some of the others here were used for other purposes as well—factory work in some cases or skilled labor in others. And they used you as their scapegoat. And now we're all being held here because they have some other use for us, but we don't know what."

"Sorry to break up the family reunion," interjects Devon. "But we have business."

"Devon told me you have a plan," Lin says to the group.

"I'll show it to you," says Devon. He walks to the back of the room and grabs a handle at the bottom of the wall. The entire wall slides upward to reveal a tunnel, carved in rock. Lin groans.

"Not another tunnel," she says. "Why is it always tunnels?" But she goes to this new tunnel and peers down it. Even with her enhanced night vision, she can't see where it goes.

"Is this part of the bomb shelter," she asks, "or the church?"

"Neither, as far as we can tell," says Sabohat. "There's a whole network of tunnels out there, and they're old. Hundreds of years older than the church. Maybe a thousand years old, even. Several parts were collapsed, but we've been working on clearing the way."

"You're planning to escape," says Lin. She's skeptical. "Are you sure these aren't Directorate tunnels? Did they really drop us here without knowing about this?"

"Many European cities had a network of tunnels below them," says the old man who spoke before. "We think it's unsurprising that the Directorate didn't bother to search every inch of the place before they imprisoned us here."

"Maybe," says Lin. "But where will you go? Won't they just round you up again?"

"We haven't finished clearing the tunnels," says Sabohat, "but we opened a space big enough for one person to get through. She reports that the tunnel extends outside the town and opens into a field. If we can arrange transport from there, we'll be free.

"But how will you arrange transport?" asks Lin.

"That's my job," says one of the men, and Lin's breath catches. She knows that voice. The man is middle-aged, barrel-chested, and clearly Rogovan.

"You're the one who was talking to me," Lin says. "The one from the slip of paper under Mom's desk." The mystery man just smiles slightly. "But how is that possible? I thought that implants don't work here."

"Senji's implant is somehow still functional every now and then," says Devon. "He's been reaching out to a few people to find out what's happening on the outside."

"That's why he talked to you," says Sabohat. "He was looking for information. I wasn't here yet then or he would have told you."

"Somehow, I'll get us out of here," says that distinctive voice.

Lin frowns. She's happy there's a plan in the works, but the risk seems very high.

"Yang Lin," says a woman. No, a girl. The speaker can't be older than fifteen. "I'm Nadya." The girl with Lin's old name smiles shyly. "I want to thank you for what you did. You saved so many of us. Not everyone, I know." Here she glances at Senji. "But many."

Lin takes in the whole crowd for the first time. Other than Sabohat, Senji, and the girl, there's two old men. One is the man who spoke to Lin earlier, the other is taller and more stooped. Both are most likely from Britton. She also sees a younger couple who look almost Earth-born, but the woman turns to the man and whispers something in Anglian, the bizarre twisted English of space stations and mining colonies. They're all giving her that look, like they expect help from her.

They always do.

Lin keeps her face expressionless.

"How long until the tunnel is ready?" she asks.

"Three more days," says Devon.

Chapter
Thirty-Four

WHEN CORMAND SMITH SPEAKS, everyone listens.

Cenric, slumped on the couch of his Denver home, flips through the news feeds glumly. In the days since the explosion at Urutu, he hasn't been able to reclaim his spirit for fighting injustice. He can't even work up a normal level of annoyance at his father.

"In the name of keeping all citizens safe, the Committee on Immigration will temporarily be managing the production of the following Xinqi, Wonju, and Hauser manufacturing facilities…" Cormand is saying on the news. It doesn't make any sense. Manufacturing plants have nothing to do with offworlder threats, and that should make Cenric angry. But he doesn't really care.

He flips through a few current events talk shows. Here and there, someone is wary of Cormand's motives, but mostly they're rallying against Rogov and the other colonies. They report on the protests worldwide and the full-blown riots in Chicago and Kinshasa. The people are angry that aliens have been allowed to live among them, that the Big Three and the Directorate haven't rid their neighborhoods of offworlders. It's what Cenric has been saying all along, but it doesn't excite him like it should.

In his listless state, it takes Cenric several minutes to notice the call buzzing his neural implant. Mohammed Al-Jabber. Cenric can't recall a time Mo has called him without Arthur's intervention, so he answers the call. Mo's official avatar looks at him coolly. Cenric just blinks back.

"How are you doing, Cenric?" asks Mo.

"You don't care," says Cenric. "What are you calling about?"

"I'm just wrapping up the paperwork for the James Lyon investigation," says Mo. "I guess it's no surprise to anyone that Rogovans were behind his murder now, given what happened at the Directorate base."

"I was there, you know," says Cenric.

"Yes, I know you're the one who found Lyon. Anyway, I need to return the items that we had as evidence now that the investigation is over. There are a couple files that he designated with your name, so they're yours now. I'm going to send them to you. We never ended up looking at them—it's just work stuff, I'm sure."

"I'm not sure," says Cenric. "Something strange is happening." Mo sighs.

"Just let me send it to you, Cenric. Don't make it difficult. I'm just trying to tick a box here."

The files arrive on Cenric's neural implant. There are two. The first is one he tried to open in Lyon's office as the man's corpse was cooling. The other gives him passcodes which—in addition to his Identification—are needed to open the first file. Cenric enters the passcodes and finds a recorded message.

He catches his breath at the sight of Lyon's face. With his eyes closed, it's just like he's sitting across the desk from his old friend. James Lyon is ducked low, speaking quietly.

"Cenric, I've uncovered something incredible. Something dangerous, and I need help. I feel, somehow, that I can trust you with it. It hardly seems like a smart choice, given who and what you are, but I know underneath all the posturing, you want to do what's right for all of us. And ironically, despite all your ties, you're not a part of the establishment. Or at least, less so than the rest of us, which isn't saying much." Virtual Lyon laughs, a little sadly.

"Did you know I had a brother? Of course you didn't. He was in the military. The Directorate military. See, I'm connected, too. His name was William, and he was Special Operations. I don't know that you even know about Special Ops, unless your father told you, but they go out among alien civilizations—colonists, criminals, the asteroid militia, you name it—and spy." Cenric remembers the alien paraphernalia in Lyon's office.

"Something happened to Will out there. I guess it happens to a lot of Special Ops people, although no one really talks about it. He started to sympathize. Not with any particular cause, just with the people." Cenric pushes aside thoughts of Yang Lin in a pool of blood.

"Well, he was wrong to sympathize. They killed him. The offworlders found him out and..." Lyon's jaw works, like he is going to say more, but he doesn't.

"Anyway, Cenric, the point is that I leapt at the opportunity to bring justice... no, revenge, against offworlders. I was eager to use my Global Oversight position to look into colonist organizations here on Earth.

"But then everything changed. You may remember that there were a couple incidents last year attributed to offworlder violence, almost always Rogovan. And they used technology that didn't come from this world. Maybe it was really Rogovan, maybe not. The point is, through my investigations, I realized that it wasn't offworlders doing these things. Not all of them, anyway. Someone on the inside is doing this."

"The inside?" Cenric asks Lyon, forgetting for a moment that the man is dead and not really talking to Cenric.

"All roads lead back to the Big Three, maybe even the Directorate," says Lyon, as if answering Cenric's question. "But Cenric..." Here his face is taut with fear. "In my investigations, before I realized what was happening, I think I tipped them off. Someone's after me. I'm recording this message just in case... Well, anyway, we have to work fast to figure out what's going on. I still don't have any idea who's behind this."

Cenric has a dark feeling he does.

***

"It wasn't Rogovans, was it?" asks Cenric. They sit in Cormand's mansion, sipping tea. Cormand was a bit surprised when Cenric invited himself for a visit, but if he's unhappy about it, he isn't letting on. He asks Cenric how he's managing at his new finance job, now that Bao Ding's team is no more, but Cenric has no time for small talk.

"It was you," he says to his father. "You did all this so you could take control of all three corporations. You killed James Lyon." His tea cup shakes. He sets it down carefully. He's been trembling since Urutu, shuddering since he got the file from Lyon. But for his plan to work, for everything to be put right, he has to remain steady.

"You do always get straight down to business," Cormand says with his obnoxiously charismatic smile.

"Well, was it Rogovans or not?"

"It was a Rogovan bomb that destroyed the base," says Cormand, still smiling. "It was Rogovan poison that killed Lyon and the Wonju representatives."

"But it was you who arranged it."

"A technicality!" says Cormand. "Remember what I've been telling you. It's all about people. How can we protect them from the alien threat if they've stopped feeling threatened? We have to remind them."

"I've been trying to protect the people."

"By doing what? Looking for offworlders one at a time? Let me tell you what I've done for the people. I've given them a mindset. I've taught them who to fear. Now, it's not just me alone, trying to fight the offworlders. The whole world will do it with me. I did a lot of good for only a few casualties."

"But you lied to them. You faked the Rogovan attack. Yang Lin didn't even plant that bomb and now you have everyone looking for her." Cenric doesn't mention his own part in bringing the Directorate down on Yang Lin.

"Yang Lin?" Cormand asks, seemingly confused. "Oh, right, the girl. I have to give you credit, Cenric, you did help us out with that one. Arden called me and let me know that you were on about some Rogovan girl who was a Hauser enforcer. He thought maybe you were high on the patches again." Cormand laughs while Cenric fumes. "But we were able to follow it all up with our own intelligence and turn it into something useful."

"So what now?" asks Cenric. His father has no idea what kind of chaos he's created. Now the entire Big Three will be acting on false information, with no way of knowing what's wrong and what's right. It's the stuff of Cenric's nightmares.

"Now you're asking the right question," says Cormand. "As you know, Cenric, my committee is running things for now. And that needed to happen. You're always on about the law, Cenric, but the Big Three created a system of laws that keeps the Directorate in power indefinitely, no matter how many poor choices they make, and it's time to change that."

"So your committee will be in charge of everyone now. You will be."

"We already are. At first it will just be temporary, because we're the experts on Rogovan attacks and the people will want experts to rely on, and so on. But eventually we'll establish a permanent organization."

"An organization? You mean a new corporation?" asks Cenric, stunned by the shine of excitement in Cormand's eyes.

"No. Something more like the old governments. Something with real authority. And Cenric... this is what the people want and need."

Cenric closes his eyes. "Tell me something," he says without opening them. "Was it also you who arranged to send the message to everyone's implants? I've never experienced that—everyone hearing a broadcast at the same time without even opening a message or a news feed."

"Yes, yes. That was me as well." Cenric suddenly worries that Cormand has played his hand too easily.

"Why are you admitting all this to me?" Cormand laughs.

"Why wouldn't I? You're my son. And also, what do you think you can do to me? If you repeat this to anyone, at best, they'll write it off as family drama. At worst, they'll think you're power hungry. And for all your flaws, boy, I know you're not after my Directorate seat. So what would you have to gain?"

"You're right," says Cenric. "I don't want to take your place. Tell me how you managed to send that message."

"I'll show you!" says Cormand. He disappears into the mansion hallways and returns carrying a flat black object. He flips it open to reveal a screen. It looks something like a very ancient computer, but without a keyboard. Across the screen is a series of numbers—a contact number for an implant, and as Cenric watches, the numbers change.

"That's all there is to it," says Cormand with a childish giggle. "Send a message to the current number, and it will go to every citizen. I had a Rogovan man make it for me—they really are skilled! Why do you ask, do you want to send something?" Cenric shakes his head. Cormand's face turns somber.

"Cenric, son, I know I've been hard on you. But you're my number one, my only offspring, and there's no one else I want by my side to bring the world into a new era. There's a place for you. Forget about Hauser. We are going to be the future."

Cenric looks at his father a long time. His portly face, his cheerful smile, the decades of power behind his eyes.

Cenric finally feels the drive for justice boil inside of him again.

Chapter
Thirty-Five

LIN RIPS OFF A tough bite of stale bread, shuddering at its sour taste. Twice each day the residents of the camp gather by the church to share the food that's been foraged. It mostly comes from restaurants and bakeries along the wall that throw their leftovers out back. Apparently, someone found a box full of ration packs and nutrition bars a few days ago. It might not delight the taste buds or keep anyone at full strength, but somehow there's always food.

Lin thinks it's suspicious that they're being fed. Sabohat agrees—it fits with her theory that they're being kept for some purpose. The camp residents are all hungry, but they've willingly pooled their food in a pile to share. One man holds a young girl, about four years old, thin, fragile, listless. Lin takes the least bruised fruit from the collection and hands it to her.

The weather is brisk, and Lin has retrieved her Directorate jacket to keep warm. Everyone knows who she is now, anyway. As she's helping pass out food, Lin hears Sabohat speaking.

"Three more days for them to discover the tunnel. Three more days for them to decide we're too much of a risk. That she's too much of a risk."

Lin follows her mother's voice around the church. Sabohat is arguing with one of the women Lin met when she arrived, the Anglian speaker.

"They won't do that," says the woman. "We're as good as dead here, so what do they care? Hurting us more than they already have would be a waste of resources." Sabohat kneads her back and looks up at the sky.

"Tallah, dear. Never underestimate what the powerful will do to stay powerful," she says.

"Ugh. You and your words of wisdom." Tallah scowls. "You have an adage for every occasion. Never trust another with what you can do yourself, those raised on harsher rations can starve longer... Blah blah blah. We've been living this miserable existence as long as you have. Listen to someone else for a change." Lin coughs, and Tallah looks at her sharply.

"You'll help us, won't you? We're leaving in three days, and we'll need people with your skills if we're all going to survive."

"We're not all going to survive," mutters Sabohat, and Tallah turns to glare at her. "Come on Lin," says Sabohat. "Let's go on a walk together."

"A walk?" asks Lin. It's obvious to her that Sabohat is in more physical pain than usual. She tries not to show it, but Lin recognizes the way her mother winces with each step.

"It's important," says Sabohat.

"OK," says Lin doubtfully. She offers her arm and Sabohat clutches her elbow and limps as she tugs Lin along. They walk down a winding path. It was probably a cobblestone road once, but now only a few pieces of that old boulevard stick through the mud. The buildings in this part of the camp are even more dilapidated than elsewhere, and Lin doesn't see any other people.

"Where are we going?" asks Lin.

"You'll see," says Sabohat, huffing as she heaves her body along without her cane. "It's something I found. No one else knows."

"What were you arguing about with Tallah?" Lin asks. "It sounded like you thought the escape plan was a bad idea."

"Of course it's a bad idea," says Sabohat. "It's a terrible idea. But what choice do we have, stay here and die?"

"So what was the argument?"

Sabohat lurches along a little more angrily. "We're ready to go now," she says. "Clearing a few more rocks isn't that important. Why spend even three more days planning and waiting and rehashing every part of the plan?"

"I thought Senji needed to arrange transport."

"It's a pipe dream," she says with a laugh. "His implant barely works and he doesn't know who to contact, anyway." Lin knows better than anyone how hard it is to have a conversation with Senji from outside the camp. And no one else's implant works at all. Remembering Rajan's success opening a message, Lin has tried to access hers, but she loses control every time. "No," says Sabohat. "We should go now, Senji's plan be damned."

"Does it matter?" asks Lin. "If the people have survived here this long, they'll be OK for a few more days."

"Will they?" says Sabohat bitterly. She stops and takes a moment to grimace and rub her hip before turning to Lin. "A week ago, these people were nothing. The Directorate and the corporations didn't care if they lived or died. Maybe they were brought here for a purpose, maybe just to starve."

Suddenly, Lin gets it, and it makes her stomach turn.

"But now..." she says.

"They have me," says Sabohat. "And I know that you didn't make the bomb, because I did, and I did it for them."

"And they have me," says Lin. "I know the truth too. And I'm public enemy number one. So..." She can hardly say the next part.

"They'll need you dead," says Sabohat. "The people believe that you attacked Earth citizens, and the Directorate will need to show them your corpse." They walk in silence. They're out beyond the remains of the old village now, where the buildings are sparse, and Lin can see that they're getting closer to another stretch of wall, which means there will be more enforcers. Wonju? Xinqi? If she came face to face with Kirs guarding the entrance of a Hauser hotel, would her friend smile? If Lin tried to shove past her, would Kirs shoot a hole in Lin's chest like Lin shot in Bogdan's?

"We need to do this strategically," Lin says. As an enforcer, this is the sort of thing she knows about; she can be helpful. "First of all, it sounds like everyone is planning to rush the tunnel at the same time. That's a bad plan. A few scouts should go ahead to make sure it's safe, and a few of us should stay behind until the end. Those in the front and the back can have the weapons."

A handful of very old guns, slow to load and awkward to shoot, had been found in the bomb shelter. Again, Lin and Sabohat found their presence more suspicious than the others did.

Sabohat gives her a long sideways look. "We think alike, Lin. Sometimes, we do."

They're approaching the wall.

"Hey, Mom, is Mr. Tomasy here? Have you heard anything from him?" Sabohat shakes her head. "I haven't heard anything about him. There's no way to know. Is this where they dump everyone eventually? I think it can't be. Too many people have been taken over the years who aren't here. Maybe there are other camps. Or maybe they're making him build bombs, like I did. Who knows what useful skills Tomasy may have had?"

They're close to the wall, but there's no building, no exit with Kirs waiting for her. Just a brick wall.

A brick wall with a hole in it.

Lin stares at the spot where the bricks have crumbled into a heap, leaving a jagged opening about a half meter wide. Creeping Terratech vines, ever-aggressive, reach their searching fingers in from the outside. Lin drops to her knees in front of the hole. Her view is mostly obscured by thick brush, but she can make out a street in the distance.

"We could get out this way?" Lin asks her mother.

"Not the group," says Sabohat. "I climbed through the hole myself a few days back and almost got caught within minutes. The people out there look like regular folks, but they're on patrol. If all of us just sprint out of here in plain sight, we won't make it a block. That's why we need the tunnel to take us farther outside the city."

"So, we'll go by ourselves?" Lin doesn't like the idea of abandoning the rest of the group.

"You can make it easily enough. Get far away from the wall before you stop anywhere or talk to anybody." Lin rises slowly, her mother's plan finally dawning on her.

"You're not coming."

"This is my fight. You don't have to fight it. I never wanted you to. I'm fighting it for you, so you don't have to. And, Lin, to have the strength for the fight, I need to know that you're safe."

"They'll kill me," she says. "You said yourself that they need to."

"You're smarter and faster than that and you know it."

"I won't get far," says Lin. "They've taken my citizenship away." Sabohat smirks.

"Citizenship is overrated," she says, and Lin has to smile too. "I got by for years without it. You'll do even better, with your accent and your height and your..." She waves a hand at Lin in an understood gesture of the intangible. "Get yourself some cosmetic altercations and live your life."

"Why haven't you told anyone else about this?" Lin asks. "Maybe not everyone could escape at once, but someone could go for help."

"I don't trust them," says Sabohat.

"Why not? My whole life you told me not to trust Earth-born citizens," says Lin. "But these people are offworlders, like us. Who can you trust if not them?" Sabohat shakes her head.

"Yes, they are a bit like us, and I do trust them more than citizens because they know us a bit. They've been through the same things. But Lin, you can't trust anyone like you can trust yourself."

"I can't go without you," says Lin.

"You can. You will," says Sabohat.

Lin looks at the hole again and swallows. If she crawls through that small brick opening, she might find anything on the other side. She could start a new life. She could be gunned down within minutes.

"OK, I'll go," she says. "I'll get myself to safety so you don't have to worry." Sabohat sags with relief, a wide smile on her face. Lin returns the smile and draws her mother into her arms, pressing back tears.

"Take care of yourself," says Sabohat, her voice thick.

"You too, Mom." Lin gives one last squeeze, then turns to the hole. The jagged edges of the opening scrape her wound painfully as she pulls herself through on elbows and knees.

She needs to get far enough away that she can use her implant. Then she'll make a plan to save Sabohat and everyone else in the camp.

***

Lin crouches behind the row of bushes outside the wall. The Terratech here has grown into thick brush with broad leaves and green berries that tickle Lin's ears as she peers through a small gap in the stalks.

In the hour and a half since she crawled through the wall, she's learned three things. The first is that the same people pass by in rotation, sometimes going one way and sometimes the other. There's a man selling snacks out of an egg-shaped bot that follows him closely, a woman jogging, and a couple carrying what Lin suspects isn't a real baby. Despite these obvious actors, she's almost certain that the town is real. Vehicles drive down the streets carrying blank-faced passengers who see only Mindlink. Lin has noticed a couple of carrier drones flying overhead, and although she squeezed herself farther into the bush to avoid detection, they seem to be carrying only food and consumer items.

The second thing Lin has learned is that she still can't access her implant without losing touch with reality. She needs to get farther away from the camp. She now understands the purpose of the long hallway from the Wonju spa to the storage room—the spa is outside of the zone where implants malfunction.

The third lesson learned has to do with the lay of the land. After she squeezed through the hole, Lin turned right and followed the wall until the row of vegetation ended in a bush sculpted perfectly round about one hundred meters behind a bakery. The discovery of the bakery was distracting. Lin smelled its warm aroma and for the first time realized that behind the ever-present gnawing of her wound, she was desperately hungry, but she couldn't exactly walk into the bakery with her blood-caked Directorate uniform and news feed-famous face.

So she followed the bushes in the other direction, still crawling low to the ground, rocks and fallen pieces of brick digging into her knees. And now, finally, she has her escape route in sight. Here, the row of bushes fades into scraggly clumps that push their way through heaps of metal shards. She's on the edge of some kind of scrapyard. Lin sees rusted-out vehicles, broken Cleanerbots, and even a huge console that she imagines might come from a spaceship. All of this rubble lies between her brushy hiding spot and a large, drab, gray building.

Most importantly, there are trucks. They rumble and clank as they come and go from the building, beds piled high with scrap metal. The trucks have no drivers, and she can't see anyone guarding the facility, so if she could slip into the back of a truck, she could ride it away from the people who patrol the camp. Hop off when she finds a good place to lay low and access her implant. But a tall fence, topped with barbwire, separates her from the road that the trucks use. Warning signs on the fence display bolts of lightning, indicating what will happen to her if she tries to climb over.

She scans the scrapyard again. She can only see one option for getting over the fence. On the side of the building, there's a ladder, its bottom rung about three meters off the ground. The top reaches the roof of the building. If she could climb the ladder to the roof, she'd have a clear view of the trucks below. A long way to jump, especially onto jagged scrap, and especially while injured. But there's no other option.

As Lin watches, a different type of vehicle emerges from the other side of the building. It's also autonomous and even larger than the trucks. It has a massive plow that gathers scrap from the yard and pushes it back around the corner, out of Lin's sight.

She assesses the area. No drones overhead, no humans to be seen. She can't be sure that there aren't cameras, but it's a chance she'll have to take. She breaks out of the bushes and runs for the ladder, one hand pressed to her injured side as she leaps over piles of junk. She makes it without incident. Now for the hard part. With Lin's enhanced strength, jumping to catch the bottom rung of the ladder and pulling herself up shouldn't be a problem. But the short dash across the yard has pulled on her wound and she feels warm blood seep through to her hand. She takes a deep breath and leaps for the rung.

The first time she tries, the pain flares and she misses. The second time, she holds tight and lets out an involuntary cry as her abdominal muscles stretch. But she doesn't let go. With a groan, she walks her feet up the wall, pulling herself fully onto the ladder.

She only allows herself a few seconds to catch her breath before continuing to climb. As she hauls herself onto the flat, brick roof, she half expects to see Directorate soldiers or enforcers waiting for her, laughing at her for daring to believe she could outsmart them. But the roof is empty.

Lin crawls to the far edge, ducking low to avoid being seen from the ground. Now that she has a bird's-eye view, she can see the city's outer limits. It's not a large town. The ancient, crumbling architecture gives way to rolling farm fields not far away from where Lin crouches. As she watches, one of the junkyard trucks winds down the road, eventually disappearing over a hill outside the boundaries of the city.

Lin turns away from the edge of the building to survey her surroundings. The roof is mostly flat and nondescript, save for one boxy structure with a single metal door. Lin walks to it. The door looks like it may have had writing on it at one time, but weather and rust have obscured the words. Lin fingers the door handle, hesitating. It's probably locked. It could even be equipped with an alarm. Or it could provide a way down to the trucks. As she's considering her options, she hears a buzz near her ear. A drone. Lin grabs for it, but it zips away from her. She's not sure if it's a news drone, a military drone, or some kind of security for this facility, but she has to assume that she's just been reported to someone. She turns the handle. The door sticks, so she pushes hard.

It bursts open and she barely stops herself from falling forward through a gaping hole. The structure was masking an opening in the roof that allows her to see into the interior of the building. A conveyor belt runs directly beneath the opening, ferrying heaps of metal toward the trucks outside. Lin hurries to the roof's edge to confirm that the conveyor belt is dumping its load directly into the truck beds. She returns to the opening, peering down. It's a four-meter drop. If she times it right, she can land on the belt between the piles of scrap.

She waits, watching the rhythm of the conveyor. When a gap appears, she leaps. The landing knocks the breath from her lungs, but she stays upright, staggering to maintain her balance on the moving belt. Just as she steadies herself, lights flash red and a blaring alarm echoes through the building. The conveyor lurches to a halt, throwing her forward onto her hands and knees. It's now or never.

Lin pushes herself to her feet and sprints along the belt toward the truck loading zone. One of the trucks is just starting to pull away, and she doesn't hesitate. Lin leaps, landing hard among the scrap with a metallic crash. Pain reverberates throughout her body, but she manages to lift a long, flat metal sheet and slide under it, hiding herself from the searching eyes of drones. From under the scrap, she sees the junkyard fade from view.

As the truck rumbles along, Lin closes her eyes, the exhaustion of everything that's happened to her since Urutu settling in. For just one moment, tucked in her rattling, metallic bed, she lets herself imagine following Sabohat's instructions. Riding the truck into the distance, far away from the strange camp and the disguised guards and any responsibility to help the refugees. She could live in the shadows, just as Sabohat and her friends always have. Lin has spent her life as a witness to such an existence. She knows that even though life would be hard, it could also be comfortable and even happy. She lets herself imagine this safe and mundane future for no more than five deep breaths before she starts planning again.

She pushes herself into a sitting position, holding the sheet of metal over her head to block drones but giving herself a view out the back of the truck. The town is already fading into the distance. On either side of the road are fields of waving grain. She can see an autonomous tractor felling the grain to her right, but no people anywhere.

After a few minutes, the vegetation changes and Lin finds herself surrounded by a breathtaking array of purple, yellow, and orange flowers. In this Terratech paradise, she finally sees what she's looking for. A greenhouse, and beside it, a small garden shed. Lin leaps from the truck, rolling as she falls onto the dirt road. She quickly gets to her feet and looks around. Not a human or a drone in sight.

Lin walks through the flowers toward the shed, slowly trailing her hands along the stems. The vibrant meadow feels so magical that she's not even surprised when the shed is unlocked. It's empty except for several rows of hand tools hanging on the wall. Lin takes a long serrated knife off of its hook. From the dirt still crusted on the blade, she can tell that it's been used to cut soil. Lin wonders what kind of person does this work by hand, and silently thanks them as she cleans the knife off on her jacket. Then, clutching the knife in her hand, she lowers herself to the dusty ground, moaning as she leans her aching body against the wall, and accesses her implant.

Chapter Thirty-Six

VEDRA IS LIVING THE life she would have always dreamed about, had she known enough to dream about it.

She dangles her foot in the pool. Her pool. Before coming to Earth, she had never seen so much water, never known how so much of it poured together could reflect the light like a gigantic mirror. A huge bowl of water for a person to swim across. Thinking of Uli turns Vedra's mood sour. She gets up and goes back inside her castle.

The castle is just a home, apparently, like the women's room of the compound or her bunk on Ghiraz station. But Vedra feels wrong calling it that, as if it isn't four stories tall, as if it didn't have more wealth within its four walls than Ghiraz and Emberaz and the compound combined. So she thinks of it as a castle.

Temar is on the second floor, leaping and flailing like a fool, large goggles on his head. He's playing a game. The house came with tons of them, which makes Vedra wonder: Did Myat ever have a child? Apparently, not one still living, since Vedra inherited the house. Did she dream of having a child? Or were the games all her own? Vedra tried to imagine how Myat occupied this place—where she sat, which of many windows she stood at to watch the sun rise triumphantly over the horizon. Vedra can't imagine it. It turns out she didn't know Myat very well at all.

She fantasizes sometimes that Myat isn't actually dead. Vedra only saw her fall to the ground. She didn't check her pulse, didn't feel her skin go cold. But if Myat had survived, if she had been riding in one of the other shuttles, she would be back by now.

Temar yells a command and leaps into the air. He's learned all this in only four days. She imagines someday soon he'll want one of those things in his head so he can play the game without the goggles, without vocalization. Vedra understands now what an implant is. She's been doing research of her own. She still doesn't like the idea of something stuck in her head, reading her thoughts, affecting her vision, but she wants Temar to have one if that's what the Earth kids have. She has an earpiece herself, a shiny blue thing that loops behind her ear so people can talk to her. Sometimes they seem to forget that she can't see them too.

"Xinqi will give you a new implant, free of charge," they told her when they gave her the earpiece and the house and the flier that she still can't fly and the warehouse full of other contraptions she's never seen before.

"I'll make sure to arrange that right away," Vedra said.

***

So far, only one person has clocked her identity. It happened soon after she arrived, when she was on a morning walk.

Vedra is used to making breakfast in the morning, but the castle kitchen has a contraption that can make all types of food by itself, with no help from Vedra and her years of experience preparing meals for others. All she has to do is say the code number for the item she wants into her earpiece. The person who gave her the house and the implant and the fliers said that the food maker was pre-programmed with custom favorites by the previous owner. Vedra can't remember the codes, so she chooses dishes at random, imagining that it's what Myat ate the last time she was here.

So one morning, not knowing what to do with her ample morning time, she went for a walk. Still amazed by the sheer scope of this world, she stood on a street corner and spun in a slow circle. From this one spot, she could see hundreds, maybe thousands of people, none of them bothering to look up and marvel at the open sky and looming yellow sun.

"Are you the one who lives at 6 Orchid Place now?" said a woman. Vedra jumped.

"Are you talking to me?" she asked. The woman was shorter than Vedra, with a cherubic face and pretty eyes framed by brunette curls. She smiled at Vedra, who smiled back but also looked around in confusion.

"I am!" said the brunette. "My name is Jeri. If you do live at 6 Orchid Place, I thought we might meet up for a drink sometime. I know you're new here, and I thought you might like a friend." She smiled again. She really did have pretty eyes.

"Sure," said Vedra. "That would be nice. I'm Vedra Ols."

"Can I get your implant number?" asked Jeri.

"Oh, right. I don't have one of those," said Vedra. She pulled the earpiece out. "I have this." Jeri looked at it.

"It says your number on the side," she said.

"I guess so," said Vedra. Jeri looked into her eyes for a moment.

"Welcome to the neighborhood," she said. In Anglian.

Chapter Thirty-Seven

"I THINK IF WE use this moment right, awareness will finally grow."

"Are you kidding? It's a disaster. Any outreach efforts are pointless after the bombing."

"Don't you see? This is the perfect time! They know about our cause now. They see us. We have to build on this."

"They hate us. They think we're terrorists. In my neighborhood people are going around painting 'death to Rogovans' and 'alien scum' on the windows and doors of any establishment they don't trust. Almost all of them are actually citizen-owned!"

"We are terrorists." A swell of murmured conversation fills the colonist virtual room. It ends abruptly when the members notice, belatedly, that Lin has joined.

"Yang Lin," breathes the silver-haired moderator. The colonists' virtual room looks the same as it has always looked, of course, and as far as Lin can tell, the discourse hasn't changed much either. "We're so honored that you've joined us." The others are quick to agree.

"Tell us, Yang Lin," says an avatar she hasn't seen before, a speckled red sphere. "Do you think that your action will bring about long-term change?" Everyone starts talking at once again.

"I think," says Lin loudly, and the crowd hushes. "That I need some help and I need it now."

"Of course!" says the moderator brightly. "What can we do?"

"There are over two-hundred colonists being held in some sort of camp here. An unofficial prison. I'm going to get them out of there, but I need your help. They need vehicles to escape the area. They need places to hide. Weapons would help if anyone has them. Even a bit of food would help—many of them are not in great health." Lin pulls up a map that hovers in the air above her avatar. "This map displays the general area where the camp is located. Work with me to figure out how to get supplies here. If you know anyone who knows anyone or even if you have any ideas, let me know."

The room falls completely silent. Lin sighs.

"Well? Let's start with this: does anyone live near here?" No one says anything.

"Bart?" says a female voice finally. "You're in Europe, right? You could get there in a vehicle overnight. If you have access to one."

"I could," says another voice that must belong to Bart. "There are a lot of cabs around here that don't check citizenship." He doesn't continue.

"Well?" says the female voice.

"Well... how would that help? I don't have any weapons except a few kitchen knives. I couldn't fit more than a couple of people from the camp in the cab with me. And that's assuming the cab accepted them at all. Plus, they can't stay at my apartment right now. My sister is sick."

"Fine," says Lin. "Anyone else in the area? Or who can get here?"

"I have a forged Hyperrail pass on my implant," says a woman, the one who was talking about awareness when Lin first joined. "I could get there."

"Fantastic," says Lin. "And if you can ride the Hyperrail, you could pick up supplies from other people who have them." Another silence.

"I'm sorry," says the woman. "I don't think I can do that. It's just too dangerous."

"OK," says Lin, trying to keep a level tone. "Anyone else?" A few of the avatars blink away, abandoning the conversation. "Got it," says Lin. "You want to spread awareness. You want to build citizen connections and take advantage of our moment, et cetera. What does that even mean? There are real refugees who are about to die, and none of you are willing to risk anything." She knows she's probably losing her audience, but she can't believe that for all their organizing and their talk and their secret codes, the group is so useless.

Finally, in the silence, one voice speaks up.

"I might know someone who could help. She just arrived, and she has a lot of planes."

Chapter
Thirty-Eight

VEDRA SITS ON AN armchair in her castle, clutching her earpiece in her hands, almost afraid to put it in and disrupt the peace she's found here. Jeri dropped by an hour ago and told her that she would be getting a call from someone who wants her help. But Vedra doesn't want to get involved, not so soon after escaping multiple fiery deaths.

The earpiece buzzes in her hand. She takes a breath and puts it in.

"Vedra Ols?" a voice asks. Without an earpiece, Vedra can't see Yang Lin, but Jeri showed her a picture. A "wanted" photo from the news. So Vedra imagines the woman from that image standing in front of her. She pictures Lin as strong and tough like Myat, but with an angrier glint in her eyes, like someone who's tired of getting the short end of the stick. Like Aria and the other kids she grew up with, like the Rogovans on the ship, like Vedra herself. She likes Lin already, just from the picture and what Jeri told her. But she can't be too friendly. She can't get involved.

"I'm Vedra," says Vedra. "What do you want?"

Lin tells Vedra about the camp and the escape plan the refugees have concocted.

"Tunnels? Food that shows up from nowhere? Weapons? It's too suspicious," says Vedra.

"I know!" says Lin. "It's some kind of trap. I just can't figure out what the point of it is."

"But they're still going to try to escape, even knowing it's a trap? Why?" But Vedra answers her own question with a soft laugh before Lin can respond. "Because they have no other choice. I understand."

"Jeri told me you were on the Rogovan ship," says Lin.

"Yes," says Vedra.

"There's a man in the camp, Nakamura Senji. He's been waiting for his brother, the ship's captain, but the last time he was able to get an update, it didn't sound good. Do you know anything about him?"

"Nakamura... Senji?" The captain was Nakamura Yusuke. Unexpectedly, Vedra feels a lump in her throat. Though she never liked the captain, she imagines his brother here on this lonely planet, waiting for his arrival, not knowing that the captain is nothing but space dust now. "I'm afraid you're right. The news isn't good."

"How did you end up on the Rogovan ship anyway?" asks Lin.

"It's a long story," says Vedra. "I caught a ride at the last minute." She pauses, meaning to stop there, but this is the first time an open ear has been offered to her, and she can't resist. Vedra launches into her tale of escaping the burning compound. Her voice catches when she tells Lin about Myat coming to her rescue and little Uli on the shuttle. Then Lin tells Vedra about her mother and the bomb that wasn't a bomb.

"Wow," says Vedra. "So that guy Javi was a spy all along? Earth is really a dangerous place, isn't it?"

They talk like old friends long into the night. Vedra curls in the armchair, closing her eyes as she tells Lin about everything from her childhood to her castle's food-maker. Finally, after their voices and stories have warmed and they're laughing together, Lin turns the conversation back to the refugee camp.

"They need your help, Vedra. Something bad is going to happen, and people are going to die." Vedra doesn't want to think about death and lives lost anymore. She's fatigued with it, and now she has a brand-new life.

"Find someone else," she says. "I've had enough battles."

"Vedra," says Lin. "Listen to me. I understand how you feel. You shouldn't have to save all of these people. I shouldn't have to save all of these people. It shouldn't have to be our job. We should be able to live our lives as happily and obliviously as Earth-born Big Three citizens. But without us... they're going to die."

Vedra sighs. She really does hate to hear about these refugees suffering under the Empire. Now she can hear the desperation growing in Lin's voice. "Nakamura Yusuke helped you. Where would you be without him? Why not help his brother?"

Vedra thinks about that. Where would she be without Nakamura? She would be peacefully dead, floating through space on Myat's junker with her, having never betrayed her. Screw what Nakamura wanted. He wanted Myat dead. But Myat wanted... Vedra thinks of Myat's endless attempts to help her. She gave her life, selflessly. Like a chump.

"Damnit," Vedra says. "I guess I have to help."

Chapter Thirty-Nine

By the time the first beam of light reaches under the door of the garden shed, Lin is ready. Her wound is already feeling better, thanks to the nanobots coursing through her blood. In her hand, she still clutches the garden knife. Around her shoulders is a shawl of thin fabric, also taken from the supplies in the shed.

Lin knows she has to find a way back to the camp without being seen. She'll be no good to anyone if she's caught before she can get back to her mother and the others. She slides the shed door open a crack to make sure the coast is clear, then heads back through the field of flowers. At the edge of the road, she crouches down, letting the tall, swaying blossoms hide her as she watches for a ride going in the right direction. Lin hopes to catch one of the trucks returning to the scrapyard, but after long hours of waiting, she hasn't seen a single one. Very few vehicles seem to pass this way at all.

Lin feels rejuvenated by her few hours of sleep on the floor of the dark shed and even more so by her conversation with Vedra. She hadn't known how much she needed to talk to someone who didn't judge her for being too alien or not alien enough. In her own way, Vedra is straddling the same worlds that Lin always has. Her reluctance to fight also mirrors Lin's. Now they'll both have to step up.

Her enhanced hearing picks up the sound of tires on gravel in the distance. She leans a little farther out of the plants and sees an autonomous taxi approaching. Not the best option, but it will have to do. Lin tucks the garden knife into her belt and sprints for the car as it approaches, hoping by some miracle that it's not carrying a passenger. She stands in the road, throws the landscaping fabric over her face, and flings her arms wide. She can see through the thin weave of the fabric, but the car's facial recognition will be too confused to match her appearance to that of the wanted terrorist. The taxi swerves right, trying to avoid the obstacle in its path, but Lin lunges to obstruct it. It tries going left, and she does the same. Its autonomous system won't let it crash into her.

The taxi has almost slowed to a complete stop to avoid hitting her, and Lin can see now that there's a passenger in the back. It's an old man, and he appears to be asleep. She can only hope he stays that way. Lin steps aside just enough to let the car go by her. It's moving slowly enough that she can toss off her fabric disguise, hop onto the car's rear bumper, and wrap her hands around the smooth chrome roof rails before it accelerates again.

Lin isn't sure if the taxi's sensors will notice a stowaway on the back of the car, but it's a risk she has to take. Thankfully, the old man is still snoring in the back seat of the taxi, his head nestled in the flab of his neck and his mouth hanging open.

As she bumps along the country road, her hair whipping around her face and her knuckles white on the roof rails, she tries to call Nakamura Senji on Mindlink. He isn't answering. She hears a rising rumble behind her and carefully turns her head as far as she dares. Two vehicles are coming up behind her. Military vehicles from the look of the large tires, small windows, and armored exterior. The taxi hugs one side of the road to let the larger vehicles pass, and Lin buries her face in her arm. Directorate soldiers won't be as easily fooled as the taxi's AI.

She holds her breath, waiting for the vehicles to slow or for someone to start firing at her, but the armored trucks blow by the taxi, leaving her choking on dust. When she raises her head again, Lin is surprised to see several drones flying behind the military vehicles. They look like news drones. None of it makes sense to Lin, but it's clear that whatever the Directorate has planned for the refugees has already started. She calls Vedra over Mindlink and puts their plan in motion.

***

A few minutes later, Lin is bumping along the worn city roads, her hands on the roof rails starting to cramp. The morning is fresh and bright and the town's early risers are already out and about. A few people stop to stare at the woman clinging to the back of a taxi and she hears someone shout behind her, but she's not worried about keeping a low profile anymore.

She recognizes the bakery she saw the day before, and jumps off the back of the car, running past the line of people waiting for warm baked goods. She hears more yelling but doesn't turn to see whether it comes from surprised locals or guards hot on her tail. She takes a hard right at the wall and runs beside it, her side wound starting to burn again, until she finds the hole. As she drops to her knees to squeeze back through the bricks, she hears gunfire ahead. She races toward the center of the camp, unsheathing the knife from her belt as she runs. A news drone drops down near her head and flies alongside her. Lin looks at it without comprehension. Why is the media here, in this secret place?

The first corpse she comes across is the father who had been holding his little girl. His arms are now empty, the girl gone to better or worse times. Lin slows and looks around. There are other bodies. Some are Directorate soldiers, but most are colonists.

Ahead of her, she sees a soldier using a crumbling wall as a barricade. He raises his rifle, aiming at someone out of her view. He's not looking her way and she barrels straight into him, wresting the gun from his hands. To her surprise, she can fire the smart weapon despite not being authorized, and she does. The soldier joins the fallen on the ground.

Lin continues toward the center of the camp. Behind a small, abandoned building, three Directorate soldiers without firearms are scuffling with Devon, who fights with a knife in each hand. He seems to be winning. A couple of news drones hover nearby. Lin dispatches the soldiers with her stolen gun, and Devon raises a hand in greeting.

"Is my mother safe?" she asks him.

"I don't know where she is," he says. "But a big group made it into the tunnel right as the Directorate soldiers showed up. She might have been with them." A shot from a nearby window just barely misses Lin and Devon's feet, and they dive around the side of the building.

"Why haven't they just blown the place up?" she calls to Devon as she returns fire. "The Directorate certainly has the firepower to destroy us in one blast." Devon laughs and indicates the drones.

"We're a show," he says. "Think about how it looks." And then Lin realizes how they'll spin it. Aliens ruthlessly attacking law-abiding Directorate troops. Citizens watching the fight on their feeds won't know that the colonists were imprisoned here before the battle started or that the Directorate shot first. They'll just see the enemies of the Big Three, proving once again that they're violent criminals. Lin takes down two more approaching soldiers, then fires at one of the news drones for good measure.

"We have to get everyone else into the tunnel," she says. "I've arranged for transport to get them out of here."

"The Directorates are guarding the church now," says Devon. "But I bet we can take them."

"Let's go," says Lin, and they take off running.

Small skirmishes have broken out everywhere. The Directorate soldiers should have been able to make quick work of the colonists, but they're sorely lacking in numbers and weapons. And wherever a colonist manages to get the upper hand, a news drone is there to witness it. Lin feels a brief pang for the soldiers who gave their lives for this charade. Then she takes down another one. She tosses the garden knife to one of the older Britton men. He seems to know what to do with it.

Lin and Devon are joined by Nadya and a young man named Jon. Both have procured Directorate smart guns. These guns are designed to be authorized to specific soldiers' implants and to refuse to fire in enemy hands, yet Jon and Nadya's guns shoot as readily as Lin's stolen weapon. As much as Lin wants to believe they've acquired the guns because they're winning the fight, she thinks it must be part of the Directorate's plan to maximize the violence and bloodshed—to put on a good show. The four of them manage to drive the remaining Directorate soldiers, their numbers falling—as was surely the intention—away from the church door. A few refugees take the opportunity to run through.

"Look," says Devon, pointing off in the distance. A familiar figure is stumping her way towards them. Unbelievably, she's propping up a much taller wounded man. Lin concentrates on picking off any soldiers who approach her mother, but at this point, they're few and far between and seem loath to come too close. As Sabohat passes through the church door, Devon instructs Jon to take the wounded man into the tunnel.

Now only Devon, Lin, and Nadya remain. Nadya's wide eyes and trembling lips make her look even younger than she is, but she holds her gun steady as the three of them wait, silent and tense, to take down any soldiers trying to enter the church. No one does. Lin finally allows herself a weak smile.

"Our turn?" she says.

"Let's go," Devon says with a nod. He leads the way, followed by Nadya and then Lin, who keeps a vigilant eye behind them. They slide down the dark passage into the church, run through the bomb shelter, and enter the tunnel.

"The others have probably already made it to the other side," says Nadya. "Will the transport wait for us?"

"Better if it doesn't," says Lin.

Lin feels a buzzing in her mind. She ignores it, thinking her implant is trying to misbehave again. The second time she feels it, she realizes it's a real call. Moll Mackenzie is contacting her. For a brief moment, Lin thinks that Moll has come to help her. Then she remembers that Moll, like all of her former colleagues, is the enemy now.

"Are you behind this?" Lin asks Moll. She's blocking Moll's avatar, but she can still hear the smirk in Moll's voice.

"I took command of this operation because I'm an expert on the terrorist leader. You." Devon notices that Lin is suddenly distracted and slows. Lin waves at him to keep going and she does her best to keep up the pace despite Moll's voice in her head. "I'm not calling the shots, though. If I were, I wouldn't accept your surrender. However, I've been informed that it's an option. I hope you don't take it. People like you don't deserve our mercy."

"How can you believe that I would bomb the base?" asks Lin. "You know me. You liked me, I think." At least as much as Moll Mackenzie likes anyone. "You know I wouldn't do this."

"It doesn't matter," says Moll.

"It doesn't?" Lin is falling noticeably behind Devon now. Maybe that's Moll's intention. "Why are you doing this if you don't know whether I'm the terrorist?"

"Do you know how old I am, Yang Lin?" Lin waits for Moll to tell her.

"Two hundred and eighty," says Moll. "I've replaced a lot more parts than you know. Do you understand what that means?"

"You remember a time before the corporations," says Lin, fascinated in spite of herself.

"It means that I remember when everyone was struggling. It was hard, but it was also an incredible time to be alive. We were all in it together, fighting to pull the Earth up out of the dark years. Almost all of us. But then some despicable, rich pigs just took off for the colonies. You don't think the friends and family I lost back then would have rather have gone to Rogov than stayed at home and starved? And now, everywhere you look, people are talking about the poor, poor, Rogovans. Now we're supposed to believe that you deserve the best of everything when you didn't die for it. We did! That's why I agreed to help cut you down." Lin has almost come to a stop now.

"What do you mean, you agreed?" she asks. "Are you saying that this wasn't an order from the Directorate? Who asked you to do this?"

"A friend," says Moll. "Who sees things my way. I couldn't be happier to join the cause."

Five meters ahead of the group, the tunnel suddenly collapses. Lin screams so loud she hurts her own ears. Devon just barely grabs Nadya in time to pull her back from the falling rubble.

"There's the bomb you were wondering about, Lin," he says.

"What have you done?" Lin asks Moll Mackenzie from her implant.

"Oh, are you still alive?" Moll asks with mock disappointment.

"Look," says Nadya, pointing upward, where the explosion has opened a hole to the street above.

"There might be soldiers up there," says Lin.

"Maybe," says Devon. "But we're close to the end of the tunnel. If we climb out here, we'll stand a chance of making it to the transport. Anyway, the only other option is going back to the church, and we can't do that." Lin hears footsteps approaching through the tunnel.

"More soldiers are coming," she says. "Do you think you can climb out?" They all crane their necks upward.

"Maybe," says Nadya.

"Go," says Lin. "Both of you. I'll hold them off." Devon starts to protest, but she waves him away. Devon and Nadya begin to climb until they're almost out of sight. The footsteps draw closer. It sounds like only a few people, probably a couple of remaining soldiers from the camp. Lin has the advantage. Bogdan's face appears in her mind.

Her murder targets are almost there.

Who will it be this time, Boyu? Kirs?

The soldiers round the corner. Lin lowers her gun.

Chapter Forty

THE SINGLE WORD SPOKEN in Vedra's earpiece is loud and direct.

"NOW." Vedra relays the message to Jeri, and in a matter of minutes, a truck pulls up to her castle and three people leap out. Two of them are tall young men. The other one waves cheerfully. It's Jeri.

"You're one of the pilots?" Vedra asks. She's reminded of Myat, but of happy memories, not the usual sad ones. Jeri salutes.

"Sure am."

"You said you have three passenger planes ready for use," says one of the male pilots.

"That's what I'm told!" says Vedra.

"Where are they? We need to move quickly."

"I wouldn't know one if I saw one," says Vedra. "But everything I own is in these garages." She starts to follow the three pilots into the first garage. The other man stops and turns to her.

"We can take it from here," he says. "We'll do our best to return the planes in top condition."

"No chance," says Vedra. "I said I would help rescue these people, and that's what I'm going to do."

"You can ride with me," says Jeri. "I might even let you fly." Vedra grins. Life on Earth might be more fun than she thought.

The planes are similar to the flier she and Myat commandeered to escape the compound, but longer and without any noticeable wear and tear. She sits beside Jeri in the cockpit as the plane soars into the sky with a smooth grace that takes Vedra's breath away. For a moment, she can see her castle below. Then they're gliding over a massive patchwork of colors and shapes like Vedra has never seen. She leans her forehead against the side window and marvels at the fact that people live in every little structure they pass.

She's so mesmerized by the journey that she almost forgets its purpose until Jeri says, "There!" The plane is circling an open field. In the center of the field is the brick outline of a building long since crumbled. And inside the building footprint is a hole in the ground. "That's where they'll be," says Jeri.

"What about those guys?" asks Vedra. Two figures in red—Directorate soldiers, Vedra knows—are standing near the hole. Jeri pulls a lever and suddenly bullets are raining down on the soldiers. They fall in a heap of red uniforms and blood.

"I guess that should do it," says Vedra.

The moment the three planes touch down in the field, a stream of people pours from the building footprint. Some are wounded and bleeding. Some are shouting in triumph, others crying. One woman holds a small girl, even younger than Temar. Jeri presses a button, and a ramp drops down from the side of the plane. Vedra rushes from the cockpit and leans out the door above the ramp.

"Come on! Faster!" she yells at the refugees while she scans the area for more Directorate soldiers. But the field is empty except for the planes and the refugees. As the colonists run up the ramp and push by her, Vedra looks for her friend Lin but doesn't see her entering any of the planes.

"We have a couple more coming!" calls Jeri, and Vedra eagerly looks up, but the two figures bounding across the field from the direction of the town are a tall blond man and a teenage girl. "Mike says there are more

Directorate soldiers coming," says Jeri. "Time to go!" Vedra takes one last look at the tunnel opening, then steps back as the plane door closes.

*****

Vedra arrives back at her castle with a heart still pounding and her face still stuck in a wide grin. The smile fades as she enters the house. The dark silence feels too full.

She fumbles for the light switch, momentarily forgetting how to turn the lights on with her voice.

"Temar?" she calls shakily as the lights come on.

"He's sleeping soundly." Vedra jumps at the sound of the voice. A figure, dressed in a red military uniform, emerges from the next room.

"Myat," Vedra exhales. Myat looks different than Vedra has ever seen her, with newly cropped hair and the straight, pressed uniform. But there's no doubt that it's Myat. Vedra throws herself into Myat's arms and Myat holds her tightly, pressing her face into Vedra's hair. "I thought you were dead."

"I thought the same about you, at first," says Myat, gently pulling out of the embrace. "When our shuttle landed, we heard that Nakamura's had been destroyed. I thought for sure... but I had to report back to my employer right away. I couldn't check on you."

"You're going to want your castle back," says Vedra, and Myat's expression, solemn until now, cracks into a laugh.

"Castle?" Vedra blushes.

"Your house, I mean. And all of your things. I'm very grateful to you for letting me live here for a while, but I can figure something else out. I understand it here now, a little bit." Myat shakes her head.

"You don't have to leave. I'm going away again. For a long time. The Directorate—that's who I work for, if you haven't figured that out by now—is sending me far away. I'm lucky to be able to keep my position at all after how the last mission turned out, with Fenton Ols's compound destroyed and most of the Rogovans making it through to Earth. They know that I... sympathized where I wasn't supposed to. So the Directorate will keep me on the roster, but send me to some backwater where I can't make trouble." She smiles. "Maybe Pluto."

The word Directorate reminds Vedra of her role in Myat's fate and a weight settles in her stomach.

"I'm sorry," she says. "I didn't understand anything. I heard the word Dongshihui—I know what the Directorate is now, in all the languages—and I only knew it was bad for people like me. If I'd had any idea what Nakamura—"

She's cut off by Myat's lips pressing into hers. She leans into the kiss, letting it warm her. Myat pulls away again.

"You don't have to apologize, Vedra. And you don't owe me anything. I made you my legal spouse so that you'd be safe here, but now that you're a citizen, we can dissolve that if you want. You can still stay at the house, regardless of... what we are. If that's what you want." Vedra runs her fingers lightly along Myat's collarbone.

"We'll talk about it when you get back," she says.

Chapter Forty-One

CORMAND SMITH IS HEADED back to Mars in the morning. Everyone important is back on Mars or on their way to Mars or making an intentional show of being too busy for Mars.

Not Cenric. He's still a member of the Congress, as he's dreamed of being all his life, but the pride in that membership died on the floor of Urutu alongside a dozen Directorate soldiers.

Last week, a video shown on every news feed showed Rogovans and other colonists waging violent battle against the Directorate army. And she was there, fighting beside a brutal man with knives. The ghost of Yang Lin. There was a moment when she looked right at him. He knows she was looking at the news drone, but she seemed to see him, and her face had no anger, no fear, only confusion.

And that's why he can't stomach the thought of going to Mars. Of standing by the statue of his ancestors and seeing what has become of what they built. He'll be surrounded by the people who run the world. But how will he know, as he talks to the VP of this or the executive director of that, if they speak the truth?

When he first saw the video of the offworlders fighting the Directorate soldiers, it fueled the old anger. The aliens were slaughtering law-abiding Directorate military men and women, gutting them with knives like savages. Ripping guns from their hands to turn against them. They were cruel. They were evil.

But was it real?

The Urutu bombing wasn't real, so how could he be sure about this? Cenric spent a full day in bed, staring at the ceiling while his insides curdled in rage and uncertainty. In the end, all he could see was the look on Yang Lin's face. Not cruel, not evil. Perplexed.

Because she didn't know why she was fighting, and why it was being filmed. But Cenric knows. The injustice of it all makes him ache for a patch of shav, but he can't lose focus now.

He will make things right. He has prepared for this. He will put things back on track, get things back to a time when good was good and criminals were criminals. When he didn't have this dark fear in the pit of his stomach.

***

Cormand's colossal mansion sits on a grassy hill surrounded by smaller homes. It's a town in its own right, with a creek that winds between the houses and fruit trees that serve up derivatives of Terratech unavailable anywhere else.

All the residents of the town work for Cormand. Technically, they work for Hauser, but Cormand has had them transferred here to maintain the grounds of his estate and do his bidding. Some of them have worked here since childhood. It's peaceful here, not like Cenric's own neighborhood, which has fallen into rioting and violence since the manufactured war first aired on the feeds.

"Two visits in a month! This must be a first," says Cormand when Cenric appears at his door. His usual genial smile doesn't entirely hide his annoyance. "You could have just called me, you know. I've got to get some sleep before I head to the Congress."

"I know," says Cenric. "It's important." He pushes past Cormand without being invited in.

"What's this about? Have you gotten into trouble again?"

"I've made a decision." He sits in one of Cormand's armchairs. Cormand reluctantly sits across from him.

"This should be good," he says.

"It is good," says Cenric. "I've decided to agree to your offer."

"My... what?"

"You said that I could be a part of your new organization."

"Of course you will be. I didn't think it was up for debate."

"Well, I would like to sign a contract."

"A... For god's sake, Cenric, we're family."

"I want an official agreement. Lots of people will want to be a part of your new group. You might change your mind."

"Fine, fine, I'll draw you up a standard contract. Officially, you'll still be Hauser, but you'll be named as a part of the Committee on Immigration. Later, when the organization becomes permanent, we'll make a new contract. If you still feel it's necessary."

"I need to read over the contract first," Cenric says. "Please send it to me." Cormand sighs and a file buzzes against Cenric's mind. He doesn't open it. "Okay," he says, "I'm taking a look. Some tea would really help me concentrate if you don't mind." Cormand's mouth falls open.

"You want me to make you some tea," he repeats.

"Yes. I'll leave as soon as I get through the document. And have some tea," Cenric says. Cormand shrugs, shakes his head, and leaves the room.

As soon as he's gone, Cenric stands and strides silently in the other direction to Cormand's bedroom. He rifles through drawers and tosses open the closet in search of the device that broadcasts into every citizen's implant. There's no safe as far as he can tell, and he knows that Cormand retrieved the device from this room. It must be hidden in plain sight.

Finally, he finds it under the pillow. Cormand sleeps with the device that gives him this power, like a child with a toy. Cenric flips it open and contacts the number on the screen.

He leaves the house with his head held high. When he gets to the streets of Cormand's little town, he breaks into a jog. It could be the end of him if he's not off of Cormand's property fast enough, but the pure elation in his soul prevents him from feeling any panic. He's just made it off the property when the audio recording starts playing in his mind. In every citizen's mind.

"It was a Rogovan bomb that destroyed the base," the recording begins. "It was Rogovan poison that killed Lyon and the Wonju representatives."

"But it was you who arranged it."

"A technicality."

Chapter Forty-Two

THERE'S PEACE BETWEEN THE four white walls of Lin's prison cell.

The walls are the edge of the world. Lin has been cut off from Mindlink and everyone she knows. No one speaks into her mind. No one speaks to her in person.

In the blankness of her cell, with her mind cut down to its natural size, she finds it easier to purge her thoughts of questions. She knows that Sabohat made it to the tunnel. She knows that most of the Rogovans made it to Earth.

She doesn't ask herself if it was worth it. She doesn't ask herself what's next for her or anyone she knows. Lin is aware that letting even the taste of those thoughts through could overwhelm her.

Her days have a rhythm. In the morning, a small opening appears in the wall of her cell, and a tray of food slides through it. Lin takes the food, and the wall becomes whole again. She eats the food, savoring the flavors only, not thinking about where it came from. Next, she does exercises. Without access to her implant, Lin's favorite games and simulations are gone. She finds a thrill in working out disconnected. She listens to her breathing, feels the sweat on her face.

Even this small peace doesn't last. After what she believes to be several weeks, a new opening appears in the wall, a dark cavern bigger than the one that offers her food. Lin stares into it. Her eyes have adjusted to the blinding light of her cell, and she can't see what's in the opening. More food?

Instead, a woman enters. She's middle-aged, with owl eyes and a face that leans too far forward. Her shoes click on the floor of Lin's cell. Lin squares her shoulders. This is it. The woman will tell Lin her fate. Death, almost certainly. She can't imagine otherwise.

She doesn't ask the woman what will be done with her, she only waits.

"Yang Lin," says the woman with a slight dip of her owly head. "It's an honor to meet you." Lin doesn't let her expression change.

"Who are you?" she asks.

"I'm Park Hosook," says the woman. "Representative to the Directorate from Wonju. Will you follow me?" Lin sees no reason to protest. She follows Park Hosook into the dark cavern, which her readjusting eyes reveal as a long white hallway. Lin thinks it's odd that the hallway has no doors, windows, or decoration, just a row of numbers. 87, 88, 89. Then it occurs to her that behind the seemingly smooth walls are cells like hers. Who is trapped behind them—criminals? Offworlders? She almost asks Park what this place is but decides she'd rather not know. Down another hallway, they stop in front of a part of the smooth wall labeled "Private." A flicker of Park Hosook's eyes and the wall slides apart. Behind it is not another cell, but a large room with a round table. At the table are two other people. One is a handsome man with a long dark ponytail, the other an older woman with glinting earrings and a tall mohawk. They both rise from their chairs, smiling, and bow slightly as Lin is ushered in by Park Hosook.

"Would you like a drink of water?" asks the man. Lin shakes her head.

"Thank you for joining us," says the woman with the mohawk. "Please, have a seat." Lin sits without saying anything. All three of them look at each other.

"Hosook has introduced herself, I'm sure," says the woman, as they take their seats. "I'm Bettis Ryan, Representative to the Directorate from

Hauser. And this is Di Wei, Representative to the Directorate from Xinqi."
They're all three smiling warmly at her, but Lin knows that attention from
three Directorate representatives can't be a good thing.

"What are you going to do to me?" she finally asks. The representatives
just glance at each other and smile wider.

"It's more about what we are going to do *for* you," Di Wei says. "First, I
want you to listen to something. This was heard by every citizen across the
Big Three." A voice fills the room.

"It was a Rogovan bomb that destroyed the base. It was Rogovan poison
that killed Lyon and the Wonju representatives." Lin bristles in protest, but
Bettis Ryan holds out a hand to silence her.

"But it was you who arranged it." Lin is so awash with anger at the sound
of "Javi" speaking that it takes a moment to register what he is saying. She
listens incredulously as the first voice affably admits to framing her and
killing colonists and citizens alike, all in the name of a power grab.

"Who is that?" she demands.

"It doesn't matter," says Park Hosook. "We'll deal with him."

"So you know that none of this was caused by me. Does that mean I'm
free to go?" asks Lin. She doesn't believe it for a minute.

"Of course, of course," says Di Wei. "But we hope you won't leave us
quite yet!" Lin narrows her eyes.

"Why is that?" she asks. Di Wei opens his mouth, but Park Hosook
jumps right in.

"Did you know that Wonju is the leader in defense systems?" she asks,
continuing before the others can interrupt. "As our share in this market
grows, we'll need people who can lead strategically. Like you."

"Lead what?" Lin is reeling from the sudden change in tack.

"I'd like to offer you a position overseeing the sales team for our largest
line of enforcement equipment. You obviously know how to connect with
people, you know all about weapons, and you're a self-starter."

"You want to offer me citizenship in Wonju?"

"Oh, not just citizenship. If you accept our offer—"

"You're Xinqi born and raised," Di Wei interrupts, then colors a bit. "Well, not born... anyway, the point is, you're one of our own, and we don't just want you overseeing boring sales and inventory counts. We'll have you training new recruits, recruiting, basically leading your own army, if you'd like to think of it that way. And honestly, don't let anyone tell you otherwise—Xinqi compensation is the best."

"Why would you give that to me?"

"Why wouldn't we? The whole world has seen video evidence of your leadership and passion. And the comments are in on the news feeds—the people like you! They sympathize with you! They're waiting to see what happens to you. We can recruit enforcers from anywhere, but it's rare to find someone who can step up like you did, not to mention someone with your popularity. We've already seen you work with the ragtag group in the video—now work with the best." Having said his piece, Di Wei leans back with a self-satisfied smile.

"You should be insulted by these offers," says Bettis Ryan. "Who cares that you were raised Xinqi? You chose Hauser and Hauser chose you. And Hauser loves you. Take any one of the positions we're reserving for you, and I think," she says this like a conspiratorial whisper, but loud enough for everyone to hear it clearly, "that you'll be a lock for Directorate Representative within ten years." Lin doesn't hear anything after that, although the bickering and interrupting continues. She thinks for a minute, imagining climbing the ranks of the Big Three. Going back to Mars. She closes her eyes and takes a deep breath, then turns to the Xinqi Representative.

"Could I have my old restaurant job back?" she asks.

***

Lin is taken to the Hyperrail station in a car with tinted windows that won't allow her implant to lock on its location. When she steps out of the car, she finds that she's in Istanbul. She immediately reaches out to Sabohat and is flooded with joy to see the silver star appear in front of her.

"Where are you?" she yells, forgetting to speak without speaking. "Are you still by the camp? I can come and get you. Are you alright? Are you in any trouble?"

"No, no trouble, and no need to launch a rescue mission. I'm back in Beijing." Lin is stunned.

"Really?"

Sabohat laughs. "What, do you think I haven't moved in all these weeks you've been away? I have many friends. I'm back in Beijing already."

"Of course you are," says Lin. "OK, I'm on my way."

"Come to Jul's," says Sabohat. "We're all here."

"What do you mean? Who's there?"

"You'll see."

Two hours later she's there too. She can hear the boisterous voices before she even knocks on the door. "I'm here," she tells Sabohat on her implant, not really wanting to walk into the fray. The door flies open and Sabohat rushes into her arms. She holds her mother close, closing her eyes and ignoring the commotion. Then she opens her eyes. She's surrounded by a throng of offworlders, none of whom she recognizes, all of whom are yelling questions at her.

"How did you escape?" shouts a man.

"Are they after you?" says a woman.

"What do you think our next move should be?"

"Does this mean something has changed in the Big Three?"

"They let me go," says Lin, and the talking swells too loudly for her to say anything else.

"It turns out that a subset of the Directorate did this," she says when she can be heard again. She explains about the man in the recording and how he fanned the flames of hate to increase his own power. Some of the offworlders seem to have heard about the situation already, while others are completely out of touch with Earth events.

Sabohat places her fingers in an obscene Rogovan gesture.

"That's what it was for? They killed their own kind, locked us away and made us fight for our lives, and framed you for their crime just to gain a little more power? When they already have so much? It's so trivial." Lin can't disagree. Despite her claims to understand Earth culture, she's having trouble with this one herself.

As the evening goes on, most of the group clears out. Only a few regulars are left—Jul, Kaori, and the other women who frequent Sabohat's kitchen. Then the door opens and Emas Day steps in. He runs to Lin and embraces her, lifting her off the ground.

"I thought you were dead," he says. "I thought I had killed you."

The small group pulls chairs together, passes beer in a circle, and discusses what's coming next.

"The citizens will turn against us again," says one New Palu man who seems especially in touch with Earth's news. "They were softening—a bit—when they learned about Cormand Smith. The rioting stopped. But there's already backlash. People liked the villain versus hero story." Here he nods at Lin. "But they still don't want the rest of us here, living beside them."

"How can that be?" asks Lin. "Now everyone knows that the attacks were faked. Shouldn't they hate us less?"

"I guess you're as naïve as ever," says Jul. "What does the truth have to do with what the citizens think?"

"What are you planning to do?" Lin turns to Emas. "What is the group talking about these days?" Emas looks around the circle and raises his beer glass.

"All I'm planning to do is enjoy that we're all alive and together." The circle of friends cheers. But Emas takes Lin's arm and pulls her into a quiet corner.

"We have action planned in Shanghai," he says. "A number of prominent Xinqi citizens are going to be at a music event there next week, including some of those that have been most vocal about executing colonists. Once they're all in one place..." Emas smiles and imitates an explosion with his hands. Lin doesn't like it.

"I don't want any part of that," she says. His smile fades immediately.

"I thought..." he trails off, looking to the side.

"What?"

"It's just... which side will you take? After all this, we're still waiting to find out."

"I don't have to choose a side," she says. "I don't have to follow anyone. I'll fight in my own way, but this isn't it."

Emas shakes his head. "Not good enough," he says. "There's a right and a wrong here. You did the right thing in the end, last time. Have you changed your mind?" Lin shrugs.

"There was never any right choice."

Emas's face hardens.

"So you're not going to help us anymore. Now that you have your mother back, you're just going to go back to your happy citizen life while the rest of us fight?" His words are everything Lin has been hatefully telling herself, but that doesn't mean they're true.

"It means I'll just keep trying to make the best decision I can, every time," she says.

"You'll come around eventually," he sighs. "Look me up then."

"Good luck," she says, and means it.

***

Lin is at work at the noodle house. She tries to focus on reservations and seating charts and pushes thoughts of lost friends and bloody battles out of her mind. She hasn't heard from Kirs and Rajan and doesn't expect to again. She only hears from Emas about the work he's doing. He's joined an offshoot of the Fourth Power and is still unhappy that she wants no part of it.

She carries a tray of food to a table and sets it down without glancing at the customer.

"Yang Lin," says the customer. Lin looks up. It's Mr. Tomasy's niece.

"Hi, Erna," Lin says cautiously. She's painfully aware of how their last interaction went.

"I got a message from my uncle," says Erna.

"What? How?"

"He escaped," says Erna. "He and some of the others were forced to work in some kind of labor camp, like an assembly line, I think, but he got away and sent me a message. But now I've lost touch with him again."

"Did he give any clue to where he was?"

"Yes, he seemed to think that he had passed through Tashkent. Lin, do you think you can help?"

"You want me to go after him?" Erna eyes her with none of the defiance of their previous argument.

"I've heard from... friends that you saved a lot of lives recently." Lin doesn't say anything, thinking of Bogdan. The memory still bubbles up at odd places. "But I also heard that you don't want to fight anymore." Around Lin, the people go about their busy lives. Some are citizens, some aren't—she can't tell which is which. And somewhere out there, Mr. Tomasy is in trouble.

"I have to go home and get my things," she says. Erna's eyes light up in the most genuine smile Lin has seen on her face.

"Thank you!" she says.

Lin leaves the restaurant, walking down the busy Beijing street with a full heart. There's always someone who needs saving, and it's always her job.

About K.B. Gazeena

K.B. Gazeena is a science fiction author. When she's not writing books, you can find her paddling dragon boats, volunteering in wildlife rehab, and thinking about spaceships. She lives in Minnesota with her husband and cat.

To hear about upcoming books and new releases, sign up for her mailing list on her website or follow her on social media.

www.kbgazeena.com
Facebook.com/kbgazeena
Instagram.com/kbgazeena
Tik Tok @kb_gazeena

www.ingramcontent.com/pod-product-compliance
Lightning Source LLC
Chambersburg PA
CBHW050528110726
47899CB00005B/1643